THE ULTIMATE REALITY SHOW

HOW FAR WOULD YOU GO TO WIN $10 MILLION?

CLAY JACOBSEN

A NOVEL

THE ULTIMATE REALITY SHOW

HOW FAR WOULD YOU GO TO WIN $10 MILLION?

INTEGRITY® PUBLISHERS
Nashville
www.integritypublishers.com

Other Books by Clay Jacobsen

Interview with the Devil
Circle of Seven
The Lasko Interview
Authentic Relationships: The Lost Art of One Anothering
(with Wayne Jacobsen)

For more information about Clay Jacobsen
visit his Web site

www.ClayJacobsen.com

THE ULTIMATE REALTY SHOW

Published by Integrity Publishers, a division of Integrity Media, Inc., 5250 Virginia Way, Suite 110, Brentwood, Tennessee 37027.

HELPING PEOPLE WORLDWIDE EXPERIENCE *the* MANIFEST PRESENCE *of* GOD.

Exclusive Representation: Blanton, Harrell, Cooke & Corzine, 5300 Virginia Way, Suite 100, Brentwood, Tennessee 37027.

Cover Design: Brand Navigation www.brandnavigation.com
Cover Images: Getty
Interior Design: Finer Points Productions

Library of Congress Cataloging-in-Publication Data

Jacobsen, Clay, 1956-
The ultimate reality show / by Clay Jacobsen.
p. cm.
Summary: "Jack Forrest is offered a chance to compete for 10 million dollars on a remote island; however he already has enough drama in his life: a budding romance with Principal Kathryn Williams—his boss, a lawsuit looming over his head and the school board breathing down his neck over a simple prayer offered for an injured player"—Provided by publisher.
ISBN-13: 978-1-59145-337-6 (pbk.)
1. Reality televison programs—Fiction. 2. Prayer in the public schools—Fiction. 3. Teachers—Fiction. 4. Islands—Fiction. I. Title.
PS3560.A2584U45 2005
813'.54—dc22

2005013826

Printed in the United States of America
05 06 07 08 DELTA 9 8 7 6 5 4 3 2 1

ACKNOWLEDGMENTS

This story was such a joy to write, and that had a lot to do with some wonderful people who shared their talents so graciously throughout the process. My heartfelt thanks belong to each of them.

Always to my Mom and Dad, Gene and Jo Jacobsen, for being the first and finest examples of how to walk with Jesus.

To Cheryl Bock, my wife's sister and my friend—thanks for sharing your expertise of the medical field.

To James Magdalin, who convinced me to hang from the rafters of stage nine at NBC Studios to gain a bit of knowledge about rock climbing—I've never seen the crew have such a good laugh. I should thank Bob and Frank, the great NBC prop guys for hanging the rope as well as getting me down without injury.

To Shelly Hazard of Puzzlers Paradise for allowing me the use of her logic problem, "Monkey Business." You can check out more of her logic puzzles at *www.puzzlersparadise.com*

To my new friends at Integrity Publishers, I'm thrilled to be part of the Integrity family. Thanks especially to Joey, Kris, Angela, and Marcus for an enjoyable and educational editing process.

To Cal Tarrant for his helpful eye with the early manuscript.

Also to Chaz Corzine and the great folks at Blanton Harrell Cooke & Corzine. God has truly blessed me with an amazing management team.

And most of all to my partner in life who God has set beside me as also my partner in writing—my wife, Cindy. Without your creative ideas and gentle nudging, this story wouldn't have been the same. Thanks for reading every line before anyone else and sharing your thoughts and heart with me. I love you beyond words.

Finally to my daughters, Sharayah and Shelby, you bring such joy into my life when you come running into my office and bug me. Don't ever stop.

ACKNOWLEDGMENTS

ROYAL HIGH SCHOOL
WHEATON, ILLINOIS

There were only a few moments of daylight left. The incoming fog had just blocked out the setting sun with all its splendid hues. The evening air was crisp, as the lengthening spring days fought to tame the harsh Chicago winter.

It was Jack Forrest's favorite time of the year, the first week of daylight savings: the signal that summer was just around the corner—and the embryonic phase of next fall's football season. Spring training.

He stood on the sidelines, intensely surveying the field before him.

It was alive.

What any bystander would see as a mishmash of hormonal teenage boys running around with no apparent rhyme or reason, Jack viewed as an intricate ballet of drills and tests designed to help him determine the potential of his varsity football squad.

Jack looked down at his clipboard, straining to make out the roster of names in the growing darkness. He glanced up at the idle bank of lights hovering high above the field. He ached to turn them on and continue into the night, but it wasn't allowed with the recent budget cuts. Irritated, Jack brought the whistle up to his mouth and blew three short bursts.

"All right, men," he yelled. "That's it for today. Hit the showers!"

Fifty-seven teenagers dressed in purple gym shorts, white T-shirts, and purple panther helmets responded immediately. A few collided in the mayhem, giving Jack reason to chuckle at the spectacle.

"So, how does it look so far?"

Jack spun around, surprised to see Kathryn Williams walking up directly behind him. She was the school's vice principal, Jack's immediate supervisor—and most recently a dinner companion a couple of times.

"It's hard to say this early," Jack said with a grin. Standing beside her, his six-foot frame dwarfed her by over nine inches. Her short brunette hair flipped in the breeze, but her normally bright and cheerful face held a serious frown. Jack instantly knew this was not a social call.

Kathryn kept her eyes trained on him. "We need to talk."

"All right." Jack turned toward his assistant coach. "Chuck, would you mind making sure all the equipment's put away for me?"

"You got it, Coach," Chuck responded. "See you tomorrow."

Jack pulled the Panther cap off his head, scratched at his messed-up hair and turned back to Kathryn. "What's up?"

"C'mon, let's have a seat."

She led Jack to the stands and settled in the second row of bleachers. Jack stood beside her, shivered, and zipped up his jacket, unsure if the sudden chill came from the settling fog, or the sense of dread coming over him.

"You've only got two more days," Kathryn warned, looking out over the emptying field.

Jack drew in a long breath, then sat down on the bench beside her, letting out a slow sigh.

"You knew this was coming ..."

"I know," Jack muttered. "I just hoped it would've gone away."

"You're not the only one."

Jack glanced away, trying to collect his thoughts as the last of his players walked toward the locker room.

They were alone.

Jack turned to her. "Will I still be able to coach this fall?"

"Coach?" She met his gaze. "I'm not even sure you'll have a job the rest of this semester."

Jack looked out toward the empty field again. "You know how much these kids mean to me."

"The special board meeting is Wednesday. It all hinges on how you respond."

Jack blinked and bit at his upper lip. "Right ... how I respond."

"I need to know, Jack. Jerry is all over me about this." Kathryn bore into him with pleading eyes.

Jack knew the words the vice principal wanted to hear—*needed* to hear. But he couldn't bring himself to say them, even to save his job.

The awkward silence was interrupted by a black Chevy Suburban racing through the main gates from the opposite end of the field. It kicked up a cloud of dust as it sped across the dirt track that surrounded the grass.

"Hey, you can't drive on the field!" Jack yelled, relieved at the interruption. He bolted from the stands with Kathryn following right behind him. Before they could set foot onto the dirt, the distinctive sound of a helicopter snapped their attention skyward.

Through the growing fog, a shaft of light bore down on them, as the thumping of rotor blades grew increasingly louder. From the corner of his eye, Jack noticed the Suburban come to a stop, followed by what looked like a camera crew piling out and heading his direction.

"What's going on here?" Jack yelled to no one in particular.

The chopper came in just above the goalpost, making its way to the center of the football field. The sound was deafening as the blades sent a torrent of wind slapping Jack with stinging bits of sand and nearly blowing his cap off.

The helicopter rotated, revealing the call letters of the local ABC television affiliate before dropping softly to the grass directly on top of the Royal Panthers logo at the fifty-yard line.

With the rotors still spinning, the back door of the Bell Jet Ranger opened and a man stepped out, keeping his head low as he trotted away from the chopper.

"Isn't that Vince Sinclair?" Kathryn's voice was excited.

"Vince who?"

"You know, from *The Ultimate Challenge.*"

As he came closer, Jack recognized the popular television host—more from the promos than the actual series. *The Ultimate Challenge* was the latest hit on ABC. It was unique among reality shows because the participants were pulled from their everyday lives without warning. Jack's brow creased as he noticed another camera crew step out of the helicopter behind Vince and head in their direction.

The TV host stopped a few paces from them. Jack thought he looked younger than he appeared on television. Dark hair, well built, with a warm, inviting smile, handsome in a rugged way that would attract women yet not be a threat to men—Vince seemed to be the perfect television host.

The crew stepped up just behind him and focused a camera and a high-powered light right at Jack. He was blinded for an instant, blinking as he brought his right hand up to shield his eyes.

Vince brushed through his wind-whipped hair with his fingers, then waited a beat for the crew from the Suburban to get their camera trained on him. He cleared his throat just as the rotor blades from the helicopter finally came to a stop.

The stadium suddenly felt deathly quiet.

"Good evening." Vince Sinclair's deep voice echoed off the empty bleachers. "My name is Vince Sinclair. I see we've arrived a bit late. We'd hoped to catch you in the middle of practice. Coach Forrest, isn't it?"

He knows who I am, Jack realized as the celebrity's eyes locked on his. *He's here for me!*

Jack gulped. "I'm Jack Forrest." He was embarrassed to hear his voice quiver.

His hand was taken in a firm handshake as Vince broke into a warm smile. "Congratulations, Jack. You've been selected."

Jack's heart skipped a beat, maybe two.

"You are the next participant on *The Ultimate Challenge*—with the chance to win ten million dollars." Vince accented each syllable, playing to the camera while trying to draw a huge reaction from Jack.

Jack felt his cordial smile collapse and his stomach lurch. Somewhere in the mental fog, he heard Kathryn mutter something, but it just didn't register.

"Ten million ..." Jack stammered. "I thought your show gave away a million dollars."

"We used to," Vince answered, his smile taking on a mischievous gleam. "But it seems a million dollars just doesn't go that far these days."

Jack shook his head in bewilderment. "I'm sorry, there must be some mistake. I haven't asked to be on your show."

"No one ever has."

Jack inhaled deeply, then slowly let out the breath of air, hoping it would relax him a bit. It didn't.

"I know you're shocked," Vince said soothingly. "That's part of the game. What you have to do right now is decide if you're going to play."

"How can I do that, I don't even know what the game is?"

Vince laughed. "That's also part of the game."

He paced a few feet to his right, then motioned over his shoulder toward the helicopter. "Jack, you'll step into that chopper and be flown to where *The Ultimate Challenge* will begin. We'll bring you back in seven days—or less, depending on your success."

Jack found it difficult to catch his breath. Why him? How could they have possibly picked a single, twenty-seven-year-old football coach from the outskirts of Chicago?

"The winner could be you, Jack. Ten million dollars."

He was speechless.

"Sounds like a great opportunity," Kathryn said beside him.

This guy is really serious, Jack thought as the reality of his predicament began to sink in. *I can't just fly off in that chopper. This whole thing is nuts!*

Vince broke the silence as if reading Jack's mind. "For a chance at ten million bucks, you're just going to have to trust me."

Trust you? You just landed that stupid helicopter in the middle of my football field, and you expect me to trust you?

"I need a little time to think this over."

"Time, huh?"

Vince looked down at his watch. Jack couldn't keep his eyes from darting back and forth from Vince to the camera's lens just over the host's shoulder. He could feel his pulse racing.

Vince looked back up at him with a smile, and then his next comment nearly made Jack's knees buckle. "Your first challenge is that you must decide to get into that chopper in the next sixty seconds, or you forfeit your position."

What does one say to an offer like that? Jack had no idea.

"I can't leave in the middle of spring training ..." Jack nearly choked on the words. "You can't expect me to just walk out."

Vince took a quick glance at his watch, then simply said, "You have fifty seconds."

Jack could feel his pulse throbbing at the tips of his fingers, the sweat dripping under his arms despite the cold breeze on his face.

This was insane.

He tried to recall what the contestants were forced to do on the show, but with the glut of reality television hitting the airwaves, he couldn't identify any events specific to *The Ultimate Challenge.* He wished he'd paid more attention.

Jack might have made a completely different decision if he had.

Ten million dollars.

God, what do I do? Jack gasped under his breath. *Could this be Your will?*

"Jack," Kathryn whispered. "You have to give this a shot. You'd be foolish not to."

"Thirty seconds, Jack."

Jack smiled nervously, feeling like he was being pushed toward the edge of a cliff overlooking a great abyss. "I don't know, Kathryn. This is all so crazy."

"Crazy, yes," she added. "But this could be a godsend."

Jack thought back to their earlier discussion. Maybe she was right—there might not be a job for him here anyway.

"But what about the board meeting?"

"I'll take care of it," Kathryn promised, caught up in the moment.

Jack's thoughts began to mesh together at incredible speed, swirling through his head.

"Your time is nearly up," Vince chimed in with dramatic fashion. "What will it be?"

Jack closed his eyes and concentrated.

Ten million dollars.

"You have ten seconds."

As a high school football coach, Jack was no stranger to pressure. But this was different. This was debilitating.

"Five seconds."

What should he do?

Breathe.

Walk away from everything he knew?

The chance to be a millionaire—ten times over.

"Time's up, Jack."

No one moved.

The only sound Jack heard was the throbbing of his pulse pounding inside his head.

He opened his eyes and took in a final deep breath before meeting Vince's gaze.

"OK, I guess I'm in."

Vince broke into a huge grin and began clapping. "Nicely done, Jack. You have chosen well."

Kathryn stepped in and hugged him. Jack felt the blood rush to his face—what had he done? The first wave of doubt hit hard.

"We have to leave now," Vince instructed.

"Dressed like this?" Jack suddenly realized he was standing in a pair of purple gym shorts, a white shirt, a purple windbreaker, and a pair of white sneakers. He surely had hat-hair under his cap—a wonderful look for his television debut.

"Just as you are," Vince answered. "Let me have your wallet, keys, cell phone, and watch, please."

Without thinking, Jack reached into his pockets and handed the items to Vince, who turned and handed them to Kathryn.

Jack watched in abject horror, surprised at how naked he felt giving up his identity and a means of escape. *I must be insane.*

"Please keep these safe until he returns," Vince said calmly.

"I'll be happy to," Kathryn said.

"Hey, don't I need my I.D.?" Jack asked.

"No I.D. No credit cards. No cell phone," declared Vince.

Jack started to complain, then shook his head. "I know, all part of the game." He turned toward Kathryn. "My mom, it's Monday night …"

"I understand," Kathryn interrupted. "I'll call her."

A young man that had been standing behind the camera walked up to Jack and handed him a clipboard with a single sheet of paper clipped to the front.

"What's this?" Jack asked.

"Standard release form," the man replied.

"Go ahead and sign it, Jack." Vince encouraged. "We need to have

Vice Principal Williams witness your signature and give her a copy, then we're on our way."

Jack glanced at Kathryn, then back to Vince. "How did you know her name?"

"We know everything … now sign."

Jack glanced at the fine print filling up the page. "Shouldn't I read what this says first?"

Vince pointed toward the bottom where his signature was to be inscribed. "It's your everyday reality show contract. We get to tape you twenty-four seven, and you have no rights whatsoever. Besides, if you don't sign, I leave you here, and you lose any chance of winning ten million dollars."

Jack glanced over the language in front of him. It would take hours and a law degree to be able to comprehend what it really said. One line jumped out at him just because of all the zeros—should he reveal any information about the event or the outcome of the competition prior to the show airing on domestic television, Jack would be liable for up to five million dollars in damages.

"A five-million-dollar fine?" Jack gasped.

Vince nodded as if it was nothing. "Just standard confidentiality language. It's the same thing CBS uses for *Survivor*. Nothing to worry about."

Jack looked at him in shock for a second.

"The only other restriction in there is that should you win and try to share the money with another contestant in some kind of alliance, we take it all back and still fine you the five million."

"Wow," Jack sighed. "You guys don't play around."

"No, we don't. But you don't sign, I can't take you with me. And then you have nothing. It's your choice."

Jack shrugged, then scribbled his name across the bottom, wondering how big of a mistake he could be making.

The production assistant took the clipboard, tore off the bottom of the contract, and handed it to Kathryn.

She smiled at him. "Good luck, Jack."

"I'll certainly need it," Jack answered, then added with a grin, "Hey, keep my job open for me while I'm gone, will ya?"

Kathryn tilted her head slightly as her eyebrows raised, seemingly understanding Jack's plea, but no answer came back in return.

Jack turned away, feeling as if a huge boulder had dropped in the pit of his gut. But his anxiety instantly changed to panic when he saw that the production assistant was now holding a handgun and pointing it directly at him.

"What's going on?" Jack cried, just as he heard the muffled spit from the gun and simultaneously felt a sharp, intense pain just below his right jaw.

"Hey!" he shrieked, as his hand shot up pressing against his neck.

Jack noticed Vince smiling beside the camera as his world started to spin and lose focus. He could see Kathryn rushing to his side, could hear her gasping in shock. But she was too late.

"You can't ..." Jack attempted to speak, but the football field faded to oblivion just before his body collapsed to the grass.

3

Amanda Forrest moved through the kitchen with grace, alternating between the stove, the countertop and the kitchen table as she completed the finishing touches for the Monday night meal with her son. With her busy schedule at the hospital, it was one of the few nights of the week when she took the time to prepare a complete meal. It had become a tradition since her husband was killed in that awful car crash.

One year—it was hard to believe that much time had passed. In many ways, it still seemed like it happened yesterday. Only forty-eight years old, the last thing Amanda thought she'd have to deal with at this point of her life was the loss of Kevin. Her friends reminded her that she was still young, that she needed to get back into the dating scene. But Amanda had no desire to open that part of her life again.

She stirred the wild rice one more time, glancing at the clock on the microwave. Jack was late—it wasn't like him. Then she remembered that it was the first week of spring training. He'd be working those kids, squeezing out the last bit of daylight before he'd let them hit the showers.

She smiled, imagining her son barking out orders, rating his new team with marks on his clipboard. He lived to coach—at least that's what he told her. But Amanda knew differently. He really loved the kids. Every year it was the same: as the season progressed, it was always less about the wins and losses and more about the kids themselves. Jack loved them and did everything he could to be a positive influence in their lives. In so many ways, Jack was just like her husband.

How she missed him.

Amanda pulled the rice off the stove and spooned it into a dish waiting on the counter. She fought back the tears, which came so easily whenever her mind drifted toward Kevin.

The ringing phone interrupted her thoughts. "You better get over here. Dinner's getting cold," Amanda jokingly said, as she picked up the receiver.

"Um … Amanda?"

"Oh, I'm sorry. I thought you were Jack."

"Not a problem. I know you're expecting him, but this is Kathryn Williams."

"Is everything all right?" Amanda asked with a familiar nervousness, her thoughts immediately going back to that night when the sheriff's office had called about her husband.

"Yes," Kathryn answered quickly over the phone, "Everything's fine. I didn't mean to worry you. I'm sorry."

"Oh, thank God." Amanda leaned against the counter. "Sorry … I guess I'm still a bit jumpy about unexpected phone calls."

"My apologies. I didn't realize …"

"No, no apology needed," Amanda reassured her. "So are you going to be joining us tonight?"

"That's so sweet of you, but I can't. Jack wanted me to give you a call. He won't be able to make it for dinner."

Amanda's brow tightened. "Thanks for letting me know, but why wouldn't he call himself?"

"Well, that's the interesting part," Kathryn explained. "He's heading out of town. He's been selected as a contestant on the next *Ultimate Challenge.*"

The kitchen buzzer went off signaling that her baked chicken in red pepper sauce was done. It was one of Jack's favorites.

"You don't mean that TV show, do you?" Amanda moved to the oven and turned off the buzzer. Grabbing a potholder and holding the phone to her ear with her shoulder, she reached in and pulled out the glass baking dish and set it on the counter.

"Yes! It's incredible. Jack has a chance to win ten million dollars."

"Ten million?" Amanda chuckled. "I doubt he'd know what to do with that kind of money."

"Good point. But it won't be easy to win. I've seen the show a few times, and it looks very intense. They even took him away in a helicopter—they say we won't see or hear from him for a week."

"I've never seen the show. I'm not much for that kind of TV. I hope he knows what he's doing."

Kathryn giggled. "I'm sure he has no idea."

Amanda stopped fidgeting around the kitchen as Kathryn's information really began to sink in. "I find it rather odd that he'd leave in the middle of everything that's going on around here."

"I kind of helped convince him to go."

"Really? Do you think that was wise?"

"Yeah, I thought it would be good for him right now."

"Things haven't been resolved with the school board, then?"

"No," Kathryn sighed. "Hotter than ever. But I can't go into it."

"I understand," Amanda answered. "I guess I'll just keep praying."

"Well, I wouldn't stop," Kathryn returned. "He really needs it right now, in more ways than one."

The vibrations were the first sensation to break through Jack's drug-induced fog. He was alive! His brain told him he was moving, but in what?

And to where?

Jack's head hadn't cleared enough to answer the first question, much less have any idea about the second. He opened his eyes and nearly heaved. His vision was tripled—blurred images seemed to circle around themselves.

He closed his eyes quickly, waiting for the nausea to subside. He struggled to focus, trying to take stock of what was happening.

The last thing Jack remembered was standing on the football field in front of the cameras. Then he recalled the gun … and the sharp pain in his neck—it must have been a tranquilizer dart, not a bullet. What a relief.

He found himself lying on the floor of … something.

The fog began to lift. It was an airplane—judging by the noise, it had to be a prop job. The incessant roar of the engines, the jerkiness of the floor as they hit turbulence … he was airborne.

Jack tried again to open his eyes. It took a second for them to focus, but at least there was only one image this time. He sat up slowly, taking in the sight around him.

He was in some kind of cargo or military plane, and it was huge. Instead of seats lined up neatly in rows of three, the large cabin had two benches along each side of the aircraft with a lot of open space in between. Jack figured it was for cargo. There were no windows.

And he wasn't alone. For a second, Jack thought this was all his imagination. There were nearly two-dozen people around him—he couldn't even make out how many were men or how many were women, since each had on goggles, a helmet, and were dressed in military fatigues. On one bench sat a group of five people wearing green camouflage. On the other bench—the one nearest Jack—four people sat dressed in the same desert colors that Jack was now wearing. The rest of the people around them were wearing black and were either holding a camera or had a miniature one mounted on their helmet.

"Ah, our last contestant has joined us," Jack heard shouted from behind him. He turned and spotted Vince Sinclair, the only one dressed in civilian clothing—a flowered blue Hawaiian shirt and khaki pants.

Jack tried to speak, but his mouth felt like he'd swallowed the Sahara Desert.

Vince offered him a bottle of water. "Don't try to talk, you'll need this first."

Jack grabbed the bottle and took a swig, swishing the liquid around in his mouth. The water refreshed him at first, then Jack felt as if thousands of tiny needles were pricking his tongue and the inside of his cheeks. When he swallowed, the burning flowed all the way down his throat.

Not pleasant, but it helped clear his head and inflame his anger.

"You shot me!" Jack's voice sounded like gravel.

"A mere tranquilizer dart," Vince answered with cold steel eyes. There was not a hint of the game show host smile he'd seen on the football field.

"Just like the rest of us," the man sitting next to Jack offered.

Jack looked down the bench. Everyone nodded.

"The game begins, Jack," Vince smirked.

One of the men dressed in black came and knelt beside Jack. He reached into a medical bag he carried and pulled out a small flashlight, shining it into Jack's right eye.

"Our medic," Vince introduced. "You'll feel better in a second."

The medic checked Jack's other eye, then reached into the bag and pulled out a stethoscope, blood pressure kit, a vial, and a syringe. He unzipped the top of Jack's fatigues and began wrapping the blood pressure band around his right arm.

Vince signaled to one of the men holding a camera to roll tape. Instantly, the inviting smile of the popular television host reappeared.

He grabbed a bullhorn and placed it to his mouth. "OK, contestants, listen up. This is the first leg of your ultimate challenge, and, as most of you know, we're not like any other reality show. There is no immunity, no tribal councils—each one of you could be sent home at any moment. You won't know what will keep you in the game, but you'll have no doubt what will get you kicked out: coming in last."

Jack took his eyes off what the medic was doing and glanced at the group of contestants—his competition. It was hard to get a read behind the goggles and helmets, but they all seemed to hang on Vince's every word, intensely focused.

"Sometimes you'll be in teams, oftentimes solo, but each challenge will test you in ways you've never been tested before—we know, we've done our homework. Seven days from now, the one who has proven worthy will be the ultimate champion."

One of the guys across the plane stood up and yelled while pointing at his chest. Jack couldn't make out what he said with the noise in the cabin, but his intensity was obvious—and slightly intimidating. Jack's stomach churned. He knew there was no way he was prepared for what was to come.

"You've probably noticed that we've split you into two groups of five," Vince continued. "One team dressed in desert fatigues, the other in jungle green."

Jack looked back to the bench beside him. His team appeared to consist of two men and three women—all in brown and tan camouflage. They seemed to be up against three men and two women if Jack was correctly judging the size of the bodies under the fatigues.

The plane hit a pocket of turbulence and dropped like a rock, causing the occupants to be weightless for a brief moment. Jack's stomach did a somersault. He shot his hand up to his mouth to force it closed.

He didn't feel anywhere near normal yet. How could he compete in this mad contest?

"Wow," Vince continued, with a broad smile evident behind the bullhorn. "That was exciting. But don't worry, you'll be off this plane very soon."

Jack felt a sharp prick on his upper right arm. He whipped back to the medic, who was plunging the contents of a syringe into him.

The medic smiled warmly. "This will counteract the residual effects of the tranquilizer."

"Thanks for the warning," Jack rubbed at his arm.

"Your first mission starts now," Vince instructed. "Each of you has a survival pack containing water, some basic rations, a first-aid kit, and a GPS receiver. On it, we've placed the coordinates of the base camp. The first team to get there passes the first challenge."

One of the women on the bench across from Jack raised her hand. "What are the rules?" she yelled.

"This is *The Ultimate Challenge*, Stacy." Vince's smile turned devilish. "There are no rules."

Jack noticed several grins emerge from under the goggles of Stacy's team. They were ready for battle. Looking back toward his own team, he thought he saw grim determination on each of their faces as well.

He felt like he was a mile behind in a two-mile race. How long had the rest of them been awake? Why was he the last to become conscious? He didn't even know the names of any of his teammates.

The medic packed his bag and stood, stepping toward the front of the plane. "He's good to go," he claimed, as he passed by Vince.

"Great." Vince grinned toward Jack, then turned to the rest of the group. "Now, all we've got left is to get you all on the ground. Everyone up, let's go."

At his words, ten men approached from the front of the plane and placed themselves directly behind each contestant. They wore a special harness that each began to strap around the person he was standing behind. Jack looked up at the man waiting above him—and noticed the parachute strapped to his back.

Great.

Jack had always had a hard time understanding why anyone would want to jump out of a perfectly good airplane.

He struggled to stand up, fighting the rebellion within his own body. His muscles ached, either from the residual effects of the tranquilizer or from the inactivity while he'd been unconscious—and he could only imagine how long that had been. Whatever juice the medic had injected into him had helped to clear Jack's head, but his body definitely hadn't caught up yet.

The man in front of him offered his hand and helped Jack to his feet.

"You'll be dropped out the back of our C-130, which is cruising at thirteen thousand feet," Vince explained through his megaphone. "We've attached you to an expert skydiver in what will be a tandem jump. We don't want to take the risk of losing one of you in the first minute of the contest."

The skydiver placed his chest against Jack's back and began strapping him into the harness. Jack could feel his heart racing, but he knew it wasn't the medication. He didn't like heights, and jumping out of a plane flying at thirteen thousand feet terrified him.

"Once on the ground, you'll be on your own. There will be teams of camera crews already on site and some covering you on your way down."

Vince walked between the two teams, making sure each member understood his instructions. "Neither the dive experts nor any of the crew will help you in any way. If you speak to them, they are instructed not to answer, only to record your every move. In the event that you encounter a life-or-death situation and their assistance is needed, then you are eliminated from the game—no exceptions."

Vince glanced at all of the contestants, then focused directly on Jack's eyes. "Any questions?"

Jack could think of a hundred, but none he wanted to express at the moment. His main thought was how he could get himself out of this.

"All right then, everyone tethered?"

Vince waited until he saw each expert diver flash him an upturned thumb. "Oh, one last thing. On the beach that you will hopefully land on, we've placed one machete, marked with a red *Ultimate Challenge* flag. It could be extremely helpful in getting your team through the jungle. The first team that finds it … keeps it."

Vince paused to allow the cameras to record the team's reactions. He looked up to the front of the aircraft and nodded. "Good luck!"

Instantly, a claxon buzzer screeched throughout the cabin as the entire back end of the aircraft opened up like a shark's mouth, revealing the open sky behind them.

The sound was intense as the roar of the engines invaded Jack's ears. The wind whipped violently around the interior of the plane, making it impossible to hear any further instruction from Vince.

There wouldn't be any.

Jack looked out the back of the airplane and could see nothing but puffy white clouds over a vast expanse of ocean. Questions flashed through his mind: What had he gotten himself into? Where on God's earth were they? Would he survive the next two minutes? Was it too late to back out?

Strapped firmly to the skydiver behind him, Jack felt totally out of control. His breathing quickened. Suddenly he couldn't get enough oxygen. Maybe he still hadn't recovered from the drugs in his system. He felt light-headed, as if he was on the brink of blacking out.

Jack turned and caught Vince's eyes, pleading without words to stop this insanity.

For a moment, it looked as if Vince understood. Then he brought the bullhorn up to his lips and with a wicked smile shouted, "Go! Go! Go!"

Jack turned his head back around as he was pushed to the rear of the plane, forced to keep in step with his dive expert. The teams stayed in single file as two lines formed heading out the back of the massive plane.

Jack's arms flailed out, as if he could grab hold of the fuselage and keep himself from being pushed out. He missed by six feet on the closest side.

Without the slightest hesitation, Jack's expert took the final steps down the ramp and leaped out the back of the plane.

And suddenly, Jack was falling and screaming as loud as his parched lungs would allow.

Breathe, Jack, breathe.

After his lungs had emptied from the involuntary scream, coaxing them into sucking air back in proved to be more difficult than expected.

The view was incredible. The ocean stretched out below him well beyond the horizon. Billowy clouds that looked like marshmallow puffs scattered over the blue-green water. But Jack was blind to it all. The wind whipped past Jack's face, tugging at his skin and stretching his cheeks. His eyes watered behind the darkened goggles.

Just when Jack thought his stomach was settling down and he might be gaining his bearings, the expert diver started tumbling. They somersaulted through the air, Jack's vision blurred between the blue of the sky and the turquoise of the ocean below.

"Hey!" Jack screamed. "What's going on?"

Jack felt a chuckle behind him, and heard the diver yell above the roar of the wind, "All part of the game."

Every time Jack rolled over, he thought he caught sight of the other contestants flipping through the air as well. His gut churned, and he was dangerously close to heaving. Then the expert brought his arms out settling he and Jack back into a steady drop.

But it didn't last long.

They went into a clockwise spin, gaining speed until the ocean and clouds below were just a blur of color. Jack was beyond sick, flashing back to when he was twelve years old and had ridden the teacup ride at Disneyland three times in a row.

What seemed like an eternity had actually taken just over a minute. As Jack's stomach continued to do flips, the dive expert stopped the rotation and pulled the ripcord.

The parachute deployed and filled with air, pulling hard at the straps connecting Jack to the diver behind him. He grunted involuntarily as the oxygen was pushed from his lungs.

Hoping to regain his senses quickly, Jack looked below. Even though they now fell gently toward the earth, his head was still spinning wildly. He pictured what it would be like when they hit the beach with all the contestants trying to find the promised machete like summer camp kids spinning in circles on baseball bats before trying to run a straight line.

Jack's expert glided them downwind, heading for a small island of green that seemed to grow from under the clouds. As his head began to clear, they dropped lower and lower. Jack noticed the air grow heavy around him. It was hot, tropical. He began to sweat under the fatigues.

Finally, they were coming down the last few hundred feet. The dive expert aimed them toward the one stretch of sand that stood out in contrast to the pounding surf against a dark lava coastline. Not a large landing area in Jack's opinion, but they glided gently over a small uprising of rocks, then the expert flared out the parachute to slow their descent.

"Bend your knees a bit," Jack heard behind him.

Jack's boots touched the sand and the momentum pushed them a few steps forward, but it was gentler than Jack could have imagined. They'd made it—Jack was the first one down from his team.

As the dive expert began to unhook him, Jack glanced around the beach, looking for a red flag. He spotted it near the center of the beach about fifty feet in front of him, but the first contestant from the green team was already unhooked and running toward it.

As soon as Jack was free he attempted to make up the distance. Stumbling through the sand, he didn't exactly make a straight line. He was still dizzy. The other contestant easily beat Jack to the flag—and the all-important machete.

With a shout to her green teammates, either still in the air or on the ground, the woman raised the prize high above her head. "We've got the machete!"

Jack stopped dead in the sand, defeated. Already sweating profusely under his fatigues, he turned back to see the final brown camouflaged contestant landing thirty feet in front of him. As her feet hit the sand, she didn't have her knees bent and the momentum forced her forward—smashing face-first into the sandy beach. Her dive expert added his weight to her misery as he landed right on top of her.

Jack ran over and knelt down beside them. "You OK?"

"Get off of me!" a voice groaned from under the pile.

The diver managed to unlatch himself from her and pull himself up, grabbing the collapsing parachute and pulling in the fabric. A camera crew arrived and positioned themselves on the other side of the diver, pointing a camera right at Jack.

"I'm gonna be sick," his teammate muttered.

"Here, let me help you up," Jack offered, gently grabbing her arm to help her sit up. His head was just beginning to clear. "Just take a few deep breaths."

He helped her remove the helmet and goggles. What was probably a pretty face, on any normal day, was ghostly white with glazed-over eyes. She had a small frame, probably not over five foot four with short cropped blond hair.

"I'm Jack Forrest."

"C. J. McCormick," she said, spitting sand out of her mouth. "Man, I feel awful."

"You must have had the same ride down I did. You'll feel better in a minute."

"I hope you're right."

"Let's see if you can walk. We need to get our team together."

Jack stood up, pausing slightly as his lightheadedness returned. But this time it went away quickly. He offered his hand and pulled C. J. to her feet.

"Wow," she sighed. "I'm still dizzy."

"Me too."

"Hey!" A voice yelled off in the distance. "Over here!"

Jack looked down the beach and saw the other three contestants dressed in desert camouflage gathered together. The man who had been sitting next to Jack on the plane was waving them over.

"Come on," Jack placed his arm around C. J. "We can make it together."

C. J. was still pretty wobbly, but Jack was able to keep her on her feet as they jogged over. The last member of their team was just being released from her dive expert as they approached. All three were glaring at him.

"Nice going—we needed that machete," the man yelled.

"I'm sorry," Jack tried to explain. "She landed before me and was closer. I couldn't make up the distance."

"Why didn't you just take the machete from her?" the man persisted. He was an imposing figure—a tall African-American, maybe six foot three or four—built like Mike Tyson with a head just as bald. He looked fit and ready; the dive didn't seem to have affected him at all.

Jack angled his head, "Vince said the first team to grab it, keeps it."

The large man glared down at Jack, "He also said there are no rules, man. Now we're screwed."

After adding some choice words directed at Jack, he looked down at his GPS receiver for a second, then started heading off toward the jungle. "Let's get this show on the road."

"Chill, man," a black woman called out after him. "Who put you in charge?"

The man turned and looked sternly back at her. "Weren't you listening up there? First team to the base camp wins. I aim to win, machete or no machete."

"So do I, but that doesn't mean we're running off blindly into that jungle," she answered. "We need to shed some clothes in this humidity or heatstroke could be a big problem."

"What are you, a nur..." the man stopped in mid-sentence when the woman zipped down her fatigues, revealing a light blue nurse's top.

"Yes, I am. I suggest we strip down to our civilian clothes, but keep the fatigues with us. We don't know what we'll encounter heading up that hill. And before we go anywhere, I want to know who's on my side. I'm Whitney Banks from Dallas."

Jack and C. J. began stripping their fatigues off—Jack revealing his T-shirt and gym shorts, while C. J. had on a stylish tan business suit.

"I'm Jack Forrest, a high school football coach from near Chicago."

"C. J. McCormick, an advertising exec from Seattle."

"Jack, you might want to keep your fatigues over your legs," Whitney warned. "It'll protect them. Just tie the arms around your waist."

"That's a good idea," Jack said. "It looks like all of us were pulled right out of our jobs."

A Latino woman was the last to pull off her goggles and helmet. Watching her shake out her long black hair, Jack surmised she would have been an extremely beautiful woman except that she was plastered in enough makeup to make Tammy Faye green with envy. She was tall, probably close to five foot ten, and looked about as shaken up as C. J. had been.

"I'm Maria Lopez, from Las Vegas."

Maria zipped down her fatigues, revealing a skin-tight, low-cut bodysuit, adorned in sequins, that left little to the imagination.

The other male contestant swore loudly, staring blatantly up and down her slender body. "We got ourselves a dancer!"

Maria responded with a roll of her eyes, then pulled the zipper back up to just above her chest. "I think I'll keep this thing on for the time being."

"Suit yourself," he chuckled, pulling down his own fatigues revealing an Oakland Raiders jersey adorned with the number eighty. "I'm Eddie Hill, a businessman from L.A." The way he stressed "businessman" made Jack wonder exactly what kind of business he ran.

"Now we've wasted enough time—let's get moving," Eddie scowled, turning to leave.

"Wait a minute," Jack interrupted. "I think Whitney had a point. Let's check our bearings before we go blindly into that jungle."

"I've already looked … the camp is due east from us, four miles." Eddie pointed beyond the brush behind him. "That way."

The group looked behind him, catching sight of the other team heading off into the lush rainforest while one of the men thrashed about with the machete.

"See?" Eddie pushed. "We're already losing ground."

"Just hold on a minute, Eddie. What elevation?" Jack asked.

"What do you mean, what elevation?"

"I mean, is the base camp at sea level?" Jack asked, pointing up to the rising hills above the jungle foliage. "Or is it somewhere at the top of those hills?"

Eddie shrugged, swearing as he admitted he didn't know.

Jack unzipped the survival pack strapped around his waist, pulling out a small, handheld GPS receiver. The unit was already turned on and displayed their position by a flashing blue dot at the bottom of the screen. There was a green outline showing part of the island, and at the top, a red target blinked, evidently showing where the base camp was located.

"Eddie's right, it's a little over four miles away," Jack said, as he kept pushing buttons.

"How do you know how to work that thing?" C. J. asked.

"I don't … just guessing." Jack played around with the menu buttons, trying to find a display that would read out the elevation of the base camp. He hit the "quit" button and the screen cycled to a compass display. One more push and Jack was looking at an elevation screen.

"Ah, here it is," Jack said.

"C'mon, we're losing time," Eddie growled.

The rest of his team gathered around Jack and looked over his shoulder. Jack moved the red crosshairs over the base camp and pressed the "enter" key.

"It looks like the camp is 512 feet above sea level." Jack looked up again at the large hill looming over them. "That looks three times that height. I think we'd have to cross over the top and hike back down to get there."

"So what are you suggesting?" Maria asked.

"Not sure yet." Jack continued to push buttons. "I want to get a wider look at the island—see how far inland the camp is."

Eddie swore again, heading for the jungle. "You already cost us the machete. I'm not waiting any longer."

"Wait," Whitney yelled. "We have to stick together."

Eddie kept walking. "Then I suggest you all follow me!"

"Eddie, come on," C. J. called out. "There might be a better way to go."

"The other team's already got a lead," Eddie yelled. "Don't you guys see that?"

"I've got it!" Jack exclaimed.

Eddie turned. "This better be good, man, he growled."

Jack walked over to Eddie. "If we head directly at the base camp, it's four miles, but we have to cross over that seventeen hundred foot mountain, through jungle brush and who knows what else. If we stay close to the coastline, we'd have about five and a half miles to go, but there'd be no mountain in the way."

Eddie glanced down past the end of the beach where the sand melted away and was replaced by jagged rocks.

"And just how do you suggest we do that?" Eddie asked.

"We walk along the beach when we can and travel through the base of the jungle when we have to. I think it'll be faster—what do you say?" Jack turned to the women.

"I'm not a great climber," Whitney said. "I say we go around."

"I agree," C. J. chimed in.

"Maria?" Jack asked.

"It's a toss-up to me. Who's to say there isn't a trail up there that leads right to base camp."

"You may be right, but looking at how wide that mountain is, I don't see how there's an easy route to get to the other side," Jack answered.

"Eddie, what about you?" C. J. asked.

"All I know is we're behind already, wasting time." Eddie looked from the mountain to the path down the beach. He then stepped up into Jack's face. "You've already blown it once not gettin' us that machete. If you're wrong and we chunk this first challenge … you'll pay."

Jack straightened his back and kept his eyes locked right on Eddie without flinching. "I'm just trying to cover all the options, man. You're free to make your own choice here."

"No!" Whitney jumped in. "Vince said the first team that gets there—that would mean all of us. If we split up, there's no telling when the last member would show up."

"She's right," Maria added. "The other team already has a jump on us through the jungle. Maybe we'll outsmart them if we go around. I think it's worth the gamble."

With a last menacing look to Jack, Eddie finally turned in a huff and walked down the coastline.

A knock on her office door interrupted Kathryn's concentration.

"You busy?" Her principal, Jerry Swift, stuck his head into the room.

With a sigh, she shook her head. "Nothing that can't wait. Come on in."

Life would be a joy if Kathryn's job simply entailed administrating and educating the two-thousand-plus students at Royal High School. But when it came to politics—embodied by her boss walking through her door, wearing his usual plastic smile—sometimes the pay just wasn't worth the hassle.

Kathryn had excelled in school administration in the Illinois public school system, rising quickly through the ranks. At the age of thirty, she was the youngest vice principal in the county.

Jerry was short and large, barely able to fit into the barrel chair that sat opposite her desk. As usual, Kathryn mentally forced herself to keep her eyes away from the off-color toupee that rested on top of his head.

"What can I do for you?"

"You know the reason I'm here, Kathryn," Jerry responded as his smile evaporated into thin air.

"Well, just to make sure, why don't you enlighten me?"

Jerry scrunched forward in the chair, closing the distance between them. "Quit the cute talk. You know why I'm here. I want to know how we're going to handle our—how do I say it—fanatic football coach at the board meeting tomorrow night. Have you talked to him?"

Kathryn stood, walked around the desk, sat on the corner and looked down at her boss. She struggled to keep her voice even. "Jack is *not* a fanatic ..."

"Mr. Forrest," Jerry interrupted coldly, leaning back in his chair and glaring up at Kathryn, "will cost the school district thousands, maybe millions, if we don't stop this lawsuit. Have you talked with him yet?"

"Briefly, last night."

"Well, what's he going to do?"

Kathryn looked down, searching for words. "We didn't get that far. We were kind of interrupted."

"What do you mean interrupted?" Jerry's voice growled.

"Well, it's kind of hard ..."

"Never mind. Just get him in here. I want to hear it for myself."

"That's going to be kind of difficult." Kathryn rose, thinking it better to return to her chair and keep the desk between them. "Let me explain."

She described the incredible arrival of Vince Sinclair to the football stadium all the way through to Jack's quick departure aboard the helicopter.

Jerry listened intently before shaking his head and standing up from the chair. "Then he's made his decision."

"Wait, please," Kathryn pleaded softly. "Jack deserves to be heard."

"He just up and leaves in the middle of a school week—the beginning of spring training for the football team? For that alone, he should be fired, much less this lawsuit hanging over our heads!"

"I was there when he made the decision ... I said we'd cover his classes. I thought I could convince you to hold off on any decision about him for another week."

"You what?"

Kathryn sighed. "Look, things have gotten out of control over this thing. I thought maybe with Jack away for a bit, people might calm down."

Jerry placed his hands on Kathryn's desk and leaned in close to her face. "You thought wrong. I'll take Jack's absence tomorrow night to mean he refuses to abide by the requests of the board."

"Jerry, please ..."

"There is no way I'm going to jeopardize millions of dollars over one religious football coach who won't agree to a simple demand that will get us out of this mess," Jerry said firmly.

Kathryn shook her head. "You don't understand ..."

"Don't let your lack of experience or personal feelings get in the way here," Jerry's eyes darkened as he interrupted her, "... or you just might find yourself out of a job as well."

With that, he turned and stomped out of her office.

The trek along the coast had been more difficult than Jack imagined. They'd only been able to travel a few hundred feet, before the jagged rocks and dangerous surf forced them into the lower part of the jungle.

The brush was thick, with all sorts of exotic plants and trees Jack couldn't begin to identify. He was sure he looked silly with the arms of his fatigues tied around his waist, but Whitney had the right idea about protecting his legs. Countless times, he'd been thwacked by sharp branches and prickly leaves across his thighs and shins. His arms had several places where the cuts were bleeding.

And what made the trip that much more surreal were the camera crews hiking right along with them. Jack had to admit they were incredible. They hadn't slowed them down in the least—and true to Vince's words, they hadn't helped at all. As the hours passed, Jack began to find it easier to ignore them.

"Any idea how much farther?" Jack heard one of the women ask from behind him.

He stopped and pulled out his GPS unit. He'd taken the lead back from Eddie once the team had been forced away from the beach. Sweat dripped off his forehead and onto the receiver. It was unbearably hot and humid. Jack glanced back at the rest of the team as they straddled the ivy-looking fauna that covered the ground, waiting.

C. J. and Whitney were dripping wet and breathing hard. Eddie stood behind them, seemingly in better shape, but still bathed in sweat. The intensity of the sun and the heat had forced Maria to abandon her modesty and remove the arms of her fatigues, tying them around her waist as Jack had done. Her perspiration had turned the thin fabric of the dancer's costume totally see-through, giving the illusion that only the adorning sequins covered her.

Jack was momentarily frozen on her image—until Maria smiled. He quickly looked down at his GPS receiver, embarrassed. "We still have over two miles to go."

"All through brush like this?" C. J. asked.

"Sure be a lot easier with a machete," Eddie shot out.

"Look, everyone ought to sip a bit of their water," Whitney suggested. "We don't want to get dehydrated."

"Who put you in charge?" Eddie scowled. "We gotta keep it in gear, man!"

No one listened to Eddie as they reached into their survival packs and pulled out their small water bottles.

"I'm outta here." Eddie walked past Jack, taking the lead.

"Eddie, wait," Jack called after him.

Eddie spun around quicker than Jack could imagine and walked up in front of him, leaning right in front of his face.

"You ordering me, Forrest?"

"Look, it's like this. I'm sure you want to win this thing—hey, we all do. And tomorrow, when there's a new challenge and you and I are on different teams, then you go right ahead and do everything you can to intimidate me."

Eddie held his ground, snorting out a breath.

"But right now, we're on the same team," Jack continued as everyone watched in anticipation of what might happen. "I suggest you back off on the attitude and try and work together here."

Eddie clenched his fists, his biceps bulging as he contemplated how to respond.

"C'mon, Eddie," Whitney added.

"There'll be plenty of time to duke it out as the week progresses," C. J. said.

Finally, Eddie backed off a step. "I can be a team player ... but I'm watching you, Forrest."

Jack sighed, letting his shoulders sag. He placed his water bottle up to his mouth and started drinking.

"Not too much now," Whitney warned. "We should conserve."

The water was warm, but still tasted like gold. Eddie finally reached into his pack and grabbed his water bottle as well.

"Looks like we might get some rain," C. J. said.

Jack looked up above and noticed a cluster of large thunderheads building. "You may be right. I think we should head back to the coastline to see if it's traversable. It might cool us off a bit too."

"I'm for that," C. J. said.

Jack looked over at Eddie. "You OK with that?"

Eddie rolled his eyes. "Just keep it movin', homey."

Jack looked down at the GPS device. "It looks like the beach is only a third of a mile away—that direction." Jack pointed to his right, directly at a large outcropping of ferns that seemed to smother the trees ahead.

Placing his water bottle back into the pack, Jack started forward. "Everybody ready?"

A few grumbles were heard as the group stepped in behind him. Jack ducked under an opening in the fern wall and stepped into the most beautiful meadow he'd ever seen. It was roughly a football field long, covered in ferns that grew from the ground and formed walls on either side, until eventually meeting above them about seventy-five feet in the air. Jack moved a few steps in to allow the rest of the team and the camera crews to get inside.

They were totally enclosed.

Jack glanced around the meadow, amazed at the multiple shades of green all around him. He couldn't see any of the trees that were the support for the ferns, just the lush green in every direction he turned. The ferns blocked the sun, allowing just small beams of light to peek through. The view was stunning.

"This is incredible," Maria voiced behind him.

"Man, what I would give for a camera," C. J. added.

"Yeah, real pretty." Eddie broke the mood with his harsh voice. "Let's keep it moving up there."

Jack double-checked his compass reading, then headed toward the other side of the enclosed meadow. He kept his pace brisk even though part of him wanted to enjoy every bit of this wonderland they'd found.

With the extra room inside the meadow, C. J. came up and began walking beside him. "So, what were you doing when Vince Sinclair interrupted your life?"

Jack laughed. "I was sending a bunch of young football wannabes to the showers."

"That's right, you're a coach."

"We'd just finished our practice for the day—spring training, you know—and in drops Vince in a helicopter, right on the fifty-yard line. How about you?"

C. J. giggled. "I was presenting this new ad campaign to the CEO of this regional bank. I was selling him, too, with charts and all this fancy animation on PowerPoint, when all of a sudden, Vince pops in, along with the blinding lights from his camera crew."

"That must have been quite a sight. What did the CEO do?"

"You should've seen the look on his face. It was as if he was being blindsided by *60 Minutes* or something. He looked terrified. Of course, I recognized Vince immediately."

"I didn't."

"You don't watch *The Ultimate Challenge*?!?" C. J. was surprised.

"No, I've only seen the promos."

"Then you really don't know what you're in for, do you?"

Jack chuckled. "You mean aside from being shot, thrown out of a plane attached to a crazy man who flips around like a Romanian gymnast, and then hiking through the Amazon?"

"Oh, this is just the beginning."

"Yeah," Jack admitted. "I'm beginning to see that. What do you think will happen next?"

"I have no idea." C. J. gave Jack an encouraging smirk. "Just that it'll be something we could never expect."

Coming to the end of the meadow, Jack took one last glance around, admiring the great handiwork of such a creative God. He didn't know where they were, just that they were on an island in the middle of some ocean—and he couldn't even tell if it was the Atlantic or the Pacific.

"Come on! Why are we stopping?" Eddie had broken his trance.

Jack separated the ferns with his hands and stepped through into a small grove of trees. It was an incredible change of scenery. The lush green slipped away, replaced by the backside of the ferns—the stems and the branches of near lifeless trees. Yet the beauty remained, just on a different canvas.

Jack heard the pounding surf off in the distance. They didn't have far to go. Then a crash of thunder bellowed above, followed by raindrops pelting the trees all around them.

Kathryn's eyes swept over the budget estimates for the fall term, but her mind drifted a thousand miles away. She kept hearing Jerry's parting words: "*Don't let your lack of experience or personal feelings get in the way here or you just might find yourself out of a job as well.*"

The words had shaken her deeply. Not his attack on her youth or the unveiled threat toward her job, but his emphatic reference to her feelings.

She leaned away from the desk, giving up on the upcoming budget concerns. Spinning around in her chair, she looked out the window to the courtyard outside crammed with students moving to their last period class. She wondered where Jack was.

She'd been shocked when they'd pulled out the gun and shot him—nearly fainting herself. As he fell to the turf, she'd lunged forward to try and catch him. The producers had kept her at bay, promising that it was just a mild tranquilizer—all part of the game.

Watching them carry his lifeless body toward the helicopter, she'd immediately regretted her encouragement that he go with them. And since then, her apprehension had grown exponentially. She'd lain awake most of the night, visualizing segments she'd seen from the show's first season: the extreme competition; the lying and backstabbing required to stay in the game; but, most of all, the sexual situations the contestants were thrown into throughout the seven days.

A soft knock on the door brought her back to the present. She turned to see one of her counselors, Tim Livingston, standing in her doorway.

"So, how'd it go with the boss?"

"You didn't hang outside my door and listen?" Kathryn teased.

"No," Tim smiled. "The only thing I heard was the slam of the door when he left. So, I assume it didn't go very well for Jack, did it?"

"No, it didn't."

"He's not going to hold off the meeting tomorrow night, is he?"

Kathryn shook her head.

"I was afraid of that. I don't want this school to lose Jack." Tim said, stepping into the office.

You don't want to lose him?

"There's got to be a way around this." Kathryn tried to keep her mind focused.

"Is there any way of getting Jack back here?"

Kathryn shrugged. "I'm not even sure it would do any good to have him here."

"What do you mean?" Tim asked.

"I could see it in his eyes last night," Kathryn sighed. "He doesn't feel like he did anything wrong. He, all in good conscience, can't agree with the board's position. And I can't say that I blame him."

"You've got to be kidding," Tim chided. "All he has to do is apologize to the family. What's the big deal?"

"It's not that simple," Kathryn argued. "The family is demanding—and Swift is going along with them—that Jack has to do more than just apologize."

"So?"

"You don't get it," Kathryn sighed. "According to the language of the agreement, Jack has to agree that Jesus Christ is just one of many ways to get to God. He's got a big problem with that."

The team arrived at the ocean's edge soaked from head to toe. The rain had poured hard for the past twenty minutes, the wind whipped around them with a vengeance. Although drenched, it had at least given the group a break from the heat. But, as the clouds passed over and the sun's intensity began to once again beat down from above, their reprieve was short-lived.

Jack looked up the coastline. The tide had gone out several feet, making this section of beach appear passable. They'd be able to make better time for the next few hours.

"Come on, team. It looks like we've caught a break for a change," Jack called to the rest of the group.

"Wait," Whitney yelled. "I don't know about everybody else, but I need a rest."

Jack looked to the west, measuring the height of the sun, "We don't have much more daylight left. Two, maybe three hours."

"We can't stop!" Eddie growled.

"My feet are killing me," C. J. said, taking a seat on a nearby rock.

"Everything hurts," Maria added. The combined sweat and rain had washed away most of her stage makeup. Through the black streaks running down her cheeks, Jack was able to get his first glimpse of how she really looked—stunningly beautiful.

Plopping down on the rocky beach, Jack pulled out his GPS receiver and pushed through several menus. Pointing toward a rock-strewn outlet, he informed the group, "The base camp shouldn't be too far around that point."

"How far?" Whitney asked.

"Looks like less than two miles."

Eddie looked up toward the mountain they'd avoided. "Looks like the storm that hit us is drenching the mountain."

"With any luck, the jungle team is trapped right in the middle of it," C. J. hoped.

"It could make their journey a bit more dangerous—slippery, hard to see through the brush," Jack added.

"What happens if we don't get there first?" Maria asked.

"I don't know," Jack answered. "Anybody who's seen this show have any idea?"

"You never know," Whitney answered. "Usually, the winning team of a challenge is safe and at least one member on the losers gets booted out. But from what I've seen, even that doesn't always ring true. The producers always want to keep the contestants guessing."

"I just know I don't want to risk being on that losing team," Eddie muttered. "Let's get moving."

For the next hour and a half, the group made their way along the rocky beach. They made good time compared to fighting through the jungle foliage, but their footing was slippery and the lava rocks were sharp. Each of them had slipped several times and either scraped their hands or bloodied their shins, oftentimes both. Everyone was dragging.

"We should be getting close," Jack said, after rounding a particularly rocky point. Looking up the beach, Jack spotted a cliff that rose a good five hundred feet above the sea and blocked their path to continue along the beach. Jack stopped and reached for his GPS receiver.

Eddie cursed. "Nice, Forrest. Now we're stuck!"

"We're going to have to head back inland," C. J. moaned, her exhaustion evident.

"Hold on," Jack said, flipping through the menus.

"We're not going to make it before dark," Whitney said.

"I think that's it!" Jack exclaimed.

"What are you talking about?" Maria asked.

"That cliff—I'm pretty sure our base camp is right on top of it."

One of the crewmen rushed over to Jack, pointing his camera right at him. "Could you say that again?"

Just when he'd forgotten that there were cameras covering their every move. "What?" Jack asked.

"I missed it, repeat what you said."

"I said: 'Our base camp is up there.'"

"No, not like that—like you said it the first time, with excitement: 'I think that's it!'" The cameraman mimicked Jack.

"Are you serious?"

"Very."

Jack looked back at his teammates and shrugged, then turned back and, with a great amount of eagerness, said, "I think that's it!"

"No, that was way over the top. Just do it like you did the first time."

With his teammates laughing, Jack tried it one more time.

"I think that's it."

"Good," the cameraman said. "Now the second line, about the base camp being on top."

Jack repeated the line, trying hard not to roll his eyes at the absurdity of this "reality television."

"Good enough," the cameraman said, backing away from Jack and returning to his position slightly ahead of the pack.

Eddie stepped up to him. "Very real sounding there, my man."

"Hey, nobody said anything about acting," Jack laughed.

"How are we going to get up there?" C. J. asked.

"We'll have to get closer and check it out," Jack said.

"I'll lead," Eddie stepped ahead without a look back. "We've probably already lost after listening to you."

The group hiked in silence, too tired to talk. The closer they got, the more intimidating the cliffs appeared above them. They paused, looking up at the jagged rocks that seemed to spill into the ocean surf from the promising peak. The lowering sun cast various shades of reds and oranges over the splashing waves, adding a surreal beauty to their dilemma.

"I don't see any way to get up there," Whitney said discouragingly.

"With this game, I'll bet they expect us to climb straight up," C. J. added.

"Maybe we should have walked over the mountain," Maria sounded dejected.

"There's got to be a path," Eddie answered from the front.

C. J. headed off, searching toward the jungle. "I sure hope so."

They split up, pulling away branches and leaves from palms and ferns, looking for some sign of a trail.

"Over here!" Whitney yelled.

The four of them quickly gathered around her, looking off into the foreboding jungle beyond. It wasn't much, but the brush looked as if it had been trampled down recently, and was heading in a direction that could take them up the surrounding hill.

"I say we take it," C. J. offered.

"We sure can't climb that stupid cliff," Whitney pointed out.

"I'm in," Eddie said, stepping into the jungle. "We still might have a chance after all. Let's go."

Single file, the team made their way away from the rock-strewn beach and into the waiting jungle. The darkness consumed them quicker than they could have imagined. Even with the sun technically still above the horizon, the dense rainforest didn't allow much light to filter through.

Eddie led them along as quickly as he could, renewed in his attempt to be the first team to base camp. He swatted at branches, pushing himself along, stumbling, at times, over stumps he couldn't see.

Passing over a fallen tree, the path seemed to take shape along a narrow meadow of low clinging ivy.

"It's looking better up here!" Eddie explained to the group.

Eddie's pace picked up to a near jog without the branches to break through. With hope that the end of their trek was near, the rest of the team fell into place right behind him. Halfway through the meadow, Eddie's left foot landed on something other than ivy-covered dirt.

The cracking sound reached his ears, but not in time to stop his right foot from leaving the hard dirt behind. The load of his weight snapped whatever was below, and Eddie was suddenly falling. Jogging right behind him, C. J., Maria, Jack, and Whitney found the path collapsing right under their feet, and they all plunged into a deep pit as their screams echoed through the jungle.

Kathryn waited impatiently at the traffic light. After the stressful day at the school, she just wanted to get home and settle into a hot bath. She hadn't been able to get back on track after Jerry's visit. She had racked her brain all afternoon, but hadn't been able to come up with an idea on how to save Jack's job.

Their relationship had moved a step beyond professional, as Jack and Kathryn had gone out a few times over the past four months. Nothing serious yet, but a solid friendship had blossomed—especially since Kathryn had recently begun her own relationship with God. Jack had even included Kathryn in the last Monday night ritual with his mother. She'd enjoyed the evening immensely, seeing a new side of her football coach with his mom beside him. Kathryn couldn't remember a night when she'd laughed so much, even with the undercurrent of the loss of Amanda's husband and the building school board pressure. After the evening, Kathryn realized her feelings toward Jack had grown stronger.

The light finally changed to green, and, on an impulse that shocked her, Kathryn made a sharp, right turn. The way home had been straight ahead. But three-quarters of a mile, now directly in front of her, was Amanda Forrest's house.

Jack's team had fallen into a pit about six feet wide, approximately eight feet deep and running twelve feet along the length of the path. Effectively hiding the pit below was a patchwork of dead branches and a thin layer of ivy. Even if it had been the middle of the day, Eddie wouldn't have noticed. With the setting sun and the long shadows, the team didn't stand a chance of avoiding the trap. The bottom of the pit was soaked with four inches of water from the afternoon rain.

"Anybody hurt?" Jack called, feeling some small creature scoot by him in the water. He didn't want to stop and think about what it could be.

His only answer was a few grunts before Maria responded, "I think I sprained my ankle."

C. J. quickly added, "I think I'm OK. Eddie cushioned the fall."

"Get off me," Eddie growled.

Jack reached out and pulled C. J. off of Eddie, as Whitney made her way to Maria.

"Let me have a look," Whitney said, then expertly pressed and turned, gently checking her foot. "It doesn't seem to be broken. Let's see if you can put some weight on it."

Whitney helped her up. Maria grimaced, but she was able to bite her lip and keep from crying out as her ankle took the weight.

"You OK?" Jack asked.

"I'm not sure," Maria answered. "It hurts pretty bad."

"How are we going to get out of here?" Eddie demanded.

"The same way we got in—teamwork," Jack responded.

He looked up and spotted the camera crews all standing above, their lenses pointing down at them. "I don't suppose they'll be much help."

"It's amazing how the crews kept out of the trap," C. J. added. "Almost like they knew it was coming."

"All part of the game, I'm sure," Jack added. He took a step toward the side of the pit as his leg broke through the twigs. One sharp stick stabbed into his right shin.

"Ouch!"

"Careful," Whitney warned after the fact.

Jack reached down and pulled the stick out of his leg, pressing his hand against his shin to stave off any bleeding. He felt along the side of the pit, looking for any spots he could use to get a grip with his hands. The dirt was smooth. There seemed to be no chance of crawling up.

"Maybe the women could get up on Eddie's shoulders and climb out," C. J. said.

Jack looked above his head, trying to estimate if the women would be high enough on top of Eddie. "That could work. C'mon, Eddie."

"Then how are we going to get out?" Eddie said, getting up on his feet.

"I'll go up the same way," Jack answered. "Then we'll figure out a way to pull you out."

C. J. was first. Eddie bent his knee and leaned down, allowing C. J. to place her left foot on his left thigh. He took her right hand in his and lifted as she stepped up. Jack helped her keep her balance until she could put her right foot on Eddie's shoulder. Then she brought her left leg up and was able to stand.

"Can you reach the top?"

"Yeah, I've got it. Just give me a shove," C. J. yelled.

Eddie grabbed her ankles and pushed upward. C. J. grabbed for something to pull on, but the ivy was slick with rain. She slipped, nearly falling back into the pit. Eddie held tight and kept her balanced. On the second try, C. J. was able to get her knee up and over the top, and she crawled out.

"Made it!" C. J. exclaimed.

Whitney was successful on the first try, with C. J. helping from above.

Maria was next. Jack helped her step onto Eddie's thigh, but when she tried to put her weight on the injured right ankle up on Eddie's shoulder, she collapsed and fell back into Jack's arms.

"I'm sorry, my ankle wouldn't hold."

"Let's try it the other way," Eddie offered, moving his other leg out front. Jack helped Maria get her weak ankle up onto Eddie's thigh, then, as she stepped up to get her other leg on top of his shoulder, Jack supported most of her weight by placing one hand underneath her bottom and pushing up. To keep her supported on Eddie's shoulders, Jack kept hold of her right shin as she kept her balance on her left foot.

"All right, everybody ready?" Jack asked. "One, two, three ..."

Jack and Eddie pushed while Maria reached up to the edge of the pit. With C. J. and Whitney above, they were able to grab her arms and drag her onto the jungle floor.

Eddie looked at Jack. "OK, your turn."

"You think you can hold me?"

"Do we have a choice?"

Eddie switched his weight back around and offered Jack his left thigh. Jack stepped up on it, grabbed Eddie's hand and pulled himself up to his shoulders. Jack's one hundred and ninety pounds was a far cry from Maria's slim dancer's body. He could hear Eddie's labored breathing beneath him.

"Hold on, Eddie," Jack encouraged. "OK, push."

Jack reached out for C. J. and Whitney, who were grabbing for his arms, then placed all his weight on his left foot while throwing his right knee over the top. He then felt himself being dragged over the ivy by the women. He was free. Now all they had to do was get Eddie out.

Jack crawled back over to the edge of the pit and stretched his hands down.

"Can you reach me, Eddie?"

Eddie reached up—their hands were a good six inches from each other. They'd have to find another way.

"Ladies, give me your fatigues," Jack said, as he rolled over and pulled his legs out of his own outfit. Without arguing, C. J., Whitney, and Maria did the same and handed their fatigues over.

"Eddie," Jack called down as he tied the arms of one fatigue to the legs of another. "We're going to send these down to you. Hold on for dear life."

C. J. caught on to what Jack was doing and did the same thing to the other pair.

"All right. Whitney, you and C. J. take one set. Maria and I will take the other. Wrap a leg around one of your arms, then we'll drop the arms down to Eddie."

The four did as Jack instructed, then they dropped the arms over the side.

"Now dig in," Jack said. They all braced themselves to take on Eddie's weight.

Eddie grabbed onto the arms, wrapping a bit of the fabric around each wrist to better hold on. "You guys ready up there?"

"I think so," Jack answered. "Try to support your weight with the fatigues and step up the side."

Eddie slowly leaned his weight onto the fabric as he put one foot onto the pit's wall. Jack glanced over as C. J. and Whitney slid a few inches toward the pit.

"Hang on, ladies. Dig your heels into the dirt."

"It's slippery," Whitney groaned.

Eddie took his weight totally off his other foot, attempting to climb a bit higher. When he did, the leg Maria held onto slipped out of her hands and, suddenly, Jack was carrying all the weight. He couldn't hold on—the fatigues slipped out of his hands. Eddie fell to the bottom of the pit with a splash, the cracking of sticks and a loud grunt.

"I'm sorry," Maria quickly said.

Jack leaned over the pit, "You all right down there?"

A series of words came spewing out of the pit, half of them Jack didn't even recognize. The ones he did know, he would never repeat.

"I'll take that as a 'yes'," Jack chuckled. "C'mon, we can do this. Throw the fatigues back this way, Eddie."

A few seconds later, the fatigues were back on top and the team was ready for another try. Jack and Maria wound the legs of the fatigues around their arms an extra couple of times, hoping to avoid what happened on the first try. Out of the corner of Jack's eye, he noticed C. J. and Whitney doing the same thing.

"All right, let's try it again," Jack called. "Just get to where you can get a hand over the top of the pit, Eddie. Then we'll try and grab you."

"All right, let's do it," Eddie said below.

Eddie stretched the fatigues out until there was no slack, then he stepped up and pulled at the same time.

It was holding.

He took his second step up the wall, his full weight now on the fatigues. Jack, Maria, Whitney, and C. J. grunted, trying to keep from slipping back into the pit themselves.

Eddie's right foot slipped, but he hung on. He struggled, until his foot took hold against the wall, then pulled with all his might.

"Pull!" Jack ordered, as the team labored. Jack could feel Eddie making his way. Then he noticed a hand reach over the ledge on his side. He kept his right arm straining against the fatigues as he reached to grab Eddie's wrist with his left.

Once he had a hold of the wrist, Jack let go of the fabric and grabbed the wrist with both hands.

"Grab his other hand," Jack called over to Whitney. She was able to grab on as C. J. kept the fatigues tight.

"Great, Eddie," Jack called. "Now try and throw your leg up here."

A foot kicked up the dirt about two feet away from Maria. "Maria grab his leg and pull it up." Jack called, "C. J. get over there and help if you can."

Together, the two ladies were able to lift Eddie's leg up out of the pit. Once his knee hit the dirt, Eddie was able to pull himself all the way out.

All five of them rolled over on their backs, exhausted, staring up into the darkening sky.

Jack chuckled.

"What?" Maria asked.

"I'm just imagining how stupid we'll look when this part of the show airs."

Maria giggled, then finally Whitney and C. J. joined in laughing.

"We don't have time for this." Eddie sat up, looking over the four of them like they'd lost their minds. "We're running out of light!"

"You're right once again, my man." Jack continued laughing, ignoring the stabbing pain in his shin. "But it sure feels good."

8

Kathryn parked across the street from Amanda's two-story brick house, trying to weigh the pros and cons of getting out of the car. She needed to talk with someone, but Jack's mother certainly wasn't the logical choice. Amanda would be too emotionally involved.

Kathryn chuckled. As if she wasn't?

The controversy had been brewing for over two months. It started when Jack held an open football clinic the first weekend in February, coinciding with the Super Bowl. As Jack had explained it to Kathryn, he'd promoted it heavily in the neighborhoods around Wheaton—Aurora, Lombard, Carol Stream, Elmhurst—hoping to draw some of the troubled kids away from the gang activity in their areas. Jack thought it would be great to show them there were other options in life.

To put it mildly, there were those in the alumni booster club who didn't think this was such a good idea. When they couldn't get the event cancelled, they made it very clear to Jack that they didn't want any of those "hoodlums" allowed on the team in the fall.

The weekend clinic had gone off without a hitch the first day. But then came Sunday afternoon. After the basics of blocking, tackling, catching, and running had been covered, Jack planned to show the kids the full excitement of the game. Full-contact football was out of the question, so Jack passed out the flag belts they used in his P.E. classes and split the kids into two teams. In flag football, instead of tackling the ball carrier, the opposing player pulls one of the flags off of his belt to end the play.

The scrimmage started off well, until a couple of kids from the wrong side of the tracks intentionally forgot to grab the flag, and gang-tackled the rich, white quarterback on the opposing team. It was a brutal tackle. One kid hit him low, tying up his legs, while the other one slammed into his chest, driving him to the ground.

Jack was on the field immediately, pulling the two kids off of Chris Swanson, a sophomore from a well-off Wheaton family. He was unconscious, having taken a hard blow to his head when it struck the turf. The offending kids were slapping high-fives and laughing until Jack yelled at them to sit on the bench.

Shouting to his assistant coach to send for an ambulance, Jack leaned over young Chris. Without hesitation, he had placed his hand on the young boy's chest and softly prayed.

A moment later, Chris opened his eyes halfway, then groaned as he rolled over and vomited.

Jack held his head through the ordeal, then helped him lie back down.

"How you feeling, big guy?" Jack asked.

"My head is killing me," Chris slurred. "What happened?"

"You got hit pretty good, don't you remember?"

"No," Chris moaned once again, "I don't."

Jack looked down at Chris's eyes: his pupils were wide open.

"Just take it easy," Jack said. "We'll get you to the hospital and have you checked out."

Jack had stayed at the hospital for several hours until the doctors had checked Chris over thoroughly. He had a concussion, but fortunately no broken bones. The good news seemingly went right by Chris's father, who continued to berate Jack for his lack of judgment in holding the clinic in the first place.

Jack went in to see Chris one last time before he left for the evening.

He wished him well and apologized profusely for what had happened to him. As Jack was leaving, Chris stopped him.

"Coach, could I ask you a question?"

Jack stopped and turned around. "Sure Chris, what is it?"

"At the football field, when I was on the ground …"

Jack stepped back toward Chris's bed. "Yes?"

"I remember hearing you … *pray.*"

Jack angled his head, looking into the sixteen-year-old's eyes. Chris was nervous, yet seemed to be sincerely questioning. Jack moved closer and sat next to him.

"Yeah. When you were unconscious, I did pray for you."

And little did Jack know, that was the moment he had become the target.

Kathryn sat in the car looking at Amanda's house, the engine still idling. She'd kept her feelings for Jack at bay while dealing with Jerry Swift and the school board. She had to stay professional and not let her personal attraction toward Jack sway any decisions that had to be made concerning his conduct.

But all that flew out the window last Monday night. She'd tripped—fallen, as some would say. She couldn't deny any longer that she was in love. What a perfectly awful time for that to happen.

Kathryn looked away from the house, placed her foot on the brake, and put the car in drive. She jumped when there was a soft tapping on her window. She turned in shock to see Jack's mother standing beside her car with a pile of mail in her hands.

"Were you looking for me?" Amanda asked.

"No … yes," Kathryn didn't know how to respond.

"Well, come on in," Amanda offered. "It's way too chilly out here to be sitting in your car."

Kathryn smiled at Amanda's invitation before she put the car back into park and shut the engine off. *Too late to turn back now.*

"Keep hold of my shirt, I think we're getting close," Eddie called out to the team behind him.

"How can you see where you're going?" C. J. asked.

"It's an obvious trail now—we're heading up the hill," Eddie said.

The team had completed their trek through the meadow, then headed up a trail that led through more jungle. As the sky grew darker and darker, they'd decided on holding on to each other in some way as they kept hiking. Eddie kept in the lead, followed by C. J., Whitney, and then Maria and Jack taking up the rear. He was walking beside her—his arm around her waist, her arm over his shoulder—trying to keep her weight off the injured ankle while not stumbling in the dark. He tried to ignore the pain in his own shin from the hole the stick had left.

As the darkness settled over them, Jack wondered if they should just stop for the night. Who knows what lay ahead on the trail they were on. Without light, Eddie could lead them right off a cliff. Plus, he didn't know what kind of damage Maria could be doing to her ankle. But that would also mean giving up on the challenge; the other team would certainly beat them to the base camp.

"Yo, we've got lights ahead!" Jack heard Eddie cry out.

Eddie picked up the pace, and the ladies and Jack struggled to keep up. Sure enough, up ahead were tiki torches illuminating a series of stone steps that hopefully lead to the top of the cliff.

"I hear music! C'mon, let's move!" Eddie yelled, breaking away from C. J.

"Careful, Eddie," Jack tried to warn him. "There could be another trap of some sort."

There was no stopping him as Eddie bounded up the steps heading for the top. C. J. was right behind him. It seemed the promise of making it to base camp, and getting off her feet, gave her renewed energy.

Whitney stayed back with Maria and Jack, looking for signs of anything dangerous. Fortunately, there were none—just a clear-lit path to the end of the trail.

"Oh my," C. J. sounded above them.

"What?" Whitney asked.

"It's incredible. Get up here."

Jack and Maria were the last ones to climb atop the cliff and get their first glimpse of base camp. Expecting a *Survivor*-type scenario where the teams had to build their own shelter and scrounge around for their own food. Jack was in shock when he stood and faced a magnificent hilltop resort. Dozens of small bungalows glowing from the flicker of burning torches surrounded a rock-creek styled, shimmering swimming pool. A large building sat off in the distance, presumably a meeting center or possibly a restaurant, overlooking the ocean below. Across the pool, with a dance floor and full bar beside them, a reggae band, complete with steel drums, was rocking away. Whatever Jack had expected in undertaking *The Ultimate Challenge*, it certainly didn't include five-star resort living. He wondered if there would be room service.

The only thing that marred the incredible vision was the five members of the opposite team happily splashing around in the pool. "Come on in, the water's wonderful," a voice in the pool called out jokingly.

Looking at the rest of his team, Jack could see the soiled faces, the scrapes and scratches running up and down everyone's legs and arms. Their fatigues were torn and tattered. Eddie's Raiders' jersey was in shambles. Maria's tights were ripped and most of the sequins had been torn off—leaving her barely covered. Her hair was a mess, curled and frizzy because of the high humidity. C. J. and Whitney stood by her appearing just as ragged.

They looked like losers.

"Welcome to base camp." Vince Sinclair stepped out of the shadows to meet them. "As I'm sure you can surmise, you have lost the first challenge."

"How long have they been here?" Eddie asked.

"It was closer than you might think, Eddie," Vince answered. "Thirty, maybe forty minutes."

Eddie swore, staring right at Jack "It's your fault, man! We shoulda hiked over the mountain."

"Actually," Vince said. "If you hadn't fallen into our nasty little trap, your team could well have won."

Jack watched Eddie stomp away in disgust.

"So now what happens?" C. J. asked.

"For now—you can all get cleaned up. We'll show you to your bungalows, allow you to freshen up. You're welcome to take a swim if you like. We'll find out which one of you is leaving us over dinner—in one hour."

"I don't think there's anything I can do to save him," Kathryn sighed, taking a pause to sip from the mug set in front of her.

Amanda had brought her inside the kitchen and boiled some water, and then made herbal tea. It didn't take long for Kathryn to open up and share what had happened that morning with the principal.

"You're right," Amanda said matter-of-factly.

Kathryn's eyebrows rose as she stared at Amanda over the mug. She couldn't have heard her right.

"There's nothing you can do, Kathryn. His career is in God's hands." Amanda reached across the table and lightly touched the top of Kathryn's hand. "It always was."

Kathryn's head shook slightly. It was just like something Jack would say. They would be talking about some ordinary, everyday topic, and he would come out of the blue with a comment that would bring God right to the forefront. She still wasn't used to it. In Kathryn's former world, God wasn't anywhere near that personal.

"If Jack would just do what they've asked …" Kathryn protested.

"Really? You've got to know by now what the school board is really asking of Jack."

Kathryn lowered her head, nodding slightly. She struggled to juxtapose the Jack she was growing to love—the one who seemed to find a way to place God at the center of everything—with the Jack who would have to declare Jesus as not being the only path to God. It couldn't be done—even to keep his job.

"I think I'm beginning to understand," Kathryn said quietly.

"It's not your fault." The warmth flowing from Amanda was soothing, even as her face became serious. "Or your responsibility."

"But I'm his vice principal."

"True, but Jack doesn't look to you, the high school, or even the almighty school board for his paycheck."

"What do you mean?"

"It's simple, and I'm sure this is exactly how Jack would put it," Amanda stated. "God is the source of Jack's finances. Right now, God has decided to use Royal High School to meet his needs. If that changes, then God will have something else for him."

"So Jack's not worried about losing his job?"

Amanda's grin returned. "Oh, I'm sure there's some anxiety over it all. He'd sure miss the kids, the football team, some of the teachers, his vice principal …"

Kathryn was embarrassed to feel her face flush.

"And it's not like he's got thousands of dollars in savings to survive unemployment. But if I know Jack, his faith isn't in his coaching job—it's in his Lord."

"The very same Lord he won't deny."

"Exactly," Amanda nodded.

"So, there's nothing we can do."

"Oh, I didn't say that," Amanda said with a grin. "We pray. And then, if God gives us a direction, we follow it."

Kathryn shook her head. "I think I've still got a lot to learn from you two."

They sat in silence for a few moments. Kathryn felt like Amanda was just patiently giving her a chance to digest everything they'd talked about.

"Oh, my!" Kathryn suddenly jumped. "What time is it?"

Amanda looked across the kitchen to a coo-coo clock that Kevin had bought on their trip to Switzerland three years before. "It's eight forty-five."

"We're missing *The Ultimate Challenge,*" Kathryn said urgently. "It's on right now."

Jack was impressed. The bungalow turned out to be a one-bedroom suite with a mini-kitchen, a large living area, and two bathrooms—one with a Jacuzzi tub. Wicker furniture with brightly colored flowered cushions adorned each room. Hanging in the closet was a complete change of clothes for Jack: a Hawaiian shirt, cargo shorts, and sandals—all in his size. There was also a pair of swimming trunks. It seemed they had thought of everything.

Before Jack could decide if he wanted to go for a swim or take a long, hot shower, there was a knock on his door. He was surprised to see Whitney holding a pile of clothes.

"Could I ask you a favor, Jack?"

"What can I do for you?" he asked.

"It's kind of crazy," Whitney seemed embarrassed. "But I have this thing about the color yellow—my bungalow is all yellow."

Jack laughed, wondering if this was some kind of strategy she was employing. "You want to switch rooms?"

"If you wouldn't mind," Whitney grinned up at Jack.

"Sure," Jack shrugged. "No problem."

"Thanks." Whitney stepped into the room. "I really appreciate this."

After packing up the clothes, Jack made his way one bungalow over. He realized it was the first time he'd been alone since Vince's helicopter had landed in the middle of the football field. He hadn't had a moment to think about Kathryn or the whole mess left behind in Wheaton. There wasn't much he could do about it now. But he was sure Kathryn was stressing over it. He wished there was a way he could reach her—he was crazy to have left on such a stupid adventure. Maybe the best thing would be if he was kicked out of the contest at dinner, and was able to go back and face the school board on Wednesday.

A shower was a definite must before then. He pulled off his soaked and tattered Royal T-shirt, taking a moment to clean up his punctured shin with one of the hand towels. The bleeding had stopped, so he didn't think it would cause much of a problem for him. He walked over and opened the shower door—and stopped cold.

Staring straight at him, from between the rows of tiles just above the water knob, was a glass bubble covering the lens of a video camera. He turned and investigated the room. Sure enough, high above in the corners were two more cameras. He stepped out into the bedroom and found another couple of lenses sticking out of the upper corners of the ceiling—one of them facing directly toward the bed. He checked the small room tucked away with the toilet. Sure enough, another camera.

Suddenly, he didn't feel quite so alone.

Jack contemplated his options. He would have to get used to having cameras covering his every move for the next seven days—if he survived. He didn't like it. He felt too self-conscious. He stepped back into the closet and grabbed the swim trunks. He looked around intently, looking for a camera.

Smiling, Jack couldn't see one. He turned out the bathroom lights, then stepped back into the closet area. He proceeded to pull off his shorts and underwear and slip on the swimsuit.

Stepping back into the bathroom, Jack turned the light back on, reached into the shower, and turned on the water. Now he was ready for a shower.

Amanda sat transfixed by the television screen, her eyes wide and unblinking.

"I had no idea …" she muttered.

The Ultimate Challenge had just ended with the cliffhanger for the week, telling viewers to stay tuned for exciting previews of the next episode.

"I'd forgotten," Kathryn sat next to her, dazed as well. "I hadn't watched the show since the first season."

"What has my son gotten himself into?" Amanda turned and looked at Kathryn.

Kathryn shook her head. "He won't last—there's no way."

"I didn't even know they had stuff like that on network television," Amanda sighed. "I've never seen so much sex, lying, backstabbing—I thought they could only do this type of thing on HBO or Showtime."

"No, but it'd be a lot worse on HBO."

"But the swearing, the nudity …"

"Yeah, notice how they bleeped the words and pixilated the video," Kathryn explained.

"A lot of good that did. I could tell every word they bleeped out. And there wasn't much left to the imagination with the distorted video either."

"I know."

The two sat stunned, the commercial blaring into the room unwatched.

"There was something else I hadn't told you," Kathryn confessed.

"What?"

"When they took Jack away, they shot him with some kind of tranquilizer."

"They *what*?" Amanda cried.

"He was unconscious when they carried him into the helicopter."

"Oh, my," Amanda sighed. "This game just sounds ridiculous."

"I'm sorry I talked him into it." Kathryn looked down at the carpet.

"Next week, on *The Ultimate Challenge* . . ." The announcer broke through their daze.

Amanda turned back to the TV, almost as if she were passing a wreck on the freeway and didn't want to look at the carnage, even though she knew she would. Next week would be more of the same sleaze. She was disgusted. She knew the entertainment industry was sinking lower and lower, but she had no idea it had gotten this bad. And Jack was somewhere right in the middle of it.

But however upset she felt at that moment didn't hold a candle to the total shock wave that slammed into her as the credits began. The first name lit the screen like a slap to her face.

Executive Producer—Zeke Roberts.

"Oh, no!" Amanda gasped.

"What?" Kathryn rushed to her side. "Are you OK?"

The credits continued to roll, but that one name was burned into Amanda's memory: Zeke Roberts. She turned toward Kathryn, her eyes flaring with fear. "We've got to get Jack out of there!"

On the second floor of the conference center, just above the restaurant, a series of rooms had been taken over by the production staff. Several housed all the camera gear, cases of videotapes, and rows and rows of battery chargers lining the walls. Three rooms had complete Avid editing suites built into them. It took another two rooms to house the electronics for the remote control cameras that had been wired throughout the resort. And the largest room at the end of the hall had a complete control room built that would rival any of the network news operations.

More than one hundred video monitors had been installed to keep real-time track of the guests over the next seven days. They were grouped according to the location in the resort: seven cameras around the pool area, twenty in the dining hall, not to mention the ten cameras in each bungalow that housed a contestant.

It was the feed from the camera pointing directly over Jack's shower that was punched up on the large, color, plasma screen in the center of the wall. The large speakers, hanging from each corner, filled the room with Jack's off-key singing mixed with the sound of water spraying against skin and tile.

The room was kept dark with the exception of small pools of light where the directing team sat in the front row. Behind them, and raised up three feet so that the row of monitors wouldn't be blocked by their heads, was a plush sectional sofa, a coffee table, and a couple of cushy La-Z-Boy recliners.

Zeke Roberts sat in the middle of the sofa, studying the image of Jack rinsing the soap out of his hair. To his left sat Vince Sinclair. To his right was supervising producer and longtime friend, Travis Diamond.

"So, who's going to be the first one booted out?" Vince asked.

"Not sure yet," Zeke said, more to himself than in answer to Vince's question. Then, with a louder voice, he called out to the front bench, "Punch up the lower angle."

With a nod from the director, the technical director reached over and pushed down on the button labeled "camera twenty-seven", coinciding with the camera positioned between the tiles right in front of Jack. The wide-angle lens had a fish-eye effect on Jack's image, making his lean torso look like he had a slight beer gut. Oblivious to the eyes watching him, Jack's hand moved above the camera, reaching for the bar of soap.

Zeke didn't let his eyes wander from the large image at the center of the room. With a hundred images to choose from, including various angles of the late arriving team, it wasn't like Zeke to fixate on one contestant—much less a male one. While the guys in the front row kept pointing out the great shots they were getting of the women changing and showering in the other bungalows, Zeke quietly kept his focus on Jack.

Vince looked from his executive producer to the plasma screen and back, "Why the interest in this one, Zeke?"

The producer took his eyes off the screen, and sunk back into the couch, smiling. "Oh, I don't know," he said evasively. "There's just something about him that intrigues me."

Vince nodded, accepting the answer—until he caught a glimpse of the dark expression from Travis's face sitting on the other side of Zeke. There was something going on he wasn't privy to.

"We've got to do something." Amanda paced the family room.

Kathryn couldn't believe the transformation. The peace and calm that Amanda had exhibited through the evening had vanished the instant the credits rolled.

"Amanda, what's happened?" Kathryn jumped up from the couch.

"It's him," Amanda blurted, walking back and forth. "He's trying to get to Jack—but I can't let him." She stopped and looked right at Kathryn. "We can't let him!"

"Amanda, calm down. What are you talking about?"

Amanda didn't respond. She just shook her head and turned, walking out of the room. She headed down the hallway toward the back of the house.

Kathryn stood frozen in the living room. She didn't know how to react. Should she follow and try to comfort, or stay and allow Amanda some time alone? Then she heard the sobbing coming from the other room. Kathryn walked slowly down the dark hallway.

Amanda had retreated into her bedroom. As Kathryn approached, she could see Amanda sitting on the edge of the bed, staring off as if in shock. Fresh tears lined her face.

"Amanda," Kathryn said softly, calmly sitting on the bed beside her. "What's going on? It's just a reality show."

Amanda sniffed, then said in a near whisper, "You don't understand."

Kathryn stayed quiet, waiting for Amanda to explain. After a moment, Amanda glanced over at her.

Kathryn was amazed at the difference. Usually, it was hard to believe that Amanda, with her bright face that showed only minor creases around the eyes when she smiled, could have a son Jack's age. But the woman sitting beside Kathryn now looked every bit of forty-eight. Something had reached deep into Amanda and frightened her to the core.

"There has to be a way to reach him," Amanda pleaded.

Kathryn shook her head. "As far as I know, he's unreachable until it's over."

"I've got to find a way …"

"What's going on, Amanda?" Kathryn asked gently.

Amanda ignored the question, rising from the bed. "Didn't you mention something about Jack signing a contract?"

"Yeah, I think it's in my car."

"Go get it, please. It must have the name of the production company on it—maybe a phone number."

It didn't take long for Kathryn to run to the car and back, holding the one-page contract in front of her.

"Let me see …" Kathryn looked at the top of the document as Amanda looked over her shoulder. "Zeke Roberts Productions … no phone number mentioned, but they do have a Beverly Hills address."

Amanda walked into the kitchen and grabbed for the phone, dialing 4-1-1.

"Yes, I'd like the number for," Amanda struggled to get out the name, "… Zeke Roberts Productions in Beverly Hills, California, please."

After a moment, Amanda scribbled out the number on a pad by the phone.

"Thank you," she said, before ending the call. She didn't even place the phone back on the cradle, but quickly dialed the 323 area code and the seven subsequent numbers.

Kathryn watched Amanda tap her foot nervously; she couldn't get over the change in her since they'd viewed the show.

"Hello, yes …" Amanda started to speak, then sighed and looked at Kathryn. "Answering machine."

Amanda listened for a few seconds, then rolled her eyes and slammed the phone back into its holder.

"Their office hours are from nine to six, West Coast time." Amanda looked at the clock on her microwave. "They went home over an hour ago."

"No emergency number?"

"No, not even a chance to leave a message, just 'Call back during normal business hours,'" Amanda repeated.

Kathryn walked over and took a seat on one of Amanda's bar stools. "You have to tell me what this is about."

Amanda shook her head, leaning over the kitchen countertop. "I'm not sure I can, Kathryn. It's too painful."

"Is Jack in some kind of danger?"

Amanda paused, weighing her words carefully. "No, not physically. Not yet, anyway."

The shower had brought some life back to Jack, but it also made him realize how hungry he was. He couldn't wait to get a plateful of anything. It was a short walk from his bungalow to the pool area. As Jack got closer, he counted the team members gathered around and realized that he was the last contestant to arrive.

"Finally, our tenth member," Vince proclaimed as everyone looked right at him.

Jack attempted a casual wave, but felt foolish. After his shower, he'd taken advantage of being alone to think through what might happen in the next few days, as well as to pray for a few moments. If the worst happened and he was the first one kicked out, he felt like he was ready.

"I'm sure you're all famished. Please, this way." Vince directed the group toward the main building.

Jack stepped in with the rest of the desert team. Everyone looked refreshed, the women looked great, but Eddie still reminded Jack of a bouncer. He was surprised to see Maria walking steadily beside him.

"Your ankle must feel a bit better," Jack commented.

"They had a doctor look at it." Dressed in her Hawaiian outfit, with her hair freshly washed and brushed, and wearing little or no makeup, Maria was stunning. Jack couldn't take his eyes off of her as she spoke. "It's wrapped up like a chimichanga, but at least I can put some weight on it now."

Jack laughed, "Good for you."

"They said if I couldn't walk on my own, I'd have been the first one sent home."

"I'm glad they got you fixed up."

"Me too." Maria grimaced with her next step, obviously still in some pain. "How's your leg, by the way?"

"It stings a bit, but at least there's no bleeding."

They walked into the main building. What would seem to have been the resort's only restaurant had been transformed into a television studio with a breath-taking tropical theme. The room was filled with a light smoke where tiki torches were scattered about, combined with moving colored lights, suspended from the ceiling, to cast wondrous magical patterns that seemed to float in the air.

The center of the room had been partitioned off with grass curtains and fake walls. Jack deduced that it was to hide all the cameras—perhaps to give the contestants less of a sense that every move they made was being recorded. As if that would help them act more natural.

On one side, there was a long table set up buffet style with an amazing assortment of salads, fruit, soup, and a couple of tasty-looking entrées. There was a five foot tall, carved ice figure of a totem pole at one end of the table and a champagne tower of glasses of equal height at the other. Two round tables were set in the middle of the room, one decorated in camouflage green, the other in camouflage brown. Between them, against one of the grass curtains, was a smaller rectangular table where Vince took his place.

"Please, help yourself to the buffet," Vince instructed. "Then make your way to your team's table."

The winning team made their way down the buffet line first. They were animated, chatting merrily as they savored their victory.

This was the first time Jack had a chance to view the team that had beaten them. It was made up of three men and two women. Unlike meeting his team, where each had been dressed in their work clothes, the green team was in their Hawaiian shirts and shorts outfits, with no hint of their occupations. Jack eyed the men first—an Asian, an African-American, and a short, preppy-looking white guy who looked like the easiest one to beat in a physical challenge. The women were both attractive, which seemed to be the one requirement for the ladies of *The Ultimate Challenge.* One of them, the blonde, was a knockout. Jack assumed she was either an actress or a model in her early- to mid-twenties. The brunette was quite a looker herself, but probably a good ten years older.

Jack's team made their way through the line patiently and quietly, each envious of the other team, and seemingly worried about soon losing the chance at ten million dollars.

"C'mon team," Jack finally spoke up. "It's not like we're at a funeral or something."

"One of us is," Eddie growled. "They just don't know it yet. And it should be you."

"I hope they don't give you a vote, then," Jack returned. He piled on the lettuce and greens, adding a bowl of some kind of soup as well.

"Conch chowder," a dark man dressed in a tuxedo explained from behind the table. "You like."

"I'm sure I will," Jack grinned. He stepped down the line, adding some minced crawfish and grouper cutlets to his plate. They seemed to be staying with the seafood theme for the night. The smells were wonderful. Jack couldn't resist any longer, grabbing a carrot off his plate and biting into it.

"If we just hadn't fallen into that pit," C. J. sighed.

"Like it was my fault?" Eddie snapped.

"No, I didn't mean that," C. J. answered. "It sounds like we might have won if we could've avoided it. That's all."

Eddie grunted at her as he headed to the table. "It would have been different if we'd had the machete in the first place."

C. J. leaned back toward Jack and whispered, "I hope he's the first to go—drives me crazy."

11

"We hope you've enjoyed your dinner this evening," Vince said, after allowing the contestants only fifteen minutes to enjoy their meals. They all expressed their appreciation, although the winning team showed a bit more enthusiasm.

"Tonight, we're left with the task of sending one of our contestants home. So, as we assess what went wrong with the desert team, does anybody want to make a comment?"

Jack looked around his table. Eddie was already jumping to his feet.

"It's all on Forrest, man." Eddie pointed right at Jack. "He was the first to land on the beach, he shoulda grabbed the machete before the other team could get it."

Vince nodded. "Jack, you have anything to say to that?"

Jack could see where this was headed. It looked like Vince was goading his team into turning on themselves. The only thing was, Eddie didn't need any encouragement.

"It wasn't his fault," Maria said, as she stood up. "I was still above Jack when he hit the beach. The other team landed a bit earlier and a lot closer to the flag."

"Then he shoulda taken it from them," Eddie added, turning to sneer at Jack. "No rules, remember?"

"Well, before we go any further,"—Vince cut into the argument —"why don't we take a look at exactly what happened?"

Vince motioned to his left where the grass curtain parted, revealing a large screen that came to life to show the last few feet of Jack's descent. The room watched in silence as the morning jump played out in living color before them. They could see Jack landing perfectly, getting unhooked from his dive expert as he looked for the flag that held the machete. From the angle the camera was shooting, you couldn't tell how far ahead of Jack the woman from the jungle team was. But as Jack attempted to run after her, it was apparent that he didn't come anywhere close to running a straight line. He zigzagged his way across the beach, stumbling and nearly falling several times as the green team member managed to beat him to the machete.

The jungle team erupted in applause with a few shouts of, "Way to go, Tara!"

Jack lowered his head. He looked like he was drunk.

The screen dimmed, and Vince looked back toward the desert team. "Actually, there were two machetes on the beach."

"What?!?" Jack's team shrieked in unison.

"Where?" Eddie asked.

"About ten paces from the other one," Vince grinned. "Half buried in the sand. You'll have to learn to not take everything at face value here at *The Ultimate Challenge.*"

Jack and several around him shook their heads. How could they have known?

"You shoulda spotted it, Forrest," Eddie shouted. "You were the closest."

"Give it a break, Eddie," Whitney spun toward him. "You want to talk about blame, how about leading us right into that pit?"

"You wouldn't have seen it either!" Eddie spun at her defensively.

"Are you saying that it was Eddie's fault you guys fell into the trap?" Vince asked Whitney.

"I'm just saying that we can't blame one person," Whitney explained. "It wasn't Jack's fault we lost."

"I agree," Maria added. "I think he was kind of like our leader."

"Isn't it the leader's fault when a team loses?" Eddie chimed in again.

"Jack used his brain rather than just blindly running through the jungle like you wanted to," C. J. argued.

"It seems like there are those who would blame you." Vince's eyes bore right through Eddie.

"If I'd landed first, we'd have had the machete. One way or another," Eddie said matter-of-factly and sat down.

The room fell silent, everyone waiting for somebody else to speak.

"We still haven't heard from you, Jack," Vince finally said, breaking the silence.

Jack stayed seated, looking first at his team, then up to Vince. He was resolved that it would probably be best to get kicked out of the game and go back to try and save his job. "What can I say, the other team beat us. I tried to use my head and find the best way to get to base camp. The team went with it, but it didn't work. We lost."

"See," Eddie pointed out. "Even Jack blames himself. He should go!"

"He should not!" Maria snapped at Eddie. "If anybody should go, it should be me. If I hadn't sprained my ankle, maybe we would've made it here in time."

"Or how about me?" Whitney joined in. "I couldn't keep up with the pace through the jungle. Maybe it's my fault."

"Me too," C. J. added. "I was so disoriented after the jump, Jack had to lead me across the beach to get to you guys."

"Oh, c'mon." Eddie shrugged. "What is this?"

"Interesting, Jack." Vince smiled from his table. "I've never seen a contestant on our show use reverse psychology so effectively."

Jack shook his head. "That's not what I was doing. I was just being honest."

Vince laughed. "Hmm, honesty. Now that would really be a first on *The Ultimate Challenge*."

A white phone beside Vince rang. He picked it up, listened for a moment, then hung up without saying a word.

"It's nearly time. Our producers would like each of you to pick the member of your team that you think deserves to be kicked out of *The Ultimate Challenge*. C. J., we'll start with you."

C. J. looked uncomfortably around the table. "I'd have to say Whitney. She slowed us down the most."

"Whitney?" Vince said.

"Wow!" Whitney flashed C. J. a wicked stare. "I didn't really mean it, C. J. I was just supporting Jack."

The jungle team laughed.

"I'd have to say give the boot to Eddie," Whitney continued. "Just for his stinkin' attitude."

"Eddie?" Vince asked.

"Jack, all the way," Eddie snarled.

"Jack, your turn." Vince said.

One vote for Whitney. One for Eddie. One for Jack.

If Jack added a second vote for Eddie, the worst he could do was tie. And that's only if Maria voted against him—which he doubted. But did these votes mean anything? Who made the real decision? Maybe he could get past this first hurdle and have a real chance at the ten million—but did he want to? The answer surprised him.

"Jack?" Vince prompted.

"I don't want to pick anybody," Jack finally said. "We all did our best."

"You have to," Vince said.

"I have to?"

"Yes, you have to."

"Well, then I …" Jack started, then stopped.

"What's the problem?" Vince asked.

"I'm sorry, I can't."

"Hey," Eddie stood up. "He's trying to pull something."

"Jack …" Vince prompted.

"It's not a trick," Jack said.

"Make him pick!" Eddie yelled.

"Jack, you have to," Vince repeated.

"All right, I'll pick Eddie for the same reason Whitney did," Jack raised his voice, then turned to Eddie. "You happy now?"

Eddie sat down with a troubled look on his face.

"OK," Vince chuckled. "Now, Maria."

"I definitely pick Eddie," Maria returned. "He's rude, and I hope not to have him on my team the rest of the week."

"Interesting," Vince said. "We have one vote for Whitney, one vote for Jack, and three votes for Eddie. But remember our show is unique. Your votes don't matter. Would all the members of the jungle team, please follow me."

With that, Vince turned and left the room as the five members of the winning team followed.

Amanda had waited for Kathryn to leave before slipping up into the attic and pulling down a box she hadn't touched since college. She carefully descended the pull-down staircase, holding the dusty memories.

After the show had ended, Kathryn had quietly stayed awhile. Amanda thought she was hoping for some kind of explanation for her outburst. But she couldn't give one.

She made her way to the kitchen table and set the box down. Cutting the tape holding the top of it closed, she then pulled the flaps open. She had to dig toward the bottom to get what she was looking for: the yearbook from her last year at Yale University, her junior year.

She pulled it out of the box and held it against her chest, pondering if she really wanted to open it and face the wounds from the past. Almost as if she couldn't stop herself, she placed the yearbook on the table and opened it to the juniors, class of 1978. She quickly flipped to the Rs and stopped at Ezekiel Roberts.

Even after twenty-eight years, the image of his young face slammed her with emotions that haunted her. What could he be up to? Why, after all these years, is he pulling Jack into his web? She brushed her fingers against the image of Ezekiel—she'd loved him once. Now the person she loved most in this world was in his grasp.

Amanda stared at the picture a few moments longer, remembering the curly dark hair that covered his ears and fell over his collar, the boyish charm and his piercing eyes. Those eyes had, at one time, poured so much love her way—before they had darkened and turned against her.

Vince led the five jungle team members into a conference room that was just off the dining area. They gathered around a large rectangular oak table with high back executive chairs as if they were in the boardroom of some Fortune 500 company. Pasted on the wall were large blown-up posters of each of the five contestants from the losing team.

"Please, take a seat," Vince instructed. "For this first challenge, we've decided that the winning team will decide which contestant will be kicked out."

Vince stood at the end of the table eyeing the two women and the three men. "So, it's up to you."

To his right was Stacy Dove, the beautiful model from New York, and Hugh Liang, a law student at Harvard. On his left was Spike Jones, a comedian from Atlanta; Tara Seacrest, an author and motivational speaker from Seattle; and Denny Armstrong, a leading stock market analyst from New York.

"How do you want us to choose?" Hugh asked.

"Any way you want," Vince smiled toward the mirror that faced him from the other side of the room, knowing that behind the one-way glass sat the producers of the show. "Think of yourselves like a jury. Feel free to elect a foreman or whatever will help you. We'll leave you to yourselves until you have a decision."

Vince walked out of the room, leaving a quiet jungle team pondering their options.

The conversation around the losing table in the dining hall had been fairly stilted ever since Vince had walked out of the room with the jungle team. Jack looked around the table, wondering what each of his teammates was thinking.

"I wonder what they're doing," Maria said.

"They're voting one of us out of the competition, idiot," Eddie snapped.

Maria rolled her eyes and shrugged.

"How long do you think they'll take?" C. J. asked.

"On TV, it's just a two-minute commercial break," Whitney chuckled. "But I've never seen them let the winning team kick out the first contestant."

"Well, I, for one, want you all to know it's been a blast," Jack said. "If I'm gone, I wish you all the best. Even you, Eddie."

Eddie looked up surprised, but only responded with a grunt.

"You sound as if you want to go," Maria mentioned.

"It's not that I necessarily *want* to go, but there are some things that are up in the air at home. It wouldn't be that bad if I'm picked first."

"What about the ten million?" Eddie asked.

Jack shrugged, "Easy come, easy go."

The girls chuckled, but Eddie didn't seem to buy it. He continued to stare at Jack as if there was something drastically wrong with him.

Vince and Travis sat next to Zeke as the three watched the jungle team ponder who would be sent home first. They had a ringside view, sitting in front of the one-way glass as if they were police detectives watching an interrogation.

"What do you think?" Zeke asked.

"I hope they don't let Eddie go," Vince jumped in.

"He's going to be great for ratings," Travis added. "The tension between him and Jack is gold."

"I agree," Zeke nodded. "Then they need to pick one of the three gals. Who goes?"

"That's tough," Vince thought aloud carefully. "None of them made any major mistakes."

"Not enough time for that," Travis said. "There's Maria's ankle."

"True, but talk about ratings," Vince argued. "Her body alone will keep the guys tuned in."

"How about C. J.?" Travis asked.

"Possibly, or Whitney," Zeke cut in sharply. "There's not that much difference between them."

"Then we just need to make sure the jungle team heads that direction," Travis stated, then turned to Vince. "Be ready to go back in when needed."

Zeke turned and watched the team through the glass. A slight smile creased his lips. Travis and Vince had played right into his hands.

"Who wants to go first?" Tara asked the group seated around her.

"Why don't you," Hugh said, sitting across from her.

"OK, why not. The way I see it, we should get rid of whoever is the most serious competition out there—and I see that as Eddie, or possibly Jack. I haven't quite figured him out yet."

"Eddie did get three votes from his own team," Hugh pointed out.

"You're just going to automatically go for one of the guys?" Spike asked.

"Sure," Tara answered. "Aren't they the most likely to win in the next challenge?"

"That depends on what it is," Spike muttered. "And who's to say I might not need a 'brother' like Eddie by my side in the next event?"

"Oh, so you're going to pounce on her for being sexist," Denny spoke up. "And now you're making it a black thing?"

Spike laughed. "It's not a black thing—I was just jivin' with ya. Trying to make a point that there might be some strategy in keeping the strongest around for a while. You know?"

"No, I'm not sure I get your point?," Tara said.

"I think I know what he means," Denny stated. "We don't know what kind of challenge will come up next—and, from what I can make of that team, the women seemed to have slowed them down more than anything. I don't want that to happen to my team on the next go round. So we should keep the strongest in the game. Right, Spike?"

"You got it, man."

"That's interesting," Stacy said. "I wouldn't have thought of that."

"That's because it's crazy," Tara said.

"Crazy?" Spike leaped up from his chair. "Who you callin' crazy?"

The room sat stunned for a moment, until Spike chuckled and returned to his seat.

"Then who would you kick out?" Hugh asked.

Spike rubbed his chin. "One of the women—but not Maria. She's too fine."

"Oh," Tara shook her head. "We're not going to decide on who might have the best chance to win this thing and get them out of the way—we're going to do it based on who turns you on?"

"It's as good a reason as any," Spike laughed, turning toward Tara. "But I wouldn't hold my breath on you making it into that group, honey."

Tara glared at him.

"Look," Hugh cut in, "I'm more inclined to agree with Tara. Shouldn't we eliminate the most dangerous threat? We're talking ten million dollars here—you can date any fine woman you want with that kind of money, Spike."

"Very good, my man." Spike held out his hand, his thumb pointed skyward and the index finger pointed at him like a gun.

"I can see both sides," Denny added to the fray. "We've got two guys over there—Eddie, obviously the more daunting, physically. I wouldn't want to go up against him head-to-head in any kind of a fight, I'll tell you that. But Jack's got a head on his shoulders. He could be tough."

"Brain over brawn, huh?" Tara asked.

"Basically," Denny continued. "On the other hand, I'd welcome either of them on my team for the next challenge."

"Maybe we need to take a vote to see where we stand," Hugh offered.

"That sounds good," Tara responded. "I'd vote Eddie out, anybody with me?" Tara raised her hand and looked around the table. Only Denny voted with her.

"Anybody for Jack?" Hugh said, raising his hand.

No one joined him.

"Why Jack over Eddie?" Stacy asked.

"Just a hunch," Hugh explained. "I think Denny's point was well made. In this kind of contest, I think I can outsmart muscle, instead of fighting another intellect."

"But he's a football coach!" Tara interjected.

"And I'll wager a rather bright one," Hugh added.

The door opened and Vince stepped into the room. "Sorry to interrupt. How's it going?"

"We're making progress, I think," Tara said.

"Really," Vince smiled. "That's good. Anything I can do to help?"

"I think we're fine," Denny said.

"OK, just one thing," Vince kept his tone serious. "The next challenge will be even tougher than what you went through today. You might want to keep that in mind."

Then he smiled and left the room.

"What was that about?" Spike asked.

"I'm sure they're listening in," Hugh thought out loud. "Maybe they don't like the direction we're headed."

"Trying to sway the vote?" Tara said.

"Maybe," Denny pushed away from the table and crossed his legs. "But it begs the question—should we seriously consider the women before we decide for sure?"

The room suddenly fell quiet. Jack looked over to the main table, and saw that Vince had returned, as the jungle team walked back to their table.

"If I could have the desert team up to the head table, please," Vince instructed.

Jack and the rest of his squad got up from their chairs and moved over to the table. Vince handed each of them a gold envelope and asked them to go back, and stand in a line in front of their table.

"Now," Vince said, "four of you will find in your envelopes a gold *Ultimate Challenge* ticket. One of you will find a plane ticket home."

Jack looked over at the winning team, trying to get a read on how they might have voted. He didn't know any of them well enough to catch a hint. His fingers moved over the envelope, attempting to sense what could be inside.

The five losing members stood as if in a police lineup.

"Let's start with you, C. J.," Vince said. "Please open your envelope."

C. J. ripped the seal quickly, and smiled as she pulled out a gold ticket.

"Now don't think that I would be so obvious as to leave the one going home for last," Vince smiled mischievously. "Maria, you're next please."

Maria nervously opened up her envelope, then jumped up and down when she pulled out a gold ticket. "Oh, thank you!" She smiled brightly toward the jungle team.

"All right, we're down to three," Vince upped the tension in the room, playing once again for the home audience. "Eddie, would you be so kind as to open your envelope."

This is it, Jack thought. *The way Vince is hyping this moment—Eddie was getting the boot, and he was stuck in the game.*

Eddie didn't think the same way as Jack, as he smiled and ripped open his envelope. It was gold. "Ah, yeah!" Eddie pumped his fist through the air.

Jack was shocked. He was sure with the three votes Eddie had received from his own team he was going to be the one kicked out.

"Now we're down to two," Vince stated the obvious. "One of you will be going home in just a few minutes. The other will still have a chance at ten million dollars." Vince let his statement hang over the room before giving the next instruction. "Whitney, would you please open your envelope."

Jack sucked in a deep breath. This was it: either him or Whitney. For some reason, the jungle team had decided one of them should go. Jack looked deep within for a moment, and as much as he felt he needed to go home, he was shocked to discover that he wanted to stay even more. After seeing the dynamics of all of the contestants together, Jack felt like he had a real shot at actually winning the whole thing.

Whitney had torn the envelope and was reaching in—it had to be a gold ticket. They'd save the airline ticket for last. TV drama. Jack was sure he was heading home, and suddenly he didn't like it.

Whitney's hand was on whatever was inside. She pulled it out slowly—it was the airline ticket. Jack was still in it. He smiled in relief, while, at the same time, feelings of empathy flooded over him for Whitney. She looked up at him, tears filling her eyes. His smile vanished.

"I'm sorry, Whitney," Jack said honestly.

"It's all part of the game, right?" She attempted to cover up her disappointment.

"Whitney," Vince broke in, stepping up to the two of them. "We're sorry to see you go."

"Why me?" she asked.

Vince smiled warmly, "You know us, Whitney. You'll find out when the show airs."

Jack watched as Whitney walked out of the room. Emotions flooded him. Just moments ago, he was ready, even excited, to think he'd be going home. And yet, the instant Eddie opened his envelope and brought out the gold ticket, Jack knew he didn't want to go home. Something sparked inside. What was it? Jack couldn't put his finger on it. Competition? Maybe he just couldn't sit back and let Eddie win the prize? Or could it be something deeper?

"All right," Vince broke through Jack's thoughts. "Congratulations to the nine of you that are left."

Cheers went up from both groups, with Jack's team now as jubilant as the jungle team. Jack was cheerful but reserved, struggling with his thoughts.

"I suggest you try and get a good night's sleep," Vince offered. "The next challenge will be an even greater test of your will and endurance."

The jungle team began to get up from their table and Jack's team headed for the door.

"Oh, one more thing," Vince spoke out again. "We've added a little mini-challenge to this year's event."

All the contestants stopped and listened intently.

"At some point during the next few days," Vince pulled a small gold envelope out of his shirt pocket, "You'll be handed one of these envelopes from someone on our staff. Make sure you're alone when you open it. Whatever is written on the card is your personal challenge. It will give you a time frame to fulfill your task—if you have not completed whatever is on the card before the allotted time, without telling another contestant what's inside, your position in the contest will be forfeited. Understood?"

Nine heads nodded, wondering what possible task would be written on their card.

"Now get some sleep," Vince continued. "We want everyone

down here in the dining hall by 8:00 a.m. sharp. If you want to get a bite to eat before that, we'll open up the breakfast buffet at 7:00. Oh, and please wear your swimming attire."

Jack was exhausted, but he lay in his bed, staring up at the corner of the ceiling. The robotic camera was silent for now, but every once in awhile, he could hear the slight purring of the servo lens as it zoomed in and out. Somebody was awake and still watching.

Everyone had made their way to their bungalows quickly, knowing that tomorrow would bring the unknown and thinking they'd better get as much rest as possible.

For the first time since he'd been snatched away from his football field, he began to think of the money.

Ten million dollars. What could he do with ten million dollars?

At first, his thoughts were altruistic. He would give ten percent, one million dollars, to his church—or maybe a combination of his favorite missionaries, charities, and his home church. Next, he'd make sure his mother wouldn't have to worry financially another day of her life. His father had been a tile layer, working for a couple of different contractors and pool companies around Wheaton. He had carried a two-hundred-and-fifty-thousand-dollar life insurance policy, and after the funeral expenses and paying off the mortgage of her house, there wasn't anything left.

Her volunteer work at the hospital had become a full-time job after the accident, thanks to a wonderfully generous charge nurse on the pediatric floor. But Jack knew she was just scraping by. If only he could win and secure both of their futures. He would probably need the money as well, the way the situation with the school board was heading.

Then Jack started dreaming of many of the luxuries he had lived without for so long, surviving on his public-school salary. A new car—maybe the new Mustang, or a Lexus. No, a Corvette—a red convertible. But why stop there? What about a new house?

He could vacation anywhere in the world. Visit countries he'd dreamed of seeing but never been able to afford. He could update his old Apple computer—get the new wide-screen laptop. When he started thinking about it, he realized there wasn't anything he wouldn't be able to buy.

Then a bit of reality crept in: taxes. He'd have to cough up probably around half the money to Uncle Sam. OK, five million dollars. That still wasn't bad. He could lower the gift to his church and charities to five hundred thousand dollars and still have four and a half million dollars left.

Jack started adding up the possibilities: the house, the Corvette, the computer, and a few vacations danced through his head like sheep jumping over an imaginary fence. In a few seconds, he drifted off.

Jack felt like his head had just hit the pillow when the claxon of an alarm screeched through his room. He jerked up in bed, totally disoriented. He didn't quite know where he was or what the blaring, off-and-on-again horn was signaling. Then the smell of smoke attacked his nostrils and his eyes popped wide open.

Fire!

Jack pulled off the covers, grabbing for his shorts and Hawaiian shirt. He stuck his legs through the shorts with the first two steps, feeling a sharp sting in his shin, as he made his way to the door. With his shirt covering his hand, he reached for the doorknob, testing to make sure it wasn't hot. It seemed normal, so Jack opened the door.

A wall of flames danced about from a strong tropical wind about fifteen feet in front of him—the bungalow next door, Whitney's. Was she still on the island?

"Fire!" Jack yelled over the blaring alarm.

The bungalow that should have been Jack's was a raging inferno. If Whitney was still inside, there was no way he could get to her. The next one downwind had caught fire as well, but was not yet engulfed in flames.

"Whitney! Maria!" Jack yelled, slipping his shirt over his back while looking back and forth between the huts.

"What's going on?" C. J. asked groggily, as she came out of her room clothed in a resort robe.

Eddie stepped out of his bungalow at the same time, naked except for a pair of boxers, but alert. "Jack, isn't that your bungalow?"

Jack ignored the question, walking around the burning hut. "Do either of you know if Whitney is in there?"

"I don't think so," C. J. answered. "She was taken off the island last night."

"We've got to get Maria out," Jack shouted, heading past the inferno toward her bungalow.

"Maria!" Jack yelled. "Are you in there?"

No answer.

The front door was engulfed in flames that were spreading rapidly around the hut's sides. If her bungalow was anything like Jack's, she'd be at the back end, where his bedroom was located—and not yet in flames. Jack ran around the building. Outside of her bedroom was a sliding glass door that led to a small courtyard. Grabbing one of the patio chairs, Jack threw it through the door, shattering the glass into a million pieces.

"Maria!" Jack yelled, rushing across the broken glass in his bare feet.

The room was bathed in smoke. He pulled up his still unbuttoned shirt and covered his mouth to try and filter the air intake. His eyes stung sharply, forcing them closed involuntarily.

He could hear C. J. yelling his name outside the hut.

Jack reached out with his hands to the right, where his bed would be in relation to the sliding doors. He felt the covers of the bed—and struck a pair of legs. Kneeling down low, Jack pulled the covers off the bed and picked up the motionless body.

He turned around and headed for the door. A "whoosh" sounded overhead as the fire leaped along the ceiling of the bungalow. Embers and sparks were falling all around Jack. He kept moving as quickly as he could, carrying Maria. His feet crunched through the broken glass, letting him know he was getting close to safety. Finally, he burst through the broken glass door, carrying Maria as far as he could onto the grass before he collapsed to his knees, laying her gently on the ground.

He sucked in a fresh breath of air, sending a searing pain through his chest.

"Is she alive?" C. J. ran over asking.

Jack looked down at Maria's lifeless body. His eyes were watering so bad he couldn't tell. He put a hand on her chest, trying to see if she was breathing, then moved to her neck to try and find a pulse. Nothing.

"Go get help!" He ordered C. J. Then he tilted Maria's head back and lifted her chin slightly. Without pausing, Jack placed his mouth over Maria's while pinching her nose and breathed into her two slow breaths. Her chest rose up as he did.

He repeated the process, then paused. Still no response.

Jack moved around and knelt in front of her with his right knee positioned between her legs. He placed the heel of his right hand just above where her lower ribs joined together. He placed his left hand directly over the top, interlacing his fingers, and then pushed down gently. Slowly, he let them release back up. Jack repeated the movement several times, yelling for anybody to come and help.

The fire continued to rage, consuming both bungalows now and starting on a third. The flames lit up the entire area around the pond. Jack saw a movement over his left shoulder. He turned to see a cameraman standing there taping the scene.

"What are you doing?" Jack screamed. "Get some help."

The man didn't move. He just continued pointing the camera right at Jack.

For the first time, Jack noticed that Maria was lying beside him clothed only in lace underwear. He moved next to her side, trying to keep his body between Maria and the cameraman. He once again pinched her nose and breathed into her lungs. On the second breath, Maria wheezed out a sick cough. Jack leaned back, placing his hand on her neck, relieved that he now felt a pulse.

She took a short breath on her own, then coughed loudly. Her eyes popped opened, filled with fear and pain.

"It's OK," Jack said softly. "You're going to be fine."

Jack took off his shirt and laid it over her.

"What happened?" she managed to get out between coughs.

"A fire," Jack explained. "It started in Whitney's bungalow and spread to yours."

"Is she all right?"

"C. J. thinks she's already left the island. I hope so," Jack sighed, looking at the burning bungalow. "Because there's no way anybody could have survived in there."

Help finally arrived a few minutes later as a group of locals, yelling in their native tongue, descended on the burning bungalows, pouring buckets of water on the flames. A man walked up a moment later with a hose that didn't have nearly enough water pressure to fight the blaze. The strong winds whipped the fire around so that another bungalow had caught fire as Whitney's had nearly burnt out. Jack noticed the five jungle team members huddled together, watching from the path that led to the pool. One of the men broke from the group and hustled over to them.

"You guys all right here?" he asked.

"I think she'll be OK." Jack answered.

"If you were in one of those ..." he pointed toward the burning bungalows, then looked back at Maria. "You're very lucky."

"Yeah," Maria agreed.

"I'm Hugh Liang."

"Jack, and this is Maria," Jack returned. Maria just nodded silently.

"Yeah, I know. How did the fire get started?" Hugh asked.

"I have no idea," Jack said. "Maybe it was done intentionally."

"Interesting. I'm going to go check it out." With that, he turned and walked away toward Whitney's bungalow.

"Let me know if you find something," Jack shouted. It seemed suspicious that a fire would start in the middle of the night during a competition for ten million dollars. And the fact that it started in the bungalow he was assigned to gave Jack more reason to pause.

C. J. walked up to them and handed Maria an extra set of clothes. "I thought you might need these."

"Thanks," Maria said, carefully grabbing the shirt and shorts while keeping Jack's shirt on top of her.

Jack turned around, glancing at the uphill battle against the fires while C. J. helped Maria get dressed. Finally, another hose arrived that looked like it had enough pressure to battle the blaze more effectively.

"You guys all right?" Jack turned around to see Vince approaching on a dead run.

"Barely," Jack answered sharply. "Maria nearly didn't make it, and we're not sure about Whitney."

"Whitney's fine," Vince noted. "She left the island an hour ago."

"That's a relief," C. J. noted.

"Are you OK, Maria?" Vince asked.

Maria still sat on the grass, now dressed in C. J.'s shorts and Hawaiian shirt. She took in a medium breath, coughing again, but not as severely. "I guess so."

"We'll have the doctor check you out in a minute." Vince looked down at the grass area by Jack. "I think we'd better have you looked after as well."

Jack glanced down at his feet. He hadn't even realized that he was bleeding. The trek through the broken glass had cut several gashes on the bottom of his feet. Blood was dripping slowly onto the grass around him.

Vince glanced at the charred bungalow with his head slightly tilted. "Isn't that yours, Jack?"

"It was," Jack nodded, "but Whitney came to my room and wanted to trade right after you left."

"Interesting," Vince scrunched his forehead. "I didn't know."

14

It took another couple of hours for the resort staff to put the remaining bungalow fires out. Jack and Maria had been sent into the main building to be looked over by the doctor. The medic that had worked with Jack on the plane had pulled out any remaining glass pieces left in his feet, then wrapped them in white bandages. Maria was still inside being cared for, while Jack, and the remaining contestants awakened in all the excitement, gathered around the pool.

Sitting with the jungle team, Jack learned the names of the rest of the competition for the first time: Stacy Dove, the outrageously beautiful model; Tara Seacrest, the author and motivational speaker—Jack actually remembered seeing her on some talk show before—then the men: Spike Jones, the African-American comedian he'd never heard of; Denny Armstrong, New York stockbroker; and Hugh. Jack made a mental note to talk with Hugh later to see if he'd found anything in his search of the burned-out bungalows.

As they sat outside at 3:00 a.m., Jack was amazed to see the camera crews were still up and working, moving around the edges of the informal meeting of the teams—like a pack of coyotes cornering their prey.

The new group was an interesting mix of personalities and occupations. Through the ordeal of being pulled out of their rooms and held together around the pool area, the friction between the two teams seemed to have evaporated. No one knew what would happen next. Would they cancel the whole thing? Delay the next challenge? Would Maria be healthy enough to continue?

Jack sat between C. J. and Eddie, who had returned within the last half-hour with no explanation where he'd been since the fire. Jack had a million questions running through his mind for Eddie, but, for now, he left them unasked.

The conversations died when Vince approached from the main building with Maria walking slowly beside him. Jack was thrilled to see her up and walking on her own. He thought she might be forced out of the competition—which, on one hand, would be good because it would be one less contestant to deal with; but on the other hand, it would be the one contestant Jack didn't want to see leave.

Vince helped her into a chair before addressing the group. "Well, I'm sure you're all wondering what happens now."

"First of all," Hugh interrupted, "do you have any idea how the fire got started?"

Vince pursed his lips and nodded. "Right to the point, Mr. Liang. I like that."

He grabbed a chair and sat down with the contestants huddled around him. "We're looking into the cause of the fire right now. Our best guess is that the wind knocked over one of the torches and it landed against the bungalow."

"Did any of your cameras catch that happening?" Hugh pressed.

"No," Vince shook his head. "Since you were all in bed, our staff was trying to get some sleep as well. We don't have any cameras covering the outside of your huts, only the inside."

"Was everybody in their rooms and accounted for at the time?" Jack asked, glancing around the group to see how they reacted.

Everyone but Eddie looked at Jack in shock for a second, then turned to Vince for the answer.

"Are you suggesting that the fire might have been deliberately set?" Vince asked.

"It's been known to happen with a lot less money at stake," Jack answered coldly. "Maria was nearly killed."

"And if Whitney hadn't left the island ..." C. J. let her comment hang in the air.

"But it was your hut, Forrest." Eddie turned toward Jack. "Who's to say you didn't switch bungalows with her, then set it on fire yourself."

"You're insane, Eddie." Jack glared at him. At this hour and after the ordeal he'd been through, he'd lost the patience to deal with Eddie. "Where have you been the past few hours, by the way?"

"Getting help, like you asked," Eddie growled.

Jack scowled at Eddie for a beat, then turned back to Vince. "Oh yeah, that reminds me. What's with your camera crew? One guy just stood there and taped us while I was trying to revive Maria, even when I asked him to get help."

"You know the rules, Jack." Vince looked deadly serious. "If he'd done something to help, Maria would be out of the game."

"But this wasn't during a challenge," Jack argued. "She nearly died."

"No exceptions, Jack. The rule applies twenty-four seven. Now, in answer to your question about everybody being in their rooms, the staff is looking at all the tapes at this time, and there's an investigation by the local authorities as to the cause of the fire. But any information about who was in their bungalow, and who wasn't, will not be shared with this group. It might affect the game."

"Affect the game?" Jack nearly came out of his chair. "So would murder, wouldn't it?"

"Calm down," Vince ordered. "We've got the situation under control, and no contestant will be in any danger, I promise."

"Tell that to Maria," Jack shot back.

Vince's eyes darkened. "If you're worried about your safety, Jack, you have the option to forfeit your position here at any time. Are you ready to quit now?"

Jack stared at Vince, taking in a deep breath. He thought for a second of just walking away from it all, flying back home, and getting on with his life. But Jack was not a quitter. Being sent home was one thing, but walking away by choice wasn't in his nature. Vince had him right where he wanted. Keeping his eyes locked on Vince, Jack finally shook his head no.

Vince continued to stare at Jack for a brief moment, then broke eye contact and spoke to the group as a whole. "I think we've all had enough excitement for the night. I suggest you get some sleep with what little time you have left. It's after four and you're all still required to be in the restaurant by eight for the next challenge."

Vince nodded as if punctuating his last statement, then got up and walked away. The nine contestants held their places for a brief moment, looking at each other, then slowly got up and made their way toward their huts.

Jack walked over to Maria. "You feeling all right?"

"Yeah," she answered. "My lungs are a little tender, but the doctor thinks I'm good to go. I just need to get rid of this splitting headache."

"Probably from all the smoke you sucked in. You really had me worried."

Maria stood up and wrapped her arms around him. "Thanks so much for being there." She brought her face right in front of Jack's and looked him straight in the eyes. "You saved my life."

Jack felt his face flush. "I'm just glad you're OK."

Maria smiled. "How about you? How are your feet?"

Jack shrugged. "He pulled quite a few pieces of glass out, but hopefully it won't slow me down any tomorrow."

"You know, if you think about it, so far, you and I are the only ones getting hurt around here."

"You've got a point there," Jack chuckled. "I think we should try to be a bit more careful from here on out."

"I'll try," Maria said smiling. "If you need anything the rest of this competition, you just let me know."

She pulled away, heading off in the direction of her new bungalow.

"Now, that wouldn't be fair, would it?" Jack asked.

"I don't care." Maria's eyes twinkled when she turned back. "I'll forever owe you."

Maria spun around once again and started walking down the path. Jack watched her go a few yards, before turning around and looking around the area for Hugh. But he was already gone.

Vince stepped into his room exhausted. Getting rousted out of bed with fire alarms at one in the morning was above and beyond his contract with *The Ultimate Challenge.* He'd be lucky to get three hours of sleep—he was going to look horrible on camera in the morning.

He stepped into his bedroom, flipped on the light and nearly jumped out of his own skin.

"Busy evening, huh Vince?" Zeke offered.

"What are you doing in my room? You nearly gave me a heart attack."

"Sorry for the drama. I didn't want to be seen, and we needed to talk."

"You could've called."

"Maybe," Zeke stated flatly, "but I wanted to make sure you understood my concern."

"Concern about what?" Vince asked.

"About Jack Forrest."

"What about Jack?"

"What do you think you were doing offering him a chance to quit?"

"Oh, that?" Vince chuckled, and plopped down on the bed. "It was just a spur of the moment thing, nothing to worry about."

Zeke rose from his chair and stepped to where he was towering above Vince. "And if he'd taken you up on your offer?"

"What?" Vince asked defensively. "Then you would have had a great television moment: the first contestant to quit—afraid for his life."

"I choose who goes and when," Zeke glared. "Not you."

"Zeke," Vince sat up on the bed, keeping his voice light, "Jack's a competitor, he'd no more quit than I would."

"You couldn't be sure of that."

"Actually, I was," Vince added. "I could see it in his eyes. He's concerned for his safety, and I don't blame him after that fire. But he wasn't going to walk away. No way!"

"Well, you had better make sure of that," Zeke demanded with a sly grin, "or you'll be joining him on that plane when he leaves."

With that, he turned and left a flabbergasted Vince sitting on the bed.

When Jack opened the door to his bungalow, he was immediately hit with the smell of smoke still permeating his room. He'd asked about moving to another one, but a producer said they didn't have any more equipped with cameras.

Jack walked back into the bedroom and opened up the glass door, pulling the screen in place to hopefully keep out the bugs. He was tempted to take another shower, having worked up quite a sweat in all the excitement and the balminess of the tropical island. But he was too exhausted. Besides, he remembered they were to be wearing swimming suits in the morning. He'd shower in the ocean.

Lying in bed with the covers off, attempting to cool down, Jack's mind raced over the details of the past few hours. How did that fire start? Could one of the other contestants have set it off hoping to kill Jack, or at least injure him enough to get him out of the game? It seemed too incredible for Jack to grasp. Then a picture of Eddie flashed through his mind. He certainly seemed capable. But there were a few contestants on the other team he wasn't too sure of either.

Jack tossed and turned, mulling over what little information he had until he eventually fell into a restless sleep.

Vince stood at his table, addressing the nine remaining contestants at precisely eight o'clock the next morning. "Your challenge today will require individual effort and stamina."

Jack was sitting at the same table he occupied the night before, between C. J. and Maria. Eddie was sitting an empty seat away from C. J., keeping to himself. The morning was a tropical postcard. The wind had settled, and the sea, beyond the cliff where the resort sat, was a calm mixture of brilliant green and blue hues, with a few puffy white clouds dotting the sky.

Jack had risen a few minutes after seven when a wake-up knock on his door had brought him out of a deep sleep. The first thing he'd done was to pull the bandages off his feet and check them out. The cuts were still tender, but the bleeding had stopped. When he stood and walked across the room, it was painful. But Jack knew it was something he'd just have to endure.

He'd put his bathing suit on, once again using the closet, added the Hawaiian shirt, then made his way to the restaurant for a quick breakfast of a half a cantaloupe, a blueberry muffin, and a glass of orange juice. They offered an omelet station, but Jack wasn't sure what they'd throw at him, and he didn't want to eat anything too heavy.

As he ate, he doubted if that was the right thing to do—what if they were going to send him to the other side of the island and make him scrounge for food the rest of the day. There was no way to know what was best.

"Our next competition," Vince continued, "is *The Ultimate Challenge's* version of the triathlon. But instead of running, swimming, and cycling, our version involves swimming, rowing, and rock-climbing. You'll be placed in a boat and taken out into the ocean, where you'll have to swim one thousand meters to get to your kayak. Then you'll paddle back here to our beach, where you'll get to climb up the rock face of our cliff."

The former desert team that had seen the base of that cliff the evening before, looked up in shock. "It's not as difficult as it might seem," Vince chuckled. "Our staff was up early this morning anchoring, and then dropping, nine ropes down from the top of the cliff. We will also give everyone a quick lesson on how to use the special equipment before we start. Any questions?"

"What if we're not that good a swimmer?" Denny shot out.

"Or climber?" C. J. added.

"There are life jackets if you want to use them," Vince answered.

"But we've done our homework. We know that all of you are able to swim, so that shouldn't be an issue. As far as the climbing, C. J., it's just a little test to see who's worthy of our ten million dollars—to see who's up to the challenge, so to speak."

"Last one to make it up the cliff is sent home?" Hugh asked from the other table.

"Basically, barring any serious injuries or someone not making it at all."

Jack looked at the faces around both tables. It looked like Vince's comment had left each of them a bit sober about the task at hand. The women looked especially worried. It did seem a bit unfair to Jack to have the women compete head-to-head with the men in this type of event. Jack was relieved that the challenge didn't require him to be on his feet all day. That would have been a disaster. He wondered how Maria's ankle would hold up.

"One last thing before you go," Vince said, interrupting Jack's thoughts. "We've got a supply shop where you can outfit yourself however you think best for the challenge. We've got wet suits, water shoes, even hiking boots, if you want to try and swim in them. Whatever you want, just take with you. So, let's get to it."

The group stood, eager to get to the next challenge. As Jack made his way toward the door, Vince stepped up to him and Maria. "We'd like to have the medic check you both out one last time before we kick this off. Come with me, please."

Standing on the beach, Jack kept looking up the cliff, imagining how hard it would be to scale up the jagged rocks. It wasn't a sheer cliff, thank God, but a tough mixture of seventy- to eighty-degree climbs with two straight drop-offs to deal with: one right off the ocean, and another at the top of the cliff. He could see the nine ropes extending over the top, ending at three different floating platforms anchored in the rolling surf.

It looked like one of the more dangerous parts might be getting from the kayak onto the platforms without being crashed against the rocks by the pounding waves. This event certainly fit the bill as "an ultimate challenge."

The medic had looked over Jack's feet and checked Maria out one last time. They were both given the clearance to compete. Jack was amazed Maria hadn't suffered any lung damage. He thought she should have been taken off the island for medical care the night before.

Sitting out about twenty-five feet from the shore, just beyond where the waves broke, a couple of men held on to a black Zodiac inflatable raft with a sixty horsepower Mercury outboard motor on the back. A bit further out to sea were four more identical boats, each crammed with production staff and camera gear.

Jack had chosen to add water shoes, swimmer's goggles and a pair of water-ski gloves along with the swim fins that everyone else had chosen. He thought the water would be warm enough to swim one thousand meters without a wetsuit, what Jack figured to be comparable to about forty complete laps in the Royal High pool.

It had taken more than an hour for the nine contestants to receive instruction on how to climb the cliff. They had each taken a turn getting strapped into a harness and, using a pair of ascenders, climbed up a rope attached to the top of the main building. One ascender was clipped to the harness that wrapped around the groin and rear end. The other one attached to a pair of stirrups, one for each foot. The ascender clamped around the rope, supporting the climber's weight. When the weight was lifted, the ascender could slide up the rope a few feet where it would take hold again. So while the climber stood on the foot stirrups, he could move the ascender attached to his harness. He could then put his weight on the harness by sitting and bending his feet to bring up the other ascender—and the pattern would continue.

Jack felt like he understood the concept, but looking up at the five-hundred-foot cliff above him, the task seemed overwhelming.

"All right everybody," Vince said, as he brought the group together. "The competition doesn't start until your driver fires the flare gun. So make your way to the raft carefully, and I'll be waiting for you back at the resort. May the best man or woman win! Good luck!"

They entered the water in a line. Jack carried the swim fins, glad that he'd added the water shoes. They provided enough protection over his sliced up feet that the rocks and sand didn't hurt. Several of the men, and all the women, had chosen wet suits. The initial coolness of the water was refreshing, but it made Jack wonder if he'd made a mistake not to have chosen one himself.

When they got to the raft, it was fairly easy to climb on board. The water was only about three-and-a-half feet deep, and they were able to spring off the rocky bottom. Once they were all on board, the driver cranked up the outboard motor and they were on their way. Looking back to the cliff as it began to shrink in the distance, it looked ominous. Climbing it would definitely be the most dangerous aspect of the challenge.

"Dr. Evans to ICU, Dr. Evans to ICU—stat." The voice blared from the hallway into the private room where Amanda was changing the bedding.

She paused, taking a moment to pray for the babies she knew were in the neo-natal intensive care unit of Good Samaritan Hospital. She listed them by name as she asked for God to intervene in their lives. One of them, little Angie, had been born four weeks premature, and Amanda knew she was under Dr. Evans's care. Amanda pictured the tiny baby lying in the incubator, with tubes coming out of her from every direction. She had a long road ahead of her, but she was in good hands with Dr. Evans. Amanda smiled at the thought that she was in God's hands as well, as she stretched the clean, fitted sheet over the mattress's corner.

The maternity ward was full. It had been an unusually busy morning. They'd just released one mother, and Amanda was in the process of preparing the room for the next mom-to-be already checking in downstairs.

Amanda had been there since seven. When Kevin had been alive, she had spent two days a week volunteering at the hospital. She'd loved those days: delivering flowers, passing out magazines, and having the chance to sit and talk with the patients who didn't have family or loved ones around.

That all changed now that she was training to be a nurse's aid. Putting in a twelve-hour shift, four days in a row, was much more demanding than an afternoon here and there as a volunteer. It wasn't easy to start over in her late forties. But through the stress and the exhaustion, she'd grown to love her new career choice.

It was the director of pediatrics, Cheryl Thomas, who had given Amanda the opportunity. They'd become friends through the years, and when Cheryl had asked Amanda what she was planning to do with her life, now that Kevin was gone, Amanda didn't have an answer. So, Cheryl had offered one.

It had been a lifeline—not just financially. The job had given Amanda a focus, or a distraction, depending on how you wanted to look at it, to help ease her through the grieving process.

But today, her mind was miles away from her work. She kept looking at her watch, or the clock on the wall, subtracting two hours to figure out what time it was on the west coast. She was planning to call Zeke Roberts Productions at precisely the stroke of nine, their time.

The Zodiac boat had bobbed and weaved through the light waves to position itself a few hundred feet from shore. From this distance, they could make out the bungalows and main building of the resort on top of the cliff. It was a beautiful sight amidst the green foliage and palm trees.

When they reached a red flag atop a floating plastic jug, the driver of the Zodiac pulled back on the throttle and turned off the motor. They drifted quietly, tilting slightly every time a wave rolled underneath them.

"This is the starting point," the driver instructed. "You'll swim toward the second flag," he pointed off into the distance parallel to the shoreline, "which is where you'll get your kayak."

Off in the distance one thousand meters away, they had tied nine kayaks around a floating buoy.

"Once you get in the kayak, you paddle back to the cliff, grab a rope and haul yourself to the top. Last man there … is out. Any questions?"

Stacy held up her hand. "How are we supposed to climb into the kayak in the middle of the ocean?"

The driver smiled. "However you can."

Stacy shook her head. "This is unbelievable. I'll never be able to make it back to shore, much less up that cliff."

"You can do it," Tara said encouragingly, then turned to Maria and C. J. "We all can. We've got to keep up with the men, ladies."

Jack could see the motivational speaker coming out in her.

The sounds of a helicopter brought everyone's attention skyward. Coming in over the camera boats at top speed was a Bell Jet Ranger, complete with a camera mounted under the belly.

It must have been the signal for the driver. He reached into a small tackle box he had at his feet and pulled out a flare gun. "All right, as soon as you're ready to go, you can jump in the water. But wait until the flare gun goes off before you begin the competition."

Each of the contestants double-checked their life vests, flippers, and other equipment, tightening straps and pulling up wetsuit zippers with nervous excitement.

Jack placed the goggles over his head, making sure they were snug against each eye socket. Then he pulled his swim fins on and dangled his feet over the side, ready to jump in.

The driver stood up, attempting to make his way toward the back of the boat when, suddenly, a loud "pop" shocked everybody. The girls shrieked as Jack whipped his head back over his shoulder to see them clumped in a heap in the center of the Zodiac.

The flare gun had gone off.

Jack stared in shock at the gaping hole, that used to be the bottom of the boat, as water swirled around him and everybody panicked.

16

Jack's ears were ringing as the mayhem engulfed him.

There was a puff of smoke where the driver had been standing. He must have dropped straight down through the hole. The women who'd been sitting in the middle of the boat were now being sucked into the same opening.

The boat began to fold in on itself as the sides deflated around them. The weight of the motor sent the back end of the Zodiac under water, pulling those trapped within along with it. Jack struggled against the force trying to suck him into the boat with the women. He leaped back as far as he could and fell into the ocean behind him.

Jack took a big gulp of air and dove underwater, swimming

straight back to the boat. He grabbed a hand and pulled out one body, sending Tara to the surface, then reached in for another. He could see on the other side of the sinking craft that Hugh was doing the same thing, pulling C. J. away from the entangled bodies.

He grabbed another arm and pulled. The woman broke free and headed for the surface. He caught a flash of Maria's face as she floated by. There was one woman still trapped, but Jack was out of air. He kicked for the surface. He sucked in a full breath as soon as his head cleared the surface. Next to him, Hugh poked through the water.

"There's one more down there!" Jack yelled.

"I know," Hugh nodded, as he sucked in a breath and dove back under the water. Jack dove right behind him.

It took a few strokes to get to the boat this time, as it continued to sink. Jack could see Stacy floating down with the boat, even though she wore a life jacket. He got to her arm and pulled, but she was stuck. She looked at Jack, her eyes wide with fear, her face panic-striken.

Hugh swam lower, going behind her back.

He signaled for Jack to stop pulling up, then brought Stacy lower, closer to the sinking boat. He reached out and yanked on the strap from her life jacket a couple of times, then let her go.

She was free.

The buoyancy of the jacket sent her quickly past Jack toward the surface. He kicked for the top, trying to stay with her. When he surfaced, Stacy was a few feet away gasping for air in between coughs. Hugh surfaced a second later.

"You OK?" Jack asked.

Stacy nodded. "What happened?"

"The driver shot the flare gun right into the bottom of the boat," Jack explained.

"And your life jacket got stuck on the throttle handle," Hugh added. "That's why you were being pulled down with the boat."

Jack spun in the water, counting the bodies around him. He only spotted six, including himself. "Who's missing?"

"No one," C. J. answered. "Spike, Eddie, and Denny took off for the kayaks."

"What?" Jack turned behind him. Sure enough, there were three male bodies swimming straight for the next buoy. "You've got to be kidding me!"

Then Jack looked beyond the other five bodies bobbing in the water. Three boats still encircled them with cameras rolling. Not one production person had jumped into the water to help. Six cameras were capturing their every move. Hanging on to the side of one of the camera boats, sporting a sly grin, was their driver.

The race had begun.

"It was a setup," Jack said.

"The boat sinking?" Stacy's voice broke.

"Yeah," Jack answered.

"But I nearly drowned!" Stacy cried.

"I don't think it matters much to these people," Jack muttered bitterly.

C. J. swam by them. "Well, thanks for the helping hand, but we'd better get going." She waved and headed toward the kayaks. The other women muttered a quick thanks, then followed off after her.

Jack moved forward, swimming alongside Hugh for a moment. "If we make it through the next couple of hours, I think we should put our heads together and see if we can figure out what's really going on here."

"You got it," Hugh answered, then ducked his head into the water and stroked forward.

Amanda entered the cafeteria a quarter after eleven—a few minutes earlier than her normal lunchtime, but a painful fifteen minutes later than she had wanted. Just as she was heading off to make her call to the west coast, the charge nurse had assigned her a patient. It was definitely the quickest sponge bath she'd ever given.

She walked over to an empty table in the back corner and pulled out her cell phone. She punched in the numbers written on the piece of paper, crumpled up in her pocket, and waited anxiously.

"Zeke Roberts Productions, home of *The Ultimate Challenge*," a bright female voice answered.

"Yes, hello." Amanda still wasn't sure what she should say. "My name is Amanda Forrest, and my son, Jack is … I guess, a contestant on your show."

"Yes, Mrs. Forrest, how can we help you?"

"I need to get in touch with him."

"I'm sorry, but during *The Ultimate Challenge*, that's not possible," the voice remained insufferably cheerful.

"But it's an emergency," Amanda said.

"What type of emergency?"

"I ..." Amanda didn't know how to respond. "Uh ... it's personal."

"Well, I'm sorry, but there is no outside contact allowed until the challenge is complete—unless there's a death in the family. Has someone died?"

Amanda thought quickly of Kevin, but a year ago would hardly apply.

"No, no one's died recently. But you have to make an exception," Amanda pleaded.

"There are no exceptions."

"Could I speak with a producer?" Amada asked.

"Ma'am," the voice took on a hard edge, "all of our producers are on site and not available."

"Then what are my options?"

"I could take a message and we'll pass it along to the production staff on location."

"Fine," Amanda sighed. "Would you please tell them that I need to speak with Jack as soon as possible. It's urgent."

Amanda left the woman her cell phone number, then ended the call. She sat quietly, staring out the window at nothing—praying.

Jack swam at a steady pace, settling into a rhythm where he'd take three strokes, then angle his head to the left to breathe as his right arm reached into the water to complete the fourth stroke. He was in pretty good shape, being the type of coach who would often run the wind sprints and drills with his team, rather than just stand there and blow his whistle from the sidelines. But different muscles were used in swimming, and after about five hundred meters, those muscles were screaming, while his breathing had quickened to every two strokes of his arms.

Jack decided he'd better rest. This was only the first of three legs.

He couldn't burn his arms and legs out now and expect to kayak and climb later. He turned over and floated on his back, moving up and down with the gentle waves as he closed his eyes against the bright tropical sun. He breathed deeply, hoping the oxygenated blood would surge through him quickly.

After a moment, Jack let his feet sink back into the water, and he looked toward the kayaks. Several heads were visible swimming steadily ahead of him, a couple of them nearly to their goal—three were now behind him. Jack had passed Maria, Stacy, and C. J, but Tara and Hugh had gained about a fifty-yard lead.

Jack sighed, then planted his face back in the water and started swimming again.

Up ahead, Spike and Eddie had reached the buoy nearly at the same time. Spike grabbed for the closest kayak, untying it from the anchored buoy. Eddie swam the few extra feet to get to the one beside Spike. Fortunately, the kayaks were the type that you sat on top of, not the ones that you had to climb into. Although still difficult to mount in deep water, it did make it a bit easier for the contestants.

"Hey, wait up!" Denny called from still a hundred feet away.

"Sure," Eddie chuckled, pulling his body up on top of the kayak and trying to keep it upright as he draped one leg over. "We'll just wait here for everybody to catch up."

"No," Denny returned. "I've got a plan."

Spike had made his way atop a red kayak and had his paddle ready. "What've you got in mind?"

Denny kept swimming toward them, finding it difficult to talk when he was so exhausted. "Untie all the boats. Let the waves send them onto the beach. The others will never catch up."

Spike looked over his shoulder at the camera boat covering their every move. "You think we can get away with that?"

"No rules, remember?" Eddie glanced over at the rocky shoreline. They'd have a tough time recovering the kayaks. He quickly started untying the closest one and pushed it toward the beach.

Spike chuckled, maneuvering his kayak to the other side of the buoy and pulling ropes. He pushed the first freed kayak toward

Denny, who was still several feet away, and sent the next one toward the shore.

"Thanks," Denny let out in exhaustion as he latched onto his kayak. "They'll never catch us now!"

"I like the way you think," Eddie said, watching the first few kayaks catch a wave and bounce toward the rocky coast.

Jack floated on his back, doing a modified backstroke which kept him moving forward while trying to rest exhausted muscles. He thought it'd be easier to swim one thousand meters; probably the lack of sleep combined with the exertion from the day before was catching up to him.

The sun was intense, beating straight down on him. Although warm and glad he hadn't worn a wetsuit, Jack was beginning to fear a major sunburn.

Jack turned in the water, ready to go at it freestyle again. He didn't have that much further to go. When the water drained from his ears, he heard Hugh shouting.

He looked up toward the buoy. Hugh was screaming, letting out a string of curses about seventy-five yards away.

"What's going on?" Jack yelled.

"The kayaks are gone!" Hugh exclaimed.

Jack put his head down and swam with all his might to catch up to them. He reached the buoy and looked around. Hugh and Tara were swimming toward the rocky shore, where the remaining six kayaks had landed. The buoy was anchored three hundred feet from the shoreline, a good mile from the resort cliff.

No time to rest now, Jack thought. He pushed off the buoy and started kicking, using the flippers to push at maximum speed as his arms stroked through the water.

Before long, he could feel the surge of the waves as they began to build near the coastline. Jack looked up to get his bearings. Hugh and Tara were off to his left. Straight in front of them were the kayaks, bashing against the rocks with each crash of the waves.

"It looks pretty dangerous," Hugh called out.

"Those idiots!" Tara cried. "They're going to get somebody killed."

Jack dog-paddled over to them, assessing the situation in front of him. The rocks looked ominous; jagged edges rose through the white foam of the waves. With each surge, the kayaks rolled over the uneven rocks, their brand new paint jobs being scratched and the kayaks themselves being dented. Going in for the kayaks looked like a suicide mission.

"We're losing time," Tara muttered.

"It's a six man race now," Hugh said. "We'll never catch those guys."

"You're right," Jack agreed. "So what do we do, stop the challenge? They can't kick all six of us off, can they?"

"I saw one episode where two of the contestants didn't make it over an obstacle wall," Tara said. "They were both kicked off that episode."

"OK," Jack nodded, looking toward the shore. "Then we'll have to find another way to get to the boats." His arms and feet had nothing left. Just treading water was becoming a concern. Fifty yards down the coast, the rocks gave way to a small section of sand.

"Hugh," Jack pointed toward the sand. "Our only chance is to come at the kayaks from the shoreline."

"Yeah," Hugh agreed. "It's the only way not to get smashed by the rocks."

"But we've still got to paddle the kayaks out of those rocks," Tara argued.

"No," Jack said. "We'll drag them over to the sandy part. Then we'll be able to push them out past the wave break."

"Excuse me," Kathryn said, getting the attention of the woman busily typing behind the main nurse's station on the pediatric floor.

"Could you tell me where I can find Amanda Forrest?"

The nurse looked up at her. "Your name, please?"

"Kathryn Williams."

"It'd probably be best if you go back down to reception. I'll let her know you're here and she'll meet you."

"Thank you," Kathryn said. She then turned around and headed for the elevator.

A few minutes later, Amanda came around the corner to the waiting area dressed in hospital blues and a pair of white sneakers. Her hair was tied back with a cap covering the top of her head. A bead of sweat reflected off her brow. She could have passed as one of the interns on the floor instead of being old enough to have a twenty-seven-year-old son.

"Kathryn," Amanda said with a smile as she stepped up to her. "What are you doing here? Shouldn't you be at school?"

"Probably, but I didn't know how to get in touch with you." Kathryn stood up as she approached. "I was dying to know if you got through to L.A."

Amanda's smile vanished quickly. "Yes, but all they would let me do was leave a message."

"I was afraid of that," Kathryn said while shaking her head. "I'm sorry."

"Yeah." Amanda motioned to the couch and took a seat. "They said 'everyone was out on location,' so I told them I needed to speak with Jack as soon as possible."

Kathryn sat down beside her. "Do you think they'll actually give him the message?"

Amanda's eyes began to water as she answered, "No … the first thing the woman said was 'no outside contact until the end of the challenge.' "

Kathryn studied her. The confidence that had been so evident the night before had vanished. It was one thing to trust God for Jack's job, but evidently quite another when it came to whatever history Amanda had with the producer of that show.

"So," Amanda finally said, "do you still have that board meeting tonight?"

"Yeah, that would be the other reason I wondered if you'd had any luck."

"Looks like we're both on our own," Amanda said with an unconvincing smile. "So what are you going to do?"

"I'll defend him the best I can—although I'm sure my principal and the president of the school board have already made up their minds."

"Remember what I told you." Amanda focused her eyes right on Kathryn. "God is in control."

Kathryn cocked her head to the side slightly, and spoke in the softest and most gentle voice. "Then why do I not get the feeling that's true for you when it comes to this reality show?"

Amanda held Kathryn's gaze for a moment, then smiled warmly. "*Touché*."

"I'm sorry …"

"No," Amanda shook her head, "don't be. You're exactly right. I guess it's just a bit easier for me to trust him with the school situation. And that's not too good, is it?"

The two sat quietly for a moment.

"So, what are you going to do about Jack?" Kathryn asked.

"I don't know." Amanda paused for a second. "I don't think there's anything I can do—but pray."

"What about asking to speak with Zeke Roberts?" Kathryn offered.

Amanda looked up quickly, her eyes gripped with fear. "Oh no, I couldn't."

"What do you mean 'you couldn't?' Whatever history you have with him is evidently playing right into Jack's fate."

Amanda didn't respond.

"If Jack's in some kind of danger, you have to call Zeke."

"I can't," Amanda sighed. "You don't understand."

"Then help me to understand," Kathryn pleaded. "Whatever you're going through, you don't have to do it alone."

Amanda brought her hands up and covered her face, letting her elbows rest on her knees as she bent over. Kathryn could see her hands were shaking. She reached out and touched Amanda's knee in support.

"Yes," Amanda whispered through her tears, "I do."

Jack, Hugh, and Tara swam parallel to the shoreline until they were even with the small patch of beach. Jack was impressed with Tara's swimming ability. She glided through the water with what seemed like no effort whatsoever, while he struggled to keep up. A camera boat was constantly right with them, and now Jack noticed that the helicopter was hovering above.

He looked over the small patch of sand they were about to head into. "We'd better be careful, there could still be a lot of rocks we can't see under the water."

"I agree," Hugh said. "Who's first?"

"I'll go," Jack suggested.

"No, let me," Tara interrupted. "I'm lighter and won't drag as deep in the water. I'll let you know if there are any rocks you need to watch out for."

Hugh looked at Jack, nodding his agreement.

"OK," Jack said. "Be careful."

Tara stroked forward, this time keeping her head above water as she looked for any sign of danger heading into shore.

"How you holding up, Jack?" Hugh asked.

"Tired, but OK. How about you?"

"The same."

"I'm worried my arms are going to be burnt out before we even start climbing that cliff," Jack said.

"Yeah, I hear you."

Tara was at the wave break, timing her swimming so that the crest of each wave wouldn't crash right over her. She lowered her head and stroked, perfectly timing another wave that carried her right to shore.

"She's good," Hugh remarked.

"Yeah, she doesn't even seem tired."

Tara stood up on shore, waving toward them and shouting something, but they couldn't hear.

"Must be OK," Hugh said.

"Then let's hit it."

The two swam toward the beach the way Tara had, keeping their heads above the water line. Within moments, they were at the point where the waves broke.

"You ever body surfed?" Hugh asked.

"No, have you?"

"Are you kidding?" Hugh laughed. "I'm from San Francisco."

"I take that as a 'yes'."

"When I say 'swim', give it all you got," Hugh instructed. "Then when you feel the wave pushing you—just hold your arms out straight and ride it in."

"Gotcha." Jack thought it was worth a try.

"OK, here comes one." Hugh was looking out away from shore. "Ready … swim!"

Jack put his face into the water and stroked and kicked for all he was worth. He felt his body rising with the water as the wave grew—then, just before it crested, Jack felt the wave grab hold and push him toward the beach, faster than he'd have thought possible.

In seconds he was on the beach as the last push of the wave washed over him, sending sand into his flippers, gloves, and swimming trunks.

"Woooo!" Jack yelled. "That was awesome." He turned over on the sand, staring up into the sky as a second wave washed completely over him. It felt so good to not be swimming or treading water.

"You're a natural, man," Hugh said with a laugh. "You rode that wave like a pro."

"C'mon, you guys," Tara said. "Playtime's over. We've got some catching up to do."

Jack removed his fins and goggles, and the three of them trekked down the beach, arriving at the sharp rocks quickly. His water shoes protected him somewhat, but on several steps, he'd hit one of the cuts just right and yelped. The camera crew continued shooting them from out in the ocean, not risking coming in near the crashing surf.

They had to climb over a pile of rocks about six feet high to get to where the kayaks were being pounded by the waves. Jack worked his way over the obstacle, then walked to the closest kayak that was stuck between two rocks. He waited for a wave to crash over, then walked in quickly as it receded. He grabbed the kayak and pulled, but it was stuck. He pushed instead, and the kayak broke free, but was that much further away from him—and closer to the incoming surge of the next wave.

Jack could see a huge one building. He grabbed the kayak and lifted it high, using his head to balance it as he turned away from the ocean. The wave hit him right above the knees and nearly knocked him over into the sharp rocks. But he held on, stepping through the water, trying to make sure each rock would hold him before putting his full weight on it. Jack was thrilled to see his kayak had the paddle still tied to it with a short line of rope.

Stepping up to the six-foot pile of rocks, Jack tossed the kayak over the top. Hugh had just done the same thing and was starting his climb over the rocks. Jack spun around and headed back for another kayak.

"What are you doing?" Hugh called after him.

"Getting another kayak," Jack yelled back, as Tara walked past him with hers. "The other women will never be able to finish if we leave them here."

Tara pushed her kayak over the rocks and shouted after Jack, "Are you crazy? This is a race!"

"You don't have to worry, you'll still be way ahead of them."

Jack walked back to the surf, eyeing his next kayak and waiting for the next wave to come in before he rushed to grab it. Just as he was about to make his move, Hugh came up beside him.

"It must be interesting to play on your football team," Hugh joked.

"Why do you say that?"

"I can just imagine you giving the other team seven points when yours makes a touchdown—just to keep it interesting."

"Not quite," Jack chuckled. "I just think what Eddie and those guys did was so out of line."

"I agree," Hugh nodded. "I just hope I don't regret this."

Jack and Hugh returned to the pile of rocks with two more kayaks. Tara was gone. Looking up ahead, she was already back to the beach stepping into the water with her kayak.

"Looks like she didn't want to help the other women," Hugh noticed.

"I can understand that. You should head off with her. I'll get the last one."

"No, it'll be easier to get the kayaks out to sea if we work together. You go get the last one, and I'll start walking these to the beach."

Jack smiled. "You know, Hugh, this is probably the only time where we can talk without being heard by them." He pointed up at the chopper hovering overhead.

"Unless they have some sophisticated eavesdropping equipment up there, you're probably right. What's on your mind?"

"The fire …"

"What about it?"

"Do you think it could have been intentional?"

"Yeah, I guess it could have been. But by who?"

"How about, Eddie?"

"Well, he was on your team," Hugh stated. "What do you think?"

"I think it's entirely possible, even probable," Jack answered. "And he thought that bungalow was mine."

"Then I'd say you'd better be extra careful."

"That's hard to do in the middle of this stinkin' game," Jack thought out loud. "What's with this 'no rules' garbage, anyway?"

"That's how this thing is run. Whoever can lie and con their way to the end winds up with the money. They should have called it *The Ultimate Cheater*."

"Then what am I doing here?" Jack asked.

Hugh smiled. "I've been thinking the same thing. Why don't we work together?"

"You mean like an alliance—like they do on *Survivor*?"

"Yeah," Hugh grinned. "You've proven trustworthy—if not a bit crazy. I'd rather be with you than against you. Besides, I don't like the way Eddie and the guys are turning this competition into an ugly game."

"Me either. You're on," Jack said.

"But how do you know you can trust me?"

"That's a good question. You're a lawyer, right?"

"I will be next year when I pass the bar."

"Then you're not a lawyer yet," Jack laughed. "Let's see if we can make it to the final two."

"OK, but I'm warning you, after that, all bets are off."

"Deal!"

19

Once Jack and Hugh got the five kayaks to the beach area, they tied the extras to the back of their kayaks, one behind Hugh's and two behind Jack's. They could see Tara paddling steadily out to sea about a hundred feet from shore.

"She's got a good lead on us," Hugh pointed out. "Not to mention the three cheaters."

"Yeah, but all that matters is that neither one of us is the last one up that cliff."

"Yeah, I just hope these women aren't expert rock climbers."

"You and me both," Jack chuckled.

They waded into the surf, pulling their kayaks behind them. As the water got deeper, it became more and more difficult to keep hold of the kayaks as the force of the waves pounded over them. Jack was deep enough to dive under the waves as they broke, but the pressure on the kayaks nearly pulled the rope out of his hand. He'd left his fins on the beach, not expecting them to help him when paddling the kayak. So even though he was kicking furiously, it felt like he wasn't making any headway to get past the waves breaking.

Pulling only one extra kayak, Hugh was making better progress and was already beyond the wave break.

"C'mon, Jack," he called. "You can do it."

Jack bore down, wrapping the rope around one of his gloves and stroking through the water. After a few minutes of grim determination, Jack and his kayak were clear of the waves breaking over them—but there were still two more kayaks being pushed back to shore by the pounding surf. Jack kept swimming, frustrated at how quickly his muscles tired from the exhausting morning.

Suddenly the load lightened and Jack sprang forward with his next stroke. For a second, he was afraid the rope had come loose, and the two kayaks would be tumbling back to shore. But when he looked up, Hugh sat beside him atop his kayak, holding onto the rope.

"Oh, good," Jack said. "I thought I'd lost them."

"It looked like you could use the help." Hugh kept the rope in his hand and paddled a few strokes away from the coastline. Jack swam beside him, grateful for the lighter load. When they were safely away from the breaking waves, Hugh stopped.

Jack held onto his kayak and tried to swing his right foot over the top. The kayak rolled in the water, and Jack fell over the top of it.

"How did you get on that thing?"

"Not like that," Hugh laughed. "You have to climb over the top of it with your whole upper body, then keep your balance while you swing one leg over. It's not that hard."

"Yeah, right."

He turned the kayak upright beside him, then leaned his weight over the top of it while keeping the kayak from spinning in the water. Jack felt like he had it balanced, so he brought his right leg up while scooting his body slightly toward the front. It worked. He was able to sit up straight and bring his legs into position in front of him, ready to paddle.

As Jack reached out and untied his paddle, Hugh asked, "Which way do we go?"

Jack pointed out to where three heads were bobbing in the water between them and the buoy. "Straight ahead. We'll drop the kayaks off for the ladies, then head for the cliff."

They skimmed above the water, easily traveling three times faster than they could swim. In minutes, they came up to C. J., with Maria and Stacy not that far beyond them.

"You guys are lifesavers," C. J. said, grabbing hold of the last kayak behind Jack.

"Over here," Maria called out. "I can't swim another foot!"

"Hold on," Jack called back.

"I'll get her," Hugh said, paddling straight at her.

C. J. had an even more difficult time getting on top of her kayak. It took Jack lining up his kayak next to hers, so he could keep a hold of it as she climbed on top. Hugh did the same for Maria, as Jack made his way over to Stacy. C. J. didn't wait around; she paddled off quickly in the direction of the cliff resort.

"Boy, that's gratitude for you," Maria said, as she pointed her kayak after her. "Thank you, guys. It looks like the race is on."

"Good luck," Hugh said to Maria, as he put his back into the stroke and quickly pulled away from her.

It took a few more minutes for Jack to get Stacy up and running. After she was set, he put his paddle deep into the water and started stroking. He came upon Maria quickly.

"Thanks, Jack," she called out to him, as he passed.

"You're welcome," Jack didn't pause, but just kept paddling. "Hang in there. You don't want to be last."

"I hear you," Maria returned. "I'll see you at the top."

Jack looked up ahead. Hugh and C. J. had already established a fairly good lead, and off in the distance, Tara was already about two hundred yards out, stroking like a professional. Slightly over a half-mile away, Jack could see the cliff looming in the distance.

From his vantage point atop the cliff, Zeke looked out over the ocean, trying to get a read on how the triathlon was going. He pulled a pair of binoculars up to his eyes, focusing where the last group was kayaking toward them.

"Can you tell who's running last?" he heard behind him. Travis had approached.

"Looks like Jack," Zeke grunted, ignoring the women who were paddling behind him.

"He's going to have a hard time making up the distance."

"Hugh isn't that far ahead. It'll be decided on the rock cliff, just like we planned."

Zeke pulled the binoculars away and looked straight down to the ocean below. The floating platforms were now full of activity as Eddie, Spike, and Denny were in various stages of their climb up the cliff's wall. Spike had arrived first, followed by Eddie. They were harnessed up and just beginning their climb. Denny was having difficulty getting off his kayak and onto the platform, as the waves kept pushing him off balance. He finally gave up and rolled off the kayak, swimming up to the platform's ladder.

Eddie was having difficulty getting the timing down between raising one ascender while keeping his weight on the other. Spike didn't seem to be having much more success. It was comical to watch. The two men dangled below them, spinning slightly on their ropes as they struggled to make headway.

Travis laughed. "This is great television. I can't wait to see Jack and Hugh's faces when the women get here. They're going to freak!"

Zeke nodded before bringing the binoculars back up to his face and looking out toward the kayakers.

"Oh, by the way," Travis said. "I just spoke with the L.A. office."

"And?" Zeke focused the binoculars on Jack's kayak once again.

"There was a message from Amanda."

Zeke grinned, then looked back toward Travis. "She wants to talk to me?"

"No," Travis answered. "She wants to speak with Jack. Says it's urgent."

Zeke cocked his head. "Really?"

"I thought you would want to know. Do I need to bring it up one more time that I think you're making a huge mistake?"

Zeke looked sternly at Travis.

"I guess not," Travis said with a grimace.

"Who's handling it?"

"Well, Kristi told her that speaking with a contestant wasn't possible until the challenge was complete—so at this point, no one."

"Good. Keep it that way." Zeke brought the binoculars back up to his eyes. "For now."

20

The muscles in his arms were screaming, his breathing more labored, but he kept at it. Paddling to his left, then to his right—over and over. Jack hadn't felt this exhausted since his two-a-day, in-full-gear, football practices in college. The sun beat down on his back—Jack knew it had to be bright red by now and would really sting later in the day, but there was nothing he could do about it. He'd managed to pull ahead of C. J. several minutes ago, but Hugh and Tara were still in front of him.

The floating platform bobbed up and down with the surf just ahead. Jack could see *The Ultimate Challenge* crew waiting on top to help them get harnessed into the rope. Hugh was just pulling his kayak alongside, grabbing onto the extension ladder and pulling himself up. Tara was already on the platform. She'd kept ahead of the guys the whole time—actually gaining on them. Jack was impressed.

He kept his paddle moving in rhythm as he took a look up the cliff. There were three bodies working their way up. The climb started with a straight vertical ascent of probably eighty to ninety feet. The section in the middle was more than three hundred feet of sharp lava rock where the ascent varied from seventy to eighty degrees. The final hundred feet were like the first—straight up to the finish point at the resort.

Jack recognized the muscular body of Eddie in the lead, moving slowly over the rocks in the middle section, as he had to move the ascenders up the rope to take each step. It looked like a time-consuming process when you weren't doing a vertical climb.

Maybe fifteen feet below Eddie was Spike, followed by Denny just completing the first section. Jack hoped his legs had rested enough to take most of the strain to make the climb. His arms felt like rubber bands. But with C. J., Maria, and Stacy still behind him, Jack wasn't worried about being eliminated. He knew he just had to take it slow and easy up the cliff, and he'd be into round three safely.

Pulling up alongside the floating platform, Jack used the surge from a wave to let go of his paddle and grab the attached ladder. Just as he was sliding his legs off of the kayak, a tremendous wind whipped around him, churning up the ocean and sending salt water right into his eyes. They closed as he squinted in pain.

The thrashing water didn't make sense until his brain finally registered the "thump-thump" of the helicopter hovering just above him. His mind was getting sluggish, impaired from the sheer exhaustion of the race.

Jack breathed in deep and stepped up the ladder. Holding onto each rung with shaking hands, he was finally able to crawl onto the platform's surface. He rolled over onto his back and looked straight up to see the helicopter pulling up and away from him—with Tara hanging from a harness below it!

The chopper ascended straight up, then began to slowly move toward the cliff—evidently giving her a ride up to the resort.

"Hey!" Jack yelled over the declining helicopter noise. "Was she hurt?"

The attending assistants on the platform looked over at Jack and laughed. Hugh, who was nearly strapped into his climbing harness, looked from them to Jack with a concerned look on his face.

One of them stepped toward Jack, holding the rope that Jack was to use to climb the cliff. "It's part of the challenge—the women don't have to climb. They fly."

Jack couldn't believe what he was hearing. "You mean none of the women have to climb the cliff?"

"That's right."

"That's not fair!" Hugh muttered as he looked up at the other three men already ascending the cliff.

"Doesn't have to be," the assistant grinned. "Was it fair to have them swim the same distance or kayak?"

"Didn't seem to bother Tara," Jack responded, as he watched her being set down gently on the top of the cliff.

"We're screwed," Hugh said. "Looks like the loser is going to be one of us."

Jack didn't answer, but looked up at the three guys on the cliff's wall. Eddie was a third of the way up the last vertical section. Spike wasn't quite there yet, and Denny was working his way slowly through the middle section of lava rock. Jack looked closely at Denny working his ascenders—he was clumsy, having difficulty keeping with any kind of rhythm. Jack had noticed the same slow process when Eddie was on that part of the cliff. The ascenders seemed designed for climbing straight up a rope, not angling up a section where your feet could just walk.

"Get goin'," Jack instructed. "Make it up that first section—then I think I have an idea."

Hugh slipped his feet into the rope stirrups and moved his top ascender as far up as he could. He then brought his feet up, moving the bottom ascender up the same amount. Repeating the process, he was now hanging four feet above the platform.

"This isn't going to be easy," Hugh called out.

"Just keep going, we can do this," Jack encouraged.

While Hugh was working his way up the rope, the climbing technicians were getting Jack into his harness. Jack was handed the foot stirrups and was ready to climb. Before putting his weight onto the rope, he analyzed the top ascender. "Now, how do you get this off the rope if you want to?"

"That would be foolish," the expert warned. "Don't do it."

"I don't care," Jack pressed. "Tell me."

The man shook his head, but pointed to the top of the red ascender and demonstrated. "If you take your weight off of the rope, you can pull this safety lever back, which will release the cam far enough to detach the rope."

Jack analyzed the piece of equipment and nodded. "OK, I got it."

"You do realize though," the man warned, "if you do that, you've given up your lifeline. As long as your harness is attached with the ascender, you'll be safe, and if there's an emergency we can come get you. But if you detach yourself from this rope, there's nothing stopping you from slipping and falling back down to the ocean and probably smashing yourself against these rocks here."

"I understand," Jack said somberly.

"So don't do it."

"Right," Jack said.

He began the process: weight on feet, move up the top ascender; weight on hips, pull up feet, and move the bottom ascender. It took Jack a few minutes to catch on. But eventually, he was able to find a rhythm and move up the cliff. He was glad he'd chosen to bring along the ski gloves.

He seemed to have a better knack for it than Hugh, because within fifteen minutes, he'd caught up to him hanging along the face of the cliff. "How you doing?" Jack called out.

"I'm getting it, but my arms are wiped out, man."

"Mine, too, but we can't give up."

"We're not going to catch those guys, Jack."

"That's no way to think." Jack kept moving upward.

Hugh laughed. "You have some miracle up your sleeve you're not telling me about?"

"Something like that," Jack answered. "Just keep your rhythm going—we're not going to be eliminated here, remember? We're a team now."

Jack kept working the ascenders, moving slightly ahead of him. Hugh grimaced and pushed himself harder, trying to keep up.

A few minutes later, they were hit with a windstorm that blew up small bits of rock, stinging their arms and legs and blinding them for an instant. Jack paused as the helicopter swooped by them before hovering over the platform once again. He looked down to see C. J. settled into the harness and being gently lifted up toward the top of the cliff. She waved at them as she floated by.

Somehow, watching the scene unfold before him made Jack's arms and legs burn that much more.

"What I wouldn't give for a ride to the top," Jack shouted above the chopper noise.

"Ten million dollars?" Hugh screamed.

Jack looked down at the ocean below them. The last two women were closing in on the platform. Maria was just ahead of Stacy, but not by more than twenty yards. They'd be flying up above them well before Jack and Hugh could make it to the top. Jack angled his head up the cliff, spotting the remaining competition.

Eddie wasn't in sight; he must have made it over the top. It was hard to tell by looking straight up, but Spike appeared to be within fifty yards of completing the climb. Their only chance was to catch Denny, who was nearing the end of the middle section, almost ready to begin the straight ascent for the last ninety feet.

They were running out of time.

"Congratulations, Eddie." Vince greeted the first male contestant back to the resort with a couple of cameras covering his every move.

Eddie's grin couldn't have been wider. "Thanks, man."

"Interesting strategy. Would you care to elaborate?"

"Just using my head. You guys said 'no rules', so we took advantage of it."

"By untying the kayaks?" Tara stomped into the interview, her voice hot, moving right in front of Eddie.

"Actually, it was Denny's idea, but what's it to you?" Eddie sneered. "You're not eliminated."

"That's not the point, you idiot! Any one of us could have been killed trying to retrieve those kayaks off the rocky beach."

Tara stared directly into his face, even though she was dwarfed greatly by the imposing figure standing over her.

Vince backed away, making sure the cameras could get close and cover the confrontation.

Eddie scowled and bent closer to Tara. "I'd back off, little lady, if I were you."

"No, I'm not going to back off," Tara pointed her finger into his chest. Eddie brushed her aside with a sweep of his arm, but Tara kept going. "Your crackpot cheating scheme was out of line, Eddie—and you know it!"

Tara turned, then glared at Vince. "And what about you guys—with that crappy little stunt with the flare gun."

Vince smiled innocently, not responding.

"What if one of us had been pulled down with the boat? Stacy nearly was!"

Vince shook his head. "No one was in danger—just part of the game."

Jack reached the top of the first section, climbing over the ledge exhausted, but thrilled to have his feet back on solid ground. The angle was steep, like trying to crawl up the roof of an A-frame cabin with jagged lava rocks for shingles. Jack looked over the edge of the cliff toward the ocean below. It wasn't deep, the waves crashed over the rocks in a steady rhythm. If he fell, there was little hope of survival.

Hugh's hand came reaching over the top of the cliff a few feet to Jack's right. He stepped over the rocks, moving toward him, and extended his hand. Planting his feet on a smooth section of rock, Jack pulled, helping Hugh to the top of the ledge.

"Thanks." Hugh sucked in his breath hard.

"You're welcome," Jack returned. "Now it's time to catch up."

"How are we going to do that?" Hugh wiped at the sweat pouring off his forehead.

"It's dangerous, but I have an idea—if you're up to it."

Hugh looked up at what lay ahead and spotted Denny working awkwardly on the last vertical section. "What have you got in mind?"

"For this section of the cliff, we'll be slowed down by the ascenders. They keep us connected to the rope, but we can only move them one at a time."

"Right ... so what are you suggesting?"

A mischievous smile grew on Jack's face. "We unhook the ascenders and walk up the cliff by pulling on the rope. We'd make much faster time—our only chance to catch up with Denny."

Hugh's eyes widened. "But if we slipped ..."

"There'd be nothing to stop us from plunging into the sea," Jack stated flatly.

"Yeah," Hugh said with a nod. "Look, you're a faster climber than I am. You could just beat me to the top. Why risk it?"

Jack's face quickly turned serious. "Those guys cheated, Hugh. One of them deserves to be kicked out of here—not you or me. Now are you with me?"

"You bet I am," Hugh grinned. "Let's go."

Jack pursed his lips. "Make sure you've got a sure footing first."

He moved farther from the ledge, finding a spot he felt was secure. He started with the lower ascender, pulling back the release lever, then the clamp. He had to angle the metal piece a bit to get the rope to pop out, but it finally came free.

"How do you get this thing to release?" Hugh called over.

Jack held his extender out toward Hugh and showed him how it released. Jack then clasped the carabiner to the harness around his waist and let the foot stirrups drag behind him.

With a quick prayer, Jack pulled down on the release of the second ascender. As he let it slip away from the rope, he held on steadily with his left hand and allowed the ascender, held on by the harness, to dangle between his legs.

"How you doing, Hugh?" Jack asked, nervously looking back over the cliff toward the ocean. It would be the last time he did that.

"I've got it," Hugh cried out.

"OK, we need to make up some time here, but keep it safe."

"I'm right behind you."

Jack bent his legs, making sure they were loose and ready. Then he started a hand over hand movement, pulling along the rope as he stepped carefully. Jack grinned as he pictured the two of them looking like Batman and Robin climbing straight up the side of a Gotham City skyscraper.

Jack was making great time heading up the rocky cliff, but now his arms—not the harness—were supporting the majority of his weight. His muscles were spent; the exertion through the morning swim, coupled with the kayaking, had blown them out. Jack wasn't sure how long he could keep pulling, but he had no choice. He tried to get his mind off the burning, to keep moving hand over hand, foot over foot, without thinking of how much farther he had to go.

He glanced behind him, looking for Hugh, and his foot slipped on a loose section of lava. The rocks went tumbling down the steep cliff as Jack slammed into the side of the hill. His left hand instinctively went out to protect his face from smashing against the cliff, leaving his right hand supporting his entire weight. The force of the blow stunned him for a brief instant, his right hand loosened, and he started slipping. The sharp lava sliced the bare skin on his arms and legs. Jack pushed back with his left hand, leaned on his side and grabbed the rope, clenching hard again with both hands. His downward movement stopped, but he swayed from side to side, the rocks biting into the entire left side of his body.

"You OK, Jack?" Hugh cried out, now a few yards above him on the hill.

"Yeah," Jack grimaced, looking down at the rocks bouncing down the cliff and dropping off the edge out of sight. There was no way Jack could have stopped his momentum if he'd continued sliding. "I'm good."

"You sure you want to continue with this?" Hugh asked.

Jack rolled back on his belly and carefully planted his feet, then looked up above. They'd traversed over half of the lava section while Denny had gained only a few feet up the vertical cliff. Jack pulled himself back up on his feet, looked over at Hugh, and smiled.

"Oh yeah. I'm sure."

"Well, then don't do that again," Hugh scowled.

"I'll try to remember that," Jack said.

He took a step, moved his hand up the rope, and began pulling again. After a few steps, he got his confidence back up and was moving faster. He could feel where he'd been scraped and bruised on his arms and legs. Even his ribs felt tender from smashing against the side of the cliff. But it seemed to help—clearing his mind and proving to be a diversion from his blown-out arms. He worked steadily up the cliff with Hugh keeping step right beside him.

"They're gaining on him," a voice cried out from the crowd.

"Someone has to stop this." Tara stood at the top of the cliff, among the others carefully looking over the edge. "They're gonna get themselves killed."

"We're not stopping anything," Vince said defiantly, standing beside her. "It was their choice to climb up the cliff untethered. We just have to see how it plays out."

"What is it with this show?" Tara turned and spat the words at him. "Our lives don't mean anything to you guys?"

"Now calm down, Tara," Vince cautioned.

"Don't tell me to calm down!" Tara exclaimed. "We've only been here a day, and there's been a fire, an apparent accident on the boat, and Jack just nearly slid off that ledge. This show is going to get somebody killed."

Vince looked back at Tara, making sure a camera was recording her reaction. "Come on, Tara. You really expect to go away from this week with ten million dollars in your pocket and not expect a little excitement?"

With a wink, Vince turned and left her standing there, not hearing her mutter, "A little excitement, yeah—being killed in the process, I don't think so."

It didn't take long for Jack and Hugh to hustle up the middle section of the cliff. Maria had passed overhead, making her way to the top well ahead of them. The helicopter had already flown back down and was hovering below, picking up Stacy.

Just below the vertical section, Jack found a fairly flat rock and stopped there. "Time to go vertical again, Hugh."

"Right," Hugh answered, pausing beside him roughly ten feet away.

"Be careful," Jack added. He kept hold on the rope with his left hand, while the right hand reached down to grab hold of the carabiner connected to his harness. His hand was shaking as he opened the clamp, the muscles spent. He moved the ascender out to the rope, wishing he could use his left hand to guide the rope into position—but that would mean certain death if he let go. He tried to attach the ascender to the rope just below his left hand, but the rope was too loose and wouldn't slip into the right position. His fingers couldn't hold the clamp open any longer and it snapped back into position.

"Oh, man," Jack gasped. He didn't think reconnecting to the rope would be such a problem.

"You having any luck?" Jack yelled over to Hugh.

"I've got my harness reconnected, now I just need my foot stirrups," Hugh called back.

"I couldn't get the rope into the right spot."

"Try to connect it above your left hand. The tightness of the rope will …"

Hugh's last words were drowned out by the helicopter noise as it flew by them, carrying the last female contestant. Jack didn't even look as Stacy floated up, but shielded his eyes from the flying rocks and sand. Hugh's instruction made sense. As soon as Jack could see, he was ready to try again.

He forced his fingers to pull open the release lever one more time, and, while still shaking, he raised the ascender. Placing it just above his left hand and close to the cliff's edge, Jack then twisted it and pulled it back toward himself. The rope stayed tight and slipped into place. He quickly released his fingers and the ascender bit into the rope.

Jack slowly let his legs bend and lowered his hands along the rope, allowing his weight to rest on the harness. It held. He was reattached.

"I've got it," Jack sighed in relief. He unleashed the carabiner that held the foot stirrups and second ascender, and easily attached it back on the rope with both hands.

"I'm good to go, how about you?" Jack called out.

"Then you better get hauling, brother!" Hugh yelled back.

Jack looked up. Hugh had already started climbing, rising a quick ten feet above Jack while he'd struggled with the rope. Further up the cliff, Denny continued his clumsy ascent. Jack had a hundred feet to get to the top, Denny had thirty. It was a race to the finish.

Jack tried to clear his mind of the image of Denny above him and concentrate only on climbing. He found his rhythm, working the rope and ascenders as if he'd been climbing for years. Hugh seemed to have found his own pace as well, and the two moved quickly up the cliff.

At the halfway point, even though Jack was climbing faster, Hugh was still holding on to second place by five feet. Jack finally took the risk of glancing to the top of the cliff. Denny was still on the rope, dangling above. It was hard to judge from Jack's angle, but he guessed

Denny was within fifteen feet of the top—Jack and Hugh were still three times as far. This was it. Either one of them was going to be eliminated, or they had to make up the distance before Denny climbed over the top.

"Come on," Jack yelled to Hugh. "We've got to catch him."

"I'm giving it all she's got, Captain," Hugh returned in a lousy Scottish accent.

Despite hanging nearly five hundred feet above the ocean surf while waves smashed against the rocky coast—his arms and legs burnt out and exhausted—Jack couldn't help but laugh. But he didn't slow down. Through the pain, he moved his arms and legs just a bit quicker. It would come down to the last few feet at the top of the cliff. Who could get their body up and over first?

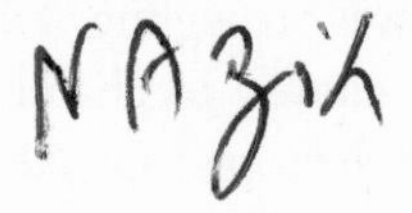

Jack kept moving—one ascender up, then the other; one ascender up, then the other—as if he were in a trance. He didn't give a second thought to Denny moving sluggishly above him, for to do that would slow his own progress and risk not catching him in time. His arms and legs had become numb—just appendages that kept him moving upward. Jack had never been a marathon runner, but he imagined he had entered a similar state that enables them to complete a twenty-six point two mile run.

Nothing mattered beyond climbing. He didn't sense the salt air swirling around him pushed by the island winds. His sunburned back, still baking as the noonday sun continued its relentless assault, ceased to hurt with each motion upward. The humidity and heat kept the sweat pouring from Jack, but it also allowed him some refreshment as the breeze whipped about.

Jack's deep concentration was suddenly broken when a black object appeared just off his left shoulder. It startled him, breaking him out of the rhythm he'd established. Jack paused in mid-stride, dangling dangerously above the ocean, standing on the stirrups, his hand ready to raise the harness's ascender. He looked over. It was a camera mounted at the end of a long jib arm that angled to the top of the cliff twenty feet away.

He was close enough to have camera coverage from the resort. Jack looked over at Hugh, a few feet below him, steadily working his way up. He had passed Hugh while in the "zone." Jack felt the weight of the race pouring over him—his arms dead, his legs like rubber bands stretched beyond their breaking point. The searing pain came in full waves from both his sunburned back and overworked lungs.

But up above, within just eight or so feet from the top, was Denny. Jack couldn't let him get there before him, or Hugh for that matter. The crowd above was cheering—he couldn't tell for whom, but everyone at the resort was anxiously awaiting the outcome.

Jack moved his right hand up and the ascender grabbed. He instantly shifted weight and moved upward. He was climbing again, and, looking up above, he noticed that Denny was struggling. His movement between ascenders had changed from clumsy to chaotic. Jack could see that the long duration hanging from the rope had taken its toll on him. They had a chance.

"Come on Hugh," Jack yelled out. "We're almost there!"

"I'm trying," Hugh cried, exhaustion evident in his voice.

Each completion of the ascenders brought Jack three feet closer to the top. After six times through the process, he was finally able to reach his right hand up to the top of the cliff. He pulled on the rope, allowing his feet to come out of the stirrups. He kicked out, getting his right foot up on top of the cliff, and pulled with all his might.

He was over the top, but in what place?

Jack rolled onto his back and brought his head around to the cliff, looking down. Hugh was just five feet below—but over to his left, Denny was reaching his hand over the top, about to kick his leg up and over as Jack had just done.

Jack grabbed for his harness, pulling down on the carabiner latch that connected him to the rope. He was free. He had a choice: run over and block Denny from climbing the last few inches, or try to help Hugh get over the top first—which seemed unlikely. Jack dashed to his left, sliding to a stop just inches from the edge of the cliff, straddling Denny's rope. Denny's right leg swung up on the top of the ledge, right in front of Jack. He pushed it off, sending it back down.

"Hey, knock it off," the exhausted voice of Denny cried from below.

Jack grabbed onto Denny's wrist and began prying his fingers off the rope. Denny cursed a blue streak as his hand let loose and he fell back below the edge. Then, hanging by his harness, Denny looked up and spotted Jack's face looming over the cliff, glaring down at him.

"What are you, crazy?" Denny screamed, reaching out to try and grab a hold of Jack.

"Yeah," Jack yelled back, keeping his hands clear from Denny's grasp. "Crazy enough to keep you from winning, you little cheat!" Jack grabbed onto the rope and yanked it from side to side with all his might. Denny swung below him, cursing at the top of his lungs.

Jack heard a scream and sensed movement behind him. He rolled to his right just as Eddie pounced where he'd been.

"You're dead meat, Forrest!" Eddie scowled at him.

Jack didn't answer, but sprang to his feet—his exhausted legs churning toward Hugh. He lined himself up with Hugh's rope and reached over the ledge as far as he could.

"Give me your hand," Jack yelled.

Hugh reached up immediately and grasped Jack's hand. His weight brought Jack forward, closer to the cliff's edge. Jack realized his mistake. He couldn't just grab on and pull Hugh over the top. He was exhausted, nearly out of strength and there was no place to anchor for leverage. Any movement Jack made would risk him sliding over the edge and plunging down into the lava rocks below.

Then he felt a weight bear down on his legs from behind.

"I've got you, Jack." It was Tara's voice. "Pull him up!"

Jack pulled, reaching his left arm over and latching onto Hugh's forearm. He groaned as he strained. Hugh released his legs out of the stirrups and planted his feet against the wall. Combining Jack's strength with his own, Hugh walked up the last few feet of the cliff's edge. With a final tug that Jack didn't think he had in him, Hugh's body came over the top and fell on top of him—ascenders, harness, and all.

A whoop went out from the crowd atop the cliff. Everyone cheered. Jack looked over to see where Denny was. He was lying face-down atop the cliff as well. Jack couldn't tell who had made it to the top first—or, more importantly, who was last.

Hugh rolled off of Jack, and the two of them lay on their backs in the cool grass, staring up at the sky.

"Did we beat him?" Tara asked, sitting beside them.

"We'd better have." Jack was spent. Now that it was over, all the cuts, bruises, muscle aches, and sunburn that had been kept at bay by the adrenalin rush were screaming for attention.

"Thanks, Jack," Hugh said, between breaths as he gasped for oxygen.

"No problem." Jack turned his head and smiled. "Partners, right?"

Hugh grinned back at him.

"What an amazing finish." Vince walked up, staring down at the three contestants.

A crowd gathered behind Vince as several cameras came in close, along with a few of the other contestants.

"They should both be disqualified!" Eddie demanded, as he stomped up beside Jack.

Jack didn't even look up at him. "Eddie, you're really starting to get on my nerves."

"You cheated!" Eddie swore.

"How can I cheat?" Jack returned. "There are no rules. Besides, I was just following your example when you released the kayaks."

Eddie shrugged. "I didn't do anything."

Vince kept silent, evidently content to let the contestants work it out themselves.

"Yeah, right," Hugh chimed in. "Like they just came untied as if by magic."

"What are you saying?" Eddie moved a bit and stood right over Hugh.

Hugh sat up, looking directly at the towering figure. "I'm saying that you, Denny, and Spike took off when the boat sank—not caring if any of us had drowned, untied all of our kayaks from the buoy, and sent them into the rocky surf. I'd call that cheating."

Eddie laughed. "Well, if the game's gettin' a little too tough for you boys, maybe it's time for you to go home."

"All right," Vince finally broke in. "I think that's about enough."

"So, who was last?" Jack asked.

"Too close to call," Vince said. "The crew is going back to look at the tapes and see if there's a clear winner—or, in this case, a clear loser."

"Oh great," Hugh sighed.

"We'll have the results soon," Vince announced. "For now—it's nearly lunchtime. You all have a half-hour to get cleaned up."

Eddie stood glaring over Hugh for a brief moment, then turned and looked straight down at Jack. "You'd better watch your step from here on out."

Jack shook his head. "Sure, Eddie. I'll do that."

Eddie eyed Jack a second longer, then turned and walked away grumbling something Jack couldn't quite make out.

"Well, I feel much better, how about you?" Jack turned toward Hugh.

"I'd be careful around him, Jack." Hugh sighed. "I don't think he's kidding."

"I'm sure he's not," Jack groaned, as he moved to get up. He ached everywhere. "C'mon, I think we deserve a dip in the pool."

Looking down at the commotion out at the edge of the cliff, Zeke nodded in smug satisfaction. Things were progressing just as he'd planned.

He stood in the control room, bathed in the coolness of the air-conditioning. He'd been able to watch both the camera feeds from the monitor wall and the live action from the cliff. Zeke had moved inside before the first contestant had made it even halfway up the cliff.

Standing in front of the window, overlooking the wondrous view out over the ocean, Zeke took special interest in Jack's struggle to stand up and walk. He knew he couldn't be seen; the staff had placed a dark film over the window before he'd arrived. He could see out, but no one could see in.

He heard footsteps approaching from behind him.

"We have a situation." Travis stepped up beside him. "It seems there's a tie."

"Really? That would be a first, I believe."

"Yes it is. Should make for a great episode. How do you want to handle it?"

Zeke kept his eyes trained out the window. Jack was walking toward him, a bit unsteady after the ordeal. Zeke turned to Travis.

"Let's look at the tapes, shall we?"

Several of the contestants had retired to their rooms to shower and change before the meal. Jack sat waist-deep in the water, parked on the second step where he was shaded from the sun by the swaying branches of a palm tree. Around him were the only contestants left by the pool: Hugh floating in front of him, and Tara and Maria sitting on the edge with their feet dangling in the water.

Jack had walked from the cliff to the pool and, without hesitation, dove into the deepest end, allowing the momentum to push him all the way to the steps where he now sat. The fresh water revived him somewhat, but he knew he was beat. If the next challenge involved muscle and endurance, Jack wondered how he would survive it. But then all the other contestants should be feeling just as exhausted. His face, back, neck, arms, and legs were somewhere close to the shade of a ripe apple. He planned to stop by the show's medic before changing to see if he could score some Lanicane or Bactine.

"So what were you doing when Vince said you could win ten million dollars?" Tara asked the group.

"That seems like it was weeks ago, doesn't it?" Jack said with a laugh.

"Yeah, it does," Hugh agreed. "I was on the twenty-seventh floor of the TransAmerica Pyramid in San Francisco—on a recruiting weekend with a law firm, right in the middle of a meeting with the senior litigating partner. You should've seen his face when the door to the conference room opened and in stepped Vince and his cameras."

"You must've freaked," Maria laughed.

"Not at first. There was no way that I could possibly imagine he was there for me. I mean, how could they even know I'd be there, you know?"

"I thought the same thing," Maria said.

"Me, too," Tara added.

"I didn't even know who he was," Jack admitted. "But when he stepped up to me and knew my name—then I freaked."

"Exactly," Hugh exclaimed. "I'm trying to stay all calm in front of these partners, and Vince asks if I'm Hugh Liang. Then I knew."

"And you're, like, supposed to be in classes this week?" Tara asked.

"Yeah, final few months of law school. I'm going to be so far behind. But I couldn't say 'no' to this. How about you?"

Tara angled her head and looked out over the water, evidently reflecting on the moment. "I was signing books after a seminar I'd given in Phoenix. Had a great crowd around the table too. Then these bright lights hit me, and Vince steps up to the table asking the obvious: 'Are you Tara Seacrest?' Kind of ironic … I'm sitting there amidst a pile of my own books with my name plastered all over."

The group laughed.

"I recognized him immediately—as did everyone around us. I just looked at him in shock."

"So, I take it you didn't sign any more books that night," Hugh said.

"Not a one. The minute I said 'yes', they whisked me away."

Jack turned to Maria. "Where were you?"

A slight blush came over her cheeks. "You may remember what I was wearing yesterday when we arrived. I was on stage at the Luxor Hotel in Las Vegas."

"Vince approached you during the show?"

"During the finale," Maria nodded. "We have this routine where all the dancers file out on the runway one last time. Just as I hit the end of it, the music stopped, Vince's voice comes booming over the P.A., and he's standing in the audience right below me."

"They must have gone wild," Hugh said.

"It was incredible. I didn't know what to do."

"He asked you right there?" Jack asked.

"Yeah—I had fifteen hundred people screaming for me to do it," Maria laughed. "Thank God my mom lives with me to take care of Teresa."

"Your daughter?" Jack asked.

Maria nodded. "Four years old. I miss her already. What about you, Jack?"

Jack splashed some water over his shoulders. It hurt, but at the same time cooled the burning. "I had just sent my football team to the showers."

"Football team, in April?" Hugh asked.

"Spring training—looking at the new talent for next year. I'm having a little discussion with the vice principal, when this helicopter lands right on the fifty-yard line."

"Wow," Hugh said.

"At the same time, this Suburban drives onto the field, a camera crew steps out of it, Vince steps out of the helicopter and walks right up to me—and I'm faced with 'leave your life for a week and you could win ten million dollars.' I still can't believe I did it."

"Me, either," Maria added.

"Then I say 'yes' and sign the contract," Jack continues, "and I immediately get shot."

"They did it right there?" Tara asked.

"Yeah, didn't they shoot you at the book signing?"

"No." Tara shook her head. "It wasn't until they took me to the limousine."

"Hugh?" Jack asked.

"Same for me," Hugh answered. "I'm sure they were a little wary of tranquilizing me in an office full of lawyers."

Jack turned toward Maria. "They probably didn't want to make a scene in the showroom either?"

"No, not until the limo."

"Well, that doesn't make sense. Why was I different?"

The four sat quietly. No one had an answer.

"What's going to happen if it's a tie?" Hugh finally broke the silence.

"I'm not sure," Jack said.

"I hope they have us vote on it," Tara brought some water up with her hands and let it pour over her shoulders. "Then you'll have nothing to worry about."

"What do you mean?" Hugh asked.

"Think about it," Tara explained. "Eddie and Spike will vote for Denny, since they seemed to have dreamed up the little kayak trick together, but that's it. None of the women will. And unless Jack's lost his mind, his vote will make it five to two. You stay, Denny goes home."

Jack nodded. "Makes sense to me."

"I wouldn't count on it though," Hugh sighed. "So far everything that's happened has been pretty far from what we've expected."

"Camera four had the best angle," the director said to Zeke. "We'll put it on the line."

The large plasma monitor above the director came to life, showing the top of the cliff. In the foreground, Jack was lying on his stomach, reaching over and shaking the rope that Denny was hanging from. Twenty yards behind them, the rope that Hugh was climbing could be seen in the distance.

"Scan forward, Bob," the director ordered into his headset.

The digital tape shuttled forward, comically showing Jack rolling away just as Eddie pounced where he'd been. When Jack made his move away from the camera and stopped to help Hugh, the director yelled, "There. Now play in real time."

The video froze, then moved forward at normal speed. Every eye in the control room looked intently as Jack reached over, taking Hugh's hand. At the same moment, Denny's foot came over the edge of the cliff in the foreground.

Zeke's eyes went back and forth between Hugh and Denny. Coming into frame at the bottom of the screen, Eddie reached out and took hold of Denny's hand. Jack's left hand reached over, grabbing onto Hugh's forearm just as Denny brought his other leg over. Then at the exact same instant, both Hugh and Denny came up over the ledge—Hugh landing squarely on Jack, Denny bringing his second leg over and squatting on all fours. It appeared to be a tie.

"Go back, and play it in slow motion," Travis ordered.

"OK, but we've looked at it a dozen times." The director gave the order to replay the last few seconds in slow motion. "They land at the exact same time."

Zeke and Travis watched the replay carefully, several times.

"I don't think we can declare a winner here," Travis said. "Unless we disqualify Jack for pushing Denny off the cliff."

"Are you kidding?" the director asked. "The animosity between Jack and Eddie is going to get us huge ratings. You can't kick Jack off."

"But we can't end it in a tie either," Travis argued.

"No, it won't be a tie." Zeke mischievously smiled as an idea popped into his head. "Let's go find Vince."

A lunch buffet consisting of deli sandwiches, salads, and clam chowder awaited the contestants when they arrived back at the restaurant. Jack had gone back to his bungalow and changed into a new pair of tan shorts and a colorful green and yellow floral shirt. Putting the shirt on had been painful, and every time he moved, the fabric would brush against his sunburn. He'd stopped by the medic's room before hitting the restaurant, doused himself with Bactine, and had the medic check all his cuts and scrapes.

The room was set up the same way it had been the night before. It was interesting to see how the contestants grouped around the two tables. Jack had picked the same table he'd shared with the losing desert team the night before. With him were Hugh and all four of the women. Sitting together at the opposite table were Eddie, Spike, and Denny. The lines had clearly been drawn.

Jack could tell Hugh was on edge. He wasn't joining in with the usual banter as they ate, instead, he nervously glanced toward the head table to see when Vince would arrive.

"Relax, Hugh," Jack tried to console him. "There's nothing you can do at this point."

"Easy for you to say," Hugh said, while sipping his iced tea.

"Maybe, but look how it's stacking up," Jack whispered. "If there's a vote, I'd say we've got their table outnumbered."

Hugh glanced over at the three guys and nodded, but his worried look didn't disappear. Jack took a sip from his soup and looked at the other table. Eddie was holding court, laughing it up with Spike and Denny. As Spike responded with some kind of joke, Jack analyzed Denny a bit more. He seemed to not have a care in the world, snickering when Spike came to the punch line.

Interesting, Jack thought. He took another sip; the soup was good and thick, just how he liked it. His thoughts drifted away, wondering what time it was back in Wheaton. He didn't know if they were in the Pacific, probably several hours behind, or in the Atlantic and possibly an hour or two ahead of Central Time. It was a strange feeling, not knowing. It kind of upset his internal clock.

Jack knew at some time that evening, the school board would be meeting, and he would be the prime topic. Jack sighed. He loved his job, but was probably going to lose it in the next few hours—and wouldn't even be there to present a defense.

What was he doing here? When he was out in the ocean or climbing up the side of the cliff, his focus was on the task at hand. During those times, Jack felt like he had a chance to win in any type of event they could throw at him. He especially wanted a crack at Eddie in some kind of one-on-one competition, something that involved some mental acuity, not just physical.

But sitting with the contestants between challenges, Jack's mind wondered how he could survive the cheating and politics to stay in the game. He was sure he would come up against situations that would require him to lie, or involve some kind of manipulation of another contestant to save himself.

He'd already cheated by pushing Denny off the cliff, although that had felt more like righteous justice. He had an ally in Hugh that Jack felt would stand whatever temptation they could throw at them, probably with Maria as well. But anything could happen in the coming days.

All this could be for nothing. Without his presence at the school board meeting, Jack was pretty sure his job would be over. There was nothing Kathryn could do.

Kathryn. Her image popped into his mind. He hadn't had time to dwell on her since the whole ordeal begun. He wondered what she was doing at the school—how far she'd stick her own neck out for him. He hoped not very far; she didn't deserve to have her job on the line as well.

"Jack." A voice broke through his thoughts.

"What?" His eyes focused back on the table in front of him. Maria was nudging his arm.

"You seem so far away."

Jack cleared his throat, somewhat embarrassed. "I'm sorry, I was thinking about something back home."

"I understand. I can't get my mind off of Teresa. Was everything OK when you left?"

Jack looked over at Maria. He was taken in by the concern written on her face. "Why do you ask?"

"I don't know, something about the sadness in your eyes."

Jack attempted to blink away any hint of his emotions. Maria smiled, and reassuringly placed her hand on his arm. "Well ..." Jack sighed, as he noticed Vince stepping up to the head table. "It looks like we'll have to talk about this a bit later."

The room went from full chatter to vacuum quiet the instant Vince took the podium. All ears were waiting for whatever decision was to come from the producers. Jack nudged Hugh and flashed him a quick "thumbs up". Hugh smiled nervously, then looked up to the head table.

"I'm sure you're all wondering what the replay showed," Vince said slowly, drawing in everyone's attention, knowing, that in the final edit, each of the contestant's faces would fill the screen as he talked. He looked through the room, analyzing the expectant expressions on Hugh and Denny, knowing that they'd get the most screen time—until he finished dropping the bomb, where Jack would be the primary focus.

"Unfortunately, after looking over the tape multiple times, we're unable to declare a winner."

A murmur went through the contestants. Looks of shock and disappointment appeared at both tables.

"That's not right, man!" Eddie complained. "I know Denny made it up first."

"Not true, Eddie," Vince said, with a raised eyebrow. "Although you won't be able to see the tape until this episode airs, you'll just have to take our word for it. It was a dead heat."

"Then Denny wins." Eddie changed tactics. "He would've reached the top first, if Jack hadn't cheated."

"If that were the deciding factor," Jack said, while standing up and facing Eddie as if they were opposing attorneys, "they'd have to figure out how many of us would've beaten you to the top, if you hadn't cheated."

Eddie stepped toward Jack. "I've had it with you, Forrest …"

"That's enough, Eddie." Vince warned. "Leave your little feud until the next challenge—that is, if both of you survive this trial."

That got Eddie's attention nearly as much as Jack's.

"What's that supposed to mean?" Eddie spat out. "I was the first one on the hill—how could I be kicked out?"

Jack stayed silent. He was sure Vince's answer would explain Jack's predicament as well.

"The producers have decided that due to some inconsistencies in the challenge," Vince teased, moving his eyes away from Eddie and looking from face to face at the rest of those seated before him, "we're going to have a vote."

"Yes," Hugh sighed. Jack glanced over at him, smiling at his reaction, but still trying to figure out what Vince was referring to between him and Eddie.

"Since Hugh and Denny did tie," Vince continued, "they'll be put up to a vote as to who will be leaving us shortly."

"Hugh, that's great," Tara whispered with a grin. "I told you there was nothing to worry about."

Maria smiled at him as well.

"And in addition, the producers have decided that since there were those who, let's say, didn't live up to the spirit of the competition …" Vince looked at the remaining men seated around the tables. "Or were creative in adding more obstacles for the other competitors, they're going to be up for the vote as well."

The tables erupted in conversations all at once. Eddie was on his feet with Spike getting up right beside him. Jack shook his head with a surprised grin on his face. This could be it, again. He was on the chopping block. The dynamics had shifted drastically. It wasn't going to be a vote between Hugh and Denny with a guaranteed outcome. He was now on the bubble with them.

"You can't do that!" Eddie shouted. "Remember, 'no rules'!"

"That's true, Eddie. And that's why you haven't been summarily disqualified. However, this is the first time we've been in a situation where, shall we say, some major unfairness has affected the outcome of a challenge."

Eddie stared at Vince, then slowly sat down, cursing all the way.

"Hey, it wasn't my idea," Spike tried to argue.

"Nice try, Spike," Vince grinned. "But the decision's final."

Spike shook his head with a scowl crossing his face, then took his seat.

"So, to make sure we're clear here, joining Hugh and Denny will be Eddie, Spike," Vince turned and looked right at Jack, "and you, Jack."

Jack rose calmly, addressing Vince in the politest manner that he could, to contrast Eddie's outburst. "Excuse me, Vince, but I'd just like to point out that when I acted on top of the cliff, I was not creating an unfair situation, but correcting one. It doesn't follow that I would be grouped among those that cheated."

Vince shook his head with a grin. "Nice try as well, but sorry."

Jack bowed slightly, hoping to accentuate his tone over Eddie's for the cameras. If he was going to lose, he wanted to go out with class.

"Now, there's just one more catch," Vince continued. "Those who are being voted upon do not get a vote in this decision."

The noise in the room erupted again, the women contestants looking around the room and chatting excitedly. Eddie, Spike, and Denny were fuming, while Jack was quickly trying to analyze which one of the five men the ladies would most likely vote out.

"Talk about not being fair," Eddie argued. "The women didn't even complete the challenge. One of them would definitely have been the last up the cliff. Denny shouldn't be in jeopardy here—none of us should be."

Vince glanced over at Eddie calmly. "Eddie, are you sure you want to continue with this argument in front of those who hold your fate in their hands?"

Eddie started to speak, then paused. His eyes opened wider and the lean face lit up as if Vince's words had just sunk in. He looked toward the women and sighed, "No, I guess not. My apologies, ladies."

"All right then," Vince nodded. "Just so we're clear on one thing, men: *The Ultimate Challenge* has never given the men an uneven playing field against the women. All are equal here. The decision to use the helicopter to fly the women up the cliff came only after the kayaks had been untied and released to the beach."

Eddie looked floored. His mouth opened and his jaw dropped. Jack could just imagine what was going through his head—if they'd just left the kayaks alone, he still would have easily made it up the cliff in no danger of being kicked out. But, as he was contemplating what Eddie was thinking, a thought slammed into his own mind.

"Wait a minute, Vince," Jack said. "Then weren't you guys basically leaving Hugh and me out to dry?"

"It could have very well worked out that way for one of you, Jack," Vince answered. "Except you found a way to beat the odds, didn't you?"

"Yeah," Jack groaned. "And nearly got myself killed."

"But what a great finish," Vince smiled. "Now it's time to vote. Ladies, if you'd follow me please."

Vince stepped away from his podium and led the women to the same room where the jungle team had voted Whitney off the night before.

Zeke sat with Travis behind the one-way mirror watching the women file into the room. This was going to be fun to watch. How would the women decide? Who would emerge as the dominant voice? And who would they pick?

The speakers above him came to life as Vince gave them their final instructions.

"Care to make a wager that your grand idea to have the women vote on this is going to get Eddie booted out?" Travis asked.

Zeke scrunched up his lips and nodded. "I'm game. A grand?"

"Sure."

Zeke laughed. "Do you think I'm that stupid? We need him."

"But why wouldn't they pick him?"

"Just watch." Zeke turned back toward the window. "You'll see."

"I don't think there's any question who we should vote off," Maria said, as soon as Vince left them alone in the room. "Eddie."

"I agree," Tara said, immediately.

"I would tend to agree with you," C. J. said. "But if we vote him off, that kind of lets Denny off the hook, and it was his idea."

"So?" Maria said. "I'm sure Eddie didn't need much prompting."

"Maybe not, and Spike was probably the same way," C. J. responded. "But think about Denny—he's the one who actually lost, despite cheating."

"Interesting," Stacy said. "I wouldn't have thought of that. Denny's the one who's on the block for two reasons: losing *and* cheating."

Maria looked around the table. What she expected to be a slam-dunk decision seemed to be slipping away. She felt like she was in a jury room heading for a hung jury.

"That may be true," Maria acknowledged. "But we need to consider what's best for us for the rest of this competition, not just decide on this challenge."

"Yeah, do you really want to continue to go against Eddie for whatever's next?" Tara added.

"Maybe," Stacy giggled. "Maybe not. I think he can be manipulated very easily. Men with tempers are so predictable."

"So you don't mind keeping him in the game?" Maria asked.

"Not at all," Stacy said. "I'd be more worried about Jack than Eddie."

"Why?" Maria, Tara, and C. J. asked in unison.

Stacy grinned. "Because Jack's smart and is playing the nice guy just a bit over the top. I don't trust him—but I know where Eddie stands."

"That doesn't make any sense." Maria shook her head.

"You're biased," Stacy argued. "You think he saved your life … and you have a thing for him."

"I do not," Maria shot back, "even if he did save my life. Besides, Hugh and Jack saved yours."

Stacy shrugged, as if being pulled to the bottom of the ocean with the Zodiac was ancient history. "I'm not going to let that rob me out of ten million dollars. You couldn't vote Jack out, even if it was down to just you and him."

"Jack isn't expecting any payback."

"Are you so sure?" Stacy prodded. "And it might not be just the game, either."

Maria's brow wrinkled, as she stared at Stacy for a second before she dropped her head.

"Are you saying we should vote Jack out?" Tara asked.

"I'm saying we should consider everyone," Stacy answered. "We have an opportunity to take one of the men out. Let's make it the one most likely to beat us."

"I'm not so sure I agree," C. J. cut in. "The competition was supposed to determine who gets kicked out. I think it should be either Denny or Hugh. One of them lost."

"If you follow that logic, then it really should be Maria or Stacy that gets kicked out," Tara argued. "There's no way either of you could have beat those guys up the cliff."

"That's not the issue," Stacy snapped.

The four sat quietly for a moment. Maria hadn't spoken since Stacy had confronted her about Jack. She had to admit she was behaving as if she was in debt to Jack. Well, she was. She could have died in that fire. There was no way, if given the chance, she'd vote for Jack to be kicked out. Now, if it was down to just her and Jack? She'd have to cross that bridge when she came to it. For now, she had to make sure he wasn't the one voted out in the next few minutes.

Behind the glass, Travis turned back to his boss and friend. "How did you know?"

"I know human nature," Zeke said with a grin. "You put four women into any room and you'll find sixteen opinions. I knew this wouldn't be easy for them."

"Very funny," Vince added, coming into the room and standing behind them.

Travis shook his head. "I'm shocked they didn't take one vote, pick Eddie, and move on."

"Well, you may still win your bet," Zeke offered. "We'll just have to wait and see."

• • •

"What do you think is going on in there?" Hugh said quietly to Jack.

Jack raised his finger to his lips, keeping Hugh quiet for a second. He was trying to pick up what Eddie, Spike, and Denny were whispering about at the other table. He caught a few phrases like "the plan" and "tomorrow," but couldn't make sense of it. They were up to something though, and it was three against two.

Jack finally brought his finger down. "Trying to see what they're up to."

"Sorry," Hugh said. "What'd you hear?"

"Not enough to know what they're planning, but enough to know they've formed an alliance."

"That doesn't surprise me." Hugh glanced over at them. "If the ladies vote me off, then you'll be outnumbered big time."

"Yeah, but if they vote one of them off—hopefully Eddie—then it's all square. And I think you and I can take on old Spike and Denny."

Hugh smiled. He liked the odds of going up against the other men with Eddie out of the picture. "So, how do you think the vote is going?"

"I'm pretty confident," Jack whispered. "I know Maria will try and get Eddie kicked out. I think Tara will as well. Even though C. J. was on my team, I haven't been able to figure her out yet."

"She was pretty hot at them for releasing the kayaks," Hugh mentioned. "You'd think she'd go after one of them."

"I hope so. Then there's Stacy—I'm not sure she cares about anybody but herself. How do you read her?"

"You're dead-on about her. We called her the "diva" through the first challenge. It's amazing we beat you guys here with her slowing us down. But I have no idea how she'll vote."

"Well, if Maria and Tara hold out," Jack contemplated, "the worst either of us could get would be two votes—a tie. Then we'd have to see what the producers do next."

"We've got to make a choice," C. J. said with a sense of weariness. "Maybe we should start with who we don't want to kick out."

"Jack," Maria said.

"There's a shocker," Stacy muttered sarcastically.

"Who would you say, Stacy?" Maria asked.

"Spike. He's done nothing to get him kicked out at this point."

"OK, we're making progress," C. J. said. "What about you Tara?"

Tara thought for a moment. "I don't think I could vote for Jack."

"Wow." Stacy cocked her head. "I'm surprised."

"What about you, C. J.?" Maria asked.

"Well, this might sound strange, but if two of you can't vote for Jack, I'd say we'd better not kick Eddie out either."

"Really?" Maria said.

"How do you figure?" Tara asked.

"I think Eddie and Jack are two of the strongest contestants out there, but they're at war. They'll be gunning for each other from here on out." C. J. paused as the other three women nodded in agreement. "If we take one of them out of the competition, the one that's left may be too difficult to defeat. If we leave them both in, we can stay under the radar while they concentrate on each other and probably make it past the next few challenges."

"I see your point," Tara agreed.

"That's interesting," Maria said. "But I still want Eddie out. He's dangerous."

"So you still want to vote for Eddie?" Stacy asked.

"You bet."

"Then that leaves the three of us," C. J. said, looking toward Stacy and Tara, "to either agree with Maria, or come together on another name to make it three to one."

"You're firm on this?" Stacy asked Maria.

"Yeah," Maria answered. "To me, there's no other choice."

"Well, I disagree," Stacy said, shaking her head.

"OK," C. J. offered. "Let's see if we can keep this moving. I know Jack's out of the question." C. J. paused to look at Tara. She confirmed her stand with a nod.

"As is Spike?"

Stacy pursed her lips and nodded.

"And what if I vote for Eddie?" Tara asked.

"Then we'd end up with a tie, unless you could convince Stacy to vote that way as well?" C. J. answered.

Stacy shook her head "no."

"OK," C. J. said. "Then that leaves either Hugh or Denny. We're back to the two who finished last."

"Hugh didn't do anything wrong," Maria pleaded.

"He didn't, and we know Denny was the source of the kayak scheme," Tara added.

"So, you could vote for Denny?" C. J. asked Stacy.

Stacy thought for a moment. Her eyes moved toward the ceiling as she ran her fingers across her lips. Maria couldn't tell what was going through Stacy's mind. She couldn't fathom how Stacy could want to keep Eddie in the competition.

Stacy looked back toward C. J. "Yeah, I could vote for Denny."

"Me too." C. J. smiled, then looked to Tara. "All we need is your vote and we're done."

"Shouldn't it be a unanimous decision?" Tara asked.

"Doesn't have to be—they never said that. Three to one should do it." C. J. answered.

"My inclination is still to vote for Eddie." Tara got up and paced the room. "Like Maria, I think he's proven dangerous." Tara stepped closer to Stacy. "Come on, won't you reconsider?"

Stacy shook her head. She wasn't budging.

Tara sighed. "We can't walk out of here with a two-two tie." She turned and approached Maria. "How about you, Maria. If I vote for Denny, will you join us and make it unanimous?"

"No," Maria shook her head, "I'm not changing my vote. And I promise you guys, you'll be sorry we didn't get rid of Eddie when we had the chance."

Tara grunted, then paced again.

"It's OK, Tara," C. J. said. "Vote with us for Denny or, heck, you could vote for Spike or Hugh—we'd still be done here. Just don't vote for Jack."

Tara looked one last time at Maria. "C'mon, are you sure?"

"I'm positive." Maria crossed her arms over her chest.

Tara seemed to deflate, then finally looked over at C. J. "All right, I'll vote for Denny."

"OK, then." C. J. finalized it with a nod. "We've made our decision."

• • •

"Ahhhh," Travis moaned. "I owe you a grand."

"Yes, you do," Zeke said with a sinister laugh.

"Never bet against the master," Vince chuckled, heading out the door.

"I don't believe it." Travis rubbed his hands in front of his face. "I thought your little scheme was going to cost us our Jack-and-Eddie feud."

"You gotta have faith." Zeke reached into his pocket, pulled out a Cuban cigar, and lit it up. Then, while puffing away, he added again for good measure, "You gotta have faith."

The women filed back into the room, taking the seats they'd left thirty minutes before. Jack tried to guess the outcome by their faces. Only Maria's gave any clue. Her quick smile and the twinkle in her eye as she looked at him gave Jack reason to relax. If she was happy, then maybe this was the last he'd have to put up with Eddie.

Vince took his place at the podium. "Well, the ladies have come to a decision. I'd like the five male contestants to stand up here by my table, please."

Jack and Hugh rose together. Jack patted him on the back as they made their way next to the head table. Lining up beside Jack came Denny, Spike, and then Eddie.

"Instead of handing you the gold envelopes like we did last time," Vince continued, "I'm going to ask the ladies to stand up and give us their votes."

The four women looked up from their table shocked. None of them wanted to voice out loud how they'd voted. But Maria's expression went beyond shock—straight to fear. Jack suddenly didn't feel as confident as before.

"We'll start," Vince paused for the drama, "with Stacy."

Stacy stood, sucked in a deep breath, and looked toward the lineup of men. "I voted for Denny." She sat back down without explanation.

"All right," Vince said. "That's one vote for Denny. Maria?"

Maria's face turned white, her head lowering to the ground.

"Care to tell us who you voted for?"

Maria stood, keeping her head low, then quickly said, "I voted for Eddie."

Jack heard Eddie swear as Maria sat back down. She was nervous, probably even scared, whereas Stacy had stood up without a care. *Maria's demeanor could only mean one thing,* he thought. *Eddie isn't getting voted off. If he were, she wouldn't be afraid. And now she's a target.*

"We have one vote for Denny." Vince's voice broke Jack's train of thought. "One vote for Eddie. C. J., who did you vote for?"

C. J. stood up as confidently as Stacy had. "I voted for Denny."

Jack glanced over at Denny, who dropped his head, shaking it slightly. Down two votes, the best he could hope for would be a tie—which didn't seem to be the case the way the women were acting.

"That leaves you, Tara," Vince said. "Would you please share with us the final vote?"

Tara stood up and faced the line of men. "I voted for Denny as well."

"Why me?" Denny burst out, breaking away from the lineup. "I would've made it to the top of the cliff in time if Jack hadn't pushed me off! Jack should be voted off—or Hugh! This isn't right!"

Vince stepped away from his podium and approached Denny calmly. "I'm sorry, Denny. But the vote is final."

"It's not fair!" Denny screamed.

Jack watched in fascination. What had been, for all intents and purposes, a calm, albeit slightly overbearing, stock analyst, was now closer to a raging lunatic. Jack thought he might burst into tears at any moment.

"Just how fair was it to release the kayaks?" C. J. asked from her table.

"I wasn't the only one who did that!" Denny screamed.

"No, but it appears that it was your idea, and you were the last up on the cliff that did it," Stacy fired back.

Denny froze, looking at the women's table with fury. Jack hoped they'd get him off the resort quick.

Vince looked back and forth between the women and Denny. He must have decided they'd gotten as much reaction as they were going to get on tape, because he nodded to his staff standing by the door. Two of the larger men from the production staff walked over to

Denny and politely ushered him to the exit. He cussed at and threatened the women all the way out of the room.

"I think you all deserve a bit of a rest." Vince regained control when the door shut behind them. "You have the afternoon to recoup. We'll reconvene at dinner."

Jack slumped in relief. He was still in the game. With each departure, Jack knew the odds increased in his favor. Hugh looked over at him, and they both smiled.

"See?" Jack laughed. "You had nothing to worry about."

"But you do, Forrest." Eddie stepped in between them.

"Eddie, give it a rest," Jack said. "Even the camera crew needs to take a break once in a while."

"You just keep it up with that lip, don't you?" Eddie stood inches away from Jack. "You and your sweet little girlfriend are going to regret ever agreeing to join this challenge."

Eddie held his position, waiting for a response. Jack chose not to give one. Two camera crews were standing on either side of them, taping the confrontation. Finally, Eddie turned and walked away.

One camera followed him, the other stayed with Jack. He was almost getting used to them being around until those moments when they'd get right into his face like that—although, given a choice, he'd take the cameras over Eddie.

As Jack watched Eddie walk out of the door, he felt a hand slip around his elbow.

"He is really starting to scare me," Maria said.

"Don't let him," Jack said to reassure her.

"Can we go talk somewhere?"

Jack looked into her pleading eyes. Nothing sounded better to him than crashing in his room and getting away from it all for a couple of hours.

"Sure, c'mon." Jack walked her toward the door. "We'll try and find someplace private."

A cameraman followed right behind them.

Back in Wheaton, the day couldn't go any slower for Kathryn if she were a student watching every tick of the clock until the ending bell would sound and release her from the torment. Everything about her job was driving her crazy. She had a hard time focusing on the subject at hand, whether she was meeting with faculty or parents. Even simple paper-pushing tasks seemed a waste of time. All she wanted to do was figure out a way to keep Jack's job.

So far that great idea still eluded her.

"Kathryn?" Tim stuck his head into her office.

"Yeah Tim," She answered. "What is it?"

"I have an idea." He stepped into the room and sat in front of her desk.

"OK." Kathryn set aside the papers she hadn't been concentrating on. "Shoot."

"Have you thought about calling the parents of the football team?"

"No, why?"

"The school board meeting," Tim explained. "If there's a public outcry in support for Jack, maybe it won't be so easy for them to fire him."

Kathryn pursed her lips, thinking. "But this is a closed meeting. No one's supposed to even know what it's about."

"The public has a right to know what's going on."

"But the school board has the legal right to hold closed-door meetings," Kathryn argued. "Especially with regard to disciplinary action toward teachers."

"Correct me if I'm wrong," he said with a smirk, "but the public could still—how do I say it—*show up* and make their support known on the other side of the door?"

"Interesting thought process you have there." Kathryn smiled, then shook her head. "It wouldn't work. Who do you think Jerry would blame for the word getting out?"

"Yeah, but could he prove it?"

Kathryn sighed. "He wouldn't have to. He's already warned me in no uncertain terms about any interference on my part."

"Jerry Swift isn't God around here," Tim grumbled.

"No, he isn't."

"Look, Mr. Swanson got his little hit squad of parents together against Jack, but no one has organized any support for him."

"That's because this has all been kept quiet. That's the way Jack wanted it," Kathryn explained.

"Well, I think at this point, keeping it quiet is just going to get Jack fired."

He was right. If she went into the meeting against Swift, Swanson, and the ACLU attorney alone, there was no way to protect Jack. Why should she keep it quiet any longer? She was sure Jack would agree—or at least she hoped he would. What did she have to lose?

Kathryn knew the answer. Her job was on the line.

"Can you get me that list of parents?" she asked.

"I have it right here," Tim said with a grin.

Her mind was made up. "Great. I'll take 'A' through 'M', you take 'N' through 'Z.' "

Jack and Maria had tried the pool area, the top of the cliff, the gardens surrounding the bungalows, but everywhere they went, the camera guy followed.

"Look," Jack finally whispered to her as they walked. "Let's go to one of our rooms, we'll still be covered by their cameras, but at least without a crew."

"Sounds good to me."

Jack walked her to his bungalow. Sure enough, when Jack ushered her into the room, the cameraman finally stayed behind.

"Wow." Maria was taken aback. "It still smells like smoke in here doesn't it?"

"Yeah," Jack said. "Let me open the sliding door and get a breeze going through here."

"I'll open the front, too." Maria went back to the front door and propped it open with her sandal. "There, that should do it."

Jack met her back in the living room. Maria sat on the wicker couch first and patted the seat next to her. Jack obediently stepped over and sat beside her.

"You know we're still being watched, right?" Jack motioned with his head toward the cameras in the ceiling.

"Yeah, I know. I don't care."

"OK, so what did you want to talk about?"

"Eddie," Maria answered.

"Oh, and here I had all these romantic notions going through my head," Jack said, smiling warmly at her, "and you want to talk about Eddie."

Maria chuckled. "Funny."

"I'm sorry," Jack laughed. "Just trying to lighten the mood."

"Seriously, I'm really worried about what Eddie might do."

"To you, or to me?"

"Both. I can't believe they made me say my vote out loud. And the way he threatened you ... I'm really worried."

"That makes two of us. But I have to believe the producers will keep an eye on him. They wouldn't let things get so out of hand that someone might actually get hurt, would they?" Jack struggled with his own words. He wanted to calm Maria's fears, so he downplayed the incidents of the previous two days. But inside, it was obvious to him: things *were* getting out of hand.

Maria sighed, her brow wrinkled as deep concern came over her face. "I'm not as confident as you. Don't forget the fire last night, and the way they staged the boat accident—Stacy could've easily drowned."

"Oh, I haven't forgotten," Jack assured her.

"And your little stunt on that cliff—when you and Hugh unhooked yourself from the rope and started scrambling up that wall. No one did anything to try to protect you. Tara said she talked with Vince and he just laughed her off, said no one told you guys to do it, that it was great for television."

"Well, in that case, he was right. It was my decision to do it, and I talked Hugh into it. Now that I look back on it, I must've been crazy. The game just grabbed hold of me and all I could think about was not losing."

"But what situation will we be forced into next? And how will Eddie use that to get back at us—or me?"

"I hear what you're saying, but it doesn't do any good to worry about something out of our control. We'll just have to take each step as it comes."

Jack looked into her troubled eyes. His words didn't seem to be helping. "Look, Maria, I'll do my best to make sure nothing happens to you."

"That's wonderful to hear, but what about you?"

"Well, Hugh and I have an agreement that makes it two against two if Eddie joins up with Spike—which I'm sure is happening. Hugh's a great kid. I think it'll be a fair contest."

"I don't think 'fair' is even in Eddie's vocabulary. I tried so hard to get him voted off in that room."

"How come the other ladies didn't agree?" Jack asked.

"Well, Tara did, initially. But Stacy thought you should go."

"Really?" Jack was taken aback.

"Yeah, in a way it was a compliment. She thought you were most likely to win, and we should get rid of you while we had the chance."

"I'll have to thank her later," he joked. The more he was getting to know the other contestants, the more he was starting to feel like he actually had a shot at winning. Then the school board decision wouldn't really matter, would it?

"But Tara and I said we couldn't vote you out."

"That's encouraging."

Maria went on to describe C. J.'s theory of keeping Jack and Eddie in the game to go after each other and how the final vote came about.

"Interesting," Jack commented. "I would've never guessed it would work out that way. I really thought you guys would take care of Eddie for us."

"I tried."

"And I appreciate it." Jack reached out and touched her hand. The spark deep inside shocked him. He could see that Maria felt something too as she looked up at him. Her hazel eyes had changed. The fear was gone, replaced with something close to longing. She was truly stunning. Without the extreme eye makeup and the showgirl outfit, she looked ten times more attractive to Jack.

"So what's your story?" Jack asked.

"What do you mean?"

"All I know about you is that you're a Vegas showgirl and have a four-year-old daughter. Ever married?"

"No. Teresa's father left when he found out I was pregnant."

"I'm sorry," Jack said.

"I'm not. It was best that way, actually."

"But for Teresa?"

"Especially for Teresa. I can't picture Mario being any better as a father than he was as a boyfriend."

"I understand."

"I dance at night," Maria continued, "and spend the day with Teresa, or I'm in class. I'm studying to get my teaching credentials."

"What do you want to teach?"

"First grade, maybe kindergarten." Maria smiled. "I love kids."

"Willing to give up the stage, huh?"

"More than willing. I'm counting the days," Maria sighed. "I don't want Teresa growing up with a showgirl for a mom."

The two sat quietly for a moment. Jack tried to imagine what a little Maria would look like. Teresa had to be a cute kid. He didn't realize he was staring at her until Maria leaned closer to him, keeping her eyes locked on his. She moved closer, and closer, then stopped.

Jack leaned in slowly as Maria waited for him to come to her. Just before their lips could meet, Jack reached his arm around her, moved his head beside hers, and turned it into a hug. She reciprocated the embrace, holding on for a moment, and then pulled away.

"Is there somebody at home waiting for you, Jack?" Maria asked.

Jack shook his head. "No, not really."

"What does 'not really' mean?"

"There's no one serious. I've gone out a few times with someone, but we haven't hit the 'exclusive' stage—we're not seeing each other every weekend or anything like that."

"Then why ..."

"Didn't I kiss you just now?" Jack finished the sentence for her.

Maria nodded.

"I don't know," Jack answered truthfully. "Maybe it's the cameras. Don't get me wrong: I think you're beautiful—and wonderful. But being part of this game, the manipulation of the producers, it just doesn't seem right to me."

"Not even one kiss?" Maria pouted, then leaned in closer. Jack was taken in by her sweet fragrance. He found himself leaning toward her, fascinated with the color of her eyes, unable to stop himself.

He grinned, and allowed his lips to touch hers, then placed his hand on her cheek as well. The kiss was soft, innocent at first, then lingered longer than he'd expected. The pit of his stomach fluttered with electricity. He didn't want it to stop—until an image flashed into his head of Kathryn sitting on a couch watching this moment replayed on television. He pulled back slowly, breaking the moment.

Maria smiled, pulling him close as she put her arms around him.

"Ouch!" Jack jumped. "My sunburn."

"Oh, sorry," she giggled.

Jack laughed as well, releasing the image of Kathryn.

"Thanks, Jack." Maria rose from the couch.

"For the kiss?"

"No, for listening," Maria said with a soft smile. "I guess we'll just have to see how this all pans out."

Jack got up and walked her to the door. "I don't think Eddie will be gunning after you. He'll be too busy trying to get me out of the game."

"Then you be careful," Maria warned.

"I promise."

"Good. I think I'm going to get some rest."

"Me too," Jack said. "I'll see you at dinner."

"It's a date." Maria smiled one last time, then walked away.

Jack lingered a moment, watching her walk away before he stepped back into his bungalow and shut the door.

With the extreme toll that the swimming, kayaking, and cliff climbing had taken on his body, Jack thought he'd be asleep as soon as his head hit the pillow.

He was wrong.

His mind first obsessed over Maria, dwelling on the scent, the feel, the touch of her lips on his. Jack had lived a fairly sheltered life through his years around Wheaton. He would never have imagined a scenario where he would be sharing a kiss with a Las Vegas dancer. But he didn't think of Maria that way—maybe it was the drama of coming to her rescue in the bungalow and while the boat was sinking, but there was a connection. He could easily imagine a relationship getting off the ground if they were anywhere but in the middle of this insane game. But then again, without *The Ultimate Challenge*, they would have never met. Despite Maria's occupation, she seemed more like the sweet girl-next-door type to him—OK, the exotically beautiful girl next door.

Jack smiled.

He lay in bed, staring into the darkness as the image of Maria began to fade, and something else stirred deep within him. He hadn't even considered her relationship with God—which, from what he knew of her past, there didn't seem to be one. That was one of his steadfast rules in dating, not getting into a serious relationship with someone who didn't share his beliefs. What had he been thinking? Before long, the growing conviction was joined by its evil cousin, guilt.

Kathryn. What would she think when she saw their kiss replayed on her own television screen? Was what he did tantamount to cheating on her? Jack didn't think so—they weren't exclusive. He didn't even know where their relationship stood. They certainly hadn't shared a first kiss yet. He was growing fond of her, true. But he'd hesitated in taking the next step. Jack had convinced himself it was because she was his vice principal. But would that really have mattered if he were in love?

But how did she feel? Jack wondered. He could see it in her behavior recently—she was falling for him. Part of him liked the attention. Kathryn was a bright, beautiful woman, and Jack cared deeply for her—which is why he didn't want to do anything that would hurt her.

Too late. *Why did he kiss Maria?* Well, Jack knew exactly why. The question was, *why didn't he have enough self-control to stop himself?* For that he didn't have an answer. *It was just one simple kiss—no big deal, right?* He would just have to be careful throughout the rest of the week.

Then his mind drifted. Stacy thought he was the most dangerous person to win. *What if she was right?* Could Jack pull off what was needed to win the ten million?

Jack thought back to the night before when he had been ready to be the first kicked off so he could go home and defend his job. A lot had happened since then. He had been able to analyze the competition, and if the challenges were anywhere near fair for the upcoming days, he was beginning to believe he had a good shot at coming away with the prize. He had a solid triangle of support: Hugh and Maria would stick with him, probably even Tara. He felt like he could continue being the nice guy of the group, and probably gain Stacy's support as well.

That only left Eddie and Spike in his way.

Hopefully, the next challenge would get rid of one of them. Jack could see the possibilities. He started thinking about the money again. What he could do with more than five million after taxes. He'd be set for life. Who cares what the lousy school board decided that night. He wouldn't need them.

Jack's reflective struggle was interrupted by a knock on his door. He was glad for the distraction as he slipped out of bed.

It was one of the production assistants with a gold envelope.

"Your personal challenge." She handed the envelope to him with a smile.

"Thank you, I think." Jack said.

She turned and walked away. Jack closed the door behind him and sat down at the dinette table. He'd forgotten about the personal challenges. He tore open the seal, pulling out a three-by-five card with a single line typed across it: *Convince Maria Lopez to sleep with you within twenty-four hours.*

Jack couldn't believe his eyes. They couldn't demand that. He couldn't—he wouldn't—comply. Even if he thought she would allow it, Jack wouldn't even consider it. He was going to have to find Vince and explain the situation here. They couldn't demand he go against his religious beliefs in order to stay in the game. There had to be an out.

The excited plans of how to spend the money, the joy of being set for life without worrying about the school board—it all came crashing down. He couldn't win, not if he had to complete this challenge to do so. He just couldn't do it, not even for ten million dollars.

Or could he? Jack thought. It's not like it hadn't crossed his mind, even though he'd fought the temptation. Would God allow one slip-up, if it could lead to financial security for the rest of his life?

Jack sighed, shaking his head, picturing Jesus on the hilltop overlooking all that Satan had offered him. He just couldn't picture Jesus saying to the ultimate deceiver, "Well, sure, OK, but only this once."

God help me be strong, Jack prayed, as he got up from the chair, tore the card into tiny little pieces, and washed them down the drain, switching on the garbage disposal for good measure. He turned the water off and headed back into the bedroom, his head down and slumped. He was disappointed he'd actually considered using Maria as nothing more than a pawn in his attempt to win the stupid game. She deserved better from him.

Flopping onto the bed, Jack's mind didn't even register the sting of the sunburn. He stared up at the ceiling, wondering how he was going to get out of obeying that challenge and somehow stay in the game. There had to be a way. But in a few minutes, the exhaustion took over. His eyes closed, and he quickly drifted off to a restless sleep.

30

Kathryn turned right onto West Park Avenue, pulling up alongside the school district office. During the school year, the school board convened on the second and fourth Wednesdays of the month, rotating between the various schools in the district. This being a special closed-door meeting on an off-week, the school board president had scheduled it at the district office, only a couple of miles from Royal High School.

Kathryn got out of her car and walked up the sidewalk. Taking a quick glance at her watch, she knew the meeting would start in fifteen minutes. Where were the parents they'd called? The street was empty, except for a few cars she knew belonged to members of the school board.

She walked into the office and headed directly for the conference room. It was large enough to hold the seven-member board and several guests. Tonight, as far as she knew, the only guests would be herself, the lawyer, and the parents of the boy Jack had prayed for.

As she entered the conference room, Jerry was already inside talking with three school board members. The conversation stopped as soon as she stepped into the room.

"Ah, Kathryn," Jerry said, looking up, smiling. "So good to see you."

Kathryn had the sense that they'd been talking either about her, or something they didn't want her to hear. She nodded at the four plastic smiles and took a seat against the wall.

In the center of the room sat a large oval conference table with seven executive chairs around it. Folding chairs were set up along two of the walls where those invited to the closed meeting could sit off to the side.

Within minutes, the remaining board members had arrived and the seats around the table were filled. Bonnie Slagle, the president of the school board, greeted Kathryn politely before taking the chair next to Jerry.

Along the opposite wall sat the Swansons and an older gentleman in a suit and tie who Kathryn knew to be Stanly Collins, the ACLU attorney.

She felt alone on her side of the room. She regretted Jack not being there to defend himself, then kicked herself for not thinking to have a lawyer there to represent Jack against the Swanson's lawyer. She had no idea what a lawyer could have done to save Jack's job, but at least she wouldn't have been alone in the fight.

Bonnie cleared her throat and got everyone's attention. "All right, I think we're all here. I call this meeting to order."

The secretary took a quick roll call, then had those not on the school board introduce themselves for the record. After a few minutes, Jerry took control.

"The president called this special meeting to discuss Jack Forrest …"

At which point, Kathryn interrupted, "And I'd like to request that we postpone this meeting."

"You haven't been recognized," Jerry spat out.

"I'm Kathryn Williams, vice principal of Royal High School."

"That's not what I meant."

"I know, but as vice principal, I would like to inform the board that Jack wanted to be here tonight but was called out of town unexpectedly, and I think we shouldn't hold this meeting without him."

"We covered this in your office yesterday, Kathryn," Jerry scowled.

"He has not responded to this board's demands—and by doing so, he has refused our demands. Whether he is here tonight or not is irrelevant."

"No, it's not," Kathryn argued.

"Where is he?" a female board member in front of Kathryn asked.

Jerry smirked. "Yes, Kathryn. Why don't you tell us where he is?"

Kathryn pursed her lips quickly and stood up. "Monday evening a helicopter landed on our football field and Vince Sinclair of *The Ultimate Challenge* TV show pulled Jack away to be a contestant."

"Really?" The woman grinned. "I love that show."

Several around the table were surprised, as were the parents and lawyer across the room. But the three board members who had been talking with Jerry when she entered the room didn't respond, neither did Bonnie.

"Jack's choice to flippantly leave his coaching and teaching responsibilities, not to mention his lack of respect for this body, only adds to the accusations against him," Jerry stated.

"He wanted to be here," Kathryn explained. "I told him it would be OK. He had a once-in-a-lifetime opportunity to be on this reality show. I thought we could delay the meeting for just one week."

"You thought wrong," Jerry proclaimed. "I've told you this already."

"Isn't there anything in the bylaws," Kathryn directed toward the president, "that stipulates Jack has to be here for this to continue?"

Bonnie shook her head. "He was here for the last meeting when we gave him our demands. Unless he's made it clear in some fashion that he's agreed to them, his time limit is up. We can act without his presence."

"Has he given you any indication that he'll do what we've asked?" Jerry prodded.

Kathryn paused, trying to find the right words. She thought back to the moment Jack was struggling with his decision to go with Vince. She'd promised she would take care of this—and now she saw no way to keep that promise.

"When we talked on Monday, he was considering the board's demands. He just needs more time. You can't go through with any decisions until Jack has a chance to respond."

Jerry opened his mouth to argue, but a knock on the door stopped him. He kept his eyes glued on Kathryn for a moment as his brow furrowed. It was as if he was trying to bore into her his words of caution the other day to not intervene. She remembered them clearly; her job was about to be laid on the line as well.

"Come in!" He yelled, then finally took his eyes off of Kathryn and looked toward the door.

It opened, revealing a large group of parents anxiously crowding the hallway and looking into the room. One man stepped forward, seemingly the spokesman for the group. Kathryn was thrilled for the distraction—and relieved that somebody had shown up.

"I'm sorry, this is a closed-door meeting," Jerry said.

"We know," the man answered. "We've come to make sure our voices are heard anyway."

Jerry's eyebrows rose at the man's bravado, then he turned his head slowly until his eyes pinpointed Kathryn. His stare bore right through her. "Is this your doing, Kathryn?"

Before Kathryn was forced to respond, the man took a step into the room. "This is no one's *doing*," he said, overly stressing the word, "but the concerned parents that stand with me tonight in support of Coach Forrest. You guys can't fire him behind a closed-door session and get away with it."

Kathryn appreciated the inflection—probably said to help alleviate the repercussions she was sure to face for putting out the word.

"Actually, we can. You don't have a say in these proceedings," Jerry said while standing to his feet, as if his small stature could intimidate the man who towered above him.

"Hold on, Jerry." Bonnie rose beside him. She looked to the parent in front of Jerry. "Excuse me. You are …"

"John Belmont," the man replied. "My son will be a senior on the varsity team next year."

"Well, Mr. Belmont." Bonnie smiled pleasantly. "We're not on a witch hunt here, but simply working through a procedure to determine what should be done about Coach Forrest. No one's been fired yet; we're here to discuss the issue tonight."

"Why wasn't this meeting posted, so those who want to have a voice in this could attend?" The woman behind Mr. Belmont stepped up beside him. Her eyes were intent, her face angry.

Jerry stepped back, shaking his head. He leaned over, right in front of Kathryn, and whispered in an edgy voice, "I warned you about this, Kathryn."

Jack slept for more than four hours, only waking up when a staff member banged on his door loud enough to rouse him. When he pulled himself from the bed, it felt like he was leaving half the skin of his back stuck to the bottom sheet. The sunburn felt raw. The outside of his arms and legs were scratched and bruised, while the muscles under the skin seemed to be on fire.

When he opened the door, the assistant handed Jack a tuxedo telling him it was required attire for the evening, and that dinner would be poolside instead of in the banquet room. After a quick shower in his swimsuit—in which the hot water seemed to accentuate every sunburned, scraped, and cut area of his skin—Jack painfully worked his way into the tux. It fit perfectly, including the brand new black patent leather shoes, which were so stiff, with each step it felt like they were cutting into the tops of his feet.

When he walked around the corner and spotted the pool area, Jack couldn't believe what he saw. The women were astonishing, dressed in lavish evening gowns that seemed to have been tailored just for them. Even their hair and makeup looked professionally done, and they all wore expensive jewelry that Jack was sure they hadn't brought with them. It was quite a contrast from how they had all looked before the break.

C. J. and Tara were beautiful—C. J. in a flowing gold dress with a beaded inset down the front, Tara with an equally impressive strapless red gown.

Stacy could have adorned the cover of *Vogue* in her pleated silk chiffon dress. But the one who really caught Jack's eye was Maria. She was mesmerizing in a long, flowing black gown, slit up the side to well above the knee, and low-cut enough to make Jack consciously force his eyes to stay on hers. They'd given her a string of pearls to wear around her neck; a matching bracelet adorned her wrist. Her hair had been curled and pinned up, leaving her shoulders bare. She was simply elegant—the worst thing in the world for Jack to get his mind off of the personal challenge hanging over his head.

Jack worked his way down the buffet line, while continually glancing at Maria who sat with an empty chair beside her. The table spread was amazing: another array of exotic salads, cold dishes, a complete salad bar, three different seafood dishes, and the evening's entrée—prime rib.

The contestants were keeping to the recent divisions. Hugh, Maria, and Tara were at one table. Eddie and Spike sat plotting together at another. Stacy and C. J. had found a table near the deep end of the pool. It was clear to Jack that the two women were keeping their distance from his group, but they obviously weren't ready to align with Eddie and Spike. Jack thought that worked to his advantage—his group of four against two groups of two. He liked the odds.

In contrast to the arrival the night before, this evening's atmosphere was classed up several notches. A string quartet played softly as colored lights and tiki torches set a romantic mood around the pool. Walking up to Maria in his penguin suit, Jack felt like it was a lovely spring evening at the prom.

"You look incredible," Jack said to her as he set his plate down. "So do you, Tara."

"You clean up pretty well yourself," Hugh joked.

"Thanks, Hugh," Jack said, then looked back at Maria, shaking his head slightly. "Really, Maria, you're stunning."

Maria's cheeks flushed as a smile creased her lips. "Thank you. I must say, you look rather dashing yourself."

The four of them chatted amiably, enjoying the lavish setting. As he ate, Jack found himself forgetting he was stuck in the dangerous game. The romantic music blended with the soft, gentle breeze, and the beautiful woman sitting next to him topped off the perfect evening. It was a night to remember.

"Welcome to challenge number three," Vince said, bringing Jack back to reality as he walked up to the eight remaining contestants gathered around the pool. The conversation around him came to a screeching halt.

"I'm sure you're wondering what we have in store tonight," Vince teased.

"Looks like a cocktail party," Hugh joked.

"More like a movie premiere or the Emmys," Stacy added.

"No," Vince laughed. "Just thought we'd class up the competition a bit. It's Las Vegas night at *The Ultimate Challenge*."

Several contestants excitedly clapped and cheered, especially Maria. Jack wasn't thrilled. He'd never been to Las Vegas and knew very little about gambling, with the exception of getting together every once in a while with some of his college buddies to play poker.

"This is a team competition." Vince brought the murmuring down and the focus of the contestants back onto the game. "Each of you will be paired up—so there'll be four teams. Tara, you're with Hugh."

Hugh scooted his chair closer to Tara. They made a striking pair, Tara in the long flowing red gown, and Hugh in the black tux with the red cummerbund.

"Next," Vince continued, "we have Spike and C. J."

Spike let out a whoop, moving over next to her and taking her arm. Jack noticed that Spike's gold cummerbund matched C. J.'s gold evening gown. He realized who he would be partnered with and he didn't like it.

"Our next team will be Eddie ..." Vince paused for dramatic effect. "And Maria."

"What?!?" Maria exclaimed. "You can't be serious!"

Eddie casually walked up beside Maria, ogling up and down her entire body. "I'm gonna have fun messin' with you."

"You touch me once ..." Maria self-consciously crossed her arms over her chest, "and I'll ..."

"You'll what, partner?" Eddie sneered.

Maria pursed her lips, her eyes fixed on his. "Just don't."

"And our last couple," Vince chuckled, enjoying the producer's strategy behind the choice of teams, "is, of course, Stacy and Jack."

Jack didn't have to move over toward Stacy; she was already by his side, wrapping her arm in his, the silver gown perfectly matching his silver cummerbund.

"Oh, Jack," Stacy flirted. "This will be so great."

Jack smiled politely, then glanced over to Maria. She sat with her back toward Eddie. The panic was evident in her eyes. Jack lifted his shoulders slightly trying to convey that he was sorry, but there was nothing that he could do. His forced smile seemed to do nothing to alleviate her fears.

For thirty minutes, the school board sat through parent after parent, standing before them, singing the praises of Coach Forrest, and giving their reasons why he should not be disciplined, much less fired.

Jerry Swift acted as if he was listening, but, in reality, he was focused on how he would make Kathryn pay for her insubordination. There was no way these parents could have gotten word about the closed-door meeting without her being involved. He had tried to get rid of them without them being heard, but the other school board members wouldn't side with him. Finally, he resolved himself to sit through it, smiling after each had his or her say, but remaining unresponsive to their fervent pleas to keep Coach Forrest.

Finally, the parade of parents was over as John Belmont stepped back into the room.

"Have we heard from everybody?" Jerry sighed.

"Yes, sir, you have," Mr. Belmont answered. "My son will be a senior next year, starting wide receiver and safety. He's looking forward to his final football season here under Coach Forrest—I don't want that to change. We hope that this board will take into account how Mr. Forrest has been a great coach, a fantastic teacher, and, most of all, a wonderful example for our children."

The parents behind Mr. Belmont cheered, emphasizing his final point.

"We certainly will," Bonnie answered before Jerry could respond. "Thank you so much for coming down here this evening."

"You're welcome," Mr. Belmont looked over to Kathryn.

"Yes, we appreciate your input." Kathryn stood, walked over to him, and shook his hand.

"Your opinions have been duly noted." Jerry stood as well. "Now if you'll excuse us, we need to continue with our business."

Mr. Belmont held his ground. "We'd like to hear how this turns out if you don't mind."

"Well, we do mind," Jerry answered rudely.

"That's enough, Jerry," Kathryn said forcefully. "I'll take care of this."

Kathryn motioned for the parents to go back down the hallway and ushered Mr. Belmont from the room. When the door had closed behind them, the first to speak was Mr. Swanson, the father of the boy whom Jack had prayed for.

"I want you all to know that I could have brought twice the number of parents into this room that would say just the opposite about Coach Forrest. But they honored the board's right to have a closed-door session to discuss this matter."

"But they have a representative in this room voicing their opinion," the vice president of the school board, Sonya Thomas, blurted out. "These parents didn't have anybody. I, for one, am glad they showed up."

A few board members shook their heads in agreement. Jerry felt like he was in danger of losing the votes he needed.

"Be that as it may," he said, "that doesn't change the problem at hand. Coach Forrest was asked to respond to this body's requirements to save the school district from a very expensive lawsuit—one that I'm sure I don't have to remind you, we can't afford."

Bonnie looked over at the boy's parents. "After what you've just heard from the other parents, is there a possibility we could convince you to not go through with your lawsuit?"

"Not on your life," Mr. Swanson declared. "Nothing in what they said makes it OK for Coach Forrest to push his antiquated religion on my son."

The parents grouped around Kathryn in the reception area. Kathryn was so thankful for their involvement, but she needed to get back in the room as quickly as possible.

"We can't let them sit in there and fire Jack," one of the fathers said.

"Showing up tonight was a tremendous help," Kathryn responded. "But the board will not allow you to stay inside the meeting."

"Ted and Marge Swanson are still in there," Mr. Belmont argued.

"Their son is at the heart of the charges against Jack," Kathryn reminded them. "Look, you've done all you can do tonight, and I'm sure Jack will really appreciate it."

"Where is he anyway?" another father asked.

"You haven't heard?" A woman next to him said excitedly. "He's away as a contestant on *The Ultimate Challenge.*"

"He's what?" The man looked at her in shock.

Kathryn knew this could go on for a while.

"Look, I need to get back in there to fight for Jack," she said to interrupt the murmurings going about the room. "Thanks, all of you, for coming. We'll make some calls as soon as we know more."

"Good luck in there, Ms. Williams," Mr. Belmont urged. "Don't let them fire our coach."

"I'll do my best." Kathryn smiled weakly, then turned and headed back to the conference room.

Vince led the contestants into the banquet hall. The room had been transformed during the afternoon and looked nothing like it had at lunch. It now resembled something you'd see at the Bellagio, Caesar's Palace, or the Mandalay Bay. In a matter of hours, Las Vegas had come to the island.

"Welcome to Las Vegas!" Vince smiled and spread his arms, presenting the room.

Slot machines lined the outer walls, while, at the center of the room, six gaming tables were positioned in a circle. Though he had no clue how to play the games, Jack recognized the roulette wheel, the long deep-pitted table for craps, and a couple of blackjack tables.

The ambience around the room had dramatically changed as well. Plants with fiber-optic lights had been placed in strategic spots, a full bar had been set up where the buffet line had been, and the room was now darker, with only bright pools of light hitting the gaming areas.

The tables were manned with dealers, all dressed alike in bright red shirts and black slacks, and standing behind each table ready to begin the gambling. A few scantily clad cocktail waitresses stood beside the bar to add the finishing touches.

Stacy still clung to Jack's arm, taking the partnership a bit too seriously, as far as Jack was concerned. Eddie and Maria stood beside each other, but several feet apart. The more Jack thought about the pairings, the more he thought this might be the best situation for Maria. Eddie might have sought revenge for her vote on the past challenge, but now that they were teammates, Eddie couldn't do anything about it. Anything he did to hurt her would only jeopardize his own chances of staying in the game.

That also meant Eddie's sole focus would probably be on eliminating Jack.

"For the next ...," Vince glanced down at this watch, "well, let's say until the sun rises, this will be your next challenge. You've been placed in teams of two. Each of you will have ten thousand dollars to start with."

Jack watched the contestants react with bright smiles, nudging each other and sharing some thumbs up.

"Ah," Vince cautioned them. "Don't think we're giving each of you ten thousand dollars, though."

The smiles faded, as production assistants walked up to the contestants and handed them papers to sign.

"The ten thousand will actually be your money."

"I don't have that kind of money," Maria complained.

"Me either," Hugh agreed. "I'm not even out of law school."

Jack didn't speak up but was thinking the same thing.

Vince continued, his television host smile gleaming. "The money is coming from your personal assets, as you'll see on these receipts."

Jack looked down at the form that had been placed in his hand. It itemized where the money would be coming from: one thousand dollars out of his checking account, three thousand five hundred dollars that he had in savings—which pretty much emptied out all the cash he had to his name. The balance of fifty-five hundred dollars would be taken out against his condominium on a second trust deed, paid back at the prime interest rate plus two points.

"You've got to be kidding me," Jack's eyes flared. "You can't do this to us!"

"Well, Jack," Vince said with a snicker. "We've found that gambling just doesn't mean anything if you're not playing with real money—*your* money."

Jack looked around the room feeling like a fish out of water. Gambling, "Vegas-style", had always been one of the things he just inherently thought was wrong. Outside of the periodic game nights with his college pals and an electronic blackjack game on his computer, Jack had no clue how to win, or, at least, beat the odds often enough not to lose his shirt. Jack knew he hadn't saved much on his teaching salary, but he had counted on that money to at least get him through the next month or two, should he be fired.

Jack stepped out of his reflective mood and looked at the reactions of the other contestants. Beside him, Stacy seemed thrilled—ten thousand dollars to her was probably a day of modeling. Spike and C. J. didn't seem to mind the challenge, grinning as if the next few hours would be a party. Hugh had already made his concerns known, but he was eyeing the tables with a look of determination. Tara wouldn't be concerned about losing the money—her books and speaking fees could cover that in a weekend, easily.

Glancing toward Eddie, who was smiling like a Cheshire cat, Jack could see Maria had turned ashen white. Jack could only imagine what she was going through. Ten thousand dollars would mean the world to her—paying for college, taking care of Teresa. She couldn't afford to throw it away in a one-night gambling binge. He had a feeling *The Ultimate Challenge* producers knew this—about her and probably about him as well.

"Please, sign the papers."

"And if we don't want to gamble?" Jack asked.

"Then it's time to go home," Vince answered. He waited for the contestants to sign. Everyone but Maria and Jack did so without hesitation. Maria glanced at Jack, who shrugged, then brought his pen down and quickly signed. Maria shook her head, then signed as well. When they turned over the papers, the production assistant handed over ten one-thousand-dollar chips.

"Very good," Vince continued. "The challenge tonight is simple.

The tables are open—gamble away until sunrise. The team with the least amount of money at dawn will be sent home."

"Both people?" Eddie asked.

"Yes," Vince answered. "You're in this together. Plan your strategy. Pick your favorite game then go for it. And by the way, any money you make tonight above your original ten thousand dollars is yours to keep."

"Oh," Stacy said excitedly, "this is going to be so much fun."

Jack suddenly wanted a different partner.

33

Kathryn opened the door to the conference room as quietly as she could, trying not to interrupt the ongoing discussion. It didn't work. The conversation stopped dead in its tracks.

"Nice ploy, Kathryn," Jerry stated coldly, his eyes hard as ice. "But it didn't work."

Kathryn quickly walked over to the chair she'd sat in earlier. The rest of the board members stayed silent, allowing Jerry to be the spokesman.

"What have I missed?" she asked.

"A lot," Jerry sneered. "We'll deal with your insolent ploy of bringing the parents here later."

Kathryn didn't respond.

Jerry shrugged, moving on. "You missed Mr. Swanson telling us how he could've filled the room with twice as many parents that want to see Coach Forrest fired."

Kathryn's brow wrinkled as she glanced toward Mr. Swanson. She didn't believe him. She turned back toward Jerry as he continued.

"You also missed Mr. Swanson's promised determination to see this lawsuit through unless we take immediate action."

Kathryn looked around the room to the other board members. "Didn't you hear what those parents said?" She stood, pleading her case. "Jack is an excellent teacher, a wonderful coach. And he's been a great asset to this school. To fire him would be a huge mistake and a great miscarriage of justice."

"We have something in this country called the *separation of church and state.*" Mr. Swanson's attorney countered. "Mr. Forrest cannot ignore that fact and go around pushing his personal religious beliefs on young, impressionable students—especially when what he preaches goes against the parents' philosophies and principles."

"That's right," Mr. Swanson said emphatically.

"We can't have any school employee trying to 'save' our students at Royal, Kathryn," Jerry added coldly.

"He wasn't pushing his religious beliefs," Kathryn argued. "This whole thing has been blown way out of proportion. All he did was pray for their child when he'd been hurt—and then answer his questions."

"Without my permission," Mr. Swanson said while standing, his face reddening. "In one moment, he shot down everything I'd taught my son over the past sixteen years."

"He was concerned for your son." Kathryn softened her voice, trying to reach him another way.

"That wouldn't have been necessary if those hoodlums hadn't been invited to the football clinic in the first place. The man is irresponsible and shouldn't be allowed to teach or coach!"

Kathryn was getting nowhere. She turned to the school board, looking from face to face as she spoke. "Are you going to let this man destroy Jack's life over this?"

"All he had to do was recant what he'd said," the vice president said. "Why wouldn't he do that?"

"That's what we were talking about when we were interrupted Monday night," Kathryn explained.

"All this would've gone away," Bonnie pointed out. "He could keep his job."

"And you might still be able to keep yours," Jerry added.

"Do you remember the language this board required him to use?" Kathryn ignored Jerry's threat.

"Yes, we wrote it with the help of Mr. Collins," Bonnie answered, gesturing to the lawyer.

"If this case goes to court," Mr. Collins said in an authoritative voice, "it'd be a slam dunk. The school district will be liable if they don't act—*now.*"

"Kathryn, may I speak with you privately?" Jerry's tone grew compassionate for the first time.

She looked at him a moment before nodding in agreement.

He led her into the hallway, closing the door behind them before speaking. "I know you want to defend Jack. He's been a wonderful addition to the school. I can see that—and the parents coming out tonight in his support says a lot. But the simple fact is, we can't let one teacher—one coach—be the cause for wasting potentially thousands, if not millions, of dollars on a lawsuit that we can't defend. One teacher isn't worth jeopardizing the resources we need to educate all of our students. I'm sorry."

Kathryn looked down, searching for the words to counter Jerry's logic. After a brief moment, she looked back up at him, her words filled with passion. "What this family is doing is tantamount to extortion. You can't fire Jack just because they threaten us with a lawsuit. He's willing to apologize to Mr. Swanson—the whole family if that's what it will take. He didn't mean any disrespect to their religious, or more precisely, non-religious beliefs."

She paused, fighting back a flood of tears. "But I'm sorry, he cannot say there is more than one way to God. He just can't."

And for the first time, Kathryn understood why.

Sitting at the bar nursing a Pepsi, Jack analyzed the seven other contestants. His partner, Stacy, had gone right for the blackjack table, betting a hundred dollars a hand. Hugh and Tara had huddled up for a bit before she joined Stacy at blackjack and he went to the craps table. Spike was playing roulette along with his partner, C. J. Eddie headed to the craps table and placed his bet as Hugh threw the dice. Maria had just settled down at the blackjack table.

"Planning your strategy?" Vince asked Jack, as he walked up beside him. "Or saving your money?"

"I'm not much of a gambler. And ten thousand dollars is a lot of money to me right now."

"I understand," Vince said. "But I think I said earlier, if you're not willing to gamble, the alternative is a trip home."

"But I also remember you saying something at thirty thousand feet before you made us jump out of a perfectly good airplane." Jack grinned, "There are no rules."

"Very good," Vince chuckled. "But not risking your ten thousand could put you out of the race for the ten million."

"Possibly. Or maybe if I don't risk my money, I'll come out the real winner."

Vince looked over to the blackjack table. "I guess that would depend on how Stacy does as well, wouldn't it?"

Jack smiled, getting Vince's point. He grabbed a hold of his Pepsi and stood. "I guess I'll just go have a little look."

"Hit me," Stacy said, as Jack slid in the seat next to her. The dealer pulled an eight to add to her queen and deuce. "I'll stand."

"How you doing?" Jack asked.

"I'm up three hundred," Stacy said without looking at her partner. "How about you?"

"Still even."

"You gonna play?"

"I'll watch a few hands first."

The dealer's face card was a ten. He flipped over his whole card, revealing a king—he also had twenty. No winner. Maria had seventeen, so she lost. Tara had nineteen and lost as well.

"This doesn't seem very profitable," Jack said, as the dealer raked the cards in.

"You just have to know when to raise the bet and when to lay low," Stacy muttered. She reached for her chips and added three black chips worth a hundred each inside her betting circle.

"Four hundred dollars?" Jack asked.

"I have a hunch," Stacy giggled.

Jack sucked in a huge breath, wanting to get as far away as he could.

34

Kathryn was getting fidgety. Nothing she heard after coming back into the room was giving her any hope that the school board would be rational about the situation. Jerry seemed to have enough votes in his pocket. There were a couple of board members who could possibly be swayed, but there was no voice of reason in the room to bring them along except for hers.

"Are we ready to put it to a vote?" Jerry asked.

Most heads nodded around the room.

"Wait," Kathryn interrupted.

"Kathryn," Jerry sighed.

"But Jack has the right to be heard," Kathryn said, struggling to find the right words to stop this.

"Then he should've been here to exercise them," Jerry grimaced. He'd won. All he needed to do was get the official tally. "All right, let's get this over with. Time to vote."

Jack's shoes were killing his feet as he walked around the room. His legs hurt and the sunburn was nearly unbearable under the tux, but he wanted to keep a sharp eye out for how many chips were in front of each of the seven other contestants. So far, he hadn't wagered a dime. Jack wasn't sure if it was because of his Christian upbringing that had taught him gambling was a sin, or simply what seemed to be the foolishness of potentially losing his hard-earned money. If his ten thousand combined with whatever amount Stacy was left with would keep them out of last place, why risk it? He could just walk around all night and protect his savings.

But it was hard to get a bead on everyone else's money. The other contestants seemed to have caught on to what Jack was doing, and they were pocketing their chips so he couldn't get an accurate count.

He stood behind the craps table watching Eddie's turn with the dice. This was a game Jack didn't understand at all. Hugh was busy laying down chips on different positions on the board, while Eddie kept being handed the dice and throwing them the length of the table. They were yelling terms he'd never heard before. It was all very animated and entertaining, but eventually Jack walked away confused.

The roulette table was much more matter-of-fact. If your number hit, you'd get thirty-six times the amount you bet. But the odds were that much against you as well. There were many other ways to bet, but Jack didn't understand them as he watched Spike and C. J. spread their chips around the table. The dealer, if that's what he was called, placed the steel ball into place and snapped it to go the opposite direction of the spinning wheel. C. J. and Spike cheered and yelled for their favorite numbers. The ball slowed down, spinning lower toward the wheel until it dropped with a pling, bounced several times, and eventually landed in the red twenty-three slot. C. J. and Spike groaned as most of their chips were cleared from the table.

This seemed to Jack like another game he would be wise to just walk away from. That left the slots, which at this point no one had decided to play, or blackjack. So Jack headed back to see how his partner was doing.

Kathryn hesitated by the phone. She dreaded making the call, but she'd promised Amanda she'd let her know the results of the meeting. As soon as the votes were counted—five votes to fire Jack, two to keep him—Kathryn walked out of the conference room. There was nothing to say. She'd fought as hard as she could, placing her own job in jeopardy at the same time. The repercussions that were sure to come would probably begin in the morning. Tonight, Kathryn just wished she could have spent the time with Jack. Maybe the bright side of the tragic news would be that their relationship could take the next step without the conflict of an employee dating a supervisor.

She cracked a smile at the thought before it was quickly destroyed by the more sinister image of Jack's loss of job actually destroying their budding romance. Her eyes moistened and a tear slid down her left cheek as her mind raced through the what-ifs. How would she be able to face Jack and give him the news when he returned?

She took in a deep breath and blew it out slowly, forcing her mind to switch gears. She had to stay strong to be a comfort for Amanda.

She picked up the phone and punched in the numbers written on the pad next to it. After two rings, Amanda answered.

"Hi, Amanda. It's Kathryn."

"Oh, Kathryn," Amanda answered. "I can tell from your tone it didn't go well, did it?"

"No," Kathryn fought to keep her voice from shaking, "it didn't."

"I expected as much. Don't beat yourself up over it. I'm sure you did all that you could."

"Well it wasn't enough. We even had over twenty parents of the football team show up and give their support, but it didn't help."

"That was sweet of them."

"You don't sound that upset," Kathryn thought out loud.

"Well, in some ways I'm very upset," Amanda responded. "I think it's ridiculous that Jack could lose his job—in this country of all places—just praying for that injured boy. But until Jack gets back from this stupid reality show, there's really nothing we can do."

"But don't you see? There's nothing for him to do even when he gets back. The board has voted. He's out of a job."

"True, the board has voted," Amanda replied. "But I don't think it's over."

"What do you mean?" Kathryn switched the phone from one ear to the other.

"Just that the school board has had their say. There will come a day when it's Jack's turn."

"But I've been told to start looking for a coach tomorrow."

"You go right ahead and do what you're supposed to do. Jack will understand, I'm sure."

"I'm not so sure," Kathryn sighed.

Amanda's voice softened, both in volume and texture. "Kathryn, you've gone above and beyond where Jack's concerned. It's not your job to protect his—that's God's responsibility. You need to know that Jack will be nothing but grateful for all you've done for him."

"I'm not so sure. I feel like I've let him down."

"You haven't let him down at all."

"I just keep hoping that he comes home with the ten million dollars, and all this won't even matter to him."

Kathryn was surprised by the laughter on the other end of the phone.

"Oh, you do have quite an imagination, don't you?"

"Have you heard anything back from them?"

"No," Amanda said. "I don't think I will, either. I've been praying all day for him, and have my prayer chain from church praying as well. I feel like that's all I can do at this point."

"Have you given any more thought to trying to get directly to Zeke Roberts?"

"I'm sure he's been given the message that I called. If he wants to talk with me, he will."

"You seem more …" Kathryn searched for the right words. "… at peace with this whole thing than you did this morning."

"Somewhat, maybe. I'm still struggling with why Zeke would insert himself into my family after all these years. But like Jack's job, at this point, there's nothing I can do but pray. And I've found that when you do, somehow there's peace in that."

"I wish I could find it," Kathryn said. "This whole thing is tearing me up."

"Then let's pray together," Amanda suggested.

"Right now?"

"Sure, why not?"

Kathryn didn't have an answer for that.

"You can just listen if you'd prefer. Father, we come to you in the name of Jesus …" Amanda began.

As the evening progressed, Jack was better able to get a read on the status of the game by judging the player's moods. Hugh, Eddie, and C. J. seemed to be faring pretty well. Spike, Maria, Tara, and Stacy were all losing. So, each team had a winner, and each team had a loser. The question in Jack's mind was, *could his ten thousand dollars be enough to insure his team wasn't in last place?* It was impossible to tell.

"The time has come." Vince's voice came over the speakers in the room, cutting through the music. "Poker is now open. No limit, Texas Hold 'Em."

It was midnight. A dealer walked over to the table that had been vacant through the night, sat down with a deck of cards, and began shuffling. The seven contestants had been gambling for more than three hours, many of them continually downing alcoholic beverages in the process. "I'm tired of blackjack," Stacy stated, getting up from the table and heading toward the poker table.

"Stacy," Jack said, while placing his hand on her arm, "what are you doing?"

"I'm gonna go play poker," Stacy slurred slightly.

"Do you know how to play poker?"

"Sure, it's easy. I watch it on TV all the time."

"It's not that easy," Jack warned her, then dropped his voice to a whisper. "How much do you have left?"

Stacy reached inside the top of her gown, without the slightest hint of embarrassment, and pulled out her remaining thousand dollar chips—three of them.

Jack's eyes widened. "You only have three thousand left?"

"Don't worry," Stacy said, pushing away from him. "I know what I'm doing."

Stacy walked over and took a seat at the poker table. Eddie was already there, as were Hugh and C. J. That meant each team had a representative at the no-limit game. On the plus side, Jack would be better able to see where the competition was. On the down side, he was sure Stacy would lose her three thousand in a matter of minutes.

Tara continued at the blackjack table where Spike joined her. Maria picked up her chips and followed Jack over to the poker table.

Vince walked up beside the dealer. "As I said, this will be Texas Hold 'Em, no limit. Blinds will start at fifty and one hundred dollars. Table Stakes rules apply."

"Are you going to play?" Maria whispered to Jack.

"No," Jack answered. "Just want to keep my eye on it."

"You haven't played at all yet, have you?"

Jack smiled. "No, I've never been a gambler."

"Everybody has a game, Jack," Maria teased, quietly placing her arm through his as they stood behind the table. "Maybe you just haven't found yours yet."

"Well, tonight I'm just trying to survive through this and keep my ten thousand. How have you done so far?"

Maria frowned. "I'm down about a thousand. That's why I'm glad for this break."

"You don't want to get your money back at blackjack?"

"No," Maria sighed. "To be honest, I'm not much of a gambler either. Actually, I never gamble. Living in Las Vegas, that can be a dangerous pastime. I can't afford to lose any more."

"Teresa?" Jack asked.

Maria nodded. "Yeah, Teresa. Plus, my tuition money for next semester."

"Not worth risking, huh?" Jack smiled.

"You got that right."

The game got off to a quick start. Hugh won the first hand with a pair of queens. Stacy lost half of her money holding onto a pair of tens. To Jack, poker was different than any of the other games around a casino. In blackjack, you played against the house—and they always held the better odds. In poker, you were playing against other people. No one had an advantage, so your money wasn't being risked with unfair percentages going to the house. It was more of a competition than a gamble in Jack's mind. If there was any temptation to play that night, poker was it.

The dealer collected the cards and dealt again—two cards facedown to everyone at the table. He pointed to Stacy, who was in the position to post the small blind of fifty dollars. She slid the chip toward the center of the table. Beside her, Eddie placed the big blind—one hundred dollars. C. J. was next; she calmly threw in a one-hundred-dollar chip. Hugh threw his cards toward the dealer, folding.

As it went back to Stacy, she looked at her cards a second time, then threw in the other fifty to call. She only had thirteen hundred left.

The dealer collected the chips in a pile at the center of the table, then took the top card from the deck and burned it, setting it aside in a discard pile. He then took the next three cards and placed them face-up on the table, presenting "the flop"—a king of diamonds, a three of spades, and a seven of spades.

It was back to Stacy to make a bet.

"I check," Stacy stated.

"Two hundred," Eddie said, tossing in a couple of chips.

"I call," C. J. said.

Stacy reached in front of her and added two more chips to the pot. "I'm in."

Another card was burned, then the turn was placed face-up alongside the three already there. It was a nine of hearts.

Stacy reached for her chips. "Two hundred."

Eddie called, but C. J. raised another two hundred. Both Stacy and Eddie called after that.

The last card was dealt—"the river," a jack of spades. Stacy looked at her cards one last time, then, to Jack's astonishment, pushed all her chips toward the middle of the table. "I'm all in."

"The lovely lady bets nine hundred," the dealer called out.

Eddie studied her face, then shook his head and tossed his cards toward the dealer.

It was down to C. J. She looked down at her own cards before smiling, then pushed nine hundred dollars worth of chips out in front of her. "I call."

The dealer pulled her chips into the center pile and asked for the players' hands. Stacy tossed her cards proudly in front of her face-up—a king and a jack.

"Stacy has two pair—kings and jacks," Vince announced.

Stacy started to reach for the money before C. J. cleared her throat.

"Hold on there." C. J. flipped over her two cards—both nines. The last card had given C. J. three of a kind.

"C. J. wins," Vince called out beside the dealer as he pushed the money over to C. J.

"Oh, no!" Stacy moaned.

Jack sighed. C. J. had just bumped her and Spike up by over two thousand dollars, while his team was down to just ten thousand dollars—his ten thousand.

"Give me some chips," Stacy said, reaching her hand out to Jack.

"No way," Jack scowled. "I'm not going to let you lose my money as well."

"Come on." Stacy slipped into her sexy voice and let her hand rest on Jack's forearm as she stepped between him and Maria. "I can win it back."

"Absolutely not."

"Fine." Stacy stalked away from Jack and headed for the bar.

"Looks like there's a little spat going on with somebody's team," Eddie chided. "Why don't you have a seat, Forrest?"

"No thanks," Jack answered. "I'd just as soon watch."

"Suit yourself." Eddie grinned, then looked over at Vince. "Didn't you say something about everybody has to gamble?"

Vince smirked, glancing back at Jack. "Yes, I believe I said something to that effect."

"Well, Forrest," Eddie said, raising an eyebrow, "don't you think you'd better get in the game?"

"I figure I'm gambling just staying in the same room with you, Eddie."

Eddie's face flared. For a second, Jack wondered if he'd crossed the line. He wanted to keep Eddie just enough off-balance that he might make a mistake, but he didn't want to push him into something violent.

The poker game went on for another hour. Jack felt several waves of intense heat as the sunburn flared under his tuxedo. He'd fight it off with a trip to the bar and either a glass of water or another soft drink, but he was itching to get out of his clothes as quickly as possible.

Each time he went to the bar, he noticed Stacy sitting in front of a fresh drink, and each time she'd try something to convince him to let her get back into the game with his money. He politely declined, not having any doubts, as her speech slurred and her language grew more abusive.

Walking back to the poker table, Jack found it painful to move. He could feel his muscles rebelling from the intense abuse they'd received in the previous challenge, and it was getting late. He was ready to call it a night.

The chip count swayed back and forth with one player taking a slight lead over another, but then luck would change and another player would step out ahead. Jack kept focused on where the money count stood—at least on the poker table. He didn't know who had what in their pockets or hidden somewhere in their gowns. Tara spent a bit of time with a slot machine, while Spike stayed at the blackjack table.

Jack began imagining how he'd play certain hands, just for the fun of it. He hadn't sat in a poker game in well over five years—probably since his senior year of college. He'd enjoyed those games, more for the fun with his friends than winning or losing the money. Back then it was college money—a huge bet was a five-dollar bill. He shuddered to think what it would feel like to sit at the table with ten thousand dollars in front of him.

Vince stepped in and interrupted the session. "We're going to give the dealers a snack break for about thirty minutes. You all are welcome to grab yourselves something to eat, then we'll rejoin here for the last couple of hours of excitement before sunrise."

As the group was disbanding, Maria walked up next to Jack. "How about a walk?"

"I'd love that," Jack answered. Maria's smile revived him like a breath of fresh air.

Jack looked over Maria's shoulder, noticing Eddie had stepped up to Stacy at the bar, saying something to her that made her laugh. Jack wondered what that was about, as he and Maria turned to leave the casino.

He led Maria out to the cliff, since most of the other contestants seemed to be heading for the pool area. The moon was shining bright, sending rippling waves of silver over the ocean waters. Maria slipped out of her shoes and walked along the grass barefoot. They did their best to ignore the camera crew walking alongside them.

She slipped her hand into the crook of his arm as they strolled, snuggling closer. Jack responded immediately to her touch, his pulse racing as he flashed back to the kiss that afternoon. He struggled, knowing he needed to stay in control this time.

"It's beautiful out here," she commented.

"Yes, it is. I'd be enjoying it a lot more if it wasn't for this stupid thing called *The Ultimate Challenge.*"

"I think you're enjoying this, Jack Forrest," Maria said with a giggle, as she pulled him closer.

"Well, sure—this part. But inside, I feel so out of place."

"You kind of look it, too," Maria added.

"Hey."

"Just calling it like I see it. I've been in Las Vegas for a while, and I've never seen anybody who looked more like a fish out of water in a gambling hall than you do in there."

Jack shrugged, pausing at the edge of the cliff, close to where he had pushed Denny off earlier in the day.

"I'm just a teacher from the Midwest—never went in for those trips to Vegas or hit any of the Indian casinos around the area."

"It's more than that," Maria pressed.

Jack turned and held her gaze. Her eyes sparkled, as Jack could see the reflection of the moon shining back at him. She paused, giving him time to answer.

"Don't let the camera bother you," Maria whispered. "I don't know if we'll get another moment like this."

Jack sighed. "I'm not sure you'll understand, seeing the line of work you're in."

"Try me."

"OK, don't be offended, but I was brought up in kind of a conservative home—Christian to be more specific. Everything that you'd think Las Vegas has to offer would pretty much be out-of-bounds."

Maria chuckled.

"You're offended." Jack reached out and touched her arm.

"No." Maria shook her head. "On the contrary, you sound just like my mother."

Jack grinned. "She doesn't approve of your … occupation?"

"Not in the least. Catholic upbringing. Ah, who am I kidding? I'm still a practicing Catholic. It's just that, right now, I don't see another way to support Teresa and my mother until I can get my teaching credential."

"I see," Jack said warmly.

"So, maybe I understand more than you think." Maria reached out and placed her hand on his arm.

"Possibly, but it's more than just my upbringing. I really feel like God wouldn't want me to risk the money He's entrusted to me in games of chance in normal life. How it'll play out in this abnormal evening remains to be seen, though."

Maria looked at him with an inviting grin growing on her face. Jack didn't know what to make of it, but he liked it. All thoughts about protecting his heart vanished.

The moment lingered, each enjoying the gentle breeze, the wondrous moon reflecting off the quiet sea, and the silence.

Maria laid her head against his chest and took in a deep breath. She fit like a glove. Sighing as she let a breath out, she looked up at him. He was already looking down.

Jack took in the sweet smell, enjoying the anticipation to its fullest —until she pushed up on the tips of her toes to close the distance. They kissed. Jack's eyes closed, savoring every sensation that flooded him. He didn't want it to end.

As the kiss grew in passion, Jack opened his eyes—to find Maria's staring right at him. She burst out laughing, breaking the kiss.

"What?"

"I'm sorry," she giggled. "I've never had anyone open their eyes and look at me like that before."

Jack felt embarrassed at first, but then laughed along with her. "Are you in the habit of staring at the people you kiss?"

Maria grinned. Her shoulders came up, as she ducked her head a few inches. "Yes," she admitted. "I always do."

"Even this afternoon?"

"Yes … always. But I've never had anyone look back at me—until just now. It was kind of freaky."

"Yeah, it was."

"But nice." Maria snuggled back into his chest.

Jack held her a moment, wondering what it was about this woman that he couldn't keep his wits about him. He never planned on kissing her—not the first time, and definitely not this time. But, man! She was beautiful. And the more he got to know what was behind the beauty, the more he seemed to be unable to resist.

A woman's voice pierced the darkness. Jack looked up and caught some movement out of the corner of his eye, like a dark shadow running away from the cliff.

"Did you hear that?" Jack asked.

Maria pulled away. "Hear what?"

"A voice. A woman's voice."

"No," Maria said, shaking her head. "You sure it wasn't the wind?"

"I'm positive." Jack walked along the cliff toward where he'd seen the shadow. "It was definitely a woman. She sounded upset, but I couldn't make out the words. Then when I looked up, I saw someone or something running that way." Jack pointed back toward the main building.

"Careful, Jack. You're getting too close to the edge."

Jack stopped, looking out over the cliff to the dark ocean beyond. Maria pulled him back a few steps, wrapped her arm around his, and snuggled close.

"You didn't hear anything?" Jack asked.

"No. I'm sorry."

"I'm sure I heard it," Jack said, more to convince himself than Maria.

"Just because I didn't hear it doesn't mean you didn't."

Jack turned away from the cliff. "We'd better be getting back."

When they stepped back inside the casino, everything seemed to be ready. The dealers had taken their positions and the poker contestants were taking their seats. Maria and Jack ambled over to the bar to grab a small plate of snacks and a soft drink before joining in as spectators. Jack spotted Eddie rushing through the main doors leading to the pool side of the resort just as Vince stepped up to the poker table.

"Let the games begin," Vince instructed. "There are only a couple of hours left before dawn. Here's where we stand at this point. C. J. and Spike have a strong lead with a total of twenty-seven thousand dollars. Hugh and Tara are second with twenty-two thousand. Eddie and Maria have twenty-one thousand. Jack and Stacy are in last place with ten thousand dollars. Good luck to all of you."

Jack grunted while the bartender poured his drink. Things were not going well. Every other team had more than double his chip count. His only hope was that somebody would lose a bunch in the next few hours, or he would be heading home.

He looked over at the crowd around the poker table. The vacant chair left by Stacy, between Eddie and Hugh, made it obvious that Jack's team was out of the competition.

"Hey Forrest," Eddie called out. "Was your partner too scared to come back?"

Jack looked around the room. Stacy was nowhere to be seen.

"I doubt that," Jack shot back. "Maybe she found a toad out back and thought it would be more entertaining than sitting beside you."

Eddie seemed to want to stare a hole through him as the contestants around the table laughed. "Cute, now why don't you show us what a real man you are and take a seat in the game?"

Jack grinned. "Nice try, but I like the view just fine from here."

"All right, let's get this game started." Vince prompted the dealer, who began passing out cards.

Jack leaned closer to Maria. "Do you see Stacy anywhere?"

"No," she answered, glancing around the room.

"That's weird."

"Maybe not. She had quite a bit to drink."

He looked back at the poker table. It was too dark to get a good view of Eddie, but Jack remembered clearly what he'd looked like stepping through the doors a minute ago. His tuxedo had been somewhat tussled, he'd undone his tie and unbuttoned his shirt. But it was his shoes that Jack remembered vividly. They had lost their spit-polish shine. Jack had noticed spots of mud caked on the sides and scuffs on the tops.

It wouldn't have stood out to Jack, except for the fact that his shoes looked exactly the same. His suspicion mounted as he thought about the moving shadow and the voice he'd heard outside on the cliff.

"What are you thinking?" Maria broke his train of thought.

"Nothing," Jack muttered, then turned towards her. "You gonna gamble anymore?"

"I'm done—especially after our talk outside. I've already lost a thousand dollars tonight. That's money I need too much back home to risk any more."

"I'm with you." Jack picked up his drink. "Come on. Let's see how this plays out."

They walked toward the poker table.

"Going to join in, Jack?" Vince asked brightly.

Instead of answering, Jack pulled Vince aside. "Could I talk with you for a moment?"

"Sure." Vince nodded his head, and the two stepped away from the table, toward the empty roulette wheel.

"Where's Stacy?" Jack asked quietly.

"I'm not sure," Vince answered, looking around the room. "I didn't realize she hadn't returned."

"I haven't seen her since the break."

"Perhaps she was feeling under the weather after losing—there's no rule that says she has to stay in here. You're her only hope now anyway, and you're running out of time."

"Could somebody check on her?" Jack ignored Vince's prodding. "I'm growing concerned."

Vince eyed Jack cautiously. "Why?"

"I'm not sure. We were out on the edge of the cliff," Jack said, nodding toward Maria. "And I thought I heard voices—then I saw someone running away."

"I'm sure you're pretty tired, Jack. You know the eyes can play tricks on you at night …"

"Just have someone check her room, OK?"

"All right, I will." Vince nervously scanned the room. "Now, I suggest you break out those chips in your pocket before the sun comes up, or you'll be on the next helo off this rock."

The poker game continued without Jack. The betting turned extremely conservative, as each of the teams' strategy seemed to have shifted from taking out their opponents to just making sure their chip count stayed above Jack's. There was a lot of folding, and few flops. As time progressed, it became obvious to Jack he had to make a choice—and his stomach began to twist into knots.

Get in the game, or he'd be gone for sure.

Jack looked out the bay window toward the ocean. There seemed to be the barest hint of a glow coming from beyond the ocean. He was running out of time.

Vince stepped up beside him. "We've checked Stacy's room. She's not there."

Jack turned his head from the table and looked at Vince. "Then where is she?"

Vince shook his head. "We don't know."

"I can't believe this," Jack sighed. "Then why aren't you canceling this stupid poker game so all of us can look for her?"

Vince stared at him. "Not on your life."

"How can you guys continue? Something could have happened to her! It's not like other strange things haven't been going on around here."

Vince didn't respond, but looked out across the room.

"Aren't you going to tell the other players?" Jack asked.

"Not until the game's over. I don't want to distract them."

"You guys are sick. Don't you have cameras everywhere?"

"We're checking through the tapes now."

"Wasn't there a crew with Stacy?"

"There was supposed to be. But her crew took a break, thinking she was still in the casino."

"What about Eddie's crew?"

"Why do you ask that?" Vince stopped dead cold.

Jack paused, looking at the floor. He didn't know if he should open his mouth or not. "Look at his shoes."

Vince shrugged. "I can't see his shoes under the table. What about them?"

"Look at mine." Jack held his right foot out. "They look the same."

Vince stared at him blankly.

"I was out on the cliff at the break—maybe Eddie was as well."

"Oh, we're back to that hearing voices thing," Vince said, raising his eyebrows.

"What if I heard Stacy, and then saw Eddie running away," Jack whispered. "He came in through the main door late, and I don't recall there being any mud out by the pool."

"You have quite an imagination—and, evidently, a growing paranoia."

"And you have one missing contestant," Jack said, as his eyes narrowed. "I would think you'd be doing everything possible to locate her."

"We are." Vince shrugged.

"You guys sure have your priorities screwed up, you know that?"

"That may be true, but right now if you don't get yours straight, you're headed home." Vince moved so that he was right in front of Jack, making sure he had his full attention. "To where the school board just voted last night to terminate your job. You've been fired, Jack."

Jack couldn't hide his shock as his eyes widened. He felt his face flush. How could Vince know this?

Vince's voice whispered urgently, "This is all you've got. You better get in the game."

Jack watched Vince walk away after dropping his bombshell. The comment definitely took his mind off of Stacy for the moment. He looked over at the poker table. Was Vince telling the truth? Or was this another of *The Ultimate Challenge's* ploys of putting the pressure on—getting Jack in the game no matter what? Jack had no way of knowing. It was his choice anyway. Play the ten thousand he would so desperately need if Vince were indeed being honest with him, or play it safe and risk being kicked out of the game here and now. The chip count hadn't changed on the table much at all. The closest team to his ten thousand was still Eddie and Maria. His best chance was to win enough to pass them—kicking Eddie out, but also eliminating Maria.

Jack pushed himself away from the bar and headed toward the table. Without saying a word, he pulled out the chair Stacy had used, next to Eddie, and took a seat. He set his ten chips on the table.

"Well, things have suddenly gotten a bit more interesting," Eddie chuckled. "Finally joining us, hey Forrest?"

Jack sat stone-faced, still struggling with his decision. The dealer took Jack's chips and exchanged half of them for a stack of black hundred-dollar chips.

"New player in the game," Vince announced. "The blinds will now be at a hundred and two hundred dollars."

The players around the table murmured. The stakes had just doubled. Not uncommon for tournament play—as the game progressed, the amount to play the game would increase to insure players would get knocked out. Jack looked at his pile of chips and compared it to the rest of the table. Hugh sat in front of the most, followed by C. J., and then Eddie—just as he imagined. He also knew Eddie had Maria's nine thousand to add to his total at the end of the night. But what he didn't know was how much Spike had to add to C. J.'s, or how much Tara could add to Hugh's total.

"All right, let's play some poker," Hugh declared.

Jack looked up at his new friend. Hugh quickly and subtly winked right at him. Jack responded with the slightest of head tilts. Was that

Hugh's way of wishing him luck? Or, was it Hugh's way of signaling their partnership was still on?

The first hand was dealt. Jack looked at his cards: a two and a six. He folded without it costing him anything. The second hand came, and Jack was now in the position of the big blind. He was forced to ante two hundred dollars into the pot. He was dealt a ten of spades and a three of clubs. Not great. Hugh folded, C. J. folded. Eddie, who was the small blind, put in another hundred to stay in for the flop. Jack now had the option to raise his bet, or check and do nothing. He checked.

The flop was placed on the table: a queen of hearts, a nine of spades, and a ten of diamonds. Jack had a pair. It was Eddie's move.

"I'll bet a hundred," Eddie said.

Jack didn't say anything, he just threw in a hundred-dollar chip to call.

The dealer laid out the next card, a two of clubs.

"I'll check," Eddie said.

"Check."

The final card came down, an ace of spades. All Jack had was a pair of tens. Eddie looked up at Jack, one eyebrow raised slightly.

"Two hundred." Eddie threw in the chips.

Jack looked at his cards again, weighing his choices. He hated to back down against Eddie. But the way Eddie had thrown in the money when the ace had shown up, Jack felt like he probably had another ace in his hand that would surely beat his tens.

Jack threw his cards to the dealer, folding.

"All right," Eddie said with a laugh as he reached for the chips. Jack had just lost three hundred dollars, and they had all gone to Eddie. He sighed, inwardly chuckling, despite the pressure he felt. His mother would have a cow if she could see him now.

Posting the small blind on the next hand, Jack was dealt two low cards. He folded, even though it cost him a hundred. The next two hands, Jack didn't have anything, and he folded as well.

Once again, he was in the position to have to put in the two hundred big blind. The kind of cards he was being dealt made Jack wonder if he was crazy to stay at the table. At this rate, he'd just dwindle away his savings and still get kicked out of the game. Jack looked outside. The glow from beyond the horizon was growing brighter. Time was ticking.

Jack eyed his cards: a seven of diamonds and a seven of spades—a pocket pair, as it was called. Nothing to write home about, but something he might at least be able to play. This time, Hugh and C. J. matched the two hundred dollars, and Eddie kicked in his hundred. All four players were in for the flop.

The dealer placed the middle cards on the table: an ace, a nine, and a jack—all of diamonds.

It didn't add to Jack's pair, but with his seven of diamonds, Jack had four diamonds. If either of the remaining cards were a diamond, he'd have a flush and a great hand. On the flip side, however, if any of his opponents had two diamonds in their hand, they already had the flush.

Jack watched the other players intently as the dealer moved around the table. Eddie was first. He played with his chips awhile, then threw out five one-hundred-dollar chips. Jack tried not to react—not breathe in deep, not sigh, or rub his chin. He didn't want to do anything to signal his worry that his hand was not the greatest.

Five hundred dollars. It pained him to have to risk it like this. There were too many possibilities in front of him. Jack wondered if Eddie had pocket aces or two other diamonds, or even if he had a hidden jack, all of which would beat Jack.

Finally, Jack shook his head and threw his cards in. This pot would get too rich for him in no time. Another two hundred dollars lost. Jack was down to nine thousand four hundred. He readjusted in his chair and pulled off his jacket. It seemed unbelievably hot in the room all of a sudden. His sunburn was throbbing.

Both Hugh and C. J. matched Eddie's five hundred, and the turn card was placed on the table: a jack of clubs. Jack forced himself not to react. He would have had two pairs: jacks and sevens. Eddie bet another five hundred, but Hugh raised it to a thousand. C. J. paused for a couple of seconds but stayed in the hand. After studying both Hugh and C. J. for a minute, Eddie called as well.

The river card came down: a five of diamonds.

39

Jack would have had the flush!

He scratched behind his head before he could stop himself. He could have won this hand, and the chips were adding up to a sizeable pot. Eddie bet a thousand dollars. Hugh didn't refer back to his cards at all, but looked across the table to Eddie.

"How much do you have Eddie?" Hugh asked him.

Eddie gasped. "What?"

The dealer quickly counted Eddie's chips. "Ten thousand three hundred."

Hugh nodded, counting out his chips. "I bet ten thousand three hundred."

Eddie's eyes looked like he'd seen a ghost. He would have to go all in to stay in the hand. That meant giving up the seventeen hundred dollars he'd already bet, or risk being eliminated from *The Ultimate Challenge.*

C. J. shook her head, then tossed her cards toward the dealer. "Too expensive for me."

Jack glanced at Hugh—did he really have the flush? Jack knew Maria had about nine thousand dollars. If Eddie went all in and lost, he'd suddenly be in third place, not last.

Hugh didn't look around at anybody, but kept his eyes glued on Eddie, daring him to call.

Eddie glanced around the room, his eyes nervously darting from player to player before he'd stare at Hugh. Maria stood behind Eddie, taking interest in the game for the first time in a while. She still looked radiant, even when her face looked worried, as she did now. Jack wondered what she was thinking, but couldn't read her. Was she rooting for Eddie so she'd still be in the ultimate game, or hating him so much that she wanted him to lose, regardless of the consequences for her?

Eddie finally pushed his chips forward, sweat breaking out on his bald head. "I'm all in."

The gang around the table clapped and hollered, cheering him on.

"All right, let's see your hands please," the dealer called out calmly. Easy for him, his fate wasn't hanging in the balance.

Hugh angled his head, nodding toward Eddie. Jack wondered if he'd been bluffing.

Eddie flipped his two cards over, showing a ten of hearts and a king of diamonds. Eddie had the flush. And with the king of diamonds, it also meant that had Jack stayed in, Eddie would have beaten his flush. Jack's shoulders sagged. What he thought would have been the winning hand was actually a loser. He was thankful he'd folded.

Now he worried about Hugh. He had wagered nearly two-thirds of his own chips. His fate now appeared to be sealed, as Eddie chuckled over his victory.

"Great hand, Eddie." Hugh nodded toward his opponent. Then his mouth widened to a huge grin, as he flipped his pair of aces face up on the table. "But it doesn't beat a full house—aces over jacks."

The table erupted. The noise in the room was deafening. All the other contestants cheered Hugh on, while Eddie cursed up a blue streak. Jack sat amazed. He hadn't seen it coming at all. He would have been just as blindsided as Eddie had been.

Hugh glanced over at Jack and smiled. They'd taken out Eddie, at least for now. It felt great—but then it hit him. Maria would be out as well.

After his tirade of every conceivable four-letter word Jack had ever heard, Eddie turned around and faced Maria.

"Give me your chips."

Maria angled her head and took a step back. "You've got to be kidding me."

"I've got to win that money back," Eddie insisted. "Come on, cough 'em up."

"No way." Maria shook her head violently. "This is all we've got left—and it's my money."

"I don't care. We're in last place after that . . ." Eddie couldn't come up with a word to describe what just happened to him. "I've got to win it back or we're dead."

The whole room watched the ongoing dialogue with fascination. Eddie overshadowed Maria by over a foot—his immense bulk making her look tiny and fragile. But she stood up to him, staring him right in the face, unwilling to back down. Jack could see her determination, knowing that she would not give in, if for no other reason than it was Teresa's money Eddie was demanding.

"You think I'm going to give you my money after that unbelievable display of stupidity? You're crazy!" Maria yelled.

Eddie spat out some of the most awful, demeaning language Jack had ever heard in a desperate attempt to intimidate her.

"Give it up," Maria insisted. "I'm not budging."

Then she pushed Eddie away, stepping past him and taking his chair at the poker table. "But I'm not ready to lose because of you, either."

Maria laid her chips on the table. "Let's deal."

Eddie stood behind Maria wide-eyed and fuming. Suddenly he was totally out of power and nearly out of the competition. Jack could literally see the color drain from his face as the shock settled in.

"You're going to pay for this ..." Eddie threatened, calling her a few more choice names before he stormed off toward the bar. Only Maria's luck, or skill, at the poker table could keep him in the game.

While the dealer was changing out Maria's chips, Jack looked at her in admiration. She was tough and wouldn't be bullied, even by the likes of Eddie. The gold card Jack had been handed suddenly flashed through his mind—his personal challenge, *to sleep with Maria.* Jack still didn't have an answer for that one yet, and boy did she look good sitting next to him in that black gown. He forced himself to think of something else to clear the mental image. There were other things to worry about now.

Jack had a slight lead on Maria by four hundred dollars, maybe five. That could easily change with one hand. Jack couldn't just get up from the game and wait for the sun to peak over the horizon. It looked like it was down to him and Maria for last place. If he didn't stay ahead of her, Jack could still be heading home.

The dealer handed Maria her chips and dealt the next hand. Vince stepped beside him and spoke to the table of players. "You guys probably have about a half-hour left. It's five-thirty now—we'll call the game at six."

Jack looked out toward the ocean. The clouds could now be seen, sporting a deep purple over the dark ocean. He thought Vince was about right—a half-hour and the sun would be cresting the sea. Jack couldn't believe the night had passed already. He suddenly felt exhausted. As he scanned the room, everyone else seemed energized with the excitement of the moment. But then again, he was the only contestant who knew Stacy was missing. He hadn't given her much thought since sitting down at the game. He looked over at Vince, who just shrugged. He took that to mean she hadn't reappeared.

The first few hands were uneventful. Maria asked a few questions as she got her bearings for the game, but didn't make any major mistakes, mostly folding before the flop. She was down a few hundred dollars in no time, increasing Jack's lead. He bet conservative, only staying for the flop when he was forced to have his money in the pot. He won a couple of times when everybody else folded and lost once to three of a kind over his queens and nines.

They were down to their last ten minutes. From what Jack could see, Hugh had taken an even greater lead, pulling some of C. J.'s chips as he and Maria consistently folded.

Jack looked at the next pair of cards he'd been dealt: an ace of hearts and a ten of hearts. *Not too bad*, he thought. It helped that they were from the same suit in case some other hearts dropped on the flop. Jack was the big blind this time, so he was already in for the two hundred. C. J. and Hugh called, and Maria added another hundred from her stack to stay in.

The flop came: a jack of spades, a queen of diamonds, and a three of hearts. Jack just needed a king to fill out his straight. But was it worth pouring money into this hand to see if one came?

Maria was first to bet. She played with her chips nervously, then finally placed two chips out in front of her. "Two hundred."

"I call," Jack said, thinking he'd go one more card. Even if he lost and Maria won, he still had her by a thousand or so.

"I'm in," C. J. followed.

"Me too," Hugh said.

The turn card was next: a king of clubs. Jack had caught his straight. He concentrated on staying absolutely stone-faced, trying not to let his body language give any hint that he liked his cards.

"I check," Maria decided.

"Five hundred," Jack said, pushing in the chips.

"I raise." C. J. reacted quickly, which made Jack run through all the possibilities that her hand could hold. "To one thousand."

"I'll call," Hugh decided.

"I'm out." Maria flipped her cards in.

Jack eyed C. J., trying to read her. She was a bit fidgety, but that's how she had been all night. She liked the king that had come down—but so had he. Maybe she had a straight as well, in which case they would split the pot and neither would be hurt by it. But what did Hugh have?

"OK," Jack smiled. "I'll call." Jack added his five hundred more.

The final card came out: a king of diamonds. Jack had to bid first.

"I check," Jack muttered, thinking they probably had the same hand.

"Not me." C. J. reached for the chips in front of her. "How much you got there, Jack?"

She surprised everyone. This close to the end, she still held a strong second place. She was willing to jeopardize that with whatever cards she held in front of her.

The dealer quickly tallied up Jack's total.

"Seven thousand, two hundred," he announced.

"Then that's my raise." C. J. counted out what was definitely most of her chips and tossed them in.

Jack would have to go all in to stay in the game. If he lost, it was all over. Last place would be his, and he'd be on his way home. If he won though, there was a good chance he'd put C. J. into last place and save Maria's position—albeit also Eddie's.

Jack studied the cards. C. J. had bet it all after the second king had appeared. There was a good chance she could have another king hidden and beat his straight with a full house.

Hugh had to act first. After studying C. J. for a moment, he counted out his chips and tossed them to the center of the table. "I'm in."

Jack struggled. He felt like he had the winning hand, but he didn't know how to play it. All eyes were on him, but he didn't care. This was it: gamble on his straight, or fold and see who had the better hand between C. J. and Hugh.

The pot was worth over eighteen thousand dollars. His total could be over twenty-five thousand if he called her bet and won—a mighty big "if", for sure.

The words from Vince rattled through his brain: *This is all you've got ... get in the game.* Jack felt the pressure to do something, to put up or shut up. But Vince's words struck a chord deep within him—it was a lie. This wasn't all he had. Whether or not Vince had been telling the truth about Jack losing his teaching job, he had so much more, including a trust in God that seemed to have evaporated with the island humidity when he arrived.

"What's it going to be Jack?" C. J. chided.

"Don't rush me," Jack answered, struggling within.

Trust God. He knew that's what he needed to do, but how? What did that mean right here, right now? Should he fold, not risking his savings to a game of chance? Or trust God in a totally bizarre way—one that he would never have contemplated before this very moment—by calling C. J.'s bet, and believing that God would supply when he returned home, even if he lost the ten thousand.

He thought he had a sure winner, but then he was reminded about what happened in the last hour when Eddie was knocked out. Jack could have drawn the flush if he'd stayed in, but he would have still lost to both Eddie's higher flush and Hugh's full house. He'd been glad he backed out of the hand when all had unfolded. And that's what settled it.

He couldn't do it. Jack pushed his cards toward the dealer. "I'm out."

"He just folded an ace high straight?" the director yelled in the control room. "What is he, an idiot?"

All the action was being captured from the poker game. They had cameras on each of the contestants, a couple of overhead cameras keeping track of the flopped cards and the chip count. They even had tiny hidden cameras at each station where a player sat, so they could see what the player had when they looked at their cards, just like the celebrity poker shows.

"Your favorite contestant is definitely not a gambler," Travis said behind the front row, watching the whole event unfold with Zeke sitting right beside him.

Zeke grunted. This wasn't going the way he'd envisioned it at all. Jack was starting to wimp out on him—something he hadn't planned on. It was beginning to both disappoint and infuriate him.

Pushing away an ace high straight nearly made Jack physically ill. But he just couldn't bring himself to risk his savings. Even without winning the pot, Jack realized there was enough money about to change hands that it might affect the outcome of the challenge. He was thankful no one at the table knew the hand he'd just folded.

Maria kept her eyes glued to Jack. When he looked up, she gave him a reassuring nod with a twinge of a smile. Jack shrugged and shook his head. He felt a bit like a coward.

"Let's see the remaining hands," the dealer instructed.

Hugh flopped over his cards: a ten, nine—he held a straight to the king. Jack's ace high straight would have beaten him. Jack physically felt his stomach lurch. He almost sprang from his chair and ran to the nearest bathroom, but he had to see C. J.'s cards. He forced the impulse back down, staring at C. J. as she shook her head and turned her cards over.

C. J. had a third king in the hole with an eight—no other pair to give her the full house. Hugh had won another huge pot, one that would have been Jack's if he'd stayed in. He felt sick and now a bit light-headed. He'd been up all night operating at near exhaustion and hadn't eaten anything substantial since seven the night before. No wonder he was losing it. The game was nearly over; he just had to hold on another few minutes.

C. J. lowered her head, shaking it slightly at what she'd done. Her chip count was now dangerously low. Looking at the stack, Jack guessed she was down to a couple of thousand at the most. He just didn't know how much Spike had on him. Would it be enough to beat Jack or Maria?

Jack did some mental calculations: the last pot had still cost him fourteen hundred dollars before he backed out. He knew he had seven thousand four hundred left. He was sure he'd dropped below Maria. His only hope was that Spike held less than five thousand dollars to keep their team in last place. If he had just gone all in, his position would have been secure. He'd blown it.

"This will be the final hand," Vince warned the players.

"Hold on," C. J. said. "Spike, over here."

C. J. got up from the table and pulled Spike off to the side where they whispered intensely for a couple of seconds. Jack could see Spike shake his head a couple of times as the conversation flowed back and forth. Finally, Spike reached into his jacket pocket and handed something over to C. J.

She came back to the table with a determined look on her face, as she took her seat and added nearly five thousand dollars worth of chips to the pile in front of her. Jack couldn't be sure, but it seemed he might have them edged out by five hundred dollars or so. Still, it was close.

"I needed a bit more leverage to continue this game," C. J. said with a smile.

Jack thought for a minute that he was OK. He just had to fold quickly, not risking any money, and he'd hang on to third place. But that wouldn't work if C. J. actually won the hand. He'd have to play this carefully.

The cards were shuffled and dealt for the last time. Jack sat in the position of small blind, so he was forced to put in one hundred dollars. He could see what the rest of the table was going to do before it would cost him the other hundred. He looked carefully at his cards: a queen of spades and a two of hearts.

A great hand to fold.

Hugh posted the two hundred dollars and C. J. called. Maria looked around the table, studied her chip count, then threw in her cards, evidently comfortable that her second-place standing would hold up. "I'm out."

There was five hundred dollars in the pot already. If Jack folded now and Hugh folded, C. J. might have enough to beat him. He decided one hundred more was worth getting to see the flop.

"I call." Jack threw in the chip.

"All right, we have three players," Vince narrated beside the dealer. The flop came: a seven of diamonds, a ten of clubs, and a four of hearts.

Jack had nothing. But the cards didn't lend themselves to anybody else having a great hand either, as far as Jack could tell.

"I check," Jack said.

"I check." Hugh followed suit.

C. J. looked at both of them, her eyes narrowing and darting back and forth between the two. "Two hundred." She pushed her chips forward.

Jack held only a queen high—not the hand he'd want to go into a do-or-die showdown against Hugh and C. J., but he couldn't let C. J. take the pot over a two hundred dollar bet and push him into last place. He called.

Hugh shocked Jack by tossing his cards toward the dealer. With the pile of chips sitting in front of him, two hundred dollars was nothing. But he folded.

It was down to Jack and C. J. for last place. This hand would seal it.

"We're down to two," Vince announced, stating the obvious. The dealer burned the top card, then placed the river card face-up on the table.

Five of hearts.

This was stacking up to be the worst hand he'd had all night. He would have folded were it not the last one. It was Jack's bet again. He looked up at C. J., hoping he put a determined look on his face—like he held something interesting. "I check."

C. J. glanced one last time at her two down cards, her brow furrowed ever so slightly as she looked back up at Jack. The room was dead silent.

"I'm all in," C. J. said, pushing in all of her chips.

41

The table suddenly came alive. Spike shouted, patting his partner on the back, cheering her on even though she'd just risked all of his money while the rest of the table murmured and stared right at Jack. What was he going to do?

That's exactly what Jack was wondering. He looked at the cards on the table: a seven, a ten, a four, and a five—two of them hearts. She didn't have a flush yet—she'd need a draw on the river to complete that kind of hand. The four, five, and seven could work into a straight if she held a six and then had either an eight or a three to go with it.

And Jack had a queen high. She could have paired up any of the cards staring up at Jack and still beat him. But what choice did he have? If he folded right here, she walked away with enough money to put him in last place. The best possible hand Jack could hope for would be for the last card dealt to be a queen, giving him a lonely pair. Maybe he should just walk away and, at least, have his seven thousand dollars to keep him afloat until he could land another job.

He'd protected most of his money all night long. Now it came down to one hand where he had to risk it all if he wanted to stay in the game and have a chance at the ten million dollars. Jack looked over at C. J., who was now sitting as quietly as she had all night. She wasn't fidgeting; she seemed to be forcing herself not to move. Jack felt in his gut she was bluffing. She had to stay in the hand just like him, do whatever it took to win the last pot, or she'd be out of the game also.

Jack breathed in deep and slowly let the breath out. Suddenly, his tie felt like it was choking him. He reached up and pulled it loose, unbuttoning the shirt below it and rubbing at his neck. He knew what he had to do.

"I call." He prayed he wasn't making a huge mistake, then pushed his chips toward the center of the table.

C. J.'s statue-like image broke as she stared straight at Jack, the look of shock clearly etched on her face. Whether she had the cards to beat him or not, she did not expect Jack to make that move.

The room cheered, loving the drama of the final hand. Maria came up behind Jack, placing her hands on his shoulders, and wishing him luck. He couldn't decide if the heat coming off her hands was due to his sunburned shoulders or the excitement of her touch. At this point, he didn't care.

The dealer reached over and counted out the chips Jack needed to call her bet. When he was finished, two hundred dollars was all that was left in front of Jack.

"All right." Vince brought the room back down to a hush. "Let's see your cards."

Jack flipped over his queen and two, embarrassed by the gasps from his fellow players. They knew he was in trouble.

"Jack has queen high," Vince announced.

Then C. J. flipped her cards over: she held a jack and a nine, both of hearts.

"C. J. has jack high," Vince added, "but could draw to an inside straight with an eight, or draw a flush if the last card is a heart."

Jack realized C. J. had been gambling on drawing to the straight until the four and five of hearts were dealt, giving her the added possibility of a flush. There were so many cards that could make her hand better than his—any heart, an eight, or even pairing up her jack or nine.

"Let's see the river." Vince hammed it up, building the drama for the television audience. From Jack's point of view, there was no need to add to the drama.

The dealer burned the top card, then slowly placed the final card on the table: a six of spades.

"Yes!" Jack shouted, clenching his fist. He didn't know how badly he wanted to win until the exact moment he had.

Spike turned from the table and cussed at the top of his lungs as the room ignited in mayhem. Jack was hugged, slapped on the back—which was very painful—and congratulated in every way possible. C. J. sat across the table dumbfounded, staring at the six of spades, as if by the force of her will she could make it morph into a six of hearts.

"I'm sorry, C. J." Jack offered.

"You played it great," C. J. returned. "How did you know?"

"I didn't," Jack said, as the room quieted down to hear the exchange. "There was already enough money in the pot for you to win if I folded. I had no choice."

C. J. nodded, then pushed herself away from the table and headed to the bar.

Maria leaned in and kissed his cheek, whispering, "You did it! Congratulations."

"Thanks." Jack blushed. "I guess we're both still in the game."

"Me too, sucker," Eddie said, as he walked up beside Jack. "Your fancy playing just kept the one man in this game who's going to kick your butt out of it."

"Bring it on," Jack said with a grin. Even Eddie's threats couldn't spoil his moment of victory.

Eddie sneered at Jack, then looked right at Maria standing on the other side of him. "And don't think you're off the hook. I got plans for you, sister."

Maria snuggled in closer to Jack. "Just stay away from me, Eddie. I've had just about all I can take of you."

Eddie held his eyes on her a moment longer before coldly saying, "You two just better watch yourselves. This thing is far from over."

"This is such great television," Travis shouted from within the control room. "How did he pull that off?"

"With a gutsy play." Zeke nodded, a smile creasing his lips.

"I didn't think Jack had it in him, the way he avoided the table all night long. Vince dangled the job thing in front of him perfectly."

Zeke chuckled. "Must have been just the kick he needed."

"Well, you've got yourself one heck of a show going," Travis added. "It was genius making the contestants gamble with their own money. I thought for sure we were going to lose either Eddie or Jack—and here we still have them both. I'll miss Spike and C. J., though."

Zeke tuned Travis's rambling out as he kept watch on the celebration going on around Jack. The kid had really surprised him this time. He was sure Jack was going to get kicked out of the game, holding on to his precious money as if it were his lifeline. But he'd come through in the end—which was a good thing, since, in this particular challenge, Zeke had no way to save Jack if he'd had the lowest money count. It had been Zeke's gamble, but it had paid off big-time, with Jack, Eddie, and Maria all staying alive in the competition.

"... don't you think, Zeke?" Travis asked.

Zeke turned to his friend with a grin, ignoring the question. "I think it's time to get Amanda down here."

Travis looked at Zeke; his exuberance instantly replaced with concern. "You're sure about this?"

Zeke's brow creased. "Yes, I'm sure. Would you quit pestering me about it, for God's sake?"

"Sorry." Travis backed off. "I just don't think it's a good idea."

"I'm well aware of that, Travis. You've made that abundantly clear. Now just do as I say, will ya? I'm going to take a little nap."

Travis turned, making his way toward the door. "OK, but don't say I didn't warn you."

When the room had quieted down, Vince announced that, indeed, C. J. and Spike had been eliminated from the competition. They received a robust round of applause from the remaining contestants.

"There's one more thing before we send you off for a well-deserved rest," Vince continued. "We have been unable to locate Stacy since the break a few hours ago. If anyone has any idea where she might be, you need to let us know."

The energy in the room was sucked away in an instant. Everybody took on a great look of concern, especially the women. Jack's eyes darted to Eddie—his eyes widened and his mouth opened as if in shock, but Jack felt like it was faked. Eddie's eyes stayed sharp, calculating. Jack was pretty sure he had something to do with her disappearance.

But why?

She had already been knocked out of the poker game and had no money to help Jack. At that moment, it looked as if she was going to be eliminated from the game—she wasn't a threat to him.

Vince changed the subject, turning on the charm. "I know it's late, and we've all had a long night. We're giving you all a break. There's a buffet breakfast set up around the pool for you, and then, please, get some sleep. We'll call you back later this evening."

With that, Vince turned and walked out of the room before anybody could ask questions. Jack was livid. They weren't taking Stacy's situation seriously, and he was afraid more people were going to be placed in danger—possibly Maria, or even himself.

As the people around him left the room, Jack took a moment to stare out the bay window. Magnificent oranges and reds splashed across the hundreds of puffy clouds scattered along the horizon. The view seemed to pull him away to another place. God's handiwork never ceased to amaze him. Sunrises were always special; but this one, in the face of the stress at hand, was especially wondrous.

When it was all said and done, Jack wound up with fourteen thousand, one hundred dollars. More importantly, he was still in the game. The gamble had paid off, but Jack was sure he'd never do it again. The anxiety of placing his hard-earned money at risk on the turn of a card exhausted him. If he did it with any kind of consistency, he was sure he'd wind up with ulcers. The adrenalin rush could be addicting, the allure of the big payoff tempting, but to Jack it just wasn't worth it. He had believed gambling was wrong all his life, but never really knew why. Now, he understood.

Hugh was the big winner, walking away with more than thirty thousand dollars. Not a bad night for a kid still in law school. With C. J. and Spike out of the game, Jack was down to one of six people who would win the ten million dollar prize. He still had a shot, and the odds kept getting better and better.

Jack turned his chips in to a production assistant, who ripped up the second loan on his condominium. He was told the original money would be placed back into his bank accounts and his winnings would be added to his savings. Watching the loan papers being destroyed was a relief. Jack just wanted to make it to his bungalow and get some sleep.

"How about something to eat?" Maria asked, as she stepped up beside him.

"I'm beat," Jack answered. "I just want to get some shut-eye."

"OK." Maria took his arm. "I'll walk with you."

They started for the door that would lead them around the pool and toward their bungalows, but were stopped by Vince.

"What is it?" Jack asked.

"Come with me," Vince stated flatly. "Both of you."

He turned, walking back through the makeshift casino and toward the door leading to the cliff top. Jack and Maria followed.

"We're being observed," Maria commented.

"Like we haven't been since we got here?" Jack motioned to the camera crew walking in front of them.

"No, I mean the other contestants."

"Oh, that," Jack said.

"I wonder what they're thinking ..." Maria paused.

Jack shrugged his shoulders. "Does it really matter? They'll think what they want no matter what we do, and no matter what the truth might be."

"You've got a point."

Vince led them out the door that faced the rising sun and to the area they'd walked in the moonlight hours before. The camera crew followed right along with them.

Vince suddenly stopped, looking back at Jack. "Show me where you were when you thought you saw something last night."

Jack silently walked toward the spot where they had kissed. Maria held onto her dress as she walked with him—the morning was starting with a strong wind gusting up from the sea. The sun was over the horizon now, as beams of light filtered through the clouds. Jack kept his pace until he was close to the edge.

"It was right about here, right?" Jack asked Maria.

Maria looked at the surroundings. "I think so."

Jack looked over the edge of the cliff. Nothing—just the surf crashing against the rocks below.

Vince watched him carefully. "Where do you think the sounds came from?"

Jack pulled Maria into his arms and positioned them as they had been earlier that morning. She looked up in surprise, as if he was going to reprise their romantic encounter. But he didn't look down at her. Instead, his eyes darted back and forth over her head.

"I thought I saw something move over there." Jack pointed about fifty feet away from them, closer to the edge. Without another word, he walked along the edge of the cliff. Vince followed.

"Why are you suddenly interested?" Jack asked.

"There's still been no sign of her," Vince returned. "We're starting to get worried."

Jack looked intently around, searching for footprints, or any sign of recent activity. Something caught his eye in the shadows just along the edge of the cliff. Stepping over to the spot, Jack leaned down and picked up a piece of fabric and held it into the light.

It was silver.

"What've you got?" Vince asked.

Jack didn't answer, but instead leaned out over the ledge and looked below.

"Oh, no!" Jack gasped, but his words were lost in the wind.

Both Vince and Maria stepped up beside him and looked over the ledge, following the path of Jack's eyes.

About twenty feet below, Stacy's body was sprawled out on a small ledge, inches away from plunging all the way down into the sea below. She lay face-down on the jagged rocks, the silver gown reflecting the sunlight brightly around her. Her head was at such an odd angle—her neck had to be broken.

"Oh my God, it's Stacy!" Maria cried.

"Quick," Jack turned and yelled to the camera crew, "go get some help!" Instead, they ran up beside him and pointed the camera to the ledge below.

"Her neck appears to have been broken from the fall," Vince explained to the group of contestants gathered back by the main building. "At this point, we think she had a bit too much to drink, and evidently, didn't see the edge of the cliff. If she hadn't landed on that ledge, we'd have probably never found her."

Jack shook his head. Even if his theory was true, what was she doing on the cliff in the first place? Did Eddie coerce her out there?

It had taken nearly two hours for the staff to get the climb experts out from their rooms, rig up their gear, and begin the difficult job of retrieving Stacy's body. There wasn't a sound from the contestants as they brought the lifeless form up from the ledge. *What a waste,* Jack thought. He glanced over at Eddie's reaction to the news. He looked as shocked as everyone else—but once again, Jack felt like he was acting. Whether it was true or just Jack's active suspicions, he couldn't be sure.

"I know this is a shock to all of you," Vince continued. "It certainly is to myself and the producers of *The Ultimate Challenge.* We want you to go back to your rooms and get some sleep. We'll reconvene later this evening, as we said before."

"You're seriously going to keep this thing going?" Maria asked. "It seems like with all that's happened, you'd be worried about somebody else getting hurt."

"We're certain this was an accident, Maria," Vince replied.

"How can you be sure?" Jack jumped in. "Were all the contestants accounted for at the time when she allegedly slipped? I know I was with Maria—does everybody else have an alibi?"

Hugh and Tara looked at Jack with shocked expressions, but Jack ignored them and kept his eyes glued on Eddie, who looked mad.

Vince turned to Jack, his expression dark. "This isn't a murder investigation. It's a simple accident. Stacy got too close to the edge and slipped. Let's not make this any more than it is."

"Right," Jack fired back. "It's not like we've had anybody nearly die in a fire, or nearly drown after a flare-gun misfired. Everything around here is running just like clockwork."

"What are you saying, Forrest?" Eddie jumped in. "That one of us killed her?"

"I don't know Eddie." Jack snapped his head toward him. "Where were you during the break?"

"You better watch what you're saying, man!" Eddie's anger flared along with his nostrils. "I went to my room and chilled."

"Then explain the mud on your shoes—where did that come from?" Jack pressed.

"You're crazy, man!" Eddie shouted right in Jack's face. The veins on his neck pushed out, his fists were clenched. He looked like he could snap any second and start pummeling Jack.

Jack stared right back at him, refusing to back down.

"All right." Vince finally stepped in. "Let's calm down here."

"You're not going to get away with accusing me of murder," Eddie snarled at Jack. Then he turned and walked away.

"Where did you find that guy?" Jack asked Vince once Eddie was gone.

Jack headed back to his bungalow with Maria beside him. All he wanted was to get some sleep.

He stopped by Maria's room, waiting for her to walk the short path to her door.

"Why don't you come in for a second?" Maria asked.

Jack angled his head.

"It's not what you're thinking," Maria grinned. Her smile was striking, almost making Jack forget how tired he was. "I'm really upset about Stacy."

Jack paused on the pathway, not sure how he should respond.

She stared at him, a serious tone coming over her face. "I'm also a bit worried about Eddie and would love the company. He really scares me."

"Yeah, I'm not that thrilled being around him myself."

They walked down the path and into her bungalow. She went directly to her refrigerator and pulled out a couple of bottles of Evian.

"How about a cold water?"

"That'd be great," Jack said, as he began a quick search through the one-bedroom unit—checking the bathrooms, closets, and even under the bed to make sure Eddie hadn't planned some surprise for Maria.

"What were you doing?" Maria asked when Jack returned.

"Making sure the room is clear—no Eddie." Jack took a seat on the wicker couch, similar to the one in his bungalow. Maria followed him with the bottles of water, handing one to Jack. He unscrewed the top and took a long swig.

Maria sat down beside him. "I still can't believe it happened—you know, with Stacy ..."

"It wasn't an accident," Jack stated. "I'm sure I saw somebody out there with her."

"You think it was Eddie?"

"I'd bet on it."

"I thought you weren't a betting man," she said with a grin. "But I question your wisdom getting in his face like that."

"Probably not the smartest thing I've ever done. But it doesn't look like Vince or the producers are doing anything about it."

The two sat quietly for a moment, reflecting on the whirlwind of events.

"So much has happened in the last three days, hasn't it?" Maria finally said.

"Has it been three days already?" Jack set his bottle on the coffee table.

"It's Thursday morning. Can you believe we were all pulled away from our jobs just this Monday?"

"Let's see," Jack recapped. "Get kidnapped on Monday, jump out of a plane on Tuesday, nearly drown and fall off a cliff on Wednesday, then gamble through the night until Thursday. Does that about cover it?"

Maria placed her bottle beside Jack's, then slid closer to him on the couch, and looked up at him with a sly grin. "You forgot one thing."

"And that would be?"

"Meeting you on Tuesday." Maria closed the gap even further, moving inches from his face. "That was the high point of the week."

Jack studied her face. Her eyes were lit up and hopeful, her skin looked incredibly smooth. Her lips parted slightly, tempting him again. His defenses were too low; he was exhausted, yet still reveling in the excitement from the last poker hand. Jack brought his hand up and caressed the side of her face. He could easily get lost in those eyes.

It was impossible for Jack not to think about his personal challenge. Would she be willing if he was? Any normal man would be crazy not to take advantage of the situation—right here, right now—and keep himself in the game. Even without the challenge, there was a growing desire that Jack was having a difficult time keeping at bay. He had to do something or he was going to slip again.

"You know what you need?" Jack had only to whisper, she was so close.

"What?"

Jack sat up straighter on the couch, turning her away from him, but holding onto her shoulders. "A back rub."

"A what?" Maria asked in shock.

"A little unwinding," Jack continued, trying anything he could think of to resist the temptation. "You know, to work out the stress."

"You're full of surprises, Mr. Forrest." Maria shook her head, allowing her body to turn and give Jack the back of her neck.

"Oh," Maria gasped, as Jack started working gently around her shoulders. "That does feel good."

"Just relax," Jack whispered, rubbing a touch firmer. Maria moaned, sliding lower in the couch. Jack adjusted, allowing her to lie down all the way. He sat on the edge of the couch beside her waist. She moved closer to the back, giving him a bit more room. He moved his hands up around her neck and rubbed for a while, then moved slowly down her back, as far as her gown would allow. Jack was suddenly having doubts that this was the right thing to do to suppress his desires. In fact, it was having the opposite effect.

He felt like he was living a James Bond fantasy. Watching the sunrise after gambling all night, dressed as the famous British spy, and now sitting in a quiet room with a stunningly beautiful woman. Jack had to get control of his thoughts, or he knew the situation would get dicey in no time.

He was a long way from Wheaton and his football team. Jack forced his mind back to what Vince had said about the school board. Did he, in fact, lose his job last night? What was he going to do after this week was over? How was Kathryn taking it? And did she blame herself?

Kathryn—how would she feel about what he was doing now? Didn't he at least owe her some kind of loyalty? Jack pictured her in his mind, contrasting the differences between her and Maria. It had just felt too weird to take that first step romantically with Kathryn, having to answer to her the next day at school. But he couldn't deny there was something going on, and it wasn't fair to either woman to not be honest with Maria.

"Maria?" Jack broke the silence.

"Ummm?" she mumbled quietly.

"You asked yesterday if there was someone back home waiting for me." Jack pushed his fingers along each side of her spine as he talked. "I need to fill you in a bit more, but it's kind of complicated. Although I wouldn't say she's waiting for me. Remember when I said there was someone that I've been seeing? She happens to be the vice principal at my school, or, at least, it was my school up until last night."

Jack paused, waiting for some kind of response from Maria.

"Maria?" He listened. Her breathing had deepened, but she didn't respond.

She'd fallen asleep.

Jack stopped massaging, allowing his hands to rest on her back for a minute. He chuckled at himself. He wasn't sure where he was going with his confession about Kathryn and his job.

He looked down at Maria for a long moment, enjoying the beautiful sight as she lay there quietly sleeping. Then he yawned, feeling the exhaustion settling in once again.

Jack finally got up from the couch and walked into the bedroom. He pulled a blanket off the bed, brought it back into the living room, and laid it on top of Maria.

He bent over her, pulling her hair back away from her face as he gently kissed her forehead.

"Sleep well," he whispered, then quietly slipped out the door.

Jack slid into his bungalow more exhausted than he could ever remember being. He shut the door behind him and locked it, then slipped the metal bar over the top hook on the door so even somebody with a key couldn't get in. He had to get out of the tuxedo—it had been more than twelve hours. He hadn't been in "a monkey suit" that long since his roommate from college got married. He slung the jacket over one of the dinette chairs while, at the same time, he slipped off his shoes. His feet were killing him. He was sure some of the cuts from the broken glass had started bleeding again.

On the way to the bedroom, he started stripping off the rest of the clothes. The cufflinks came unclasped, the shirt unbuttoned, and by the time he reached the bed, his pants were on the way down. He didn't care a bit that cameras were all around him; he just wanted to be in the bed as quickly as possible.

He went about his business clad only in his underwear—brushing his teeth, turning on the air conditioning, and then finally pulling back the covers and crawling underneath. The cool sheets felt like a taste of heaven, even as the sunburn twinged a bit. He laid on his back with his eyes closed, and uttered a quick prayer of thanks for getting through the day. He knew he should pray more—about the challenges ahead, about Stacy and her family, probably about Maria and Kathryn, even about the job situation back home—but he was just too tired to mentally push through. Before he knew it, he was drifting off.

A knock on his door—no, must be a dream. Jack kept his eyes closed, willing his body to stay asleep.

A fist pounded on the door. This time Jack's eyes flashed open. Who could be bugging him now? They were supposed to be on a break.

Jack grunted as he pulled the covers back and forced his legs out onto the floor. He walked to the closet, grabbing the white terrycloth robe provided by the resort and slipped it over him as he headed for the door.

Opening it, there stood before him a man he hadn't seen before. He was about Jack's height, smartly dressed in a white polo shirt, dark blue shorts, and a pair of leather sandals. He was one of those handsome types where it was hard to guess his age. He had the look of experience, yet just the beginnings of gray along the temples of his dark brown hair, and a hint of wrinkles around his eyes when he smiled—which he was doing now from the other side of the doorway.

"I'm so sorry to interrupt," the man offered. "I'm sure you must be exhausted. But may I speak with you a moment?"

Jack sighed and stepped back from the door, allowing the man to enter. "Why not?"

"My name is Zeke Roberts," he said, as he walked past Jack, stopping at the dinette table.

Jack didn't say anything, but decided he didn't want to be on his feet, and sat across from him at the table.

Zeke watched Jack carefully, then sat down as well. "That name doesn't mean anything to you?"

Jack wasn't in the mood for games. "Should it?"

Zeke angled his head slightly, then grinned. "No, I guess it shouldn't. I'm the executive producer for *The Ultimate Challenge*."

Jack nodded. "Oh, I see. Sorry, I didn't recognize your name."

"It's quite all right. I try and keep a low profile around here."

I guess so, Jack thought. He hadn't seen him on the island once.

"You were amazing in the poker game tonight," Zeke said. "I have to hand it to you calling C. J.'s bluff."

Jack shrugged. "I really didn't have a choice."

"True, but you could have walked away with your savings intact."

Jack looked across the table, wondering where this was going. If Jack hadn't been so tired, he might have enjoyed the conversation with the show's producer. He seemed nice, had an easygoing way about him that Jack found refreshingly different than Vince or the staffers he'd been surrounded by the past few days.

"Look, you need some rest," Zeke offered. "So I'll get right to the point."

"That would be appreciated. Does this have something to do with Stacy?"

Jack could see that he'd caught Zeke off-guard. His brow creased, showing clearly more wrinkles than Jack had first noticed, placing his age, in Jack's mind, more toward his late forties. His eyes left Jack's for an instant.

"Why do you ask that?"

"I figured Vince told you I'd seen something on the cliff last night."

Zeke nodded, overtly so. "Yes, that's right. I remember. But that's not why I'm here."

"Aren't you checking into it?" Jack leaned closer across the table. Maybe this was his chance to make his point. "You guys have cameras tucked away in every nook and cranny around here. I've found six in this room alone. You can't tell me you don't have exactly what happened to Stacy on tape."

"We're checking into every possibility—and we've taken appropriate measures, Jack," Zeke said. "You have to trust me on this one. I can't tell you any more at this time."

Jack shook his head. "Then why are you here?"

"To talk with you about your personal challenge."

The personal challenge. He had been doing just fine blocking it out of his mind and getting some much-needed sleep.

"Oh, I'd forgotten about that."

"It occurred to me you might have, after leaving Maria's room not long ago," Zeke offered with a wink.

Jack didn't respond.

"There's some wonderful magic going on between you two, Jack. On camera it shines like …" Zeke searched for the right words, "like Tracy and Hepburn, Astaire and Rogers or … Gere and Roberts in *Pretty Woman*."

"Aren't you exaggerating just a bit?"

"Not at all," Zeke pleaded. "You two have the whole staff talking. It's like watching Sam and Diane on *Cheers*. Every reality show hopes to spark something like this—and, with you two, we've got it. The chemistry between you and Maria is a gold mine."

"For your ratings, you mean," Jack said.

Zeke smiled. "Yes, for my ratings. I won't lie to you about that. But also for you, Jack. I've been in this business a long time, and I know when something is 'right.' You two are meant for each other, and yes, I want to capitalize on that for the sake of the show. This could be huge. But I also want it for you—and her."

Jack seriously doubted Zeke's altruistic intentions. "What's between us has nothing to do with your show."

"We both know that's not true," he said. "But be that as it may, I thought I'd come to you with a little incentive to help you fulfill your challenge. We don't want to lose you."

Zeke paused a moment, making sure he had Jack's full attention.

"We know about the school board's decision last night, and we're sorry you seem to have lost your job. We don't want you to go home from this game with nothing, should you not make it to the end. So, I'm offering you a bonus: one hundred thousand dollars, if you complete your task with Maria."

"You've got to be kidding me." Jack rose from the table, his anger boiling under the surface.

"I'm deadly serious," Zeke answered, his eyes darkening and remaining on Jack. "I'm extending your deadline another twenty-four hours. And should you succeed, you'll have one hundred thousand dollars to help get your life in order again—whether you win or lose the ultimate game, that money will be yours."

Jack paced in front of him. "You're unbelievable. Are the ratings for your precious show all that matter to you?"

"No, I told you, this is a win-win situation for both of us. You and Maria could walk out of here the new Charles and Diana of the world."

"Exactly," Jack snapped. "Look how they turned out. Do you think there'd be any relationship with Maria if I did what you're attempting to bribe me into doing, and she finds out about it?"

"She'll never find out," Zeke argued. "This conversation will never air—it's off the record. How would this make my show look if I let it out, huh? I'm not crazy. What we air has to look like it's real or we lose everything."

Jack was furious. "And what does your offer make Maria—just a piece of meat to be bartered over by a couple of men for a hundred grand?"

"No." Zeke looked shocked. "It's not like that at all."

Jack wanted to hit him. "I'm not interested in your offer. You can take your hundred thousand dollars and ..."

"Now, don't be hasty, Jack." Zeke's voice was calm and controlled as he interrupted. "Spend some time and think about this. You have nothing to lose."

Jack shook his head, trying to calm his rage. "I thought you researched your contestants."

"We do."

"Yet you know so little about me that you would make this disgusting offer?"

"I don't understand."

"No, you don't," Jack sighed. "There is so much in my life that is more important to me than money—maybe you worship it, but I don't. I worship something far greater. And I have a heck of a lot more respect for Maria—for women in general—than you obviously do."

Jack walked over to the front door and opened it. "You can forget your offer. Now get out!"

Zeke rose from the table and walked slowly to the door. "You're making a mistake, Jack. Think it over. I'm sure you'll come to your senses."

"You think it over," Jack said as he passed by. "Think about the fact that you're dealing with two lives here—two people who deserve respect, not two objects that are yours to manipulate by whatever means necessary to win your next sweeps period. You should also be thinking about the life that was lost this morning because of your stupid reality show. Stacy was more important than your game."

Zeke stepped outside, then turned to face Jack. "I apologize. I didn't do this to upset you, but thought it could be a way to help you out when you return to Wheaton, win or lose."

"Well, you thought wrong," Jack stated coldly, just before he swung the door closed with a bang.

Amanda was up bright and early, getting to the hospital before the sun had risen over the Chicago suburbs. The routine helped get her mind off of Jack and whatever weird plan Zeke had behind the reality show. She knew it was much more than Jack being a contestant. The odds were far too great for this to be some innocent coincidence. She just didn't know what it was.

She so wished Kevin was still alive so she'd have somebody to talk this over with. There was no one in her life who knew the dark history of her time with Zeke. Kevin had been the only one—and even he hadn't known all of it.

She changed the bedding in room 422, then rolled her cart down the hall to deliver the old sheets to the laundry chute.

"Amanda." The front desk nurse stopped her. "You've got a call."

"I do?" She was surprised. The only person who ever bothered her at work was Jack. She rushed over to the phone.

"Hello?"

"Mrs. Forrest?" a strange voice asked from the other end.

"Yes, this is she."

"My name is Philip Weston. I'm one of the producers on *The Ultimate Challenge.*"

"Oh, so you finally got my message, huh?" Amanda snapped.

"Well," the voice sounded confused. "Actually, no. I wasn't aware that you left a message."

"Then why are you calling?"

"You are aware that your son is with us on the latest challenge, right?" he asked.

"Yes, that's why I was trying to get in touch with him."

"Oh, I see. Well, then maybe I have some good news for you. We have a plane waiting for you at DuPage Airport. Do you think you could get away for a few days and fly down here to join us?"

Amanda held the receiver in shock, not responding.

"Mrs. Forrest?"

"Yes, I'm here," Amanda answered. "I'm just trying to comprehend what you've said."

"We want you to come and join us, to see first-hand how your son is doing."

"Where will I be flying to?"

"We can't let you know that information," the voice said. "Security and all. The pilots know where to take you though. Just bring clothing for warm weather ... and you might want to throw in a swimsuit."

"I'm not sure I can get away." Amanda looked around the hospital. The administrator wouldn't be in for another couple of hours. "How can I reach you when I know for sure I can come?"

"No need to." The voice sounded confident. "When you've cleared your schedule, just head over to DuPage. You do know where it is, don't you?"

"Yes, I do."

"Our plane will be obvious. The pilot will be waiting for you."

"But what if I can't go?"

"I'm sure you'll be able to figure out a way, Mrs. Forrest. Your son is counting on you."

She heard a click.

"Wait!" Amanda gasped. "What do you mean ..." But the line was dead. Jack was counting on her. What was that supposed to mean?

Amanda looked at the clock over the nurse's station—it was 7:15 a.m. Out of the corner of her eye, she noticed a guy standing in the hallway with a video camera pointed right at her. It wasn't unusual for someone to be running around with a camera—with all the new fathers taping their child's first moments. But why tape the nurse's station?

She walked over toward the man. He didn't back down or try to hide the camera; he just kept taping her, the red light glowing on top like a beacon.

"Excuse me," Amanda started politely. "Would you please turn that camera off?"

"Can't, lady," the man replied. "Sorry."

"What do you mean you can't? You have no right to shoot me without consent."

"Just what I said. I can't," the man answered coldly. "I'm going to be your shadow until you get on that plane, Mrs. Forrest."

"So you're with the show, I take it?'

"Yeah, just try and ignore me." The man moved his head from behind the camera and smiled. "It'll be easier for you that way."

Amanda had to wait for her supervisor's arrival to get permission to leave work. She had gone about her duties with the camera guy following her every move, except when she went into a delivery room. He tried the first time and found himself face-to-face with the largest security guard in the hospital.

It was a little before nine when Amanda spotted Cheryl going into her office. She'd managed to make it a point to walk by her door every five minutes.

"Cheryl," Amanda knocked lightly on the open door, "can I speak with you for a minute?"

"Sure, Amanda." The director of pediatrics waved her in. "But I've got just a couple of minutes before a staff meeting, so make it quick."

Amanda stepped into the room, with the camera guy stepping in right behind her.

Cheryl looked at him, concerned. "What's with him?"

"That's part of what I want to talk to you about," Amanda said. "My son has been chosen as a contestant on *The Ultimate Challenge*."

"OK … and …?" Cheryl prompted, having a hard time keeping her eyes off the guy with the camera.

"I've been asked to fly to where they're doing the taping and see him," Amanda answered.

"And when would you go?"

"Right now, if it's all right with you," Amanda said. "I know it's short notice …"

"Short?" Cheryl cut her off. "How about *no notice*?"

"I know." Amanda ducked her head, searching for the right words to say.

"We're short-handed enough around here."

Amanda nodded and looked back up to her boss. She couldn't keep the tears from pooling up in her eyes. "It's just that I really feel like I need to go and be with him."

Cheryl cocked her head, waiting for further explanation.

"I can't go into detail right now, but I'm seriously concerned for what's going on with Jack."

"It's just a stupid reality show, isn't it?"

"Well, I really don't think so, but I can't explain more. I'm sorry." Amanda felt like she was blowing it. She had to convince her to let her go. "Please, Cheryl. I'll make it up to you, pull double shifts without overtime, fill in on holidays—whatever it takes."

"OK, OK," Cheryl finally said. "I guess we can make do." Then she turned to the cameraman. "Do you know when she'll be back?"

"She should be back by Saturday, Sunday at the latest," he answered.

"Thank you so much," Amanda said to Cheryl.

"Have Tina call in a replacement for you before you leave."

"I will," Amanda said. She turned and walked out of the office before Cheryl changed her mind. Stopping by the nurse's desk, Amanda asked Tina, the charge nurse, to call in someone who could replace her for the next couple of days. Tina wasn't happy about it until Amanda told her why—she was a big fan of the show.

Now there was only one thing left to take care of. She picked up an extension at the end of the desk, and dialed Jack's school.

"Ms. Thompson, please," Amanda said. "It's Mrs. Forrest calling." A few seconds later, Kathryn came on the line.

"Amanda, have you heard anything?"

"In a way," Amanda answered. "I'm flying somewhere to meet him."

"Really?"

"Yeah, I just got the call, and some guy's been following me around with a camera all morning."

"Is everything OK?"

"As far as I know, things are fine." Amanda paused. "Look, I need a favor."

"Name it."

"I need you to set up a meeting at three this afternoon with your principal and the president of the board at the school."

"I'll try," Kathryn said. "But what for?"

"I can't tell you that. Just make up some excuse, but get them together."

"Amanda, this doesn't make any sense. I need some excuse."

"Um," Amanda thought. "If you have to, tell them I'm going to be with Jack and we'll try and call in."

"Do you think that's possible?" Kathryn sounded hopeful.

"Probably not, but you have to trust me."

"What have you got planned?"

"It's really better that you don't know," Amanda warned.

There was a pause before she heard, "OK, I guess. And Amanda ..."

"Yes?"

"You don't know what you're getting into—be careful."

"I will." Amanda smiled. Kathryn was such a sweet woman. Jack had found himself a winner in her eyes. "I'll call if I get the chance."

"You better. I'm dying to hear what's going on with Jack. This whole week is turning into such a mess."

45

Amanda didn't waste any time getting out of the hospital. She stopped by the house to pack a quick bag, then headed to the small airfield in West Chicago, just a few miles from Wheaton. The irritating camera guy insisted on riding along, taping her every move. It was more than a bit unnerving.

She didn't know the airport well and wondered where she'd find the plane. But as she drove by the DuPage Flight Center, it became obvious. Sitting off to the side was a jet as large as a Boeing 737 painted in shiny, metallic black with brilliant gold lettering on it: *The Ultimate Challenge.* Underneath it, in smaller gold script, read *Zeke Roberts Productions.*

"Pull in over there," the camera guy instructed as he pointed to a chain link gate between her and the beautiful jet. She pulled over, and a man stepped up to her window.

"Are you Mrs. Forrest?"

Amanda nodded.

"Great. Right this way, then."

He walked back to the gate and opened it. As she drove through, he pointed her toward a parking spot next to the flight center. She got out, grabbed the overnight bag from the back seat, and started toward the huge aircraft.

"You're all set, just head on up the stairs," the man instructed. As she walked, the cameraman followed right behind her.

She paused at the base of the rolling stairway, looking up at the magnificent aircraft. It all seemed impossible. Zeke had come a long way in the twenty-eight years since they'd seen each other.

There's no turning back now, Amanda thought, and took her first step up.

The flight crew greeted her at the top of the stairs and then politely moved to the side to allow her into the plane.

It was incredible.

The few times she had flown before had only been in passenger airlines with the usual three chairs crammed closely together on both sides of the aisle. But even the first-class sections in those jets looked like a run-down inner-city bus compared to the luxuriousness in front of her.

The first section contained a white, wraparound, leather couch to her left, and a pair of matching recliners with a small table to her right. She felt as if she should take her shoes off before walking down the plush, light beige carpet. Looking farther down the plane, she could see an office setting that could pass for the conference room of any Fortune 500 company, complete with eight matching high-back, leather chairs around a glossy, dark maple table that matched the rest of the wood trim throughout the interior of the cabin.

Another camera crew was waiting inside the plane, shooting her every reaction.

"Mrs. Forrest." A man in a captain's uniform approached her. "I'm Captain Bell. Welcome to *The Ultimate Challenge.*"

"The plane or the television show?"

The captain smiled, and motioned to the camera crew behind her. "I guess both."

"This is quite a plane," Amanda said.

"It's the new Boeing Business Jet," he answered proudly.

"Is this Zeke's private jet, or is it used for the entire production?"

The captain was taken aback. "Do you know Mr. Roberts?"

Amanda grinned, while trying to quickly come up with something to hide her blunder. "I just saw his name on the side of the plane."

"Oh, I see." The pilot wasn't convinced. "It's used by both, ma'am. Please, make yourself comfortable and we'll get underway. If you need anything at all, you just ask one of our flight attendants and they'll take great care of you."

"Where are we going?"

The captain shook his head slightly. "I can't tell you that—or how long the flight will be. But you'll have time for a movie, if you'd like. We have a large selection on board. Have a pleasant flight."

Amanda watched the captain leave before settling down on the plush couch. *I'm sure I will*, she thought.

"Would you like something to drink?" A young woman walked up wearing an outfit that resembled a flight attendant's uniform, but with a Hooters twist. The skirt was exceptionally short, and the top sunk way too low for Amanda's taste. But it wasn't hard to imagine Zeke sitting back and enjoying the view.

"Some ice water would be fine, thanks." Amanda smiled at the young lady.

"Coming right up."

She sank into the couch, praying for a whole list of things: wisdom, guidance, protection, and, especially, peace. Her anxiety level was high: sitting on a plane with Zeke's name on the side was enough to unnerve her, but knowing she was flying straight toward him, sent her into utter panic. She knew she was flying right into his trap, but what else could she do?

Jack was already in it.

Kathryn noticed that the school board president had arrived about ten minutes early. It was nearly 3:00 p.m. and she would have to make her way into the principal's office any minute.

She didn't know what she was going to say. Jerry hadn't been eager to go along with the idea of the meeting, so Kathryn had been forced to use Amanda's idea that they might hear from Jack. Yet, she knew by the way Amanda had talked, that no call would be coming.

How could she have let Amanda talk her into this?

It was time.

Kathryn made her way down the short hallway to Principal Swift's office, interrupting the quiet conversation she could hear beyond the door by tapping lightly.

"Come in," she heard.

Kathryn opened the door and stepped into the room. "Jerry, Bonnie, thanks so much for being here."

"Not a problem," Bonnie replied politely, but the scowl across her face belied her words. "Anything to get this mess straightened out."

"You say Jack should be calling in soon?" Jerry jumped right to the point.

"I hope so ..." Kathryn's response was interrupted by a voice coming over Jerry's intercom.

"Mr. Swift, there is a Mr. Walker here to see you." The voice echoed through the office.

Jerry's eyebrows rose as he spoke loudly toward his phone. "I'm in a meeting, Sally. Could you find out what he wants and make an appointment?"

"He says he already has an appointment, 3:00 p.m. today."

Jerry stared up at Kathryn, his eyes darkened. "Is this another one of your little tricks?"

"No, I promise," Kathryn answered honestly. But in the back of her mind, she knew Amanda was up to something.

Sally's voice came through the speakerphone again. "He says this has to do with Jack Forrest."

Jerry's eyes turned black as coal as he bore into Kathryn, but he answered Sally, "Send him in, then." He turned to Kathryn and asked again, "You know nothing about this?"

"No, I don't. All Amanda said was that she would have Jack call in. She didn't say a thing about someone else coming to meet us."

"If I find out you're lying ..." Jerry let the words hang in the air as he rose from his desk and headed to the door.

Kathryn allowed him to pass, then stepped further into the office by Bonnie. In seconds, Mr. Walker was at the door.

"Mr. Swift," a silver-haired, middle-aged man dressed in a navy blue suit said with a smile. He extended his hand. "A pleasure to meet you."

"Mr. Walker." Jerry shook his hand. "Let me introduce the president of our school board, Bonnie Slagle, and my vice principal, Kathryn Thompson. If you'll excuse me, I'll just go grab another chair."

The man entered the room and shook hands with both of them, while Jerry stepped away briefly and returned, rolling in another office chair.

"Please, have a seat," Jerry offered. Kathryn sat next to Bonnie while Jerry returned to his desk and the mysterious Mr. Walker sat quietly in the chair the principal had brought in.

"Excuse my frankness, Mr. Walker," Jerry began. "But I wasn't expecting your arrival. What is this about?"

Mr. Walker smiled warmly. "I'm a lawyer with the American Center for Law and Justice. I would have liked to have been at your meeting last night, but another matter kept me from getting there in time."

"I don't understand," Jerry responded coldly. "You have no standing in this matter."

"I beg to differ," Mr. Walker said. Kathryn noticed that he kept his voice light in contrast to Jerry. "If I understand the position the school board has adopted, you voted to fire an employee last night in the misguided hope that you would divert a lawsuit planned by Mr. Swanson. Am I correct?"

"There's more to it than that," Jerry said.

"There certainly is a lot more to it." Mr. Walker nodded once to emphasize his point.

"Have you been retained by Jack Forrest?" Jerry got right to the point.

"Not directly yet; he's currently out of reach."

"Then why have you inserted yourself into this school's business?"

Kathryn watched Jerry sparring with the lawyer. Whatever rudeness Jerry seemed to fire out didn't affect him at all. He kept composed and well-mannered.

"Actually, I could be here to represent your school," Mr. Walker offered to Jerry.

He then turned to a shocked Bonnie. "And your school district, Ms. Slagle."

"What are you talking about?" Jerry snipped.

"Now you've got my attention," Bonnie added.

"Good, now getting back to the Swanson's lawyer. I'm sure you heard all about the dangers of *separation of church and state* in conjunction with Mr. Forrest. Am I correct?"

Jerry nodded in the affirmative.

"And I can assume that he was associated in some way with the ACLU?"

"As a matter of fact, yes," Jerry responded. "But I don't see how ..."

"Then I can also assume that you have not had any discussion on Mr. Forrest's First Amendment right to freedom of speech?"

He paused and looked around the room. Kathryn followed his eyes; there was no response from either Jerry or Bonnie.

"Ah," Mr. Walker continued. "I thought not. I'm sure you didn't hear that the Supreme Court, in *Tinker v. Des Moines Independent Community School District,* ruled that state employees don't—and I quote—'shed their constitutional rights to freedom of speech or expression at the schoolhouse gate,' close quote. And I believe that would also apply when Mr. Forrest was in a hospital emergency room on his own personal time."

"What Mr. Swanson and his lawyer were arguing," Bonnie took the lead, "is that the *separation of church and state* issue overrides Mr. Forrest's First Amendment rights."

"Clearly it doesn't," Mr. Walker argued.

"This is not the forum for this argument," Jerry interrupted the lawyer, looking clearly at him. "This is not a court of law. And by the way Mr. Walker, I'm still unclear as to why you think you can invade our meeting. You have no standing here."

"I'm simply here to inform," Mr. Walker answered. "Should you continue with the decision to terminate Mr. Forrest in an attempt to avoid Mr. Swanson's lawsuit, I wanted to make sure that you knew you could be met with a wrongful termination lawsuit instead."

"So, you are threatening us with a lawsuit?" Jerry demanded.

"Not threatening, Mr. Swift. No, sir. I'm simply informing you of the possible liability. But I also want you to know that should you decide to rescind the aforementioned termination of employment, and there is a lawsuit filed on behalf of Mr. Swanson from the ACLU, we would be willing to represent this school and the school board on that matter—free of charge."

"What?" Jerry leaned forward on the desk, seemingly not believing what he'd heard. Kathryn had to admit she was a bit surprised by his comment as well.

"That's what we do," the lawyer smiled. "We protect religious and constitutional freedoms at no charge to our clients. We would represent you in defending Jack Forrest's First Amendment rights."

Kathryn sat in the room amazed at what was taking place. Perhaps there was some hope after all—and Amanda had protected her by arranging this meeting without her knowledge. Was this the answer to their prayers? She hoped so.

"Well, this is crazy," Jerry grunted dismissively, turning and giving Kathryn an evil look that she knew meant he would be after her later.

"No, it isn't," Bonnie shot back. "I'm glad you've come, Mr. Walker. I'd like to hear more."

47

Jack woke up with a splitting headache. He had no idea what time it was or, for a brief moment, where he was. His curtains were pulled shut, allowing little sunlight into the room, but he could tell it was still daylight outside.

He sat up in bed, moving gingerly. His aches and pains from the previous day had quadrupled. It was always the day after overexerting muscles that the soreness really kicked in. He groaned, as he pulled his legs out from under the covers and over to the side. His back itched, which he hoped was a good sign that his sunburn was healing.

After a few minutes of shaking off his grogginess, he slowly got up from the bed and made it to the bathroom, recalling the weird conversation he'd had with the producer of the show. It seemed so unreal now. Did the guy really offer him a hundred thousand dollars to sleep with Maria?

Jack followed his normal routine of hiding in the darkened closet to change into his swim trunks, used the toilet, and then stepped into the shower. Despite the pain, he let the hot water pound away at his overworked muscles. He wondered if there was a place to jog around this resort to work some of the soreness out later—if there was time. But did it matter? He was pretty sure after the confrontation with Zeke, he'd be the next one cut from the game.

He hated to admit it, but he was depressed. After all he'd sacrificed, missing the school board meeting, losing his job—it looked like it was all going to be a waste. This whole interruption of his life was getting out of hand. Plus, there was Stacy to think about—the game had taken her life. How could the producers, especially this Zeke Roberts guy, not be responsible?

He was also struggling with his thoughts toward Maria. If they had met in any other circumstance, would a natural relationship have developed? As it was, being forced together by this insane game, they would never have a chance for a real start. Any feelings they might have, as intense as they might be, were manipulated by the pressure and false situations they'd already encountered. He was her savior from the fire, her rescuer from the sinking Zodiak. She held an emotional attachment that had morphed into romantic feelings. He couldn't say he wasn't flattered, and he had to admit, he was extremely attracted to her *and* having a hard time holding back his own heart.

But where was she with God? That had always been Jack's litmus test for the women he dated. Recently, that priority had begun to slide—as evidenced in his attraction toward Maria. Jack knew very little about her spiritual condition, but as he thought about it, he realized he'd begun his relationship with Kathryn the same way. As Jack was getting older, was his priority for a woman who loved God waning? At least Kathryn was now a believer and her interest in godly things was growing.

What about Maria? Jack didn't know much about Catholics, but he decided he'd have to find out.

Mr. Walker had spent the last half-hour explaining to Kathryn, Jerry, and Bonnie how the First Amendment rights of state employees, especially schoolteachers, are not trumped by church-state separation. In fact, there was no mention of the *separation of church and state* anywhere in the Constitution or the Bill of Rights.

The phrase, he explained, actually came from a letter Thomas Jefferson wrote on January 1, 1802, to the Danbury Baptist Association of Connecticut. The congregation had reacted to a widespread rumor at the time that Congregationalism was to become the national religion. Jefferson made it clear in his letter that their fears were unfounded.

"The wall Jefferson cited in his letter was one-dimensional: it protected the church from having the government establish a national religion, or attempt to tell men how to worship God. Jefferson would roll over in his grave if he could see how that phrase is being used to strip God from our culture today."

"Be that as it may," Jerry retorted, "we can't have our teachers running around praying for kids, and then trying to convince them that their religion is the only way."

"I understand your concerns," Mr. Walker said. "But Mr. Forrest wasn't acting as an agent of this school when he was at the hospital with the boy showing his personal concern. For you to require him to renounce his religion in some way, to amend this situation, is in direct conflict with his First Amendment rights."

"I don't care," Jerry's voice rose. "He'll either say what we've told him to say, or he doesn't have a job around here—it's that simple."

"No," Mr. Walker replied. "It's not that simple, actually."

"The language wasn't our idea." Bonnie stepped in trying to calm the discussion. "The lawyer and the boy's father came up with that in order for them not to go forward with the lawsuit. Once the ACLU stepped in, we didn't know what to do. We're barely managing to keep our sports programs going, or enough books in the students's hands. There's no way we could find the money to pay for a lawsuit."

"I understand," Mr. Walker nodded. "I really do. But that doesn't mean you can run Mr. Forrest out of town and trample on his rights either. You have to decide—do you want to basically give in to blackmail and fire a really good teacher and coach, or let us help you stand up for Jack's rights. It's your call."

Kathryn had quietly watched the entire debate. She didn't feel like it was her place to jump in—until now. "We haven't even given Jack a chance to defend himself. We should've delayed any decision until he returned, anyway."

"I'm beginning to agree with you, Kathryn," Bonnie stated. "What about you, Jerry?"

Jerry shook his head, bringing up his hand and scratching the back of his neck—which he often did when thinking over a tough decision. "To me, Jack crossed the line and is getting what he deserves. If we listen to Mr. Walker here, he's going to want us to have our science department stop teaching evolution and bring back creationism. This whole thing is getting out of hand, and I'm not willing to let this school be trampled on by the religious right."

"Mr. Swift," Mr. Walker sighed, evidently choosing to ignore the latest tirade. "I'm sure we could have a very interesting discussion on the merits of evolution, but that's not what I'm here about. What if I could get the other side to see this thing more reasonably? Would you be willing to delay the school board's decision until I could set up a meeting once Jack returns?"

"That'd be great," Kathryn exclaimed. "I know Jack would apologize—he's very sorry for upsetting the family. It's just that he can't bring himself to say what they want him to say."

"No!" Jerry slammed his fist down. "A decision has been made, and I plan to stick with it."

"Calm down, Jerry," Bonnie said, then turned to Kathryn. "Do you know when Jack will return?"

"They said it wouldn't be any more than seven days—less if he got kicked out. So, he should be back on Sunday at the latest."

Bonnie looked back to Mr. Walker. "How about if we give you a week to attempt some kind of solution that will keep us out of court. But for now, Jack is officially suspended without pay until a different resolution can be presented to me. Would you agree to that, Jerry?"

"I guess we can give it a week," Jerry grumbled.

"A week it is," Mr. Walker said with a nod, then stood to leave. "Thank you all for your time."

Kathryn watched with a thin smile as Mr. Walker walked out. Remembering how the Swanson family had been the night before, she knew he had his work cut out for him.

After the door had closed, Jerry looked over at Kathryn with a cold, hard stare. "You swear you had nothing to do with this?"

Kathryn shook her head. "I told you the truth, Jerry. This was all Mrs. Forrest's doing."

Jerry sighed, as his eyes darkened. "That doesn't excuse how you've gone against my decision every step of the way on this. Now get out of here before I fire you as well."

Amanda looked out of the window. Her best guess was that they were somewhere over the Caribbean. They'd flown over what she thought to be the Gulf of Mexico hours ago. The sun was still up, giving her a view of the magnificent multicolored ocean, and also a bearing on what direction they'd flown—due south, perhaps a bit east as well.

The staff had gone out of its way to accommodate her, offering refreshments every thirty minutes, serving a gourmet meal halfway through the flight, and continually offering entertainment. She didn't feel like watching a movie, but was comfortable just sitting with her thoughts, which, for now, were on her college years—especially that sophomore year when she first met Zeke.

He was tall—she remembered him being around six-two, with long hair flowing over the ears and down over his collar in the back. That was the style in the seventies: flared Levis and silk shirts—the disco years. It was past the radical time of the sixties, but not by much. There was still a lot of discontent on college campuses. And Yale was no exception.

He'd sat beside her as if he owned the world. Amanda hadn't thought about it in years, but the memories came flooding back like it was yesterday. She'd been sitting in the library, studying, and not wanting to be bothered. He plopped down next to her, dropping his books on the table as if the noise announced his grand entrance.

She wasn't impressed at all, but did everything she could to tune him out and continued studying. It wasn't easy. He was quite handsome, even if irritating.

"Studying for a test?"

"I was before you came crashing in," she responded.

"I'm sorry ..." he let his sentence trail out, expecting her to fill in her name.

She didn't.

It took a half a dozen meetings like that. He'd find her in different locations around school, but mostly in the library. It got to where she was disappointed if she completed her studying and he didn't come up to aggravate her.

The day she finally offered her name had been one of those times. Just when she thought he wasn't going to show, Zeke snuck up as usual, nearly making her jump out of her skin.

"Oh my!" she gasped.

"It's me," he said with a smile, brightening her day. "Did you miss me ..."

His last word trailed on, just like the first day they'd met.

"Amanda," she said, before she could stop herself.

Zeke's grin widened. "Yes ... Amanda. Nice to meet you—*finally.*"

The lurch of the plane touching down on land brought her back to the present. She had blanked out the good times with Zeke, choosing to only remember what caused them to separate over the past decades. It might have been the way most people handle the pain, but Amanda suddenly realized it was the only way she could keep herself from still loving him.

It had been so intense that her conscious mind had buried the memories. Deep enough that she hadn't had a second's thought of regret about her decision to marry Kevin. He had come into her life when she was a wreck. He'd given her hope, led her down that path which brought her right to Jesus. He had been her mentor, her friend, and finally, her lover. She missed Kevin greatly—but thinking back on it, they had never come close to the heights of passion that her year with Zeke had brought. At least, that's what her rekindled memory was telling her.

She looked out the window to see palm trees lining the runway, separating the long blacktop from white sand beaches and a turquoise ocean just beyond.

Jack walked out of his room, this time dressed entirely in black: black T-shirt, black cargo pants, even black socks and tennis shoes. The clothes had been left for him by one of the production assistants with the explicit instructions to wear them to the next gathering.

He didn't really know where he was going, but he wanted to walk around and clear his head. The sun was dipping in the skyline—probably getting close to seven o'clock. He realized that he was starving and wondered what the menu was for the night.

"Hey, Jack. How you feeling?" Hugh called, sitting in a lounge chair by the pool. Jack casually walked over to him. He was dressed in all black as well.

"Groggy, like I'm hung-over—and I don't even drink. All I had last night were soft drinks." Jack grunted, as he sat in the chair next to Hugh.

"You sore too?"

"Very," Jack chuckled. "I've got muscles aching that I forgot I had."

The moment quickly turned quiet as they both watched the water in the pool ripple and reflect the reddening sunlight.

"It's awful about Stacy," Hugh offered.

"I know. I can't get my mind to really wrap around it."

"You really think Eddie had something to do with it?"

Jack explained what he'd seen on the cliff's edge that night, and then mentioned Eddie's shoes.

Hugh sighed. "Pretty circumstantial."

"Listen to the lawyer coming out in you," Jack said with a grin, as his eyes remained glued to the mesmerizing water. He looked back up at Hugh. "You sure know poker."

Hugh smiled at him. "Helped pass the time in law school. Texas Hold 'Em was very big on campus."

"We used to play a lot of seven card stud—Texas is a different game."

"You came out OK."

"Maybe, after I was nearly knocked out. But you were the one to take out Eddie."

Hugh snickered. "Yeah, that was sweet."

Jack leaned closer to him. "You remember the hand you won with, a straight to the king?"

"Sure. That knocked C. J. nearly out of the game."

"I folded with an ace high straight."

"You what?" Hugh sat up in shock.

"I had an ace and a ten. When the king came out, I had my straight."

"You would've won—taken all of C. J.'s money and a heck of a lot of mine." Hugh shook his head. "Unbelievable. Why'd you let it go?"

"I just couldn't bring myself to risk the money at the time." Jack analyzed his own behavior as he talked, realizing it was Vince's prodding that finally got to him to risk it all at the end.

"So you wait and gamble it all on a queen high on the next hand?"

Jack flashed a smile. "That's poker, isn't it?"

"Yeah, that's poker," Hugh laughed.

Jack felt his stomach growl. "Man, I'm starving. You know what's going on around here?"

"Vince came by about an hour ago. They're going to call everyone into the room around eight and explain our lovely attire. Dinner's set up, you can eat anytime you want."

"Care to join me?"

"No, thanks. I already ate." Hugh leaned back in the lounge chair. "Just relaxing, trying to imagine what they'll have in store for us tonight."

"We're still partners in this?" Jack asked, standing up.

"You bet," Hugh said with a nod. "In this next challenge, I'm just looking for a way to get Eddie out of the game. He's dangerous."

Jack noticed Eddie coming from the bungalows dressed just like them and walking in their direction. "Speak of the devil," Jack whispered. "Anyway, I'll see you in there."

"OK." Hugh laid his head back down and looked up at the blue sky.

To get to the restaurant, Jack had to go right by Eddie. He stopped as Jack approached.

"You really outdid yourself last night, Forrest."

Jack tried to pass, but Eddie blocked the way. He looked even more ominous standing above him, dressed as if he could be hiding in an alley and ready to mug him.

"I'm talking to you," Eddie declared.

"I have nothing to say to you."

Eddie ignored Jack's rebuff. "You got lucky last night."

"For once, I'd say we're in agreement," Jack stated. "I did get lucky. Unfortunately for you, you didn't."

"I'm still in the game, though."

"I'm sorry," Jack said.

Eddie looked around the pool area, then leaned in closer to Jack. "I've got a proposition for you."

Jack angled his head without responding.

"I think you and me are the obvious ones to make it to the final two. What do you say we form an alliance to make sure it works out that way."

Jack was speechless.

"If it comes to any more votes, you promise to not vote me out, I'll do the same for you."

"You're serious?" Jack asked.

"You bet," Eddie said with a grin. "Then it'll all come down to one final challenge—you against me, one-on-one."

"I'll have to give it some thought," Jack said. "But I want one thing from you."

"Name it."

"I want you to lay off Maria. She hasn't done anything to you."

"I'd say trying to vote me out isn't nothin'."

"Yeah? Then tell me what Stacy did to you."

Jack didn't wait for an answer, but quickly stepped around Eddie and made his way toward the main building.

"How was your flight, Mrs. Forrest?" the young man asked Amanda, as she made her way down the stairs carrying her small travel bag.

"It was fine, thank you," Amanda answered. The plane had taxied away from what appeared to be a small terminal and parked on the opposite end of the airport. A black helicopter sat fifty feet away.

"I'm Josh," he said. "We'll take you right to the resort."

Amanda didn't think Josh was older than twenty-five, maybe even younger. He wore a safari shirt with matching cargo shorts.

"It's nice to meet you, Josh. Are you the one taking me to see my son?"

"Yes, you'll be able to see him tomorrow."

"Why's that?" Amanda asked, trying to mask her disappointment and irritation.

"They're out on a challenge and won't be back until then," he answered, as if that was all that needed to be said. "Is there any more luggage?"

Amanda motioned to a bag she'd set at her feet. "This is it."

He reached over and picked it up. "Great, then right this way."

"Where are we?" Amanda asked, as he led her across the tarmac toward the waiting helicopter.

"Can't answer that."

"Can you at least tell me why I have to fly in that?" Amanda pointed nervously toward the chopper.

Josh smiled. "You're full of questions, aren't you? He's not on this island, but a smaller one, more isolated. It's quicker to fly over than taking a boat ride this time of night."

Amanda looked around. Beyond the immediate vicinity of the airport, there was nothing but a long stretch of sand and tropical foliage. The terminal didn't even have any markings that she could read from this far away. She still had no idea where she was.

Josh reached the helicopter and opened a back compartment, laying Amanda's bag inside. He closed the hatch and faced Amanda. "Even though you've been invited to join us, Mrs. Forrest, it's imperative that when you see Jack, you don't know where you are—where he is."

Amanda listened intently.

"You'll be kept in an isolated room for the night—no phones, no TV, no outside contact. At the appointed time, I'll come and get you, and you'll be able to see him."

Josh opened the helicopter's door and motioned for Amanda to climb in.

"We'll make sure you're fed and have whatever you need." Josh raised his voice to be heard over the whine of the turbines kicking up as the rotor starting spinning above them.

"But if you don't follow the rules," Josh continued in a serious tone, "*all* of them, you'll be sent back home and won't get to see your son at all."

Amanda looked at him as he gave her a smile. "Is that all?"

"That's it," he said.

Amanda felt like the situation was getting out of control, but there was nothing she could do but go along for the ride and keep praying.

After finding the medic and convincing him that several extra-strength aspirin were in order, Jack made his way to the banquet room to see what the evening meal offered. Evidently, most of the contestants had already eaten, since the room was empty except for Maria sitting alone. She was also dressed all in black—and still looking incredible.

Jack picked up a plate and piled on a healthy salad: a mixture of carrots, broccoli, and cauliflower, and the main course that evening, mahi-mahi.

"How'd you sleep?" Jack asked, as he approached Maria's table.

She looked up at him and smiled. "OK, I guess. Why'd you leave?"

Jack grinned. "It seemed the proper thing to do."

"Thanks for the blanket."

"Not a problem," Jack said, as he sat down beside her.

"And how did you sleep?"

"Not well. I've had this headache ever since I woke up."

Maria gently placed her palm against his cheek. "I'm sorry."

Jack placed his hand over hers. "I just took some aspirin. Hopefully, it'll kick in soon."

He let his hand rest on hers for a second, then pulled away. She slid her hand down, letting it rest on his leg. Jack's mind flashed back to his thoughts when he'd woken—about her and Kathryn. He felt like he needed to clear the air with her, but he didn't know how to approach it.

"How did you sleep?" Jack asked after he'd swallowed.

"You already asked that," Maria said with a giggle.

"Oh, yeah." She was getting to him.

"I woke up wishing you'd stayed." Maria's face reddened as her eyes dropped.

Jack smiled warmly. "Maria …"

She must have sensed something in his eyes. "What?"

"I don't think we should get carried away in the middle of this game."

Maria recoiled slightly and pulled her hand off his thigh. She lowered her head. "I'm sorry, I didn't mean to ..."

"Listen," Jack whispered, not wanting the staff to hear—then realized there were cameras and microphones everywhere anyway. "It's nothing you've done—you've been perfect." He scooted closer and waited for her to look up at him. "You are so incredibly beautiful, and one of the most desirable women I've ever met."

"Then what's the problem?" Her voice had grown colder, matching her eyes.

"There isn't a problem." Jack wished he could drop this whole conversation. "It's just that any relationship we develop here isn't based on reality. We're in the midst of this ... game. We're being manipulated, pushed together in so many ways. I don't want either of us to feel something, and then when this week is over, we go our separate ways and never see each other again."

"That doesn't have to happen." Maria's eyes began to water.

Jack sighed. "No, I guess not, but ..."

"Jack, last night was something very special," Maria said with her eyes glued to his.

"Nothing happened last night."

"Exactly. Any other guy I've ever been with before would have tried something. They would have taken advantage of the late hour and my tiredness. You didn't. You were the perfect gentleman."

Jack broke into a sly smile. "Don't think it didn't cross my mind."

Maria tilted her head. "Then you did ... think about it?"

Jack laughed. "I wouldn't be a red-blooded American male if I hadn't thought about it, being with you as much as I have the past few days. But that's part of what I'm trying to explain. I've got another priority that drives my decisions—something more than just being a perfect gentleman."

"What?"

The doors to the restaurant opened and the rest of the contestants barged into the room. Several staff members and camera crews followed behind them. Their intimate conversation was over.

Jack turned back toward her and shrugged.

"You're off the hook for now," Maria smirked. "But believe me, we'll finish this later."

"Good evening, contestants." Vince walked up to his podium as everyone in the room quieted down. "I hope you've all had some decent rest."

Jack glanced around the room. It was down to five people. He knew where Eddie stood. And he knew where Maria, Hugh, and probably even Tara stood. It was four to one, but could they manage to get Eddie out this round?

"Before I explain your next challenge and the beautiful matching outfits you're all wearing," Vince said with a chuckle, "we've completed our first wave of personal challenges, and it's time for an update."

Jack leaned back and muttered, "Oh, brother," before he could stop himself. Evidently, Mr. Roberts had pulled the extension he'd given Jack to complete his challenge—one he had no intention of completing anyway.

It was time to face the consequences.

He looked over at Maria. A look of fear flashed across her face, and she looked away. She must have not completed her challenge either. He wondered how she was going to react when she found out what his was.

"First of all, we have Hugh." Vince grinned. "Would you care to share with us your challenge?"

Hugh smiled and stood. "I was supposed to steal one thousand dollars worth of poker chips from Eddie."

"What the ..." Eddie said, standing up.

"Are you serious?" Tara gasped beside him.

"And did you accomplish your assignment?" Vince asked.

"Yes," Hugh answered with a sly grin before he sat back down.

"What do you mean 'yes?' " Eddie was right up in his face.

"Calm down, Eddie," Vince warned. "It's all part of the game."

Eddie spun around toward Vince. "He ripped me off, man! I coulda still been in the game if I had another G."

"You touch him, you're off the island," Vince threatened, then looked at Hugh. "We have it all on tape, Mr. Liang. Very impressive."

"You've just jumped to the top of my list," Eddie growled at Hugh.

"Eddie," Vince cautioned, and then brightened. "Care to go next?"

Eddie didn't respond.

"Eddie?" Vince prompted.

"Mine seems a bit weird now," Eddie said.

"I know. Go on."

Eddie shrugged. "My challenge was to convince Stacy to spend the night in my bungalow."

Jack stared at Eddie in shock. It all made sense—his motive for pushing Stacy off the cliff. She must have refused.

"Needless to say," Eddie said uncomfortably, "I never got the chance to complete my challenge."

Jack wanted to jump up right there in the room and shout, *No, because you killed her, you jerk!* Eddie was the focal point of everything that had gone wrong on the island so far. He had motive for the bungalow fire—he hated Jack. He had opportunity and motive for Stacy's "accident," and now she was dead. Jack wanted desperately to know what the tapes showed when Stacy left the casino.

"So, Eddie," Vince stated, "you still failed."

"Hey." Eddie's anger flared. "That's not my fault, man. We'd made plans as soon as the gambling was over."

Jack watched in amazement. He sure wasn't a good liar. So much of him wanted to confront Eddie right then and there, but that would risk retaliation. Jack glanced around the room—with all the camera gear and Eddie's every action being recorded, how could the production people not know exactly what was going on?

"Sorry, Eddie, you failed your challenge." Vince wouldn't budge. "But you're not the only one—Tara?"

Tara looked down, scratching quickly at the base of her neck. She stood slowly. "My challenge was impossible," she argued. "I was supposed to convince the women to all vote for the same guy when we kicked Denny out."

Maria looked at her with mouth agape. "Is that why you were pushing me so hard?"

Tara nodded. "But you wouldn't budge, and neither would Stacy." She sat back down.

Jack pondered the new development. Would he be thrown in with Tara and Eddie to be voted off for not completing their personal challenges? He thought back to when he'd been given his challenge—in his room, alone. When could Tara have received hers, if the decision for the women to vote on who gets kicked out after the triathlon was such a spur-of-the-moment thing? At least, that's what the producers had wanted them to think.

"That leaves us with Maria and Jack," Vince stated. "Who wants to go next?"

Jack lowered his head. He didn't want to go through this, either for Maria's sake or his.

"One of you was successful; the other failed," Vince added. "Maria, why don't you tell us what you were forced to do."

Jack noticed how Vince had stressed the word *forced.* He hadn't used that word with anybody else, and his inflection made it sound ominous.

Maria took a final look at Jack, her eyes trying to convey something to him. He wasn't sure what she was trying to indicate. But Jack was sure that whatever it was, he wasn't going to like what she had to say.

She stood, taking one step away from the table and separating from him a bit. "My challenge was to seduce Jack enough ..." She paused, too embarrassed to look at Jack, and instead kept her eyes on Vince. "To make him kiss me."

51

The flight was actually enjoyable—Amanda was amazed as she stared out of the window. The view, flying across the blue-green sea as the sun dipped below the horizon, was one of the most beautiful sights she'd ever witnessed. As they approached the rocky cliff, she could spot the lush resort sitting on top. The colored lights hitting the buildings, and the tiki torches illuminating the pathways and pool area, were nothing short of spectacular. The cliff top seemed to beckon to her. Somewhere below, Jack was in Zeke's clutches—and with God's help, she was going to free him.

• • •

"Oh, that must have been difficult," Hugh said with a laugh, after hearing Maria's admission.

Jack looked up at her, but she didn't turn her head. The kiss was part of her challenge? She played him that night. She needed to talk, worried about Eddie. He replayed the kiss in his mind, how she'd leaned into him—pouted when he'd turned it into a hug—until he fell for it.

"That's not even a challenge," Eddie chided. "All she had to do was get a kiss? What's fair about that?"

"Nobody said this game was fair," Vince responded.

The sounds of a helicopter approaching filled the room, interrupting the exchange between the contestants. Jack tracked the sound as it flew over the banquet room and apparently landed on the grass area by the pool. Unfortunately, the windows on that side of the room had the drapes drawn. He couldn't see who was arriving.

"Just some expected guests." Vince answered the unspoken question, then turned back toward Maria. "Getting back to your challenge, Maria. Were you successful?"

"Oh, she was successful, all right," Jack answered for her.

She spun toward Jack, her eyes pooling with unshed tears. "It wasn't like that, Jack."

"You played me perfectly." Jack couldn't stop himself. Here he was conflicted about how far the relationship had grown and to her, it was all just part of the game. "What was our time on the cliff, extra credit?"

Maria couldn't have acted any more hurt if Jack had slapped her across the face. Her eyes sunk, the color drained instantly. "You don't understand," she cried and turned away.

"And now that leads us to you, Jack." Vince recaptured the moment. "What was your challenge?"

Jack stood, his anger overcoming his embarrassment. "To make Maria sleep with me."

Maria snapped back to stare at Jack, the anger flaring in her eyes. Then she turned to face the head table, shouting at Vince, "How dare you!"

Vince smiled, as Maria stepped closer to his podium. Jack could just see his wheels turning, knowing they were getting great footage for the show. This would probably be the teaser for the end of the episode the week before. Jack was proud of Maria; her outburst was righteous, her anger pure.

"You have no right to demean me or Jack in that way," she yelled, stepping right in front of Vince. "*Ultimate Challenge* or not, that was way over the line."

Vince didn't back down. "You didn't seem that upset with Eddie's challenge."

"I wasn't Eddie's challenge!"

"Now that would have been sweet!" Eddie remarked.

Maria turned and stared at Eddie with a vicious scowl.

Vince seemed to be enjoying the moment. "So, Jack, don't keep us in suspense. Did you succeed?"

Jack rolled his eyes. "No—I knew the minute I read your challenge I wouldn't do it. If that gets me kicked out of your little game, then so be it. I'm not willing to sell myself, or Maria's integrity—even for ten million dollars. I agree with Maria, your request was way out of line."

"Very well said, Jack," Vince mocked, while clapping lightly. "However, that doesn't let you off the hook."

"Wait a minute, I'm not done," Maria said. She turned back to Jack. "Exactly how was your challenge worded?"

Jack rubbed his chin, trying to get the exact words. "I think it just read, 'Convince Maria to sleep with you.' "

"You sure?" Maria asked.

"Yeah." Jack nodded. "But I tore up the stupid thing right after I read it."

"Then you haven't lost." Maria grinned mischievously and turned back to Vince. "Check your tapes, Vince. My room—last night. I slept with Jack."

"What?" Jack asked. But the moment he said it, he realized what Maria was alluding to.

"I've seen the tapes." Vince pursed his lips. "Nothing happened."

"Oh, don't be so sure." Maria turned and walked back to the table. "We were talking, Jack rubbed my shoulders a bit, and I fell asleep, right on the couch. Jack covered me with a blanket and left the room.

But for awhile, however long he stayed in the room, I was sleeping with Jack!"

Hugh broke out laughing, and Jack couldn't help but chuckle. She was right. To the letter of the challenge, Jack had completed his.

"I don't know what to say," Vince stammered.

"There's nothing to say." Maria held her arms out. "I confess, I slept with Jack."

"But that's not what we meant," Vince argued.

"It doesn't matter." Maria was on a roll now. "He convinced me to sleep with him—it was the backrub that did it. Very tricky, Jack. Nicely done."

Maria smiled at him, then took her seat. She had put on quite a performance, and one that just might save his position in the game. But all the fears about their relationship in the midst of this game came crashing home. How could he trust her after this? How could she trust him?

The stupid game.

Vince bit his lip for a second, then spoke. "So, you're saying that falling asleep on the couch while Jack is rubbing your shoulders is the same as sleeping with him?"

"Yes," Maria said flatly. "I slept—with him."

"No," Vince countered. "We meant for you to have sex with him."

"That's not what your challenge said." Maria grinned.

Vince rolled his eyes. "Jack wasn't sleeping with you. It doesn't count."

"Yes, it does," Jack retaliated, stepping forward. "I remember the wording exactly. *Convince Maria to sleep with you.* That's what it said—that's what I did."

"Just a minute ago, you said you failed," Eddie shouted.

"A minute ago, I thought I had. But Maria's right."

The room sat in silence for a minute.

The white phone beside Vince rang. He picked it up, obviously now connected to the producers. Without saying a word, Vince listened, then set the phone back down.

"It seems our producers have ruled. Jack completed his challenge."

"That's not right!" Eddie stood again and shouted. "I object."

"This isn't a court of law," Vince laughed.

The doors to the banquet hall burst open. All eyes turned in their direction as three men in uniform marched into the room. Two of them brandished automatic weapons strapped over their shoulders and seemed to be of lower rank. The man in the middle had gold braids on his shoulders and only carried a pistol attached to his belt. The uniforms were dark green: military looking, not police-like. The three all had dark skin, matching the resort's staff. Jack tried to place the nationality. They weren't quite as dark as most African-Americans, possibly closer to Jamaican, or some other Caribbean island.

"Who's in charge here?" the one with the braids demanded, in heavily accented English. Jack couldn't place its origin, but it had the formality of the British Isles.

Everyone looked up at Vince, as did the three men.

"I guess that would be me," Vince said. "What's going on?"

"We must speak," the official said, then turned and stepped out of the room.

Vince eyed the soldiers that stayed, suspiciously guarding the room, then addressed the contestants. "If you'll excuse me." He stepped off of the platform that his podium sat on and walked to the back of the room. Jack took the diversion to quietly slip back down into his chair. Maria followed suit.

The soldiers stepped aside to allow Vince to walk through the doorway, then came together shoulder to shoulder, pulling their automatic weapons from off their shoulders and holding them chest high to guard the door.

"What's going on?" Hugh whispered to Jack.

"Silence!" one of the soldiers shouted, also in a heavy accent.

Jack shrugged, not wanting to risk the repercussions of answering him vocally.

The room waited in strained stillness.

Jack looked around the room. All the contestants seemed anxious. The resort staff didn't move a muscle, but stood quietly where they'd been when the soldiers had interrupted the session.

After a few minutes, Vince walked back into the room, followed by the military leader. They whispered something to each other before the soldiers turned and exited. Vince walked through the room quietly, then stepped up to his podium.

"Nothing to worry about." Vince's words contradicted his furrowed brow. "It seems there is a minor conflict brewing on the island. Some gunfire has broken out in the village on the north shore. General Manfried has assured me that they are getting things under control, but they wanted us to be aware of the situation."

"Did he say what kind of conflict?" Hugh asked.

"He was rather vague about that," Vince answered.

"Hey," Tara said, "if there's some political unrest out there, I think we have a right to know."

"Under normal circumstances, you'd think so," Vince answered. "But part of the charm of this game is to keep you guessing."

"Forget your stupid game." Jack could feel the surge of anger deep within as he interrupted. "We've lost Stacy. A bungalow burned down—what was supposed to be my bungalow, nearly causing Maria's death. Now armed soldiers show up, and all you're worried about is the game? Are you guys crazy?"

"It's all under control, Jack," Vince said. "Just a few more days and we'll have our new champion."

52

Amanda relaxed with her back against the headboard, reading her Bible. They had taken everything out of the room that might have given a clue where they were located: no telephone, no television, no magazines or books of any kind—no clues whatsoever. When the helicopter was coming in for their landing, she'd spotted a green, military-style jeep driving toward the front entrance of the resort. Josh had ignored them, but as they got out of the helicopter, three armed soldiers walked briskly toward the main building.

It didn't help set her at ease.

She knew Jack was somewhere on this island, and she wanted nothing more than to be with him and figure a way out of this mess. But she also knew that somewhere within the buildings of this resort was Zeke Roberts—and that scared her more than anything. She had no desire to see him again, but seemingly had no way that she could avoid it either.

The one-bedroom suite was beautiful, elegantly decorated in tropical themes and wicker furniture. She'd freshened up first, then tried to relax on the bed. If she hadn't carried along her pocket Bible, there would have been nothing for her to do but sit and stare at the walls.

Josh had promised to return with a plate of food shortly, as he ordered her not to leave the room for any reason. She felt like a prisoner. And it helped her better understand Paul's frame of reference in the section of Colossians she was reading:

> *Devote yourselves to prayer, being watchful and thankful. And pray for us, too, that God may open a door for our message, so that we may proclaim the mystery of Christ, for which I am in chains. Pray that I may proclaim it clearly, as I should. Be wise in the way you act toward outsiders; make the most of every opportunity. Let your conversation be always full of grace, seasoned with salt, so that you may know how to answer everyone.*

Amanda went back and reread the portion of Scripture, once again amazed at Paul's passion for spreading the message God had entrusted to him. Even in prison or "in chains," as he worded it, he was asking for people to pray—not for his freedom, but for him to be able to proclaim his message clearly.

It humbled her. And it made her wonder what God had in store for her through this whole ordeal.

She continued reading. The last few verses seemed to leap from the page as her eyes passed over them a second time:

> *Be wise in the way you act toward outsiders; make the most of every opportunity. Let your conversation be always full of grace, seasoned with salt, so that you may know how to answer everyone.*

A picture in her mind formed of Zeke, the last person she wanted to think about. She was here for Jack and Jack alone. But the words she'd read seemed to be sinking deep within her—*make the most of every opportunity; let your conversation be full of grace, seasoned with salt.*

Amanda sighed, shaking her head as her heart opened to God's prompting. Praying silently for strength, she looked up toward the ceiling, as a tear formed at the corner of her eye.

She didn't notice the camera pointed right at her through the fake smoke alarm hanging in the corner above.

"Now it's time to move on to the next challenge." Vince stepped away from his podium, and moved over to the large video screen they'd used on the first night to embarrassingly show Jack's failure to get to the machete first. The screen came to life, revealing a detailed map of the island that showed a small village to the north of the resort.

"This is Martiese, a small fishing village about five kilometers from us," Vince explained. "Your challenge this evening is to make your way into the village and complete *The Ultimate Challenge* scavenger hunt."

The black clothing finally made sense to Jack.

"You'll be given a list of items that must be collected and brought back to the resort," Vince continued. "The last one back here—or those who don't bring back all the required items—will be sent home."

"What about the personal challenges?" Hugh interrupted.

"Glad you asked, Hugh. I was just getting to that. Those who failed their personal challenge, namely Eddie and Tara, will be given additional items to collect, making their task that much more difficult."

Eddie swore, obviously not worrying about letting his displeasure show.

Jack wondered what kind of items they would have to search for. Sneaking through a foreign village in the dead of night wasn't exactly something Jack was looking forward to.

"And on this mission," Vince added, "we won't be sending along any camera crews—that would be too obvious for the townspeople. We have these vests for each of you to wear."

Vince reached into a box sitting beside the screen and pulled out a black sleeveless vest. "They're equipped with infrared and standard miniature cameras sewn into the shoulders. We'll be able to monitor your progress, and record everything for the show, without having a crew along with you. We also have helmets that will have a camera facing back toward your face to get that great close-up for the show."

Vince grabbed one of the helmets with a weird extension where a small lipstick camera was perched coming off the top.

"We're going to look ridiculous," Maria commented.

"Well, the whole point of this exercise is not to be seen," Vince said. "If you get caught, you lose."

"What about the soldiers that were just here," Tara asked. "Aren't we heading right into the middle of the conflict?"

Vince flashed his million-dollar smile and pointed to the map. "Actually, the general was referring to another village on the tip of the island—up here. You'll be in no danger."

"Like we haven't heard that before," Jack muttered.

"This is it," Vince continued. "We're getting down to the wire. And just to give you something a bit more to think about ..." Vince stepped away from the screen so that he wasn't blocking it, as the graphic representation of the island faded away and was replaced by five different images from rooms similar to their bungalows. Each picture showed people in the rooms, whether they were sitting on a bed, in a chair, or doing something in the kitchen.

Jack analyzed the images: the first one had an African–American man sprawled on the couch; the second had a beautiful young girl with an older woman sitting at the dinette table; the third had a woman reading on a bed—then it hit him. The woman was his mom.

She was on the island. Jack could hear the other contestants recognizing their loved ones as well.

"We've brought members of your family here to the island to join our little adventure," Vince stated with a large grin, seeming to love the reaction he was seeing on the faces of the contestants.

Jack had a hard time focusing on the words. He was too shocked at seeing his mother calmly relaxing on the bed, reading her Bible. The other two images showed an older Asian couple and a single white man. Each of the images seemed to match with one of the remaining contestants.

Jack figured he was getting his first look at Teresa, Maria's four-year-old daughter. She was as cute as Jack thought she'd be, but his eyes kept tracking back to his mom.

Suddenly the images vanished, and Vince once again had everyone's full attention.

"I want to make this next point very clear, so listen carefully." His voice took on a seriousness that Jack hadn't heard in the three days of the challenge. "Each of you has a secret in your past."

Jack's stomach dropped, as if he'd driven over a small hill on a road and suddenly gone weightless. What secret could Vince possibly be referring to?

"The people you saw on the screen are here at the resort," Vince informed them. "They either have a deep secret that you have never been told, or they've been kept in the dark on something you've hidden from them."

Maria gasped, lowering her head and closing her eyes.

Jack reached over and took her hand in his, thinking he would comfort her, but finding solace himself in the warmth of her fingers intertwining with his.

"The four of you that make it through the scavenger hunt tonight ... will have to face that secret. You'll have the choice to have it revealed on national television—or the option to go home. Because, the only way to keep it hidden, is to forfeit your position and lose the chance at the ten million dollars."

53

The room was as quiet as a schoolhouse on Labor Day. No one said a word as Vince waited for the cameras to record each of the contestant's shocked expressions.

"There is one way to protect your family, however. That is if you come in first tonight," Vince said, finally giving them a dash of hope. "Then your secret will remain safely between you and your loved ones."

Jack felt Maria squeeze his hand. He figured there was something she was deathly afraid would be revealed to Teresa, or her mother, or maybe both. He looked at the other contestants. Hugh looked troubled, with furrowed brow, keeping his eyes on Vince. Eddie looked defiant, like whatever it was, he could handle it. And then there was Tara. She looked as devastated as Maria.

Jack wasn't sure how he felt. He couldn't think of any dark secrets he'd been holding from his mom with his quiet life as a schoolteacher, so it must be something she had never told him. He couldn't imagine what it could be, but he knew one thing: he wouldn't let this game hurt her in any way. He was happily surprised the personal challenge didn't get him kicked out, but he'd still forfeit his position in a heartbeat before he'd let them expose his mom.

Vince stood before them, a smirk coming over his face. "We thought it would add a bit of intrigue for this evening's competition to let you in on the next phase of *The Ultimate Challenge.* Any questions?"

It took a moment before any of the contestants spoke up. It was Eddie. "What do we have to find?"

"Ten items." Vince motioned to the screen, which came back to life. "Twelve, if you didn't complete the assigned personal challenge."

There was a list of ten items lined out on the left edge of the screen, with two additional objects listed at the bottom under the heading "Penalty Items." The first ten: a live chicken, a coconut, a beer bottle, a fishing hook, a fishing net, a pack of cigarettes, a bathing suit, a child's toy, a folding chair, and a tire. The penalty items were a garden tool and a bicycle.

It took a moment for the contestants to read down the list. A few loud sighs could be heard mixed in with a couple of chuckles.

"How are we supposed to get this stuff back to the resort?" Hugh asked.

"Each of you will be supplied with a van and a driver. You will determine where the van parks as you go about the village collecting your items. Sneak the items into the van, and when you've completed your list, get back to the resort. First one back here with everything gets the exemption from their deep, dark family secret."

"I've got a question," Jack spoke up.

"Sure, Jack. What is it?"

"You mentioned the word 'sneak'. I take it we aren't to enlist the villagers' help in getting the items, is that correct?"

Vince smiled. "That is correct. You'd have a hard time convincing them to give up their chickens."

Laughs filtered through the room.

"I also assume this is a pretty poor fishing village?"

"Yes," Vince answered.

"Then, why are we taking these things from them? It seems to me, losing some of these items might be quite a hardship on these people?"

"That's probably a very good reason for you to avoid getting caught."

"Then you're asking us to steal," Jack stated.

"Well, I think Jack finally gets it," Eddie smirked.

"Your concern for the natives of this island is touching, Jack," Vince said flatly. "But it doesn't change your challenge." He turned to the rest of the contestants. "In the event you get into any trouble with the locals, your driver will be there to help you out; but, like getting assistance from any of the crew, it will also mean your disqualification. Everybody understand?"

The rest of the contestants nodded while Jack stared at Vince and shook his head. It looked like he was in for quite an interesting night.

"Mrs. Forrest?" The voice came from the other side of the door, after a couple of knocks.

Amanda pulled herself off the bed and walked to the front door, suddenly realizing how hungry she was.

It was Josh, but there was no food in his hands.

"Hello," Amanda said. "I thought you were bringing me back something to eat."

Josh nodded. "I did say that, but instead, I bring you an invitation."

Amanda's smile thinned. "To what?"

"Our executive producer has asked for the pleasure of your company for dinner." Josh smiled, as if he had just bestowed upon her the highest honor in the land.

Amanda felt her stomach drop, and was sure her face had just turned ashen white, as Josh gave her the strangest look.

"Are you all right?" he asked.

Amanda tried to recover quickly. "I'm fine." *How can I get out of this?* she thought.

"Well, are you ready to go?"

"Now?"

"Sure. Aren't you hungry after your long day of travel?"

I was a second ago.

In the midst of her panic, the Scripture she'd just read pierced through her thoughts. God was trying to speak to her—but at the moment, the last thing on Amanda's mind was listening. She just wanted to flee.

"If you'd give me just a minute," Amanda requested, then turned and quickly headed toward her bathroom.

"Take your time, I'll just wait out here," Josh called out after her.

"Jack, I can't go through with this," Maria whispered in a panic. Her eyes were wide, her breathing labored. He hadn't seen her anywhere near this upset since they'd arrived.

Vince had ended the briefing, and each of the contestants was to head out to the portico of the resort and get into his or her van. The race would begin soon.

"What do you mean?" Jack asked.

"The next challenge," Maria answered. "There's something my mother and Teresa don't know."

Jack looked down at her and tried to smile reassuringly. "I kind of figured that."

"I don't know what to do."

"I'd say don't worry about it until you have to. I'm fighting the same thing about my mom."

Maria looked up at him, her eyes wide. "Really?"

"Not that I've hidden something from her, but there must be something she doesn't want revealed. I won't let that happen."

"Oh." Maria dropped her head.

"There's only one way for us to protect them," Jack added.

"Come in first?"

"Yeah."

"But we both can't come in first," Maria said with a sinking tone.

"I know."

"Let's go, folks," Vince yelled back into the banquet room. Only Jack and Maria were still inside.

"Coming," Jack called back, then turned to Maria. "We've got to get going—just give it all you've got. Don't think about the next step."

She looked up at him, tears pooling in her eyes. "I'll try."

Jack smiled reassuringly. "Oh, and Maria, I'm sorry about what I said—you know, about the kiss and extra credit and all."

Maria nodded. "Please believe me, Jack, it wasn't what you thought."

"I know," Jack said. "At least I think I do. I just got so upset at their manipulation—of both of us."

Maria didn't answer but nodded silently, wiping the tears away from her eyes.

They walked out together, seeing five identical white Toyota vans lining the circular drive at the front of the resort. Eddie stood by the first one, with Hugh and Tara taking the next two. Jack politely motioned for Maria to take the next one, leaving him the last one.

Jack sat down in the passenger seat, meeting his driver for the first time—a young native named Palau. He didn't look old enough to drive.

A production assistant walked up to Jack, helping him with the camera vest and the silly-looking camera helmet. Once he made sure the recording machines had been turned on and were working properly, he turned toward Vince and gave him an "OK" signal.

"There is a list of the items in each of your vans," Vince called out through a bullhorn. "Remember, get all of them into the van, do not get caught, and the first one back here is off the hook with the family secret. The last one is going home. Good luck."

As Jack closed the door, Palau started the engine. He revved the motor, looking back toward Jack with a mischievous grin. Jack smiled back, grabbing the seat belt and buckling in.

"Ready ..." Vince held his right arm up. "Go!"

Eddie's van took off with the other four following close behind. Palau punched the accelerator, turning Jack's van to the left as if he could pass Maria's van on the one-lane road. When the van instantly started scraping against the bushes lining the path, he pushed down hard on the brake and fell back in line.

Palau laughed. "We back first," he said in his broken English. "You see."

Jack chuckled nervously. "Just get me back alive, and I'll be happy."

Amanda walked with Josh along the pathway, ignoring the lush landscape around the resort. The flames from the tiki torches cast eerie shadows off the bungalows and shrubbery, adding to her anxiety as she approached the man she hadn't seen in twenty-eight years.

It had taken more than ten minutes in her bathroom to calm herself. She kept going over the Scripture in her mind. God must have planted those words in her just before being asked to meet with Zeke for a reason. He didn't want her to lash out at him at first sight. But how could she stand before him and be full of grace?

That was impossible. God had asked more of her than she could deliver.

This might be the most difficult test she'd suffered since the whole issue with Zeke in the first place—*her* ultimate challenge. Could she stand through it? Would God be faithful to her?

She couldn't delay any longer. Josh was waiting.

She'd applied a fresh layer of makeup, brushed her hair, and glanced at herself in the mirror—comparing the Amanda that stood before her to the twenty-one year old college junior that Zeke would remember. She was still within twelve pounds and one-and-a-half dress sizes since then. Her hair color was the same, thanks to Clairol, and she thought the wrinkles along the edges of her eyes were minimal for a forty-eight year old. All in all, not too bad. Then she silently scolded herself for even caring how she looked for him. After what he'd done to her, he didn't deserve it.

Maybe that was it though, she grinned. Wanting, *needing* to show him what he'd passed up—what he could have had as a partner all these years.

Amanda sighed, trying to calm the conflicting emotions. *God, be with me*, she prayed.

"How well do you know the village?" Jack asked, as the van weaved back and forth down the road leading to the small village.

"Very good," Palau answered. "Like back of foot."

"Back of hand," Jack corrected.

"Yes." Palau smiled. "Like back of hand, sorry."

"It's OK," Jack said, smiling to himself. The kid seemed determined to help Jack with his challenge, and driving like a maniac seemed to be part of his plan. "Take me to the richest part."

Palau looked at him, confused.

"Watch where you're going!" Jack screamed, as the road turned sharply to the right.

He turned hard, keeping the front wheels on the road, but the back left wheel slid off into the loose rocks along the edge. The wheels spun for a second before they finally grabbed and propelled the van back onto the road.

Palau drove on as if nothing had happened.

"I want to go," Jack said slower, as if that would help the language barrier, "to the part of the village where the people have more money."

"All the same," Palau answered. "Everybody fish or work here."

"Then get me close to where the boats are docked," Jack sighed. He'd hoped to pull this off by playing a bit of Robin Hood.

"OK, man." Palau nodded up and down excitedly. He was in it to win.

As they approached the main building of the resort, Amanda wanted to run. She couldn't do it. She didn't want to face him.

"It's a beautiful evening, isn't it?" Josh asked innocently.

Amanda didn't respond right away, until Josh repeated himself. "Yes, it's lovely. Can you tell me where my son is right now?"

"Only that the contestants are away from the resort on one of the challenges. They'll return sometime late tonight, and I believe you'll be able to see him tomorrow."

"I'd prefer to see him now," Amanda stated.

"I understand, but I have my orders—and he really isn't here anyway. Besides, you're in for quite a special evening."

"Really?"

"Certainly," Josh said excitedly. "Mr. Roberts is an amazing man. It's been my dream to work with him. I would think a dinner with him would be an incredible experience."

"Maybe you'd like to take my place."

Josh laughed as if she was joking, then walked up and opened the big glass door that led into the banquet hall. "Right this way."

He led her away from the large room where the meals had been served to the contestants and brought her to a smaller room on the other side of the entryway.

"Please." He stopped at the door, opening it to allow her through. "Have a pleasant meal."

Amanda stepped into the room and the door closed behind her. The room was lit only by candlelight—maybe a couple dozen scattered about the room. A single table was at the center, draped in a white tablecloth, with a setting for two laid out in fine china. Along one side, was a long window overlooking the bay, the moonlight adding to the flickering candles.

Standing beside the table was Zeke, his hand outstretched in an offering for her to come join him. The sight of him brought back waves of memories. He hadn't changed that much—a bit wider at the waist maybe, but still in good shape. A little graying at the temples, if the light wasn't playing tricks on her, but still very handsome.

"Amanda," he nearly whispered. "I'm so glad to see you again."

She stepped toward him, having no idea what would happen next, but loathing him inside. Her head lowered slightly as she acknowledged him, yet she remained silent.

"Please, have a seat." He politely pulled her chair back.

She stood next to him, studying his face, his lips, the familiar nose, his eyes. They seemed hopeful.

"You look well, Ezekiel," she finally said.

One side of his mouth tilted upward, his "half-smile," as she'd termed it. "No one has called me that in nearly thirty years."

"It's been a long time," Amanda agreed, taking her seat so he'd move away to the other side of the table.

He helped push her chair in and then walked to his chair. "And you look incredible," he said, as his eyes sparkled. "As beautiful as the day we met."

"Albeit a few decades older," Amanda added, struggling to stay calm. "To what do I owe this evening?"

"I'm sure you have many questions," he replied, dodging the first one. A waiter appeared from the darkness. "But I'm also sure you're famished after the long flight in."

A dark-skinned man in a tuxedo stepped up beside her and placed a fresh green salad before her.

"What kind of dressing would you like, madam?"

"Whatever you have is fine."

"It's our house vinaigrette," he smiled, placing a small cup of it beside her salad.

"And for you, Mr. Roberts?"

"Italian, please."

"As you wish," the waiter responded, placing both a salad plate and a cup of Italian dressing in front of him.

"I'll be back with some hot bread," he said.

They were alone again.

Amanda bowed her head and prayed silently, not caring what Zeke would think. She needed to collect her thoughts more than ask God's blessing on the meal. But she did both, and, once again, asked for His direction.

To his credit, Zeke politely sat there, not saying a word until her head popped up.

"Interesting," he said. "I don't remember you doing that before."

"I didn't," Amanda said matter-of-factly. "A lot has changed."

"I'm sure it has," Zeke sighed. He appeared nearly as uncomfortable as Amanda. She hoped he was more so.

"I guess I should start with 'I'm sorry,' " Zeke said.

Amanda picked up the dressing and poured it around the top of her salad—anything to keep her hands busy.

"It was really awful what I did to you, and how we parted," he continued. "I'm truly sorry."

Words she cried herself to sleep hoping to hear twenty-eight years before now seemed so hollow. She stared at her lettuce, moving the pieces around with her fork, not yet ready to take a bite.

She looked up at him. His expression did portray a certain amount of sorrow—his eyes soft, the wrinkles above his eyebrows deepening as he held her gaze. Just let him talk, she told herself, as she forked in a mouthful of salad.

"I wished I'd never let you go." He reached across the table to touch her hand.

Amanda pulled away reflexively. He moved his hand back, emotional pain creasing his face.

"Why am I here?" Amanda asked. "Do you expect me to run into your arms after all these years?"

"No," Zeke answered. "I don't know what to expect. This is awkward for me ..."

"Like it's not for me?" Amanda stated flatly. She forced herself to stay in control, trying to run the words of Paul through her brain to keep her calm.

"I know," Zeke said warmly. "And I'm trying to apologize to you. You don't know how many times I've thought about you over the years—what we would've had between us, what should've been."

"Was that after wife number one, two, or three?" Amanda stared across the table.

Before he could respond, the waiter returned with a basket of bread and a bottle of wine. He presented the label to both of them, and Zeke smiled proudly. Amanda just shrugged. They sat silently as the waiter went through the wine-opening ritual, until he had poured them both a glass, and left.

"So, you've kept track of me?" Zeke grinned.

"Actually, no. Just a quick Internet search when I found out you were behind bringing Jack here."

"Oh, I see," Zeke sighed. "You're not making this very easy on me."

"Did you make it easy on me?" Amanda didn't raise her voice, but kept it warm, probing in a way that hopefully wasn't accusatorial.

"No, I'm sure I didn't."

"When you left me, everything I thought I loved left right along with you."

Zeke nodded without interrupting.

"But you couldn't take my baby away from me." Amanda fought back the lump swelling in her throat. "Heaven knows you tried, though."

"That's why I wanted to see you, Amanda." Zeke pulled his chair around the side of the table, moving closer to her. "I was wrong back then. I know it now."

Amanda grabbed her water glass to keep her hands busy and stared over the rim at him. "It took you nearly thirty years to realize that?"

"No," Zeke confessed. "I knew it back then, but didn't want to face up to it. I was convinced my career was more important."

"But you let me go."

"Yes." Zeke lowered his head. "I did."

"And left me alone," Amanda continued. Zeke just nodded. This wasn't what she'd expected.

"I didn't want to, but you wouldn't listen."

"I listened," Amanda argued. "I just wouldn't do what you wanted me to do."

"Right," Zeke said. "I was such an idiot."

They were getting too close to the pain. Amanda wanted nothing more than to flee as far away as she could. What good was his apology for demanding she get the abortion? It didn't change anything. There was so much he still didn't know. The more important issue was why was he forcing his way back into her life now?

Jack had Palau drive into a dirt alleyway a few hundred feet away from a bar that was open. A few of the locals were singing loudly and cheering as they passed the evening hours with drinks in hand. They were just a few hundred feet from the small cove that held most of the fishing boats anchored out in the water. There was a long dock jutting out into the bay with a couple of boats tied to it. The water was calm. There must have been some kind of natural wave break at the entrance to the cove.

"This good spot," Palau exclaimed.

Slipping out of the van while making sure the camera, extending off his helmet, didn't slam into anything, Jack ran quickly across the dirt road and down to the beach. He thought it would be best to pick up the easy stuff first to get a feel for sneaking around and acting like a thief. Then, he might have success with the more difficult items. He noticed another of the resort's white vans parked along the dirt road near the cove. He wondered whose it was.

Keeping his body low, he ran along the sand to the entrance of the dock. There was no gate, and, as far as he could tell, no local standing by guarding the boats. He sprinted down the wood planks, feeling like he was making too much noise. He stopped at the first boat, ducking down low by a pair of crates as he looked for any signs of life within. There were no lights on, but Jack saw some movement on the boat's deck. Somebody dressed all in black was searching the back section.

Jack decided to let them have this boat and sprinted farther down the dock to the next one. It was an old cabin cruiser with the pilot's wheel up above on a high deck. It had the name "Jumpin' Lady" painted on the back. Jack jumped aboard quietly, pulled out the small flashlight he'd been provided, and started looking along the deck for any loose fishing gear. He found a couple of rods and reels lying on the back end. He quickly pulled the Swiss army knife they'd given him out of his pocket and cut the fishing line at the end, gently placing the hook into his vest pocket.

One down, nine to go.

Along the side of the boat there was a storage bin that doubled as a seat. Jack lifted the padding up—no lock. He looked inside, moving the flashlight around briefly. He was in luck. There was a short handled net inside. He pulled it out, thinking it was time to get out of there before he was spotted. But sitting right in front of him was a small folding chair, like the kind he'd see back home on a picnic or at the park. The fabric was old and frayed at the edges, but would suit his needs just fine.

Jack folded it together and stepped out onto the dock. Keeping low, he ran back toward the beach. Before he could reach the first boat, the contestant in it stepped out onto the dock. It was Hugh.

"How's it going, Jack?" Hugh whispered.

"So far so good," Jack whispered back. He didn't like stopping to talk, feeling vulnerable out in the open. He kept his pace heading toward the sand. "Good luck."

"You too," Hugh returned, turning the opposite direction and heading deeper down the dock.

Jack figured he still needed to find more stuff. Maybe it had been a blessing that Hugh had already found the first boat. The fishhook was no big deal, but Jack felt bad about taking whoever's net and chair he'd just stolen. He made a mental note of the boat, praying he'd have the chance to come back to the dock and make amends when it was all over.

"It's as if you haven't changed." Zeke tried to move the discussion forward after an uncomfortable silence had enveloped him and Amanda. "I could see you just like you are now, sitting in the library studying."

The reference brought the image immediately to her mind.

"Remember how long it took you to even tell me your name?" Zeke asked.

Amanda couldn't hold back the smile. "You were persistent."

"I knew it would be worth it."

Zeke let the comment hang between them.

"I've changed a lot more than you know," Amanda finally said. "Not just on the outside."

"What do you mean?"

Amanda paused, the words filtering through her thoughts: *speak full of grace.* "We were so radical back in those college years—and they were a lot of fun. But reality hit." Amanda chuckled. "Kind of ironic, using that term to the king of reality television."

Zeke laughed from across the table. "Yeah, when you put it that way."

"I was so distraught after we broke up." Amanda dabbed at the corner of her mouth with her napkin, willing herself to stay focused. "I thought my life was over—my career plans shattered, the love of my life had just rejected me. I had nothing to live for, or so I thought."

Zeke chose not to respond, but just kept watching her intently.

"Except for the life growing inside of me." Amanda patted her belly without thinking, as if Jack was still there inside of her. "Something just wouldn't let me go through with what you wanted. I had no idea what that was until later in life. But I now know, it was God."

Zeke stared at her in disbelief. "God, huh?"

"Yeah, believe it or not, I found God—well, Jesus, to be more specific. But I think it was more like He found me."

Zeke seemed deep in thought, as he took a sip of his wine. "Have you had a good life?"

"An interesting question," Amanda thought out loud. "You know, I wouldn't change it for the world. This last year has been the hardest though, after losing Kevin."

"Please accept my condolences," Zeke said warmly.

"Thank you." Amanda took a drink of her water. "He was a lifeline after I dropped out of school. He was a wonderful husband and a terrific father to Jack."

Zeke smiled, his eyes lit up with a twinkle. "He's been pretty amazing, you know—Jack, that is. He's done well thus far into the game."

"And why is he here, Ezekiel?" Amanda asked. "Why are you doing this after all these years?"

Zeke placed his silverware down on the table and stared intently at Amanda. "You want to know the truth?"

"Of course I do."

"I wanted to see you."

"You couldn't have called?" Amanda shook her head, her voice took on an unwanted edge. "Dropped into town after some meeting in Chicago? You had to pull my son into your twisted reality television show and parade him to the world like this?"

"You wouldn't let me," Zeke said. "I've tried over the years to help with Jack—sent cards, gifts, money—they were all returned."

It was true. When Zeke had started finding success in television after graduation, he'd tracked down where Amanda was living and tried to offer support for Jack. She refused every time. Jack didn't even know about the attempts—or anything about their past relationship.

"You thought he was your son," Amanda said softly.

"Come on, Amanda." Zeke's voice rose. "Stop playing games. We both know he's my son. And you've kept me away for twenty-seven years. That's why you're here. That's why Jack is here. It's the only way I knew to bring us all together."

Amanda didn't say anything, looking at her past lover with detached numbness. Maybe it was God working—or maybe there was nothing left to feel after all the years of pushing the memories away.

"He's not your son, Ezekiel," she finally said.

"He's not my son?" Zeke stayed calm, his voice even. "We both know that's not true."

Amanda lowered her eyes. She couldn't look at him. After all these years, it was too difficult to face.

"Amanda?"

She closed her eyes, as if she could shut out the past.

"I should have the DNA results tomorrow." Zeke rose from his chair, moving it to the side of the table, right next to her. "Not for me, mind you, but for Jack. It'll prove beyond any doubt that Jack is my son—our child."

Amanda looked up at him, shaking her head. "No."

"I had some blood drawn the first day we picked up Jack. I don't want him to have any doubts. Too many years have gone by, Amanda." Zeke reached out and placed his hand on her arm. "Jack needs to know who his real father is."

Amanda pulled her arm away. "Jack's real father died twelve months ago."

"Not his biological father," Zeke argued.

"You don't understand," Amanda whispered.

"Then help me." Zeke rose, pacing around the table. "I know Kevin was Jack's dad, and from what I now know of Jack, you two did an incredible job raising him. But he should know who his flesh-and-blood father is, don't you think?"

"No," Amanda stated flatly. "I don't."

Zeke stared at her, dumbfounded.

"You gave up any claim to him when you handed me that three hundred dollars and demanded I get an abortion. 'Jack was just a mass of tissue,' you said, 'and you weren't going to let that stand in the way of your career.' I had to choose between the baby and you."

Zeke opened his mouth to speak, but Amanda silenced him with her hand.

"I remember those words as if you'd spoken them yesterday, Zeke. And when I finally made my choice—the most difficult one I'd ever made—you would have nothing to do with me. I never saw you again.

Now, twenty-eight years later, you think you can walk into my life and pick up as if that never happened?"

"Amanda," Zeke pleaded, "I haven't lived a day since then that I haven't regretted what happened, that I haven't wished I could take back every word I said. I so desperately wanted to have you by my side—with our son."

Amanda watched his face, amazed to see his eyes reddening.

"Why do you think I had three failed marriages?" Zeke continued. "No one could measure up to you—we had something so special. Every other relationship couldn't hold a candle to it. So, I became a workaholic. That was the only thing that I seemed to be good at, and it kept my mind off of you."

"I find that hard to believe," Amanda muttered.

"It's true. I wouldn't lie to you." Zeke's eyes confirmed his words. "I found out where you were a few years after we'd separated. Learned you'd gotten married, had a son. I kept track of everything he did—his birthdays, football victories—I even quietly slipped into his college graduation."

Amanda didn't know what to say to that.

Zeke walked toward her again, this time kneeling beside her chair. "I can't tell you how many times over the years I've thought about the day we met in the library, the moment you finally agreed to go out with me, our first kiss, our plans to get married after graduation … even the last day I saw you."

He paused, as if the memories were too raw. "And, as often as I dared, I dreamed about this day—when I could see you again, hear your voice, smell your hair, touch your skin."

He reached his hand out toward her but stopped a few inches away. She looked up, beholding his face. It was as if the years hadn't separated them; as if she was twenty again, sitting in the library when this handsome stranger interrupted her studying. The layers of anger were peeling away, revealing feelings she didn't know still existed.

Amanda sighed. "Why didn't you …"

"Contact you?" Zeke finished the question. "You were happily married. I couldn't interfere with that. And hey, I figured you hated me. You returned everything I tried to get to Jack."

"Yes," Amanda said softly.

"And to be honest, I didn't want to mess up your life like I'd done with mine."

Zeke bowed his head, while at the same time reaching out and taking her hand. This time, she didn't pull away.

"I have three ex-wives who probably wish I'd just die. My children are strangers to me." He looked back up at her. "Watching you and Jack from a distance, I fantasized how wonderful your life must be—and I knew that if I somehow touched it, it might be ruined."

"Then what changed?"

"When I heard that your husband had died, it got me thinking," Zeke admitted. "What if?"

"What if you roped Jack into your reality television show?"

Zeke grinned, slowly rising from the floor as his knee creaked. He pulled his chair close and sat beside her. "No, not at first. I wanted to get on my fancy plane, fly to Wheaton and show up on your doorstep. But that wouldn't have worked."

"I don't think so," Amanda said, lightening the mood.

"That's what I figured. I agonized over what to do—or even if I should do anything. I knew you'd gone back to work, but I had no idea how you were grieving, when it would be the right time to see you. But eventually, I couldn't wait any longer."

"And you just happen to have this *Ultimate Challenge* coming up." Amanda shook her head.

"Yeah, I thought it would be a great way to see just how well you and Kevin raised Jack."

Their solitude was interrupted with the waiter entering the room, carrying their dinners.

As Jack made it to the waiting van, Palau was there with the back door already opened. He grabbed the chair and shoved it in the back of the van.

"Where now?"

"Stay here," Jack said, throwing the net into the van. "I want to check out that bar."

Jack carefully removed the fishing hook from his pocket, then made his way back to the end of the dirt alley. He stood with his back flat against the wall of the bar or cantina—or whatever they called them on this island. He felt like a really bad thief—trying to be quiet and stealthy, but every noise he made sounded like he was announcing his arrival to the world.

The street was clear, and the patrons inside the bar sounded busy. Jack ducked under one of the windows and made his way around the back. The back door was open, and he could hear music coming through and the sound of dishes clanging. The light spilled onto the dirt parking lot and hit three trash cans lined up against an old brick wall.

Jack trotted along the wall, jumping over the trash cans and hiding in the dark. He pulled one of the containers out of the light and into the darkness of the corner of the wall. Keeping the can between him and the door, he turned on his flashlight and searched through the refuse.

He found several empty beer bottles. He set one aside, scrounging deeper into the trash. The smell was atrocious. They probably hadn't washed out the can in months. But it was better than stealing. He figured anything in a trash can was fair game.

He mentally went through the list; nothing seemed to match as his hand pulled through leftover food, tissues, fruit peelings, and all sorts of mushy stuff he couldn't identify. He put the first can back in place and pulled the second one back into the darkness.

Nothing of any value in that one.

He started on the third when somebody walked out the back door of the bar. Jack heard him coming. quickly turned out his flashlight, and froze. The man was walking right toward him. Jack hoped he was enough in the dark that he couldn't be seen, because it was too late to hide. Any movement and he'd be spotted for sure.

The man staggered slightly, walking as if he was drunk. He probably wasn't a worker but one of the patrons, Jack thought. Hopefully, he wouldn't recognize that one of the trash cans was missing.

He continued straight at Jack, stepping to the side of the last trash can and facing the brick wall just off to Jack's left. Jack heard the sound of a zipper, and then a spattering of liquid hitting the bricks. The man was urinating less than three feet away, and Jack's camera vest was capturing it all on video. Jack stayed frozen, not even daring to breathe. If his eyes moved to where Jack was, he was sure to be spotted.

The man kept looking down at the wall, completing his business, then zipped up and turned back toward the bar. Jack waited another ten seconds before letting his lungs clear and sucking in a much-needed breath of air. That was close.

He double-checked to make sure nobody else was headed his direction, then flipped his flashlight back on. The third trash can was a winner. They'd thrown away some bad fruit: a couple of pineapples and a very valuable, although overripe, coconut. Jack set it next to the beer bottle and dug around one last time. There was also an empty pack of cigarettes—Jack held onto it, not sure if the list made it clear it had to be full of cigarettes or not.

He put the last trash can back in place and looked back toward the bar entrance. There was a pile of *something* off in the darkness on the other side of the door. Jack pocketed the pack of cigarettes and the empty bottle, then held onto the coconut as he crept along the brick wall. Once he was past the area illuminated by the open door, he angled toward the pile. It was a stack of lumber and old scraps. Jack didn't see anything useful, but as he took a step closer, his foot caught on a metal pipe, and he fell into the pile. He froze, sure that the noise he'd made would bring somebody out of the bar. But no one came.

His left hand rested on something that felt familiar covered by the stack of boards—an old tire.

Jack worked as quietly as he could, moving the boards off of the tire until he could free it from the pile. As he worked, he realized there were two tires mixed in with the mound of garbage. He knew he didn't need both tires, but he grabbed the extra one anyway. It was too good to pass up.

He pulled them up beside him, wrapped his left arm through one of them, and then passed the coconut to his left hand, allowing his right hand to grab onto the other tire. It was awkward, but he made his way back toward the brick wall, keeping his eye on the door to the bar the entire time. When he got to the corner, he turned and slowly moved along the side of the building. Ducking under the window proved to be difficult, as he tried to keep hold of the tires and coconut in his arms. He made it back into the alley, and to the van, without running into anyone else.

He now had seven of his items, plus an extra tire thrown in for good measure.

Once the waiter left them, Amanda and Zeke ate in silence. The food was delicious: the same grilled mahi-mahi the contestants had been served earlier in the evening, along with a bed of rice and some steamed vegetables.

Amanda used the chewing time to reflect. Zeke was a total shock. She expected to be met with the same arrogance and selfishness he'd shown her the day they parted. He was different, softer. The years had changed him. But how would he react if he knew the whole truth?

"The mahi-mahi is excellent," he said from across the table.

"Umm," Amanda agreed, then startled Zeke with a question that came out of nowhere.

"Are you happy?"

"An interesting question," Zeke responded, picking up his napkin and wiping at his mouth. "Professionally—sure. I love what I do. The show's success has been unbelievable, allowing me to do pretty much whatever I want."

"That's not what I asked," Amanda pressed. "I asked if you are happy."

"I'm doing what I love. Doesn't that equate to happiness?"

"You tell me. I enjoy my job at the hospital most of the time. But that's what I do, not who I am. There's a big difference. At the end of the day, you leave your big-time executive producer job and go home. Then you're left with who you are—at that point, are you happy?"

Zeke blinked a couple of times, apparently faced with a question he hadn't considered. He finally shook his head. "No. When you put it like that, I guess I'm not."

"I didn't think so," Amanda said warmly. "But you know what? You won't be happy with me either."

"What are you saying?"

"That the fantasy of rekindling your first love won't get you what you're looking for."

"I'm not following you."

"Look at you." Amanda spread her arms out toward Zeke. "You're at the top of your game, the number-one-rated TV show in the nation. You have jets and helicopters at your disposal, a staff ready to do your bidding. Yet, you've gone through three divorces, and admit to having no real relationships with your kids. The one thing you do have going for you is that you're at least wise enough to look at it all and admit you're not happy."

"And you are?"

"Yes—I am," Amanda said confidently. "Sure, I'm sad over the loss of Kevin. I miss him terribly. But my peace, my purpose for being—my happiness—doesn't come from money, jets, or tropical islands. It doesn't come from any external force."

"Oh, I get it." Zeke glanced away. "This is where you start preaching."

"No, no. I'm just sharing some of my life experience."

Zeke looked back at Amanda, his eyes widening with passion. "We were happy back then, Amanda. The world was at our fingertips. Nothing was going to stop us. We were in love and we had each other."

"We weren't in love, Zeke. How we ended proves that. There was no foundation." Amanda shook her head. She could see the hurt darken his face as if a curtain had been brought down. "We were passionate about each other. In lust? You bet. But love? I'm not so sure."

Amanda paused to let the words sink in slowly. She could see the pain etched into his eyes as he sat silent before her. "Love isn't selfish. I've learned that over the years. It's selfless. Love doesn't demand; love gives."

"You have changed," Zeke said.

"More than you know."

"But your memories of the past, and how you present it—it demeans what we had." Zeke's voice broke and he stopped for a second. "It was more than lust—so much more."

"What happened to us was as much my fault as it was yours. It finally dawned on me: I didn't understand a thing about love, until I came face-to-face with how God loves me."

"Then what hope is there for a middle-aged Jewish guy like me?" Zeke muttered.

Amanda's heart cracked, she struggled inside as she read the pain in Zeke's face. She reached out and touched his hand, smiling gently.

"There's always hope, Zeke."

Palau drove through the small village, turning wherever Jack told him. They were a couple of dirt roads in from the bay where tiny mud huts and wooden shacks lined the road.

"I need to find chickens." Jack didn't even realize he'd spoken out loud.

"You need chickens?" Palau got excited. "My cousin has chickens!"

They came up against another white van barreling down the tiny one-lane road. Palau had to dodge quickly to his right to avoid a collision, nearly sideswiping a motor scooter parked in front of one of the houses. Jack caught a glimpse of Eddie laughing in the passenger's seat as the van shot past them.

Palau turned up the next street.

"OK," Palau said with a huge grin. He seemed to be having the time of his life.

The van pulled a few feet up the next drive before Palau pulled off to the side, in between two small shacks.

"Cousin next house up street—he have chicken. Shed in back," Palau said, as he turned off the motor. "I wait here."

"You do that." Jack grinned. He opened the door, irritated by the dome light that came on and exposed them in the darkness.

He closed the door quickly and ran up the street. He silently slipped past the house he thought Palau meant and stood in the back yard. There were a few small patches of grass, but most of it was dirt. In the back was the pen, fenced in by chicken wire set up in a square around a small wood shack. There was a low water trough that looked promising. Some kind of animal was housed in the shed; Jack hoped it was a couple of chickens.

There was a gate wired shut toward the middle. He didn't want to deal with figuring out how to open it, so Jack decided to step over it. He got up on his tiptoes and placed his right leg over and onto the dirt on the other side. His left leg followed suit and he was in the pen. Jack kept his body low, nearly crawling toward the shack. He pulled out his penlight, shining the beam into the darkened interior.

Two red eyes pierced the blackness as the beam of light flashed across the face of a snarling dog.

Jack struggled to stay calm.

"Nice doggie," Jack whispered.

"When do I get to see him?" Amanda asked, after the waiter had poured some coffee and left the room.

"Soon," Zeke answered. "Probably tomorrow morning."

"Why not tonight?" Amanda pleaded.

"Can't."

"You expect me to come all this way and then not be able to see him right now?"

Zeke shrugged. "All the contestants are out on a challenge. We're not sure when they'll return, and the plan is for the family members to see them tomorrow."

"So, I'm not the only family member here?"

"No, you're not."

Amanda contemplated his answer for a minute. "Then, I'm not here because I asked to speak with Jack. There's another reason?"

It took a moment for Zeke to answer her, as a look of concern crossed his brow. "Yes. You're part of the game now. It was the only way I could get you down here without raising suspicions with the staff."

"They don't know about our history?"

"Only my supervising producer."

Amanda looked up at him intensely. "So, now I'm involved in your reality show?"

"I'm sorry, Amanda. But yes."

"What are you expecting me to do?"

"It's not a matter of what we want you to do; it's more about how Jack will respond with your presence here on the island."

Amanda's voice grew cold. "Just when I think you might have changed—why am I not surprised that you've only brought me here as a pawn in your grand scheme."

"Amanda, that's not true," Zeke pleaded softly.

But it was, and she was devastated. As the evening had progressed, part of her had been enamored by Zeke's attention. After all these years, it looked like he still loved her and had set up this whole scenario just to see her again. Her heart had softened, reigniting feelings that had been squelched for so long. But that was all shattered in an instant—when it became clear that she was just another part of the game.

"I'd like to go to my room now." Amanda rose from the table.

Zeke got up quickly and helped pull her chair away from the table. "Amanda, please."

"No," Amanda snapped. "I want to see my son now."

"I told you, he's not here …"

"I'm not sure I believe you anymore."

"It's true." His eyes shifted as he felt challenged by her accusation.

Amanda read the defiance in them and tried to take the edge out of her voice. "Then I think you've given me enough to think about for the evening."

The Scripture kept running through her head about making her conversation full of grace. That might be all well-and-good to a stranger, but her earlier softness might have played right into Zeke's trap. Her anger had been a wall of protection. Letting that down had cost her—dearly.

"Please, stay," Zeke asked. "Give me a chance to explain."

"I appreciate the offer," Amanda stated flatly. "But right now, I'd just like to be alone."

The dog growled, taking a step toward Jack. He could see the hair on its back bristled upward. It wasn't that big, about the size of a golden retriever with short black fur, but with its mouth curled back, the fangs and all surrounding teeth were staring menacingly right at Jack.

One bark and he would be discovered. One leap from the dog, and Jack could get hurt badly. What was he doing here?

He thought about turning and running, hoping he could jump over the fence before the dog clamped onto his ankle. Then he'd probably have to deal with the barking and whoever lived on the other side of the hut's walls. Then he heard a clucking sound off to his right. There were chickens in the pen.

The dog stopped his forward movement, but a low growling continued coming from deep within its throat.

Jack stayed frozen, hoping he wouldn't startle the dog. Beyond that, he was out of options.

"Toko." Jack heard a whisper from outside the shed followed by a soft whistle. The name was repeated again, followed by a string of words Jack didn't understand. But he knew the voice—it was Palau.

The dog angled its head, looking at Jack, then outside the hut. It stepped forward, sniffing Jack's arms, his legs. Jack breathed as shallow as he could, trying not to move.

"Toko," Palau called again, the voice sounding closer. Jack could sense Palau coming up behind him, but he didn't move. The dog looked past his shoulder and started wagging its tail.

Palau came up beside him, calmly petting the dog.

"I forgot about Toko," Palau explained. "Thought I should come help."

"Thanks," Jack sighed.

He carefully moved his flashlight ever so slightly around the shack, still not wanting to move drastically in the event the dog decided he was a threat again. There were six chickens settled comfortably on their nests for the night. Jack wondered how Toko would react if he reached out and grabbed one of them.

He heard a chirp to his left. He cautiously turned his head and let the beam of light follow. There, at about eye level, was a hen sitting on her nest. The chirp sounded again, coming from right underneath her. Her eggs were hatching.

Jack had an idea. He slowly reached up toward the chicken. Lifting her wing, Jack moved his hand under her. She pecked at him, breaking the skin with her beak. It hurt, but Jack fought the impulse to cry out.

His fingers touched the newly hatched chick, and felt another cracked egg about to hatch. He groped around, feeling an egg that was still intact. He wrapped his fingers around it, and gently pulled back from under the hen's wing. She pecked at him one last time, letting out some kind of warning sound as Jack palmed the egg, trying to hide it from her. Inside was a live chicken—Vince hadn't said how old the chicken had to be. Jack hoped the poor family wouldn't miss one unhatched chicken.

He carefully placed the egg into the pocket of his vest as Palau continued to pet the dog.

"Nice dog," Jack whispered, as he started to back out slowly.

The dog watched him intently, even with Palau by his side. Jack made it outside the shed, inching his way toward the fence and thinking he was going to make it. Suddenly, the still night was shattered by the sound of a horn honking short shrill blasts coming from just in front of the house.

The dog reacted instinctively, barking before lunging away from Palau and right at Jack. Jack dodged to his left and the dog flew by, his mouth snapping and missing him by inches. Before he could make a second pass, Jack ran the few steps to the wire fence and leaped over the top. He sprinted as fast as he could toward the corner of the hut, knowing that the dog could easily jump the fence as well and expecting his pants, or worse the meat of his calf to be caught in its steel-like jaws. He saw the source of the honking when a white van, with tires spinning in the dirt, pulled away from the house. Jack thought he heard Eddie's laugh as the van sped away; he must have doubled back to this street to try and give Jack some grief.

It worked.

Jack made it to the side of the hut without the dog locking on to any of his body parts. With his back against the wall, Jack looked back to see Palau holding an angry Toko in his arms. The dog was still barking profusely, but he was inside the fence. Jack heard voices coming from the front of the house as the occupants had gone outside to see what created the commotion.

Jack and Palau were sitting ducks if they came back to quiet the dog. A male voice yelled, evidently at the beast. It didn't listen.

He was trapped. His only hope was that, after seeing the van leave, the people would head back inside. Jack held his breath, slinking down to the dirt, making as small a presence as he could.

The couple started talking about something; the male's voice was agitated. A cry from a child interrupted the exchange, and the wife headed back inside the hut. The male screamed one more time at the barking dog, then followed his wife.

Jack let out his breath, this was his chance. He crept along the side of the house, wanting to get a view of the front before he dashed off into the darkness. His foot kicked against a small rubber ball, sending it a few feet out by the front of the home. Jack froze again. He peeked around the corner—no one was there.

Jack made his move. Taking long strides, he reached down and scooped up the ball as he made his way down the dirt road and away from the hut.

He collapsed against the side of the van, breathing hard. In a few minutes, Palau came running up as well.

"You glad I come?" Palau whispered.

"Very," Jack said between breaths. "You did great."

"Me happy to help."

"Me happy too," Jack said with a quiet laugh. "Come on, let's get out of here."

Before Jack could get back into their vehicle, another white van came charging down the dirt road. It slammed on its brakes right beside them, stopping in a cloud of dust.

"Jack!" Maria smiled from the passenger side.

He grinned, shaking his head. "I thought you were Eddie, and I was getting ready to clobber you."

"Why, what did he do now?"

"Just about got me devoured by a rabid dog. How are you doing?"

"Pretty good." Maria grinned. "But I can't find an old tire to save my life."

"You've got everything else?" Jack asked in surprise.

"All except one thing, but I'll get that back at the resort," Maria answered.

"What's that?"

"My bathing suit," she answered proudly. "I haven't found one yet, so I thought I'd throw mine in when I get back. They never said where the items had to come from."

Jack laughed. "That's a great idea. That's all I've got left too, I think."

Maria's face turned ashen white. "No, I've got to be first, Jack. I can't let Teresa find out …"

Jack could see the overwhelming fear clearly in her eyes. Whatever she was hiding from her mother and daughter would be disastrous. Without hesitating, Jack opened up the back of his van and reached for the extra tire.

"What are you doing?" Maria asked.

"Getting you out of here." Jack pulled on the tire, dragging it out of the van.

But you need that, don't you?"

"I grabbed two—this one's yours."

"Oh Jack." Maria climbed out of her van and ran to hug him. "You're a lifesaver, again."

Jack half-hugged back, then pushed the tire into the back of her van, being careful not to hit the chicken flapping its wings behind the driver's seat. "Just go before I change my mind."

Maria kissed him on the cheek, then ran to the front of her van and jumped in.

Jack grinned as she drove away, then rushed back to his own van.

"Let's go," Jack said to Palau as he opened the door. "But don't pass them."

Josh escorted Amanda back to her bungalow.

"How was your dinner?"

Amanda walked on, not sure how to answer. "The food was delicious, thanks."

He seemed wise enough not to pry as they walked in silence.

"Well, here we are," he said, as he stopped at her room.

"Thanks, Josh." Amanda smiled at him.

"You're very welcome," Josh returned, opening the door for her. "I'll come by and get you in the morning, when it's OK for you to leave your room."

Amanda stepped into the room, then turned and looked up at him, her eyes narrowing. "When it's OK to leave my room?"

Josh lowered his head slightly. "Yes. We have to make sure none of the family members see each other until the right time. You'll be locked in—I'm sorry."

"This is ridiculous!" Amanda raised her voice. "I just want to see my son."

"You will, Mrs. Forrest." Josh tried to console her. "But you'll just have to wait, or you'll risk causing Jack to forfeit the competition."

"I don't care about your stupid competition."

"I would think you'd be thrilled that Jack was chosen. He's done quite well."

Amanda didn't answer.

"You need to stay in your room until I come to get you. Breakfast will be brought to you in the morning, and if you have any kind of emergency before that ..." Josh pointed to a red button that Amanda hadn't noticed before on the wall by the door. "Just press this and someone will come running."

"Wonderful," Amanda returned, with sarcasm.

"I'm sorry for any inconvenience, but if Jack wins, won't it all be worth it?"

"I doubt it," Amanda said, reaching for the door. "Good night."

"Good night, Mrs. Forrest," Josh returned just before the door closed on him.

Amanda heard the door's lock click into place without her touching the knob. She tried to turn it, and it wouldn't budge. True enough, they'd locked her in the room. Could this night get any stranger?

Then, suddenly, music began playing in the room. It sounded like it was piped in through some intercom system. She knew what it was from the very first note.

It was Rod Stewart's "Tonight's the Night." It had been their song. Amanda's shoulders sagged as Rod's voice instantly took her back to 1977. She stepped further into the room, sitting on the dinette chair nearly in a daze. Then she noticed the card, with her name on the front, leaning against the flowered centerpiece.

She shook her head, knowing that Zeke was playing games with her, but that didn't stop her eyes from tearing up. She reached out and grabbed the envelope, opening it as Rod's gravelly voice filled the room.

The note was simple and handwritten:

Amanda,
Just a quick note to let you know that I'm so glad you're here. I hope you'll give me a second chance to show you how sorry I am for my past mistakes, but also how excited I am for what the future could hold. Thank you for having dinner with me. I hope that "Tonight's the Night" for a new beginning. Sleep tight, I'll see you in the morning.

Zeke

She held the note in her hands for a few moments, wondering what her life would have been like if things had turned out differently. There was no way to know. She didn't move until the song ended, the memories floating through her mind.

Just as Zeke planned.

The two vans made a mad dash back up the winding path toward the resort.

"I can beat them," Palau yelled, as they rocked over the bumpy road.

Jack thought about it. He'd reacted quickly when Maria looked so frightened. But should he give her first place in this event, and the exemption from having the family secret revealed? That would just about ensure Jack would quit the competition—he didn't think he could put his mother in the position of revealing something from her past on national television.

Maria's van skirted the corner in front of them, nearly sliding off the road and down a dark embankment. But the driver caught control just in time and bounded up the next part of the road. Jack didn't see any way Palau could pass them on this narrow winding road. The resort was just another mile and they'd be there.

"No," Jack finally answered. "Let her stay in front."

"But we could win ..." Palau wouldn't give up.

"I know," Jack said softly. "I know."

A pair of headlights flashed through the back window. Somebody was not that far off in third. Then again, Jack wasn't sure if there was another van waiting at the top of the hill already in first. He thought he'd gotten his ten items fairly quickly, but he couldn't be sure. At least it looked like he wasn't going to be last. But both he and Maria still had to run to their rooms and grab their bathing suits. If whoever was behind them had all the items, they could be in trouble.

"Hurry," Jack called out. They were almost to the resort's entrance.

"Now you want first?" Palau turned to Jack, taking his eyes off the road for a split second.

"Watch out!" Jack yelled.

Palau turned back just in time to swing the wheel to the left and miss two men standing along the side of the road by an old pickup. Jack caught a glimpse of them as they passed, and he didn't like what he saw.

"Did you see that?" he asked Palau.

Palau answered excitedly in his native tongue before he caught himself. "Sorry, I not see them."

"No, I meant did you see what they were carrying?" Jack prodded.

Palau shook his head.

Jack was sure, as they'd flashed by the two men, they'd been holding machine guns. What would they be doing in the middle of the night standing guard along the road up to the resort?

He couldn't think of any good reason, unless it had something to do with the military guy who showed up earlier. Could these men be his? Unlikely—they weren't in any kind of uniform like the dark green outfit the general had worn.

"Is there another entrance to the resort?" Jack asked Palau, as he sped up the winding drive to the resort.

"Yes. Side road lead to service entrance." Palau pointed to a split in the road up ahead.

"Stop!" Jack ordered.

Palau obeyed and slammed on the brakes. The van stopped dead in the middle of the road.

"Palau." Jack turned to his driver, his pulse racing. "Do you know why men with guns would be coming from a village up north?"

Palau shook his head. "No, but at times drug lords on island fight. Could be it."

Jack had to think quickly; he only had a moment before the next van would be on their tail.

"Wait here," he said, as he opened the door and sprinted up the service road. The front of the resort was visible another fifty yards up the hill. Jack placed himself there, beside the base of a palm tree, and watched intently.

Maria's van pulled into the portico, but before she could even open her door, she was immediately surrounded by four men carrying the same type of rifles Jack had seen the men down the road holding. In the light of the resort entrance, Jack could see that they were AK-47s.

One of the men quickly grabbed the passenger door and yanked it open, yelling something Jack couldn't quite distinguish as he pulled her from the van. He held onto her arm and roughly escorted her off toward the main building. Jack had caught a glimpse of Maria's face as she was yanked from the van. She was deathly afraid.

Keeping down low, Jack made his way back toward Palau just as the lights from the other van could be seen coming up the road behind them. Jack waved for Palau to pull off onto the service road, then ran beside him and told him to turn off the lights.

The other van had Jack in its headlights as it barreled toward him. Jack waved his arms, praying it was one of the other contestants. The driver slowed down and then stopped right in front of Jack.

Jack dashed over to the passenger side as Eddie rolled down the window.

"What the …" Eddie began.

"Quiet!" Jack ordered in a forced whisper. "There're some guys up there with guns, they just pulled Maria out of her van and rushed her off."

Eddie looked at Jack, then up to the resort and back. "You're out of your mind, Forrest."

"Eddie, I'm not kidding."

Eddie shook his head, the mounted camera on his helmet dangling in front of him. "Yeah right. This is just some kind of stupid trick to get me out of the game."

"No, I swear."

"Well, it's not going to work." Eddie turned to his driver. "Let's go."

"Eddie!" Jack grabbed hold of the door handle. "You've got to believe me."

"Not on your life," Eddie laughed, rolling up the window.

Jack had to let go as Eddie's driver started up the hill. Jack quickly got out of the road and ran up the service road to the spot where he could view the portico. Just like with Maria, as soon as Eddie's van stopped, four men surrounded the van with their weapons ready. Eddie was pulled out and roughly pushed toward the main building. Jack could see Eddie looking back over his shoulder. His eyes pleading for help from Jack.

But what could he do?

Maria's van was still parked in the portico, leaving Jack to believe that Hugh and Tara were still out there.

He headed back down the hill.

60

Jack stopped beside Palau. "Drive up the road a bit and hide the van."

"Why?" His eyes opened in fear. "What going on?"

"Nothing good, I'm afraid. Pull the van up the road, then wait for me."

"OK," Palau said and drove ahead.

Jack studied the road before him. He needed a place where he could see a vehicle driving up and make sure it was a contestant van. He didn't want to just jump out in front of the first headlights he saw and risk confronting any of the men who had taken Eddie and Maria hostage.

Up ahead, there was a right-hand turn. Jack figured he could hide in the brush, get a look at what was coming up the road and jump out at the last minute. It would have to do.

He scrambled up the driveway, tripping several times over rocks or dips in the road that he couldn't see in the dark, and eventually found a hiding place. Sitting in the jungle brush, Jack pulled off his helmet, looked at the cables that connected the camera to his vest, and yanked them out. The game was over.

It was the first moment Jack had to regroup since he'd spotted the armed men. What was he going to do? His mom was somewhere in that resort—as was Maria, her mom, and little Teresa. He had no way of knowing what had been done with Vince or the rest of the production staff from the show. They could be dead as far as he knew.

Jack had no military training. He was alone against men with automatic weapons. He didn't even know where he was, or how he could even get off the island. All he could do was pray.

So pray he did.

Jack wasn't sure how much time had passed, but he heard another vehicle approaching. He got up on one knee, staring intensely at the road. As it came around the bend below, Jack got a good enough view of it to see that it was another white contestant van. Jack shot out from his hiding place, waving his hands in the air in the middle of the road.

As soon as the van stopped, Jack ran over to the passenger window. It rolled down, revealing a concerned Hugh.

"What's going on?" Hugh asked.

"I don't know, but it looks like the resort's been taken over," Jack explained quickly, keeping his voice low. "As soon as Maria and Eddie pulled up, four guys surrounded each of them with AK-47s and took them into the building."

"What?" Hugh's eyes flared. "Are you serious?"

"Deadly. Did you see a couple of guys hanging around a pickup down there?"

"Yeah, didn't think much of it."

"They had guns as well," Jack pointed out. "I think what that military guy warned Vince about is happening. Somebody raided the resort while we were gone."

"What do you want me to do?"

"I hid my van up the service road about a tenth of a mile back. Have your driver do the same thing, and we'll wait for Tara."

Hugh nodded, then opened his door and got out of the van. They both helped the driver back down the road until he could turn off into the service area, then they ran back up the road to the hiding place.

The moon had settled on the backside of the cliff, leaving the area pitch-black. Jack sat a foot away from Hugh behind a thick bush but couldn't make out his face. They were well-hidden from the road but had quick access should another contestant van drive by.

"What are we gonna do?" Hugh whispered.

"I don't know. First thing is to get that silly camera helmet off of you."

Hugh pulled the helmet off while Jack reached around and pulled out the wires connected to his vest.

"That feels much better," Hugh sighed.

"I want to make sure Tara doesn't get caught," Jack said. "Then we'll have to figure something out."

"Did you get all the stuff on the list?"

Jack nodded, then realized Hugh couldn't see him. "Just about. I still need a swimsuit. Maria thought we could get our own suits back here."

"Great idea."

"How about you?"

"I found it all—but evidently didn't do it quick enough," Hugh answered. "How long ago did you guys get back?"

"Ten, maybe fifteen minutes ago."

"And Maria was first?"

"Yeah," Jack answered. "Eddie was third. I tried to stop him ..."

The sound of a vehicle approaching from above cut Jack off mid-sentence. It came down the drive slowly—a pickup with three men in the back pointing their AK-47s to each side of the road. They were speaking in the native tongue as they drove by. Jack wished he could have understood what they were saying.

Once on the access road, the pickup stopped and a couple of the men jumped out. They quickly searched the area with flashlights before jumping back into their vehicle and driving up the road toward Palau and the other van.

"What if they find our vans?" Hugh whispered.

"I think they may already know about us," Jack said. "If they have radios, the truck down below would've told them four vans had driven up."

"Great," Hugh muttered. "Now what do we do?"

"Wait it out. See what happens."

A few minutes later, the sound of automatic gunfire erupted into the still night, echoing through the hills.

"That doesn't sound good," Hugh whispered.

Jack's mind immediately imagined Palau and Hugh's driver lying beside their vans in a pool of blood. Jack clenched his fists, wanting to run to their rescue but knowing he was powerless to do anything about it.

The truck came back about ten minutes later. It turned slowly from the access road, pointed back up toward the top of the cliff and drove past them. The men in the back were laughing and still speaking in their foreign tongue. One of them pointed his weapon right at their bush as they passed, but evidently didn't see them. Jack waited until the truck was out of sight before he spoke.

"We've got to check on our drivers."

"What if they left someone back by the vans?" Hugh asked.

"We'll just have to be careful," Jack answered, stepping quietly out of their hiding spot.

Just as they reached the turnoff for the access road, the sound of a vehicle approaching from below hit their ears.

"Hide!" Jack warned.

He dove behind a couple of low palm trees, cutting himself on the sharp branches at the base. Hugh slammed beside him as the headlights flashed across them.

Jack was blinded, dying to see if it was Tara's van or more of the rebels.

"I think it's Tara," Hugh whispered.

"Are you sure?" Jack still couldn't see.

"Yeah." Hugh stepped out from behind the trees, waving at the approaching van. It slid to a stop right in front of him.

"What are you doing?" Tara's voice cut through the night.

Jack leaped out onto the road and ran up beside the van.

Hugh was at the window first. "Get out, quick!"

"What's going on?" Tara asked.

Hugh opened the door for her as Jack explained the situation.

Tara looked at him in disbelief, then shock. "What are we going to do?"

"Hide," Jack answered. "Have your driver back into the service road. We might need to make a quick getaway."

Jack left Hugh to help get Tara's van parked up the access road and ran to see if he could find out what had happened with Palau and their vans. The road was dark, and Jack was afraid of giving himself away if the rebels had, indeed, left someone at their vans.

He walked along the edge of the road, ready to duck into the jungle foliage at the first hint of any trouble. About a hundred feet up the road, Jack could make out a couple of white blotches—evidently the vans parked off to the side.

He stopped dead in his tracks and listened. The jungle noises were deafening once he concentrated on them. There were more varieties of insects and animals making their nocturnal noises than Jack imagined existed. He should be able to sneak up without being heard.

He progressed slowly, stepping lightly to make as little noise as possible along the dirt road. There seemed to be no movement ahead, so he continued carefully.

Jack walked up behind the second van, pausing to listen again. He jerked back when something moved inside the van. He ducked down, low to the ground, and waited.

There, he heard it again. A fluttering, followed by a clucking sound. It was Hugh's chicken. Jack grinned despite the fear. He kept low and snuck up along the side of the van.

Nobody was around. Both drivers were gone, and the vans were empty except for the items they had collected. Jack reached through the open passenger window of his van and grabbed the flashlight he'd used on the challenge. He quickly scanned the area around him, thankful that he didn't spot any dead bodies. He turned the flashlight off and headed back to the main road.

Coming up on Tara's parked van, Jack didn't see anybody around.

He whispered strongly, "Hugh, Tara, where are you?"

"Over here," he heard from the brush to his right.

Jack walked over and found the two of them crouched behind the foliage with Tara's driver.

"We weren't sure it was you," Hugh explained.

"You did the right thing. We have to be careful," Jack said.

"What'd you find?" Tara asked.

"The other drivers were gone. I don't know what happened to them."

"We're on our own then," Tara muttered.

"I think so," Jack responded.

"My husband is up there," Tara pointed out.

"My parents," Hugh added. "What are we going to do?"

"I wish I knew," Jack answered.

The three contestants sat in silence, contemplating their fate. There seemed to be nowhere to go. If the armed men in the van weren't at the bottom of the road, they could get in a van, drive into the village, and try to find some help—but where? Or, they could head up to the resort and attempt to rescue their family members. But they were outnumbered and hopelessly outgunned.

"Do you have any military training?" Jack asked Hugh.

He shook his head. "No. Do you?"

Jack shrugged. "No, but I wish I had some now."

"We can't just sit here and give up," Tara argued. "We've got to do something."

"Yeah, we do." Jack said. "Let's find out what we're up against, what do you say?"

"How?" Hugh asked.

"Take the access road up to the resort, at least we can see what's going on."

Jack led them past the two parked vans, continuing up the road until the back of the resort was in view. There was an old stone retaining wall about four feet high that separated the road from the back lawn as it wound down to the loading dock.

The three of them ducked down as they walked quickly toward the resort. From this angle, they could see into the back of the dining hall and the hilltop area where they had climbed up the cliff—and where Stacy had fallen to her death.

Jack got as close as he dared, then stopped and poked his head above the wall. They would have had a great view into the restaurant from where they were, except the curtains were drawn.

Jack ducked back down. "Can't see anything."

"Do you think they're holding Maria and Eddie in there?" Tara asked.

"You'd think so—it's the biggest room. They could have the whole staff in there with them for all we know."

"I don't see any guards," Hugh said, after glancing over the top of the wall.

"I didn't either," Jack said. "I'm gonna try to get a peek inside."

"What should we do?" Hugh asked.

"Stay hidden back here," Jack answered. "If I get caught, or don't come out after ten minutes, make your way back to the van and go get some help in the village."

"How do we get by the guards at the bottom of the hill?" Hugh asked.

"I don't know ... just blow right by them as fast as you can," Jack instructed. "I don't think they'll be ready for anything like that."

"This isn't the movies," Tara argued. "We can't just bust through their little roadblock with their guns a-blazing and not get hit—it doesn't work that way in real life."

"Well, if you think of something better, then do it," Jack said.

"Be careful, Jack," Tara said.

"You too," Jack wished to both of them.

"Jack, Tara, and Hugh." The loudspeakers on the outside of the building roared to life. The voice was heavily accented, like most of the locals spoke. Jack froze in place. Hugh and Tara looked at him with fear etched on their faces.

"We know you're out there," the voice continued. "We don't want anybody to get hurt. Please show yourself and come in immediately."

"What do we do?" Tara asked.

"Shh!" Jack motioned, with the wave of his hand.

"If you don't, we have Maria and Eddie and members of your family in here. I'm sure they won't enjoy any hesitation on your part. Walk up to the main building immediately."

The speakers went silent, followed by a sudden burst of light as the floodlights came on, bathing the back of the resort in a bluish light. The three contestants stayed behind the wall, covered in the shadows for the time being.

Jack silently prayed. He didn't know what to do.

Peeking his head up over the top of the wall, Jack analyzed the building. There were still no bodies walking around outside. But as he glanced above the dining hall, he noticed a flickering glow of light coming from a room on the second floor.

"Hugh." Jack dropped back down to the ground. "Look up at the second floor and tell me what you see."

Hugh nodded and poked his head above the wall for a moment, then dropped back down.

"It looks like somebody is up there watching TV," Hugh answered.

"Exactly," Jack said.

"So?"

"So there isn't any TV in this resort—just *The Ultimate Challenge* crew."

"Then what's up there?" Hugh asked.

"It must be their control center, which means the rebels have access to the cameras shooting all over this place."

"Then sneaking around could be really risky," Hugh realized.

"But we need to get a peek inside," Jack said. "To see what we're up against."

"Are you crazy?" Tara asked. "You're going to get yourself killed."

"No, I'm gonna try to get some answers." Jack pointed to some trash bins sitting just off from the loading dock. "You guys hide over there and wait for me."

The speakers clamored again. "You have five minutes to comply —or we will start killing the hostages!"

"Oh my god!" Tara cried.

"Wait, Jack," Hugh said. "What if you get caught?"

"Then stick with the plan," Jack said somberly. "And go get help."

"But they'll kill our families." Tara stopped him.

"Think, Tara. They're just trying to scare us into giving ourselves up. If we do, then there's nothing we can do to help our families.

Jack left a scared and trembling Tara as he scrambled down the pathway and bounced quickly up the concrete steps to the top of the loading dock. He moved quickly into the shadows and hid behind a crate of boxes. He tried to calm his breathing so he could hear what was going on around him.

He had to be close to the dining hall. The kitchen would be right off of the loading dock, if this resort were like most others that he'd encountered. And the kitchen had to be connected to the restaurant they had been using.

All was quiet, which amazed him. Why wasn't the place crawling with armed men, instead of a single pickup truck full of guys grabbing people at the front of the resort?

He moved from his hiding spot, angling for the double doors that led into the building. They opened automatically as he stepped on the black rubber mat in front of him. It caused Jack to jump back, fearing somebody was coming through the doors from the other side, but the hallway was empty.

Jack passed through quickly, following the worn path on the floor caused by countless dollies and foot traffic. It led him straight to the kitchen.

It was empty—so far, so good. Jack kept moving, nearing the door he hoped would lead into the dining hall. He heard voices and ducked quickly behind the sink, just before one side of the double doors swung open. Jack was a sitting duck if they walked around the counter.

He heard two voices, this time speaking English without accents.

"You think they're really out there?"

"From what I hear, the vans have returned and they found the drivers—but no contestants, so they must be on the premises. Grab me a beer, would ya?"

"Sure thing." One of the men walked over to the refrigerator that was at the end of the counter Jack was hiding behind. Jack could see his pants and shoes. If he took one more step, he would surely see Jack.

"What do you think they're going to do if they don't show up?" he asked as he reached in for the beer.

"Who knows—it'll sure make for an interesting twist, don't you think? But they'll come in. They have to. It's almost as dangerous out in that jungle at night as they think it is in here."

The first man laughed, shutting the fridge door. "Nice."

"Come on," the second voice urged. "We better get back on camera."

"Right."

The door opened again, and Jack found himself alone. He walked the length of the counter, past the refrigerator, and stood by the doors. They were the typical restaurant variety, one side for going into the restaurant, and the other side for going into the kitchen, so waiters wouldn't crash into each other with armfuls of dishes. There were circular windows in the center of each door, so Jack risked leaning in and getting a view into the next room. It was dark, except for a large window that opened to another room beyond—the one where all the events and dinners had taken place each night for the contestants.

He could see the two men who had just walked out of the kitchen, chugging their beers as they stood behind a couple of cameras that pointed into the next room. It was the view in the next room though, that Jack was interested in.

Maria and Eddie were tied to a couple of chairs, bound and gagged like a couple of kidnapped Westerners on an Aljazeera news report. Standing on guard beside them was one of the rebels holding his automatic weapon. Jack zoomed in on Maria's face: it was full of fear as tears streaked the side of her cheeks. He moved his eyes to Eddie, who also looked scared, but mixed with a good dose of irritation.

The whole setup suddenly looked like a Hollywood stage, with gun-toting actors parading around as the camera crew patiently waited for the excitement to begin.

It was all a hoax.

Evidently, Jack's next hurdle in *The Ultimate Challenge*.

Jack ducked his head down and quietly made his way toward the back of the kitchen. He opened up the door leading into the hallway and peeked out.

A couple of production assistants were casually walking his direction. Jack thought back to the men in the pickup, laughing as they made their way back up to the resort. It was all adding up.

He quietly let the door shut toward him and ducked around the corner just in case. Nobody entered the kitchen, so after a minute Jack tried it again. The coast was clear.

He headed down the hallway, and was about to step out onto the loading dock, when he spotted a set of stairs leading up to the second floor—to the control center. As he started up the stairs, Jack imagined walking in and shocking Mr. Zeke Roberts with his knowledge of their attempt to fool the contestants.

"You have one minute left," the voice over the speakers echoed down the hallway.

Jack stopped. He couldn't leave Tara and Hugh out there thinking their family members were about to get shot. So he headed back down the hallway and out to the loading dock. He jumped off the platform and ran over to the trash dumpsters. Hugh and Tara were huddled behind the second one.

Jack settled in beside a panicked Tara.

"We've got less than a minute," Tara said frantically. "What are we going to do?"

"Nothing." Jack looked at her, catching Hugh's shocked reaction as well. "It's all a trick—part of the game. There are no armed rebels. They're actors."

"What are you talking about?" Tara looked confused.

"Your time is up!" The speaker shouted at them again. "Show yourselves now."

"I snuck into the kitchen," Jack continued, ignoring the threat. "Got a look into the restaurant. The camera guys are still hanging around, drinking beer and shooting through this one-way window into our dining area. They've got Maria and Eddie tied up, but none of our family members are in there."

"How can you be sure it's not real?" Hugh asked.

"It's obvious," Jack stated. "It's all part of this challenge. Our scavenger hunt was just a setup to get us all off the property while they set up this armed takeover."

"If you're wrong, you could be putting Maria, Eddie, and our families in even greater danger," Hugh mentioned.

Jack flashed a smile. "I'm not wrong. There were production assistants roaming the hallways, camera people taking breaks in the kitchen, and no sign of Vince—that wouldn't be happening if the resort was under siege."

"I hope you're right." Tara choked back tears.

“So what are we going to do?” Hugh asked.

“Let’s put our heads together and turn the tables on them,” Jack said with a grin. “And see how they like playing the game.”

The white van came speeding up to the portico with lights flashing and horn blaring. The men guarding the front of the resort sprang to life, running out to the circular drive with their AK-47s ready. But the white van didn’t stop, instead taking the circular drive with its tires screeching and bounding back down the hill.

Inside the dining hall, everyone scurried. Two of the guards went out to see what the commotion was all about. A couple of cameramen rushed to the window to capture it all on tape. It was what Jack and Hugh were waiting for as they spied through the window of the kitchen door.

“Let’s go,” Jack whispered. He pushed the right door open.

Hugh was directly behind him as they slipped around the back of the darkened room. There was so much commotion amongst the crew, the two went unnoticed moving quietly against the wall.

Jack made it around to where a curtain separated the equipment room from the restaurant. He held the black curtain back, peeking into the room. Maria and Eddie were right where he’d last seen them: tied to chairs and sitting in front of the main table. There were two guards left in the room—one standing beside Maria with his back to Jack, the other standing by the door, glancing back and forth from outside to inside the room.

Shouts were coming through the door from the men in the front of the resort as the blaring horn from the van returned. As lights flashed across the door, Jack knew it would be Tara’s second pass around the portico—and their next cue.

He waited for the man by the door to move, which he finally did, going outside to help the guards in the front of the resort.

Without looking back, Jack dashed into the dining hall as quietly as he could, running behind the remaining guard, pushing the handle of a ladle into his back. It was the closest thing he could find in the kitchen that might feel like the barrel of a gun.

“Freeze!” Jack ordered.

He was relieved when the man did what he asked. "Drop the weapon!"

The guard evidently spoke enough English to understand Jack's instructions. He dropped the AK-47 to the floor.

Instantly, Hugh rushed in, grabbed the gun, and handed it to Jack. He threw the ladle away and took hold of the AK-47. It felt foreign in his hands—something that exemplified such power but was harmlessly loaded with blanks.

The guard took one look at the ladle Jack had been holding to his back and shook his head in disgust. Jack winked at him, then turned his attention to the hostages.

Hugh moved behind Maria and started loosening the gag and the ropes around her.

"Jack," Maria said as soon as her mouth was free. "Thank God you've come."

"Not now," Jack whispered to her with a grin. He then turned to Hugh while keeping the AK-47 pressed into the guard's back.

Jack knew the crew was recording it all, but he still wanted to get out of the restaurant as quickly as he could. Hugh undid the last knot keeping Maria's hands bound behind her and brought the rope over to the guard. He positioned the man's hands behind his back and went to work.

"We've got to get moving," Jack whispered urgently, stepping over to Maria and helping to get her feet free. Eddie was mumbling through the cloth stuck in his mouth and jerking his chair up and down. He wanted to be freed. Jack looked over at him and grinned.

"How does it feel, Eddie?" Jack whispered.

Eddie's eyes bulged as he screamed something unintelligible through the gag.

"Cat got your tongue?" Jack chuckled. "After all you've done, I can't think of one good reason why I shouldn't just leave you here."

A mumbled "no" could be heard through the gag as Eddie shook his head violently. He blinked several times and his eyes softened.

Jack's didn't.

Without explanation, Jack turned his back to Eddie to help Maria get out of the chair—receiving a gripping hug in the process. As he touched Maria, Jack was hit with a flash of doubt: was this really a hoax, or could he have been mistaken? He didn't want to hang around to find out.

Eddie screamed at the top of his lungs, which came out through the gag as a muffled but extended grunt.

Jack pulled away from Maria and turned back to him. "Too bad, Eddie. Sometimes you just reap what you sow."

With that said, Jack turned back to Hugh, who was finishing up with the guard. "Time's up. Let's go!"

Hugh nodded, and the three of them dashed for the back door. At the same moment, a commotion broke out at the front entrance. The guards were coming back.

"Go!" Jack ordered, pushing Hugh and Maria out the back door toward the grass cliff. He turned back into the room as he fidgeted with the AK-47, hoping he had found the safety switch.

The entrance doors burst open and two armed men ran into the room. Jack aimed the weapon above their heads and pulled the trigger. The sound was deafening, as a volley of shrieking pops shattered the silence. The charging guards dove for the floor, taking cover. Jack glanced up quickly, pleased to see that no damage had come to the ceiling—he had been right. The weapon contained blanks. His final doubts were extinguished as he turned and sprinted out the door.

Hugh and Maria were running along the walkway to his right, heading for the loading dock at the back of the building. Jack took off in a full sprint after them. He was sure the guards would be on the move in seconds.

As Jack turned the corner to the loading dock, he saw that the white van was in place, facing the direction of the access road. He caught a glimpse of Hugh and Maria ducking into the dark corner where he'd hidden moments before. He ran toward the van as voices shouted at him from behind. Jack didn't stop, but simply slapped the back of the van, which roared to life, tires squealing as it accelerated forward. Jack leaped up the stairs to the loading dock and dove into the darkened storage area.

His timing was perfect, crouching down just as three men came running around the corner after him. But their attention wasn't on the storage area; they were yelling after the van escaping down the access road.

Jack breathed heavily, sucking in oxygen from a combination of sprinting around the building and the tension of the chase. He could hear Maria, Hugh, and now Tara panting beside him, each of them trying to make as little noise as possible. It wasn't a problem, however, as the actors playing the role of the rebels fired off bursts from their own AK-47s to try and stop the fleeing van. A cameraman came around the corner after them, shooting the whole scene.

When the van didn't stop, the three men jumped off the loading dock in fast pursuit of what they believed to be the four contestants. The cameraman ran after them.

Jack didn't move for a moment, waiting to make sure they were alone.

"It worked," Hugh whispered.

"Yeah," Jack said with a smile. "It did. Good work, Tara."

"My driver was great—once I convinced him the guns weren't really loaded."

"Which must have taken some doing," Jack added.

"The guns aren't loaded?" Maria asked, amazed. "Then what the heck is going on?'

"All a setup," Jack answered. "Part of our challenge."

"But they told us they'd killed all the production staff."

"All a lie," Hugh said. "So we're turning the game around on them."

"Oh my," Maria gasped. "So what's next?"

"You'll see." Jack grinned, getting up on his feet. "Follow me."

"How did this happen?" Zeke was screaming in the control room. "We've got to stop them before they leave the resort!"

The director and associate director were both yelling instructions into their headsets. Vince and Travis were sitting beside Zeke watching the room turn into total chaos.

"Their van just left the loading dock," the director turned and told Zeke.

"Don't we have any cameras on them?"

"No, the contestants were never supposed to go back there," the director answered defensively.

Zeke swore. The whole game had blown apart. The scenario was supposed to play out in the dining hall, as each contestant returned from the scavenger hunt to be captured by the rebels.

"We've got to stop them at the entrance. Get everybody we have down there!" Zeke yelled.

His orders were relayed through the communications channels to every staff member connected either by headset or walkie-talkie. Everybody was heading out to cut off the runaway van.

"Give me the mic, quick." Zeke stepped up to the front counter, grabbing the microphone tied into the speakers throughout the resort.

"Jack, Hugh, Tara, Maria, listen to me." Zeke spoke forcefully, but slowly into the microphone, hoping the occupants of the van could hear him. "This is the executive producer of *The Ultimate Challenge.* Do not leave the property. There is no rebel takeover—it was all part of the game. You are safe here. We need you to not run off."

Zeke paused as he watched the center screen with a picture of the front entryway to the resort on it. Headlights from the contestant's van were shining into the camera. Zeke could see the fake rebels at the bottom of the hill, standing in the middle of the road waving their arms frantically. The van wasn't slowing.

"They can't hear you," the director informed Zeke.

Everyone in the room watched in silence as the van approached, apparently willing to run over the two men to get out to the main road. Then at the last instant, the van slammed on its brakes, sending a cloud of dust into the air, engulfing the camera.

"What's happening?" Zeke demanded. The dust was too much for the camera in the darkness of the night. All they could see were the bright beams of the headlights shining through the thick cloud of dust, as if in a dense fog.

"Hold on," the director raised a hand to silence Zeke. "I'm getting a report."

"Put them on speaker!" Zeke shouted.

The technical director reached over and punched a button on the director's communications panel and a voice blared through the small speaker in front of them.

"We've got the van stopped and we're checking inside … there's just the driver. I repeat, there's just the driver. No one else is inside. The contestants are gone."

Zeke slammed his fist down on the console, shouting out a string of curse words that filled the room. "Where are they?"

Jack watched it all from the doorway as he and the other three contestants had snuck up the stairs to the back of the control room. Still carrying the AK-47, Jack aimed the gun at the ceiling and shot off a long burst of gunfire.

The reaction was priceless.

The director and his staff flung themselves out of their chairs and hit the floor, ducking under the console. Vince and the man next to him, watching from the couch, screamed as they jumped two feet before putting their hands over their heads in total fear and surrender.

Zeke spun around, swearing as he turned until his eyes caught sight of Jack—and then his face went from shock into a look that could kill. His eyes darkened, his brow creased.

"What the …"

"Don't talk!" Jack interrupted, his ears still ringing from the gunshots. "We're taking you hostage!"

"Don't be absurd." Zeke shook his head. "That gun's not loaded."

That brought the director and his staff peeking their heads out from under the console.

"Maybe not." Jack kept the weapon in his hands, pointed just above Zeke's head. "But before we give you back control of your silly little game, we have some demands."

Zeke angled his head, looking at Jack as if he'd lost his mind. "You what?"

"First," Jack continued undeterred. Even though the AK-47 was just a prop, holding Zeke at bay with it felt good. "Seeing that Eddie seems to be the only one still tied up and gagged, we declare he loses this challenge and is out of the game."

Zeke's eyes narrowed as he stared a hole right through Jack. A cameraman pushed his way into the room and started taping the confrontation.

"Second," Hugh said, standing just behind Jack. "The four of us demand to see our loved ones who have been brought to this island, immediately—before any new challenge commences."

Zeke started to step toward them. "You're both crazy. You can't come in here demanding ..."

Jack pointed the gun upward a bit and shot off a few more rounds. Whether there were bullets flying out of the barrel or not, the noise was intimidating enough for Zeke to jump a foot in the air before stopping dead in his tracks. The rest of the staff ducked for cover again.

Maria smiled, pushing closer to Jack. "And finally, we want the cameras in our rooms turned off when we talk with our family members. No recording."

Zeke didn't move, waiting to see if his group of renegade contestants were finished.

"Is that it?" he finally asked.

Jack turned to his other three companions, who all nodded, and then turned back to Zeke with a grin. "Yeah, that about covers it."

Zeke shook his head, a sly grin appearing on his face. "I have to hand it to you four. You're the first contestants we've ever had to pull one over on us—very well played."

"Thank you." Jack motioned his head toward the three people behind him, as if in a bow.

"Right." Zeke's eyes scanned over each of the other contestants, holding an extra second on Hugh. "Good job, all of you."

"Now about our demands?" Jack pressed.

"First of all, why don't you put down that ... very loud gun in your hands, so I know you won't go off half-cocked and blow my eardrums out again."

Jack shrugged. "Oh, I don't know, it's kind of growing on me."

"Please?"

Jack smirked, then tossed the gun on the couch next to Vince. "It's all yours, Vince."

"Good," Zeke sighed. "Now, why don't we all go down to the dining hall and talk this over, shall we?"

"What's to talk over?" Jack looked to his three allies standing beside him, then back to Zeke with a shrug. "You've heard our demands."

"Like I said, Jack." Zeke's voice grew cold. "It was very well played, but don't forget who controls the prize money, OK?"

Jack held his ground, staring back at Zeke. He knew they had nothing to push their demands unless everyone was willing to quit the game. That certainly wasn't the case, but he'd hoped their spectacular rescue would allow some leniency from Zeke, to at least get some time with his mom before her secret would be revealed.

"Downstairs." Zeke's eyes darkened. "All of you, now!"

Nobody moved. It seemed Jack's rebellious group was willing to wait for his cue. Jack stared into Zeke's eyes for just a moment longer, recalling his sadistic offer of a hundred thousand dollars to sleep with Maria. He was sure that whatever secret his mom was hiding, the man before him would not hesitate a heartbeat to reveal it to the entire nation—simply for his own benefit.

For the first time in his life, Jack experienced utter hatred for another human being. He suddenly wanted nothing to do with this man, or his game—and especially his money. The escape had been a rush, and Jack had gotten completely caught up in the excitement of it all. But as the adrenaline waned, he realized it was over.

Jack was ready to go home.

He blinked, breaking eye contact with the personified evil in front of him and shrugged to the other contestants. "Let's go."

The four of them headed down the hallway, and to the stairs that would take them back to the dining hall.

The control room was deathly quiet as everyone waited for Zeke's reaction. He stood frozen, shaken to his soul by the passion in Jack's eyes. He felt the pit of his stomach churning, as right before him, Jack had morphed from the playful adversary to an impassioned man that seemed to loathe him.

The son he had so much hope for, now hating him just like the others did.

With an act of true willpower, Zeke forced his voice out. "Was there a camera in here to record the beginning of that?"

The director pulled himself off of the floor and answered sheepishly, "No, sir."

Zeke swore before turning his head toward Travis and Vince. "Then we'll just have to recreate the beginning of that scene, won't we?"

When they got back to the room, nothing had been disturbed. Eddie was still in his chair, tied up and gagged, as was the local guard lying on the floor. The crew had stayed behind their fake wall, unwilling to compromise the scenario until they'd gotten official word from the director. But they had enjoyed listening in on the confrontation between Zeke and the contestants through the director's headset.

Jack was the first to walk up to Eddie, whose eyes were as wide as silver dollars at seeing him approach.

Jack reached for his gag. "It's OK, Eddie. There aren't any rebels."

Eddie held nothing back as soon as his mouth was free. "What kind of stunt you think you were pulling, leaving me here, man?"

Hugh stepped in behind him, working the knots out of the rope. "It was all a hoax—part of the game. You weren't in any danger."

"The hell I wasn't," Eddie continued. "I ought to kill you all for leaving me here."

"Hold on there, Hugh," Jack said. "I'm not so sure we should untie him, are you?"

"Now that you bring it up, he does seem kind of volatile."

"Hey, don't be playing games, now." Eddie softened his tirade. "I'm just letting off some steam—I've been tied up like this for way too long. Get me out of this thing, please."

"Only if you're good," Tara said, as she leaned in front of his face.

"I'll be good," Eddie promised.

"I say leave him be." Maria turned her back toward him. "What'd he ever do for us?"

"That's true." Jack looked at him. "Eddie, how would you answer that?"

"Just untie me," Eddie spat back. "And quit playin' around!"

"Temper, temper," Maria said, with a giggle.

The doors opened, and in walked Vince and several of the production staff.

"All right, let's gather around," he instructed.

After untying Eddie, the contestants sat around the table waiting for word on what was to happen next.

"It's been an interesting evening," Vince began. "One that will go down in the record books as probably the most bizarre night on any of *The Ultimate Challenges.*"

Maria, Hugh, and Tara cheered. Jack laughed, eventually joining in. Eddie sat stone-faced.

"The producers have decided that they have some regrouping to do. Needless to say, this challenge didn't exactly turn out the way they'd expected."

"What about seeing our families?" Maria asked.

"We're getting to that. It's very late, and we've all been through so much, we've decided to suspend the game until noon tomorrow—give our producers a chance to figure out what they're going to do, as well as give you guys a chance to rest."

Jack didn't even know what time it was. It had to be after three in the morning; noon probably wasn't that far away.

"We're also going to stop all in-room recording—go off the record, so to speak—for the rest of the night. You'll have to trust us on this one."

Jack shrugged. He trusted Zeke about as much as he did Eddie.

"And this will play heavily into the rest of your evening, because now, even though you know there is a family secret that could be revealed in the next challenge, we are allowing you to see your families tonight and spend time with them unmonitored."

"When we reconvene at noon, we'll have the results of the scavenger hunt, which will determine who is exempt from the next challenge, as well as who will be sent home."

"Wait a minute," Jack interrupted. "How can there be a decision on the scavenger hunt after the whole armed rebellion thing?"

"We're going through your vans tonight to see who completed the list and who didn't," Vince answered. "We'll also take into consideration the order of who made it back to the resort."

"But all that changed when you had armed thugs capturing the contestants as they returned," Jack stated.

"Be that as it may, it'll all be part of the judging. Now, one of our staffers will escort each of you to the bungalows where your family members are being kept."

Jack shook his head. Still counting the scavenger hunt was ridiculous—but what did it matter? He'd be heading home tomorrow anyway, right? He turned and nudged Maria before she got up to leave. She turned toward him, her eyes troubled.

"Maria," Jack whispered. "Don't trust them. Make sure you don't say anything in your room that you don't want broadcast all over the nation."

Maria nodded. "I know, thanks."

"Go be with Teresa," Jack smiled warmly. "I'll be praying for you."

Her eyes stayed on him for a moment, tearing up before she nodded.

Jack started to get up from his chair when he heard a cracking sound. It was faint, but loud enough to grab his attention.

He heard it again, and at the same moment, realized what it was.

The egg!

Jack had totally forgotten about putting it in his vest pocket. In all the commotion, he was shocked it hadn't been crushed. He gently reached in and pulled it out.

The side of it was cracked, and a tiny beak was punching from the inside, breaking a hole in the egg.

"Oh," Maria sighed. "How precious."

A cameraman ran up and pointed his lens right into Jack's hands.

"What have you got there, Jack?" Vince called over as Jack looked up and smiled.

"Item number one on my list: a live chicken."

Zeke stood up from his couch, stretching out his arms and yawning.

"Well, that's a wrap. You can all call it a night," he said to the control room staff sitting across the counter in front of him. "Get some rest. You deserve it."

The director and his team pushed themselves back from the counter. They didn't have to be told twice. It had been a long night.

Zeke grinned as he watched them exit the room. He could see on their faces that they were still unnerved by Jack's semi-automatic gunfire attack in the booth earlier.

Travis, as always, stood by his side. "You're not going to listen in on the family discussions?"

"Nope," Zeke answered. "We told them this one was off the record—so it is."

Travis cocked his head. "You sure?"

"Yeah, big day tomorrow," Zeke added. "I need you to supervise the scavenger hunt judging while I try and figure out how to adjust the next challenges. We'll talk after that."

"OK," Travis said.

"Come on." Zeke led him to the door. "I'll walk you down."

They were the last two leaving the control room, heading down the hallway as the head technician walked by them to shut down all the equipment. Zeke paused, snapping his fingers.

"Ah, shoot," Zeke suddenly muttered. "I left my briefcase in the room. I'd better get it before he locks the door. You go on, I'll catch up with you later."

Travis agreed and turned down the stairs.

Zeke made sure he was out of sight before he turned back down the hall. He made it back into the control room as the technician was sitting on the console, turning off all the monitors.

"Go ahead and leave it all on, Mark," Zeke said to interrupt him. "I've got a bit more work to do in here."

"Yes, sir," he said. "Not a problem."

The production assistant led Jack around the pool in the opposite direction of where his bungalow was. He felt his heart rate increase and his hands grow clammy as they headed to his mother's room, which surprised him. He hadn't been nervous about seeing his mom since that night in high school, when he'd come home at dawn. How was she going to respond when he brought up the threat of some dark secret in her past? And did he really want to find out what it was?

"Here you are," the production assistant said as they came to the room's door. He pulled out a key and unlocked the door before turning and leaving Jack alone.

"Mom?" Jack called into the darkened room. "Are you awake?"

Jack took a step into the bungalow. It had the same design as his, so he knew where the bedroom would be. "Mom, it's me, Jack."

"What?" he heard a groggy reply.

Jack stepped toward the bedroom and flipped on the light switch.

"Jack?" Amanda sat up in bed, reaching out her arms. "Thank God you're OK."

Jack leaned over the bed and took hold of his mother. She was shaking slightly, repeating over and over her thanks to God that he was all right.

He pulled back, sitting next to her on the bed. "Of course I'm OK. Why are you so worried?"

"Why am I worried?" Amanda tilted her head. "Could the sound of gunshots all around this place while I'm locked inside this room have anything to do with it?"

"Oh," Jack laughed. "I guess I can see where that might be a bit stressful."

Amanda punched him lightly in the arm. "It's not funny."

Jack explained why she'd heard the gunshots, continuing to make light of her worries, as sons are prone to do.

"You don't know what I've been through since you disappeared," Amanda protested.

"Disappeared? Didn't Kathryn tell you?"

"Oh, she told me all right." Amanda smiled, as the relief began to settle in. It was so good to see him. "We've had some interesting discussions since you've been gone."

Jack wondered what that meant, but he decided to let it go.

"How did you get down here?"

"Well, after I called Hollywood, trying to find you …"

"You called looking for me?"

"Yes."

"Why?"

Amanda paused. This was going to be difficult. "I figured you were in trouble."

"Trouble? It's just a reality TV show."

"It's not just any show." Amanda reached up and placed her palm against Jack's cheek. "It's Zeke Roberts' reality show."

Jack felt his face flush at the name. "What do you know about Zeke?"

Amanda blinked and lowered her head. "A lot—and it's time that I finally told you."

"You know him?'

Amanda looked up and nodded. "From a long time ago, yes."

"Oh my," Jack sighed. Life was suddenly getting very complicated.

"I'll tell you everything, Jack," Amanda whispered. "You deserve to know."

"No." Jack stopped her. Whatever she had to share, Jack did not want it recorded by the show and broadcast throughout the nation. "Not yet, not in here. I don't trust them."

"Oh, that's right." Amanda looked around the room. "The cameras."

"You've found them?"

"Yes, in the shower, the bathroom, over the bed. It's disgusting."

"How about getting dressed," Jack suggested. "We'll go for a walk."

"But I'm locked in," Amanda said.

"I don't think so," Jack got up from the bed and walked back to the front door. It opened when he turned the knob. "Get your clothes on. I'm sure we have a lot to talk about."

Zeke watched from the control room, listening to every word. He was alone, sitting at the center of the front bench where the director was usually stationed. They were leaving the room—he knew enough to be able to punch up the cameras in the room on the large plasma, which would then automatically route the microphones from that room into the control room speakers. But once they left and walked around the resort, Zeke didn't know enough about the equipment to be able to follow their conversation.

He reached for the walkie-talkie sitting on the console in front of him. "Zeke, for Mark."

A few seconds later, he heard Mark's voice. "Go for Mark."

"Mark, I need you to meet me back in the control room if you could."

"Be right there."

Zeke leaned back in the chair, smiling. "You won't get away from me that easily, Jack."

Amanda walked in silence beside her son, holding on to his arm while searching deep in her soul for the right words. It was a bit cool this early in the morning and Amanda shuddered, but she knew it was more from nervousness than being chilled.

Jack led her beyond the pool and around the back of the main set of buildings.

"Where are we going?" she asked.

"Hopefully, where nobody can eavesdrop on us," Jack said. "They've got cameras everywhere around here, but picking up what we say will probably be a lot more difficult out on the cliff."

The scenery was incredible. From the cliff's edge, the moon shone off the surface of the ocean like a mirror. She could hear the waves breaking down below on the rocks. The soft tropical breeze offered the faint tinge of salt coming off the sea.

If we were only on this island for another reason, she thought.

Jack laid down a blanket he'd carried from the room, and the two sat facing the vast ocean.

"It's beautiful," Amanda remarked.

"Yeah, it is."

They sat quiet for a moment, Amanda collecting her thoughts; Jack, patiently waiting. She took a second to pray, asking God for the right words, and for Jack to have the right heart as he listened.

Amanda gazed off at the bright moon. "I met Zeke in college ..."

"They're on the cliff," Zeke spat out as soon as Mark entered the room. It'd taken him too long to get back. "I need to hear what they're saying!"

"Uh ... who?" Mark replied, as if he'd stepped into the tail end of a conversation. Zeke pointed to Jack and Amanda on the plasma screen, and hurriedly repeated his request.

"I can try," Mark said. "But we don't have any microphones placed out along the edge, just close to the building. The only way to hear them is if we had one of them wired."

"Well, we obviously can't do that—I just have to hear what they're saying," Zeke ordered. "Now!"

"I'll see what I can do." Mark turned and headed through a small door that led into the audio control room.

Jack sat quietly listening to his mom tell her story. His mind would wander, trying to figure out how the tale would end and what it would mean for him.

"He finally convinced me to go out with him a few times," Amanda sighed. "And I fell in love—or at least what I thought was love back then."

Jack wasn't surprised. As soon as she'd admitted that she knew Zeke, he figured it had to be a past love, although he couldn't imagine his mom with the shady man Jack had encountered.

"I was very different back then, what you might call a bit wild," Amanda admitted.

That explains a bit of it, Jack thought.

"It was before Christ," Amanda continued. "My B.C. years. It wasn't until I found your father that I also found God."

"I know," Jack smiled. He'd heard the stories growing up of how his dad had led his mom to the Lord.

"But there's a lot you don't know, honey." Amanda turned toward him. "Things we should've never kept from you."

Jack pursed his lips, fighting the urge to just get up and run. He wasn't sure he wanted to hear anymore. Perhaps ignorance was bliss after all. Whatever his mom was about to say, she had hidden from him for a reason. Could anything good come out of it if she was only telling him now because Zeke Roberts had his hands all over it?

Zeke watched in frustration on the plasma monitor from the robotic camera aimed at them, as well as through the window, peeking around the curtain and seeing the two with his own eyes. Even with all the sophisticated equipment they'd brought to the island, the wind and surf noise overpowered their expensive audio gear. He couldn't hear a word Amanda was saying to her son—to his son.

He was tempted to walk out onto the cliff and make the family complete. But then he saw, in his mind's eye, the expression Jack had shot at him before returning to the dining hall. He would be the last person Jack wanted to see. The image still left a hole in the pit of his stomach. All he wanted to do with this session of *The Ultimate Challenge* was reunite with Amanda and get to know his son. His chances at either one of those was rapidly slipping away, and for the life of him, he couldn't figure out a way to stop it.

"You're obsessed with that woman, Zeke." Travis had slipped into the room behind him. "It's been nearly thirty years, and you still can't let her go."

Zeke stared at the plasma, his anger seething. He whipped around. "What are you doing in here?"

"She's going to destroy you again." Travis ignored his question. "You've got to let it go."

"No!" Zeke snapped. "I've come too far with this—I can't let it go."

Travis shook his head and calmed his voice. "She wasn't worth it then, she's not worth it now."

Travis let his words hang in the room a moment, then turned and walked out, leaving Zeke alone.

Zeke stared at the fuzzy picture of them sitting on the grass—mom and son sharing the secrets of his birth, talking about *him.*

Zeke hadn't felt this helpless since the day Amanda told him she was pregnant. He'd give half of his wealth to be able to hear how she was telling their story to Jack. He thought the meal had gone well—she was more receptive to him than he could have imagined. He even felt like he had been gaining ground with her, that her heart was softening as they talked. That was until he blew it and mentioned there were other family members on the island.

It would be his undoing, unless he could find a way to convince her how sorry he was for his mistake. He now regretted playing games with her instead of being honest.

As he contemplated his strategy, he noticed movement on the screen in front of him. Jack's arm had reached around his mother's shoulder as he pulled her close to him. She shuddered under his embrace, obviously sobbing.

Zeke felt his heart break. Emotions flooded through him stronger than he could believe. He wanted to be the one comforting her, yet that was a dream that seemed impossibly out of reach. How could he recoup what they had so many years before? How could he convince her to let him love her once again?

Amanda and Jack were getting up now, heading back down the path around the main building. Zeke watched them through the window until they dropped out of sight, then turned back to the array of video monitors and watched them walk around the pool area. They were headed to her bungalow, back to where he could hear everything they said.

Zeke sat down in the director's chair, turning up the knob that fed his speakers with sound from Amanda's room. He could feel sweat break out on his forehead and under his armpits, realizing he was afraid of what he might hear.

66

"You haven't said much," Amanda said, as they entered her room.

They had walked back in silence, Amanda giving Jack time to deal with all that she'd told him and Jack opting to say nothing at all. The news had come as a shock—not so much that his dad hadn't been his biological father; there had always been little clues when he was growing up. Nobody ever said he looked like his father—only his mother. But still, the shock of facing twenty-seven years of not knowing the truth hit hard.

Jack was also greatly affected by how deeply his mother had been hurt during that time in college, and how painful it was to see those wounds ripped open all these years later. If anything, it made him appreciate ten times over what his dad had done for him—for his mom.

"I'm sorry, I just don't know what to say, Mom." Jack closed the door behind him. "It's all pretty shocking. I mean, I can sure see why you and Dad decided to not talk about it."

Amanda sat down on the couch. She looked exhausted. Jack kicked off his shoes and sat beside her.

"It's just so hard to believe Dad wasn't my biological father," Jack said, staring straight ahead.

"But that doesn't change a thing about who you are," Amanda said softly. "You are who you are in spite of your biological father. Kevin adopted you and treated you as his own from day one. He couldn't have loved you any more."

Jack nodded.

"I'm sorry it had to come out this way." Amanda's eyes were bloodshot from crying. "I should've told you at some point. It was wrong of me to hide the truth all these years."

"If you had done what Zeke wanted you to do, I wouldn't even be alive."

As Amanda reached out and grabbed her son's hand, her eyes pooled again. "I would go through it all again in a heartbeat, Jack. As painful as it was, I couldn't bear to think of what life would be like without you."

Jack squeezed her hand, looking at her and fighting back his own tears. "God had a plan. What you thought was a desperate tragedy might've been the one thing He could use to get your attention."

Amanda nodded, a smile creasing her lips. "I would probably have never heard His voice if I hadn't gotten pregnant. I was so full of myself at the time. But I ended up coming out of it with two gifts—well three, actually. You, Kevin, and then God."

Jack smiled. "Yeah, Dad was quite a godsend for you, wasn't he?"

"He loved you so much, I don't think it could've been any different if you had been his own."

"I know." Jack paused. "Why didn't you have any other kids, though?"

Amanda sighed. "We tried … even went through all the testing. But we just didn't have the money to go through all the fertility treatments. So we just spoiled you instead."

"Right," Jack chuckled.

He let the laughter hang in the room for a second—it felt good. "You know, Mom, Zeke won't reveal your secret on the show. I won't let him. I'll quit first."

Amanda shook her head. "It doesn't matter anymore. The only person that I care about knowing is you, and maybe it was better this way. I don't know if I ever could've found the courage to tell you the truth. Whatever else happens now, it's ancient history. I can leave it in the past."

"I hope so," Jack sighed. "You've suffered enough."

"You know, once the truth is out, the power of the secret is gone. Zeke has no control over me. He never really did. I only allowed it by trying to hide something."

"Even still, I don't want to have anything to do with him. He hasn't changed. The way he treated you back then is no different from how he's treated Maria this week."

"Maria?" Amanda asked.

"Yeah, another contestant. You'd really like her, Mom."

"Oh really?" she angled her head.

Jack felt his face blush. "That's another story, a bit long for tonight. I'll introduce you tomorrow."

"OK. But what about Kathryn?"

"Oh, I've thought a lot about her this week as well," Jack admitted.

"Well, I can tell you she's certainly thought a lot about you. She really went to bat for you back home. She did everything within her power, and beyond, to try to keep your job—putting her job on the line in the process. She even had a bunch of parents show up at the board meeting to support you."

Jack lowered his head. The guilt he felt about his attraction to Maria slammed him hard as he heard about Kathryn's attempts to save his job. But before he could deal with his emotions, Amanda's next words devastated him.

"But it didn't work, Jack."

Jack had hoped the producers had been lying about losing his job just to get him in the poker game.

"You know about the school board's decision?"

Amanda frowned. "Yes. She called me after the meeting."

"Then it's true." Jack's shoulders slumped, as he slid lower into the couch.

"I'm sorry, honey. But how did you know?"

"The producers told me last night—actually sometime early this morning."

"How would they know?" Amanda asked.

"Believe me, they know everything."

"What are you going to do?"

"I have no idea." Jack shook his head. "Just try and live through this week first, I guess. Then, maybe I'll apply over at the Christian high school. But I'll really miss those kids at Royal."

Amanda looked up at him and grinned.

"Is there something I'm missing?"

"It's not over until the fat lady sings, my boy," Amanda said with a wink.

"Huh?"

"I set up a meeting between your principal and a lawyer with Jay Sekulow's organization—the American Center for Law and Justice."

Jack's eyebrows shot up. "You what?"

"I'm sure they got an earful about your First Amendment rights, and how they can't terminate you for expressing your religious beliefs."

"Oh my gosh." Jack shook his head. "How am I going to pay for that?"

"You don't have to," Amanda answered. "They don't charge. We'll just have to see how the meeting went when we get back."

"You're incredible, you know that?"

"I've been told that a time or two," Amanda said with a smile.

Jack was thrilled to see a spark light up in her eyes.

"You know," Amanda continued, "I've spent a lot of time with Kathryn these past couple of days. I really think she's falling for you."

"Really?"

"I could be wrong, but all the signs are there," Amanda said gently. "You'll have to tell me more about this Maria."

Jack sighed. "I will. We have lots to talk about when this is all over."

"Yes, we do."

"You need to get some sleep, though." Jack got up from the couch.

"You do too. Who knows what tomorrow will bring?"

"As soon as they reconvene the game, I'm out of it," Jack stated flatly.

Amanda got up and walked him to the door, holding on to his arm. "Whatever you think is best. But don't do it on account of me."

Jack turned and gave her a hug. "You're amazing. I'm glad you're here."

"Me, too."

"Now go get some sleep—we both need it." She kissed him on the cheek and sent him out the door.

Zeke dropped his head down and rubbed over his eyebrows with his right hand. He'd lost them both. Amanda didn't want to have anything to do with him—and neither did Jack.

Where did he go wrong? He thought he had the perfect plan: bring Jack to the island, let him see the wealth, power, and fame that his real father could bring him. What man could resist? Jack should be running to him right now, looking to take his place as his firstborn son.

And Amanda—he still didn't get her. He thought this would be the perfect time to reach her—a year after losing her husband. Time enough to get over the grieving and just when the loneliness would have settled deep.

He thought he'd had her at dinner, only to see the wall go back up between them. He had to do something. There was one day left—one day to pull out all the stops to recapture the love of his life.

It would take a brilliant plan, one that was just starting to take form in the back of his mind.

Travis staggered down the walkway, heading toward the production office at eight in the morning. He'd gotten maybe two hours of sleep before the production assistant pounded on his door, yelling that Zeke wanted him in the office.

Most challenge weeks were like this—little sleep, taping the contestants basically 24/7 to get the best footage needed to make their number one rated show. But this week had drained him beyond the limits.

The production office was empty with the exception of one other production assistant at the coffee machine. Travis walked over, poured a cup, adding about four tablespoons of sugar to it, then headed to Zeke's office.

"About time," Zeke stated, as Travis stepped into the room.

"Did you sleep at all?" Travis asked groggily.

"No time," Zeke answered sharply. "We had the game blow up in our faces last night, and you think we have time to sleep?"

"Blow up?" Travis angled his head. "I thought it was great television. We just need to recreate the first part of the contestants barging into the control room like you said and we've got an amazing show. And besides, you said …"

"Your idea of great television makes me look like an idiot," Zeke grumbled.

"If that's what it takes," Travis said with a smirk.

"Shut up! This isn't just about the show and you know it."

"Well, it should be, Zeke. This could be the highest rated series in our history—in the whole history of television. When word gets out about this one, we'll be able to charge a million, maybe a million five for each commercial. We'll make a killing …"

"All you care about is the money!" Zeke screamed.

Travis stopped, waiting for his friend to calm down.

"There's more at stake here," Zeke said softly.

"You're losing it, pal." Travis shook his head. "You've got to come to grips with this whole thing. You can't live in the past. What was between you and Amanda is ancient history. I told you this was a bad idea from the beginning. How else did you expect it to end?"

"I need your help. We have to finish this," Zeke pleaded.

"What's your plan?"

"One final challenge," Zeke stated firmly. "I'm afraid I'm going to lose Jack if we let this continue any longer."

"So?" Travis argued. "Let him go—he's served his purpose. We could finish as scheduled with the other four. There are still three challenges to go."

"No," Zeke said. "I won't jeopardize that. Jack is the game, remember?"

"Maybe to you."

"Forget the three challenges, combine them in some way." Zeke ignored him. "I want to have one great finale."

"I'm not sure we have enough cameras to cover something like that."

"Just talk to the director and make it work," Zeke spat out. "I've got to figure out a way to give Jack the incentive to stay in the game."

It didn't take Jack long to find out that family members were once again off-limits to contestants. His mom was sequestered back in her bungalow, while Jack had the run of the resort. It didn't matter much though; he hadn't gotten out of bed until after eleven o'clock. There wasn't much time left before the noon deadline and the restart of the competition. He grabbed a late breakfast, then walked around the resort mulling over the events of last night.

He spotted Maria sitting on the edge of the pool, dangling her feet in the water. She looked up and waved Jack over.

"How are you this morning?" Jack asked, sitting down beside her.

"I'm OK," she responded. "How about you?"

"I'm great." Jack smiled, a bit relieved that this whole ordeal would be over soon. "How's Teresa?"

Maria grinned. "She's great. It was so good to see her."

"I can't wait to meet her."

Her eye caught the sun just right and sparkled, as her grin grew wider. "I'd like that. How about your mom? Everything all right?"

"Yeah," Jack answered without explanation. "It's all OK."

They sat, watching the reflections off the shimmering water.

Jack leaned closer to her, whispering quietly. "Did you talk about anything with your family?"

Maria looked at him, staying close. "No. I couldn't do it."

Jack saw the pain revealed in her eyes. "I'm sorry." He reached over and placed his hand on her arm.

"Thanks." She looked down. "I'm just praying since I was the first one back at the resort, I'll get the exemption."

Jack pulled her chin up to him, smiling warmly. "I hope you do too."

She reached over and put her arm around him, pulling him into a hug. "Thank you so much, Jack."

"You're welcome. Is there anything I can do?"

Maria let him go, keeping her face close to his. "Let me win?"

Jack laughed. "If I could I would. But I won't be competing any longer."

"What? You're kidding."

"I had a long talk with my mom last night," Jack explained. "What's been hidden for years will stay that way. I won't allow this show to spread her secret nationwide. I'm done with it all."

"Oh, Jack," Maria whispered. "I'm so sorry."

"Don't be. I was crazy to get involved in the first place. This game gets to you in ways you don't expect. Look how suspicious I was of you as soon as I found out about your personal challenge."

"I don't blame you for that. You wouldn't believe the mixed emotions I struggled through every time we were alone."

"Oh, I can believe it." Jack grinned. "You kind of have a way of stirring emotions."

Maria blushed as they sat quietly. A moment later, Jack heard footsteps coming up behind him.

"What are you guys talking about?" Hugh asked.

Jack looked up at him with a grin. "I was just telling Maria I hope she wins."

"What about me?" Hugh spread his arms out in front of him. "I thought we had a deal."

"I'm afraid our deal's off. I'm dropping out."

"You're what?" Hugh's eyebrows rose in surprise.

"It's over," Jack repeated.

"You can't do that, man."

"Yes, I can."

"No, seriously, you've got a great chance to be ten million dollars richer." Hugh's voice grew serious. "How can you walk away from that?"

"I thought you'd be happy," Jack said with a grin. "One less person standing in your way."

"Well, now you've got something there." Hugh rubbed his chin. "Then, if they bump Eddie out for last night, that'll just leave me and the women—all right!"

Maria and Jack laughed.

"Attention contestants!" The loudspeakers sounded around the pool. "Please convene in the dining hall immediately. *The Ultimate Challenge* resumes!"

"Here we go," Jack said. "I can't wait to see Eddie again."

Vince stood before the assembled contestants, who sat around a circular table. They waited anxiously for the final word on the scavenger hunt, and what ramifications would come from the hostage rescue.

"Good afternoon," Vince began. "We have some business to take care of before we begin our day. First of all, to our hostage rescuers—the producers wanted me to let you know that although they allowed all of you time with your families, your demand for Eddie to be bounced from the game for being the only contestant still held by the rebels has been denied."

"You guys tried to sell me out?" Eddie fumed, glancing over at Jack with disdain.

Jack just nodded politely—it didn't matter anyway.

"We are however," Vince continued, "prepared to declare a loser from the scavenger hunt, who will be leaving immediately."

Vince paused, allowing the camera crew to get close-ups of each of the contestants as they reacted. These were the moments he relished the most—drawing out the tension for both the home audience and those in front of him.

"The following contestants did not complete their list of items: Tara, Maria, and Jack."

Maria stood up quickly. "That's not true!"

Jack followed her. He might as well go out with a bang. "We had everything listed."

"So did I," Tara added.

"Jack," Vince began, "you didn't have a live chicken or a bathing suit."

"The live chicken wasn't in the van, it was in my vest—and I handed it over to one of your production assistants last night."

"I remember the hatching egg—not exactly what we asked for."

"But did I, or did I not, bring back a live chicken?" Jack asked rhetorically.

Vince paused, then nodded. "OK, I'll give you the chicken. But that still leaves the bathing suit—that both you and Maria failed to acquire."

"I'll answer that one," Maria said stepping forward. "The bathing suit is on the premises—I just didn't have time to add it to my items before I was taken away at gunpoint."

"What do you mean?" Vince asked.

Maria reached behind her and pulled out of her shorts the bathing suit she'd worn on the first day at the resort. She held the two-piece bikini in front of her like a prize. "Here it is. I just didn't have a chance to get it in the van last night."

Vince's head shook from side to side. "That's your bathing suit, Maria. I don't think that's what we meant."

"I'm sure you didn't mean an egg for Jack either," Maria argued. "But this was in my possession last night, just not where your staff was looking."

Vince turned toward Jack. "And I can assume your bathing suit was in your room as well?"

"Yep," Jack said with a grin. "I was unable to place my final item in the van—seeing that we were busy rescuing those contestants worthy of being saved."

Jack's insult had the intended effect, as Eddie scowled and glanced back at him.

Vince chuckled. "Highly irregular, Maria and Jack." He turned toward Tara. "Do you happen to have a fishing net in your possession that we don't know about, Tara?"

Tara's mouth dropped. "A fishing net? My list said a fishing pole."

"No," Vince stated. "I'm pretty sure your list matched everyone else's. You were supposed to get a fishing net."

"Oh no!" Tara brought her hand over her mouth.

"I'm sorry, Tara," Vince said without any further discussion. "You've been eliminated."

Tara started to argue, but whatever she saw in Vince made her back down as her shoulders sagged.

"Wait a minute," Jack said to Vince. "What if I drop out, then can Tara stay in my place?"

Jack felt every eye in the room—and probably every camera lens he couldn't see—suddenly zoom in on him.

But Vince handled his question calmly. "No, Jack. The decision has already been made, and your sacrifice wouldn't help Tara."

"But you'd still have four contestants to continue. And it's my choice if I want to," Jack argued.

"No," Vince stated flatly. "Besides, you'll change your mind in a moment if you'll just hold on. At this point, the decision is final—Tara has been eliminated. We have four contestants left."

Jack looked at Vince as if he'd lost his mind. They can't force him to continue. If he wanted to quit, what could they do?

Tara walked up to Jack, giving him a quick hug. "Thanks for trying."

"I wish you great success," Jack said somberly. Hugh and Maria came up to console her and wish her the best as well. Eddie just stayed in his chair, focused on Vince. When Tara had left the room, Vince continued.

"Now on with the game."

Maria raised her hand and stood.

"Yes, Maria?" Vince asked.

"What about who came in first—they were supposed to be exempt from the next challenge."

"Ah, yes." Vince grinned mischievously. "Something was mentioned to that effect. However, that has been rescinded, thanks to the brilliant hostage rescue made on your behalf."

"What?" Maria asked.

"Yes, you guys changed the rules—now, so have we," Vince stated proudly.

"But ..."

"Sorry, Maria," Vince interrupted. "No arguments. Sit down."

Maria had no choice. She looked over at Jack, as if he could make it better, but all he could do was shrug at her. He was as surprised as she was.

"Now, here's what's going to happen," Vince continued. "Each of you had a chance to spend some time with your loved ones—unmonitored, as we promised. So we don't know what was said. Perhaps each of you talked about the deep dark family secret with your loved ones, perhaps you chose to stay silent about the past—or, as I suspect, there was probably a combination of the two. But I digress."

Jack took his eyes off of Vince and studied the three other contestants. Vince had their full attention. It seemed as if each of them had something in their past that they wished to remain hidden, if he was reading the worried looks on their faces correctly.

"There's only one way that you can keep your family's dirty laundry from being revealed—and that's to win the game outright," Vince stated, then stared directly at Jack. "If you lose, or even drop out, then the dark part of your family's history will be prominently displayed on the show this summer."

Jack felt Vince's eyes bore right through him. He couldn't even walk away from the game without risking his mother's past being broadcast across the nation. They had managed to find a way to trap him until the very end.

"The winner, however, will not only walk away with the ten million dollars," Vince projected with his game-show host smile, "but will also be able to bury their little secret forever. We call it our 'winner-take-all' challenge. There will be no alliances, no helping any other contestant—it's either win it all, or lose it all. Now it sounds like we've got some incentive, don't we? Not only to win—but also not to lose. Still thinking about quitting, Jack?"

Jack didn't have anything to say.

Maria looked over at him with a horrified look. The color had drained from her face. Her lips were pale and her eyes looked dark and lifeless. Hugh didn't seem thrilled either—only Eddie looked excited.

Jack shook his head, wishing he'd never agreed to get involved in the first place. He seemed to be boxed in with nowhere to turn—exactly where Zeke wanted him to be.

"So let's get to it." Vince evidently gave up on Jack replying. "You have thirty minutes to get your swimsuits on and report back up here on the cliff's ledge."

69

Amanda spent a restless morning confined in her room. After waking up around ten-thirty, she'd dressed and had planned on taking a walk around the resort, only to find her front door once again locked from the outside.

A half-hour later, Josh had showed up with a tray of breakfast and coffee. It was much appreciated, but he did not have any news on what was happening with the game, or when she could see Jack again.

Sitting on the couch meditating on her daily reading in Psalms, she bolted upright when a knock on the door disturbed her silence. Maybe it was Jack.

She quickly set her Bible down and moved toward the door. As she approached, the knock repeated.

"Amanda?" She heard Zeke's voice. "It's me, Zeke."

Her stomach dropped, the excitement instantly replaced with apprehension. She paused at the door, realizing she couldn't open it for him; he would have to open it for her.

She braced herself, praying quickly once again before she spoke. "Come in."

The door opened in front of her. Zeke stood beyond it, smiling warmly, holding a bouquet of tropical flowers in his hand.

"For you," he offered.

Amanda smiled despite her true feelings, and took the vase from him. "That's very sweet. Thank you."

"It's the least I can do after last night," Zeke said. "May I come in?"

"Sure." Amanda stepped away from the door, moving to her dinette table to place the flowers down. "They're beautiful."

"A mixture of flowers indigenous to the island," Zeke explained. "I thought you might like them."

"I do." Amanda sat down, leaning over and taking in the fragrance of a tall orange and yellow flower. "Please, sit down."

"Thank you." Zeke took the seat across from her. He didn't say anything at first, but looked right at her for a moment.

"What?"

"It's amazing how beautiful you still are," Zeke answered. "Usually, reality can never compare to the memories we hold in our minds. But in this case, you have greatly exceeded them."

Amanda smiled, feeling her cheeks flush and imagining them to be crimson red. Despite the anger over Zeke's forced manipulation in her life, it had been a long time since she'd heard words like that.

"Zeke . . ." Amanda said.

"Wait," Zeke held up his hand. "Before you respond, there's something I want you to know."

She paused, nodding her head in permission for him to continue.

"I am so sorry about this whole thing," he began. "The game, bringing Jack into it, and, especially, bringing you into it. I was wrong. I just wanted to find some way to get to know Jack, and be able to see you again. I should've found a better way."

Amanda sighed. "Yes, you should have."

"I know." Amanda could see he was uncomfortable, struggling with what to say next. "Well, I would imagine that Jack mentioned one of the reasons why you were brought here?"

Amanda nodded. "It did come up that you were planning to shout our history across the nation."

Zeke bit on his upper lip, something she remembered him doing whenever he was stressed. "Yeah, well, after our talk last night, I kind of had a change of heart."

"Really?" Amanda cocked her head.

"Yeah. I changed the game this morning."

"Well, isn't that grand of you." She let the sarcasm drip through her voice. "After uprooting Jack's life, manipulating it so that I end up down here to be part of your game, people are getting hurt, one woman is dead—and you now have a change of heart?"

"I deserved that," Zeke admitted.

Amanda scowled. "I can't believe what you've become. Is this stupid game of yours really worth it?"

Zeke lowered his head, then backed away from the table and started pacing the room. "Look, this isn't working."

Amanda was amazed at the change in his demeanor. The façade he'd been keeping before her vanished in an instant. She could see him struggling deeply. Then he stopped and leaned over the table in front of her, his eyes softer, his voice pleading.

"The whole game—me, it's not what you think."

"What do you mean?"

She could tell he was searching for words, completely out of his element and uncomfortable. "I can't tell you everything, yet—but I will. You just have to trust me."

"Trust you?"

"Yeah," Zeke shrugged. "I know that's a stretch. But I have a good reason for everything."

Amanda looked at him struggling, wanting to understand. "Why?"

He sighed, looked down and rubbed at his forehead. "It was kind of a test."

"A test?"

"For Jack—for you, I guess."

"For me?" Amanda's voice cracked.

"Don't be mad, Amanda. You made something out of your life. All I've ever done outside of this show was mess up mine. You had a successful marriage and you still have a great relationship with your son. I wanted to see if Jack was really any different than my kids. I wanted to find out why you were so different from me."

"You could've called and asked."

Zeke didn't answer; she could see he was drained.

"I was never going to reveal any deep dark secrets on the show—especially yours. It was just the leverage I needed to break Jack down and find out what's at his core."

"You could've mentioned that before you sent him to my room last night," Amanda said, rolling her eyes. Her first impulse was to be furious with him. But she held back for a second. Would keeping her past a secret for the rest of her life have been the best for her?

For Jack?

Maybe God had a plan. Maybe he used Zeke, of all people, to push her along. An interesting thought she'd have to contemplate later.

"The whole thing just got carried away," Zeke sighed. "I didn't know how to stop it. I'm sorry."

"It sounds like you've just described your whole life."

"I know. Trust me, I know."

"There was a much better way, Zeke." Amanda softened her voice, reaching across the table and taking his hand. "Instead of bringing us into your world for your silly bit of testing, you should have just come to ours. I don't know what you expected to discover by putting Jack through all this."

Zeke intertwined his fingers in hers. "Actually, you'd be amazed at what I've learned. I want what you guys have—I want to have a purpose in my life, other than myself."

Amanda felt a lump growing in her throat. Could he be serious?

Or was this just another of his carefully orchestrated attempts to push her in the direction he wanted. She was tempted to believe him.

"That's a discussion I'd be glad to have with you—once I know you're serious."

"Oh, I'm serious," Zeke said. "You don't spend the kind of money this whole game has cost me if you're not serious about finding some answers. You mentioned the other night that there's always hope, even for me."

"It's true."

"Then I'm counting on it, Amanda." She was shocked to see Zeke's eyes filling with tears. "I'm really counting on it."

Amanda sat, stunned at the broken man before her. So much time had passed between them. In her wildest dreams, she could never have imagined the encounter that was taking place. There was always something special in her heart for Zeke, her first love. Wouldn't it be something if God used Jack to bring Zeke into a relationship with Himself?

Zeke seemed to appreciate the quiet moment to collect himself. He wiped at his eyes, then looked up at her with a renewed hope in them.

"Did you like the music last night?"

Amanda grinned. She thought it was just another way for Zeke to manipulate her like when her room filled with the sounds of Rod Stewart the night before. Now, with him sitting in front of her, looking up at her with his puppy eyes, she realized it had been his attempt to sweep her back to 1977, when they were lovers.

"It worked," Amanda admitted. "And your card was sweet."

"I meant every word. I really did."

"I know." Amanda smiled thinly.

"Will you come watch the last challenge with me?" he asked.

"I'm not under house arrest anymore?"

"No, you'll be my guest," Zeke said with a smile. "Come on."

"Why don't you just end the game?" Amanda pressed. "You should know pretty much what Jack is made of by now."

"True," Zeke agreed while standing up. "But the finale is going to be incredible. Besides, I still have a show to deliver to the network, you know."

"Oh, right," Amanda teased. "The show must go on ..."

Jack stood on the grass at the top of the cliff, waiting for the instructions with the other remaining contestants. It seemed odd to be dressed in their bathing suits overlooking a five-hundred-foot-plus drop to the ocean below. He feared they might be taking this to the next level, and they were about to engage in a cliff diving event.

He was on the outside; to his left was Maria, then Hugh, and at the other end Eddie. Jack stood barefoot with just a pair of swim trunks on, as did the other men. Maria was outfitted with a bright red one-piece. She looked like a lifeguard from *Baywatch*—only better. She glanced over at him and smiled nervously. Jack knew she needed to win to be able to keep her secret from Teresa and her mom. Unfortunately, Jack didn't have any choice but to try and beat her to protect his mother. Add Eddie and Hugh into the mix, and it was definitely going to be an interesting competition.

Jack peered over his shoulder at the assembled production staff and crew from the resort looking on. His eyes suddenly widened in shock. His mom had joined the crowd, standing in the shade of the dining hall next to none other than Zeke Roberts. She flashed him a tentative wave, as if she were on the sidelines of one of his football games. It didn't make sense.

Vince stepped in front of him and caught his attention. The cameras were everywhere, hovering around each of the contestants as events began to unfold.

"Well, here we are, the last challenge," Vince stated in dramatic fashion. "Each of you has proven to be a fantastic player—Eddie, coming in first on the triathlon; Hugh, winning poker night and that marvelous finish for next-to-last place climbing up this very cliff; Maria, the first one back on the scavenger hunt; and Jack, never coming in first, but always at the center of the excitement, no matter what the challenge."

"This will be your toughest test yet. It'll tax every muscle in your body as well as your brain, if you so choose. Here's what we're going to do. In a moment, two helicopters will fly right above us with two ropes hanging down from each one."

Vince held up what looked like the end of a single-handled water-ski rope. "You'll have to hold on to the handle at the bottom, which will look like this. Now men, at first you'll be able to hang on with both hands, but that's just until the chopper gets you down to sea level. When you get five feet above the water, you're only allowed to hang on with one hand. Maria, you'll be allowed to hang on with both hands the whole time. It's our attempt to equalize the competition."

"That's not fair," Eddie charged.

"Live with it, Eddie," Vince snapped back.

Maria glanced back at Jack and grinned.

"You'll be flown parallel to the beach," Vince continued, stepping up to the edge of the cliff and pointing down to the sand below. "The longer you can hold on, the less you'll have to either swim or run along the beach to your next destination. But once you drop from the helicopter, you must make it as quick as you can to the flags at the other end of the beach."

Jack looked off in the distance. At the far end of the beach where his team had come out of the jungle and spotted the resort at the top of the cliff for the first time, there were three flags waving in the breeze. It had to be nearly a half-mile away. It was obvious that you'd want to hang on to the rope as long as possible.

"There will be four water coolers sitting on a table under the flags. Whoever gets there first will have his or her choice." Vince paused, letting the contestants think about his instructions.

"Whatever is in that cooler, you must eat."

The guys all moaned and Maria gasped, "Oh, no."

"Oh, yes," Vince chuckled. "We'll have a couple of large dice on the table as well, just to make it more interesting. Whatever number you roll, that's how many of whatever is in your cooler you have to eat."

Jack started praying to roll a one right then.

"When you've finished your 'lunch,' a member of our staff will signal by waving a red flag over you. Then, you have to make your way down the beach, back this direction for the next station."

Jack looked down the beach, spotting another set of flags set up around what looked like four piles of brick.

"At this point, you'll have a choice to use your brains or your brawn. We have a mental challenge that will involve logic and math, or you can use your muscles to move twice your body weight in bricks fifty feet up the beach toward the jungle."

"Moving the bricks will take several trips, but you have no way of knowing how long it will take you to solve the mental challenge. Your choice could be critical."

Jack thought that was an understatement.

"The final leg of this challenge will be to make it through our short obstacle course. Should two of you be close at that point, it should make for an exciting finish."

Jack looked closer to the cliff where they'd set up what looked like a kids playground area. There were two identical courses set up side by side that started with a net to crawl under, monkey bars to get across, a wall to scale, and ended with a sprint along the sand of about fifty yards to the finish line.

"The first contestant over that finish line wins ten million dollars," Vince stated proudly. "And I'm sure I don't have to remind you, will also be the only player exempt from having your family secret revealed on the show."

Jack didn't need to be reminded, and he was sure Maria didn't as well. He looked back to the other contestants, who seemed anxious and ready to go. He liked his chances with what was ahead. Sure, Eddie had the muscle and athletic advantage, but there seemed to be only one part of the challenge that relied on sheer strength, and Jack thought his best chance to beat him would be to opt out of that for the mental test. The obstacle course looked something like what he'd set up for his team every fall, and whatever he required of his team, Jack always did as well. If he could just be close when he got to that point, he might have a chance to win it all.

It wasn't about the money anymore—not that it ever really was. Now it just boiled down to winning the game to protect his mom.

71

"All right, let's do it!" Vince moved off the cliff in front of the contestants at the same moment as two helicopters came over the main building from behind. The sound was deafening as they flew in formation only fifty feet above them. A production assistant moved Jack and Maria off to their right, and Hugh and Eddie were led to their left.

Only seconds remained before the competition would start. Jack moved close to Maria, knowing that the helicopter would make it impossible for the crew to pick up his words.

"This is it," Jack yelled to her. "Don't hold anything back."

She looked at him, her hair blowing around her face. "Don't worry about me. I'll be waiting for you at the finish line."

Jack laughed. The girl definitely had spunk.

True to Vince's word, one of the helicopters stopped just above them and two ski ropes were lowered. Jack began stretching out his shoulder muscles immediately, alternating between rotating his arms around in a wide circle, then crossing them in front of his chest. Maria took notice and started warming up as well.

The ropes slowly dropped down until they were below their heads, stopping just about belt high. Somebody in the helicopter shouted down at them through a speaker mounted on the bottom of the craft. "On my mark, grab on to the ropes, and then we'll start our ascent."

Jack looked up at Maria and shouted above the noise, "May the best man win!"

"Or woman!" She smiled. "If I don't win, I hope you do."

Jack chuckled. "You, too."

"Ready ..." The voice above broke through the whine of the turbines, as the wind whipped all around them. Jack was thankful they weren't on the beach with bits of sand adding to the fury.

"Set ..." the voice continued. Jack reached out, ready to grab hold of his rope.

"Go!"

Jack placed both hands side by side, one wrist facing him, the other facing away. Immediately the slack on the rope tightened as the helicopter ascended. In seconds, Jack's legs were dangling as the grass moved further and further away.

The strain on his arms and shoulders could be felt immediately. His muscles hadn't fully recovered from the week's abuse. At first, the stretching felt kind of good, but Jack knew that wouldn't last long.

"You doing OK?" Jack called out to Maria.

Across from him, Maria was hanging on for dear life. Her face was etched with fear as her hair flapped around her face, at times covering her eyes. She was too scared to answer.

Jack looked below him just as the cliff top gave way to the pounding surf below. The helicopter didn't stay at five hundred feet for long. As soon as they cleared the cliff, it dropped slowly down to sea level. Jack hoped they'd planned on flying at a good speed toward the end of the beach—he didn't think he could hang on with two hands very long and was worried how it would feel when he had to drop one of them.

Within seconds, they were hovering above the water. The sound of the waves crashing mightily against the rocks, mixed in with the whine of the turbine and the "whop-whop" drone of the rotors, surrounded Jack. The water was thrashed up further by the whipping winds, stinging Jack's skin as the salt pelted him.

Jack's pilot held his place above the water, waiting for the second helicopter to drop beside him. Jack could already feel his shoulders straining, and his hands wanting relief.

He could see Hugh and Eddie floating down into view behind Maria. As soon as they were all about the same height over the water, the speaker above him came to life once again. "On my mark, the men will drop one of their hands."

Here we go, Jack thought.

"Ready, set, now!"

Jack released his left hand slowly, not wanting to risk swaying below the chopper. His right hand held steady, but the strain on his right shoulder doubled. He grimaced in pain.

"Hold on, Jack!" Maria encouraged.

The helicopter began to move forward slowly—much slower than Jack wished.

Glancing beside him at the coastline, about a hundred yards up ahead, the rocks faded away, and bright white sand covered the rest of the beach. He had to at least hold on until the rocks were behind him.

Jack knew he had to think about something besides the pain he was feeling in his hand and shoulder. He tried to guess how fast they were flying. With the rotors whipping the air around him, it was hard to judge by the wind speed; but seeing how fast the water was moving underneath him, he guessed they were only flying between three and five miles per hour—a painstakingly slow pace.

He looked up the beach to their destination ahead. Estimating the length of the beach, combined with the speed they were traveling, it seemed to Jack that it was going to take somewhere around fifteen minutes to get there.

Fifteen minutes of holding on, stretching his shoulder, all the while exhausting his grip. He didn't like the effects it would have on his body. But if he could get to the beach, run along the hardened, water-soaked part of the sand, he could make much better time than the snail's pace of the helicopter. *A slow jog has to be more than five miles per hour,* he thought. *A four-minute mile is running at fifteen miles per hour.* He was sure he could probably run at least twice as fast as the helicopter was flying.

Jack made his decision.

He started groaning, half-acting that his hand was cramping.

"You OK?" Maria yelled.

"I'm losing my grip," Jack shouted back, looking off to the side to see if they'd cleared the rocks on the beach. They were now right beside him, the beach seconds away.

Jack kept his eyes on the shoreline, wanting to time it just right. He let go with an added scream for effect, dropping the five feet to the ocean below. He didn't waste a split second as he ducked his head into the water and started swimming directly to shore.

He couldn't hear or see what he'd instigated above, but he was sure Eddie was laughing at his apparent misfortune.

In moments, Jack caught a wave just right and was bodysurfing quickly to the beach.

Standing along the cliff, Amanda watched in horror, bringing her hands up to her mouth. "Oh, no! Is he OK?"

Zeke laughed, shaking his head. "He must have figured it out."

Amanda saw Jack's head pop up out of the surf. Feeling better, she turned toward Zeke. "What do you mean?"

"The helicopters," Zeke pointed out, "they're traveling too slow. He'll be able to run on the beach faster than they're flying. Watch."

Amanda turned back to the beach, amazed that Jack was up and running, already having caught up with the helicopters and moving past them.

"Interesting," Amanda said with a grin.

Jack felt like he was flying. The minute he'd gotten to his feet on the beach, he started running, catching up with the helicopters faster than he'd thought possible.

He raised a hand toward Eddie as he passed him. "You just keep hanging around, Eddie. I'll see you at the finish line."

Jack could hear him swearing even over the groan of the choppers. Then, almost in unison, the three of them let go of their ropes and dropped into the water.

Jack turned his head and pushed his legs harder. The race was on.

"It didn't take long for them to figure out Jack's plan, did it?" Amanda asked.

"No, but he's got a good lead now. How is he at disgusting food?"

Amanda laughed. "Not that great."

"This should be interesting then."

Amanda noticed someone coming up toward them. The sun was at his back, so she couldn't get a glimpse of the face. She turned back to watch Jack sprint along the coastline, as the man stepped up beside Zeke and spoke into his ear.

"Amanda." Zeke pulled her attention back to him. "You remember Travis, don't you?"

"Travis?" Amanda turned and felt her jaw drop as the intense feeling of panic that she'd felt on arriving on the island returned in a blinding flash.

"Hello, Amanda," Travis said politely. "It's been a long time."

Not long enough, she thought. *What is he doing here?*

"You OK?" Zeke asked.

Amanda caught herself. "Um, yes … just surprised. I didn't realize there was somebody else here from our past."

"Travis has been with me from the beginning," Zeke said with a smile. "I don't think I'd be where I am today without him."

More than you know.

"Didn't I tell you about my supervising producer?" Zeke asked.

"You said something about the title, but you didn't mention it was Travis."

"Well, it's nice to see you again," Travis said politely.

Amanda nodded back, resisting the urge to turn and flee.

"I'm sorry to interrupt," Travis continued, "but there's something I need to speak with Zeke about."

"Please excuse me," Zeke said to Amanda and stepped away.

She watched them walk off in utter shock. He must have been on this island the whole time. Emotions flooded through her as the memories of the past came crashing down.

"What is she doing out here?" Travis snapped at his boss.

"She's my guest," Zeke answered flatly. "What's your problem?"

"You're losing all perspective on what's important out here because of her—just like you did twenty-eight years ago."

"You're out of line," Zeke warned, his brow furrowing.

Travis rolled his eyes and sighed. It was like they'd time-warped back to 1977.

"What's so important?" Zeke asked.

"Your DNA test just came back." Travis held up a piece of paper in front of his eyes. "I thought you'd want to know."

"Really?" Zeke excitedly grabbed the paper, searching through the medical mumbo-jumbo until he caught the conclusion at the bottom.

Test results negative: Subjects are not related.

"What? How could this be?" Zeke stared at the mind-numbing words.

"Easy, she's a slut," Travis stated flatly. "Just like I told you back at Yale.

"We've been friends a long time," Zeke said, as his eyes burned a hole through Travis. "But you better be careful about what you say right now."

Zeke looked back at Amanda standing on the cliff. He was so sure that Jack was his son. "I don't believe it." He crumpled the results in his hand. "There must be some mistake."

"Don't be a fool," Travis sneered. "This whole thing has been one big mistake. I told you to stay out of their lives. Now you've risked our whole franchise on this stupid fake challenge. The best thing to do is let it end and get them out of your life forever. Jack's not your son—why care? And Amanda—she wasn't worth it then, she certainly isn't now. All this could do is mess up your life."

Zeke let the words spill over him like vomit. He couldn't fight back. Everything he thought of her was instantly shattered. She had cheated on him—just like wives numbers two and three, probably even wife number one, though he never found any proof. Amanda—the one woman he had kept on a pedestal all these years—had actually been the first to betray him.

"Trust me, Zeke," Travis whispered to him. "You're better off this way."

Zeke wasn't so sure. He'd fallen in love all over again.

Jack started to feel winded, his legs driving well but the bottom of his feet and toes burning from pounding through the gritty sand. He glanced over his shoulder. Eddie was already up and running a good two hundred yards behind him. Hugh was struggling in the surf. There was no sign of Maria. She must still be in the water, in last place, Jack thought.

The flags were about a hundred feet away. Jack could make out the four coolers lined up on a table in a row. He wouldn't waste any time choosing—he decided to go straight for the purple one, the color of Royal High, and deal with whatever was in it. His stomach already started churning at the thought of it. This was not going to be fun.

"Bad news?" Amanda asked, reading the ashen look on Zeke's face as he stepped up beside her.

"Yeah, you could say that," he responded coldly.

"What is it?"

"Nothing, really. Business stuff," Zeke answered, looking up toward the beach. "How's it going?"

"Jack is just about to the end of the beach," Amanda pointed out. "He's way out in front, though."

Jack had to leave the wet sand close to the surf and trudge through the deep, soft area to get to the next station. The sand was hot, and, after a few strides, he could feel the pain growing as his feet dried.

He made it to the table huffing away, sucking in as much oxygen as he could. He doubled over for just a second to catch his breath. He knew he'd need to be in control to deal with whatever was next.

He stood up tall, took in one last huge breath, then walked to the end of the table, passing the red, yellow, and green coolers before flipping open the purple one.

The stench hit him instantly, even before the image focused in his brain. He stepped back, already gagging. There were six small plastic cups full of wormy creatures. They were colored white and brown, and were in constant motion.

"Maggots," the production assistant explained with a smile. "Since they're so small, each cupful will represent a number on the die."

Jack forced his eyes back down to the cooler. There had to be twenty or thirty maggots in each cup. His queasiness was growing.

The production assistant handed him a large red die.

Jack grabbed it and shook it in his hand. It rolled out of his hand, onto the tabletop.

Three.

Jack closed his eyes and tilted his head straight up.

Three cups of maggots.

He didn't know what else was under the other three coolers, but right now Jack thought they had to be better than what he was facing.

Jack glanced over his shoulder. Eddie was coming up fast.

He grabbed the first cup and brought it to his lips. He'd have to do it quick, or just give up now.

Jack held his breath, tilted his head back, and poured the contents of the cup into his mouth like he was taking a shot. He nearly panicked and spit them out when he felt the little creatures move all through the inside of his mouth. The urge to gag was instinctive and strong—but he resisted.

His mouth watered, as he fought to keep his stomach under control, using the saliva to swallow several times.

The production assistant held up a bottle of water. "Show me an empty mouth and you can drink this."

Jack worked through, swallowing twice more, then opened his mouth.

"Great, here ya go."

Jack unscrewed the bottle and started chugging down the water.

Two more to go. He wasn't sure he could do it.

Eddie came up behind him, breathing as hard as a fullback after a ninety-yard touchdown run. He didn't wait, however, but stepped to the other side of the table from Jack and opened the red cooler.

He swore loudly. Jack glanced over and caught sight of what looked like hundreds of huge cockroaches scampering about inside his cooler. They were huge, but Jack wondered if the dry insects would be preferable to the slimy grubs he was forced to endure.

"Your die," Jack heard beside him. He wasn't about to waste any more time worrying about Eddie. He grabbed his second plastic cup and poured the contents into his mouth.

Eddie swore again. "Four! You've got to be ..."

Jack blocked it out as he fought to hold back his natural gag response, enduring the second wave of maggots tickling his tongue and gums.

Hugh came flying in behind him, quickly rushing up to the yellow cooler. He yanked it open as he panted like an overworked dog.

Jack opened his mouth for the production assistant before sucking down more water from the bottle. He could hear the crunch of Eddie chewing the cockroaches as he heard a disgusted moan from Hugh.

Jack couldn't help himself and glanced over at Hugh's cooler. Six squishy octopus tentacles were arranged neatly in a circle. He couldn't help but laugh as Hugh turned and gagged.

He only had one cup left—but he'd come closer to heaving during the second one. This was getting harder, not easier.

Hugh cheered as he rolled a two just as Maria arrived.

Eddie was chomping quickly, grabbing for another cockroach. Jack brought his focus back to his own dilemma. He reached for the final cup of maggots and brought it to his lips. This time, he couldn't hold back the gagging reflex and he dropped the cup as he bent over. He was able to stop himself from throwing up, but barely. The maggots started furrowing in the sand at his feet.

Maria opened up her cooler and screamed. Jack lifted his head and saw a moving mass of earthworms.

Eddie shouted, opening his mouth for the production assistant and receiving the wave of a red flag over his head. He grabbed a water bottle, chugging down the refreshing liquid as he turned and ran down the beach.

Jack had lost the lead. He couldn't look over at Hugh—viewing the octopus tentacles might be just enough to bend him over again. Jack decided to repeat how he'd gotten through the first cup.

He picked it up, then closed his eyes and held his breath. He tipped the cup and poured the last group into his mouth. His stomach churned as he felt the bile coming up. Jack didn't think he could stop it and, without thinking, he spat the mouthful of maggots into the sand, but just in time to stop from throwing up altogether.

There were only two cups left. He was running out of maggots if he couldn't get this last cup down.

Maria rolled a five and nearly vomited right then. Jack felt sorry for her, but there wasn't anything he could do. He had to catch up with Eddie.

He picked up the next cup, held his breath, quickly tilted his head, and tossed them into his mouth. He gagged as his stomach threatened to send back up the first two cups of maggots. But he held on this time.

He swallowed again and again until he felt like the last disgusting maggot was finally down his throat. He opened his mouth for the staffer and got the red flag over his head. Jack wolfed down half of the water in the bottle attempting to wash the taste out of his mouth, then he turned back to his friends as he ran after Eddie.

"Let's go, both of you!" he yelled. "We can't let Eddie win this thing!"

Hugh gave him a thumbs up with a tentacle hanging out of his mouth. Maria responded by reaching into her cooler, pulling out five worms all at once, and stuffing them into her mouth.

Jack groaned, then turned and sprinted as fast as he could through the hot sand.

"Jack's completed checkpoint two—heading on to number three," the walkie-talkie strapped to Zeke's belt rattled off.

"He's still behind Eddie," Zeke updated Amanda. "But he might be able to catch him on the next challenge."

Amanda nodded. It was difficult to follow the contest from atop the cliff. The action was so far away. She looked over at Zeke. He'd grown extremely quiet over the last several minutes, ever since Travis showed up. *Something's happened,* she thought. *Something serious.*

Then again, she hadn't wanted to talk after Travis showed up, either. Zeke suddenly turned and caught her staring at him. She felt her stomach drop. His eyes had grown empty and distant, almost as if he'd retreated from the present and was once again engulfed in the anger of the past.

Amanda quickly looked away and saw Jack struggling in the sand to catch up with Eddie. The sun beat down on her back and the humidity had to be nearly ninety percent, yet a cold shiver ran up the entire length of her spine.

Jack pushed his legs through the sand as his calves began to rebel. Eddie had already made it to the next station while Jack still had another fifty yards or so to catch up. He plunged on, ignoring the churning sensation in his stomach. If his mind went back to what he'd just eaten, he was sure he'd be forced to …

He plunged to his knees, unable to hold back any longer. He heaved; throwing up the instant his hands hit the sand. He retched a second time, refusing to look at what was coming out of him. Then, he was up and running again as fast as he could, trying to clear the image of maggots from his mind.

When he finally reached the flags, Eddie had already started moving the bricks up the sand toward the edge of the jungle where the producers had placed a large scale. He was drenched in sweat, his powerful muscles bulging out, as he carried a load of bricks in his arms. He was too strong for Jack to compete head-to-head in a physical stunt like this. Jack had no choice but to go for the mental challenge.

"Brain or brawn?" one of the four production assistants under the flags asked.

"Brain," Jack huffed.

"Brain it is," the man replied. He reached around and handed Jack a clipboard and a pencil. "Here you go. When you're finished, hand it back up here, and I'll check your answers."

There were four lawn chairs set up under a couple of umbrellas to give the contestants a bit of relief from the baking noonday sun. Jack plopped into the first chair, thankful for the chance to get off his feet. If he could complete the problems before Eddie, he might gain the advantage for the obstacle course with fresh legs.

Jack tried to ignore the nasty taste of bile in his throat and concentrate. Eddie had already dropped off the first batch of bricks and was running back to load up more. Running along the sand toward them were both Maria and Hugh. The race was tightening up.

Jack took a deep breath and focused on the clipboard. There were four problems to complete. He looked at the first one: it was a series of numbers, and he had to figure out the next logical one in the sequence.

2 5 17 71 ___

Jack didn't know any other way to figure out these kinds of problems than to just do the old trial and error method. He analyzed the first two numbers, trying to find their relationship, and then applied his theory to the third number to see if he was correct.

Add three—doesn't work.

Times two and a half—doesn't work.

Multiply by two, add one—doesn't work.

It was more difficult than just a single step for each pair of numbers. There had to be an increasing pattern in the formula between numbers of some kind.

He could hear Eddie struggling to grab as many bricks as he could for his second trip. Jack could feel himself tense up; he was starting to panic.

Hugh sprinted by him, kicking sand all over his legs. Jack was running out of time. He looked at the numbers again, forcing himself to focus.

Increasing pattern, he thought.

Multiply by two, add one. What if he increased that formula by a digit?

Multiply by three, add one. The next number would be sixteen, didn't work. Then it clicked in—multiply by three, add two. That worked for seventeen, but did it work for seventy-one? Jack quickly did the calculation: seventeen times four would be sixty-eight, add three and you've got seventy-one. He had it!

Jack scribbled on the side of the sheet, seventy one times five and got the total three hundred fifty-five, adding four he got the final answer: three hundred fifty-nine.

Hugh plopped down in the chair next to him and jumped right into the problems as Maria ran up to the production assistant. There was no time for pleasantries.

Jack looked at problem number two. It was the classic: If train A leaves New York traveling at fifty miles per hour, while train B leaves Los Angeles traveling …

Jack quickly made note of the pertinent information and started calculating. In twenty seconds, he had the answer and moved on to problem number three.

Eddie was back for more bricks. Jack got sidetracked trying to figure out how many trips it would take him, when Maria walked in front of him and sat beside Hugh, bringing Jack's focus back to the task at hand.

He looked down at his clipboard—mad at himself for continuing to get distracted. Problem three was staring back at him, as if taunting him. It was a logic problem.

Jack hated logic problems.

There was little to see from the cliff top, as three of the contestants sat under the umbrellas working on the math problems. The only activity was Eddie running back and forth through the sand either loaded with bricks or sprinting to get more.

"This load should get him to two hundred pounds." Zeke kept the play-by-play going for her, but there was no other conversation, even though there certainly was time for it.

What could Travis have showed him that's put him in such a funk? Amanda thought. She had seen the piece of paper handed across but, for the life of her, couldn't figure out what could set him off like this. Then it hit her.

The DNA report.

Zeke had mentioned that he would have the test results back sometime today. *Could that be what set him off? Does he finally know he really isn't Jack's father?* Amanda was afraid to ask, but it seemed the only thing that made sense.

Jack sighed, wondering if he'd made a mistake by not moving bricks. When he took his S.A.T. tests back in high school, he did great on the English sections, but struggled when it came to some of the math problems. Something about the time pressure made it difficult for him to see the clues on logic problems. He tried to block out the past, as he read the problem in front of him.

> Mrs. Robinson's 4th grade class took a field trip to the local zoo. The day was sunny and warm—a perfect day to spend at the zoo. The kids had a great time and the monkeys were voted the class favorite animal. The zoo had four monkeys: two males and two females. It was lunchtime for the monkeys, and as the kids watched, each one ate a different fruit in their favorite resting place. Can you determine the name of each monkey, what kind of fruit each monkey ate, and where their favorite resting place was?
>
> 1. Sam, who doesn't like bananas, likes sitting on the grass.
> 2. The monkey who sat on the rock ate the apple. The monkey who ate the pear didn't sit on the tree branch.
> 3. Anna sat by the stream, but she didn't eat the pear.
> 4. Harriet didn't sit on the tree branch. Mike doesn't like oranges.

I hate logic problems, Jack thought yet again.

He looked down the clipboard to see what the last problem was. He thought it might be best to leave the logic problem for last. He was feeling the pressure build as Eddie groaned while moving through the sand with his third load of bricks piled high in his arms.

Jack glanced down at problem number four and his heart skipped.

Compute pi out to ten decimals.

When Jack was in the eighth grade, as a special math project he memorized the value of pi out to thirty decimals. He wondered if he still remembered, until his brain automatically started running through the sequence: 3.14159265358979323846 …

He still remembered.

Jack smiled and wrote down the first ten digits after the decimal point, then added a few more just to show off.

Now, he was back to problem number three. He made a three-by-four grid on the side of the page, listing on the top of it: name, fruit, resting place. Then he re-read the problem and started fidgeting. He was nervous this wasn't going to work, which made it that much harder to concentrate.

He looked at the first clue: Sam who doesn't like bananas, but likes sitting on the grass.

In the top left box of the grid, Jack wrote *Sam*, and then followed across and wrote underneath the resting place *grass.*

Just for good measure, he drew a line from Sam's fruit box off the chart and wrote, *no bananas.* He looked at clue number two and tried to figure out what else he could write down.

The monkey who sat on the rock ate the apple.

He couldn't place a name yet, but on the second line of the grid he wrote *apple* and *rock.*

He read the rest of clue two—the monkey who ate the pear didn't sit on the tree branch.

That didn't tell him much yet, so Jack made a notation to the side. At least he was making progress, but so was Eddie, who had just returned to load up more bricks.

Hugh scribbled away beside him, evidently having no difficulty figuring out the first two questions. Maria worked furiously as well. They were both still in school and were used to dealing with this kind of pressure.

Jack shook his head; he needed to stay focused. He moved on to the next clue.

Anna sat by the stream, but she didn't eat the pear.

Jack placed Anna's name down in the third row and added *stream* under her resting place. Then he made a line from her fruit box and wrote *no pear* off to the side.

He looked at the fourth clue.

Harriet didn't sit on the tree branch. Mike doesn't like oranges.

He wanted to scream. He hated the negative clues. He scribbled the notes off to the side and looked at his grid in confusion.

Eddie was loaded up with bricks. As he turned to run up the beach, he yelled out, "I'm almost done, losers!"

75

Jack tried to ignore Eddie's bravado, but he had succeeded in breaking Jack's train of thought.

"How are you guys doing?" Jack looked over at Hugh and Maria.

"Halfway there," Hugh answered.

"Me too," Maria added.

"You guys on the monkey problem?" Jack asked.

They both nodded.

Jack had an idea.

"I figure Eddie has two more trips, tops." Jack observed, based on the small pile of bricks left. He leaned closer in, whispering so Eddie couldn't hear them. "If we're all stuck on these problems when he unloads the last brick, he'll win. We can't let that happen."

Hugh looked up at Jack. "What are you suggesting?"

"We work together—then see who wins the obstacle course between us. At least that way Eddie doesn't take home the ten million."

"I'm in," Maria said.

"Hugh?" Jack asked.

Hugh looked over at Eddie, who was dropping off the bricks, and then turned back toward them. "Are we allowed to do that?"

"No rules," Jack grinned. "Remember?"

Hugh nodded. "OK, let's do it."

Jack got out of his chair and showed him the grid he'd started. "I've gotten this far."

"Hey, you've already done problem number four," Maria noticed.

"Don't worry, just copy my answer."

Hugh looked over what Jack had written for the third problem. "That looks good so far. Now let's see what we can deduce."

Maria looked closely at Jack's clipboard. "You've got Sam on the grass, Anna by the stream ..."

"And look at clue four, it says that Harriet didn't sit on the tree branch ..." Hugh noticed.

"So Mike has to be on the tree branch," Jack realized.

"Which leaves Harriet on the rock!" Maria's voice was excited, as she pointed to Jack's grid.

"Hey, you guys can't work together!" Eddie screamed behind them as he started grabbing his next load of bricks.

Jack turned around and looked at him. He was filthy, with red stains all over his arms and chest. He looked exhausted. He was going to have to reach really deep to beat Jack in the next challenge if it was at all close.

"Don't you remember?" Jack sneered at him. "No rules."

That might have been a mistake. Eddie squatted down, scowling at Jack like he was a rabid dog. Jack saw a determination in his eyes that frightened him, as Eddie began piling up the bricks.

"Come on," Maria yelled at Jack. "Don't worry about him."

"Right." Jack was happy to turn away from Eddie. The look in his eyes was cold, deadly. Jack had a quick flash of Stacy lying dead on the ledge of the cliff. He wondered if Eddie had the same plans for him.

Jack wrote Mike's name in the bottom row, adding *tree branch* to it. Then, he moved up quickly, and wrote in Harriet's name in the second row. They now had all four names and all four resting places. All they needed was to figure out what fruit each of the monkeys ate.

Eddie groaned loudly off to the side, barely able to stand with nearly double the load of bricks in his arms. He slowly made it to his feet and began trudging across the sand once again.

"Come on, Jack." Maria saw him watching Eddie. "Focus!"

"I'm trying," Jack snapped. "This could be his last load."

"Then let's get to it," Hugh said, looking back at the clues.

"We know Sam doesn't like bananas." Jack looked over his notes off to the side.

"It's the pear . . ." Maria pointed to the clues.

"What do you mean?" Jack asked.

"The monkey who ate the pear didn't sit on the tree branch, so it's not Mike," Maria said, pointing to clue number three. "And Anna didn't eat the pear. That only leaves Sam."

"She's right," Hugh said.

Jack wrote down *pear* next to Sam's name. They had two boxes left to fill: Anna's and Mike's fruits.

They all looked up when they heard Eddie drop an armful of bricks.

"What else do we know?" Jack looked back down to the clues.

"Yeah!" Eddie screamed up the beach. Jack glanced up to see a production assistant wave a red flag over Eddie's head. Eddie didn't hesitate as he started running back toward them to begin the obstacle course.

"Clue four," Jack noticed. "Mike doesn't like oranges—so Anna gets the orange."

"And Mike gets the banana!" Maria exclaimed. "We did it!"

"Quick." Jack looked up to see how close Eddie was. "Write the answers on your papers. Here comes Eddie."

Eddie was running through the sand with a triumphant look on his face, but Jack could tell he was exhausted. Did he have enough reserves to make it to the finish line first?

"OK!" Hugh yelled. "We got 'em. Go!"

Jack grabbed his clipboard and slapped it on the table. The first production assistant began looking over the answers.

He looked to his left; Eddie was running straight at him. He had only a few yards and he'd hit the beginning of the obstacle course.

"Come on, hurry!" Jack yelled. The production assistant had checked the answers to problems one and two and was looking through

Jack's grid on the logic problem. Hugh and Maria placed their clipboards on the table as the other staff members started checking their answers.

Eddie turned, trying to make the sharp corner into the obstacle course. He slipped in the sand and fell right in front of Jack. Jack could hear him cursing as he scrambled to his feet, kicking sand in the air behind him.

"Come on!" Jack screamed.

Eddie ran by, diving under the cargo net, the first obstacle on the course.

Finally, the production assistant lifted the red flag over Jack's head.

Eddie had a slight lead on him, already crawling under the cargo net and moving sideways through the sand like a crab.

Jack ran to the second course, just to the right of the one Eddie was on, and dove under the net. He pushed his muscles with everything he had, doing a G.I. Joe-type of crawl, and having to keep his butt low to avoid his swimming trunks catching on the net.

Hugh and Maria were right behind him; Hugh on Eddie's course and Maria on Jack's.

Jack either had to pass Eddie, or figure out a way to slow him down—otherwise, he would lose.

Jack scrambled out from under the net, rushing to the start of the monkey bars. He jumped up and grabbed the first metal bar, using the momentum to reach out across two bars before grabbing again. He looked over and saw that he was now even with Eddie.

They both completed the monkey bars at the same time and sprinted for the wall. It was going to come down to whoever could get over the wall the fastest.

The wall was about ten feet tall with a rope hanging down the middle to help each contestant get over. Jack leaped when he was about two feet away from it and latched onto the rope as his legs pumped to keep the momentum going up. He was just about to reach his hand over the top of the wall and grab hold, when he suddenly felt a great weight land on his shoulders. He couldn't hold the weight and his hand let go. Jack landed hard on the sand in a heap—with Eddie right on top of him.

He heard Eddie swear at him as if in an echo chamber.

Jack couldn't breathe. He doubled over as Eddie left him on the sand. "No rules, Forrest!"

Fighting the panic that comes from having the wind knocked out of you, Jack tried to get up—he had to keep moving. He knew it would pass and he'd be able to breathe again, but he couldn't afford to wait. Eddie was already working his way to the top of his wall.

Forcing himself back on his feet, Jack reached for the rope. Not having the momentum from running up to the wall, he had to start from the bottom. Finally, the first breath came as Jack sucked in deep. He didn't hesitate, but grabbed the rope with both hands and started pulling. He placed his feet flat against the wall and tried to walk up as he pulled.

Eddie was almost to the top. Jack was running out of time.

He pulled with all his might, not realizing that Hugh had cleared the monkey bars and was running to the wall. Eddie was able to reach his hand over the wall and pull his feet toward the top just as Hugh leaped at him.

Hugh slammed into the wall, his outstretched hand missing Eddie's right foot by inches. The hit made it too hard for him to hold on to the rope, and he fell back down to the sand.

Jack's hand reached the top of his wall just as he heard Maria come up below him. He didn't look back, but quickly pulled with all his might until his right leg made it over the top. Knowing there was soft sand on the other side, he flung himself over the wall like a high jumper and braced himself for the ten-foot fall to the beach below. After shielding the impact with his hands and rolling, he instantly spun to his feet and started running.

Eddie was up ahead to his left, churning through the difficult beach with a five-yard lead over Jack. There was nothing left for Jack to do except run as hard and as fast as he possibly could.

Jack pushed his legs hard, angling toward Eddie instead of running straight for the finish line. All he had to do was get close.

He could feel the sand kicking up behind him as he dug for every bit of speed he could get. Eddie had too much of a lead to actually pass him. His only hope was coming up from behind, but he'd have to time it just perfectly.

He concentrated on Eddie's rhythm, the pumping of his legs—right, then left, right, then left. He'd have one shot.

When he thought he had it timed, Jack leaped forward, stretching out as far as he could with his right hand and slapping across the back of Eddie's legs. Jack felt the palm of his hand make contact just before he fell to the sand. He'd hit skin—Eddie's right ankle. The force of Jack's slap sent Eddie's right foot across the back of his body, tripping him as it crashed into his left leg. Eddie slammed to the sand, cursing violently.

Jack was already up on his feet, churning his legs to get past Eddie as he lay sprawled out on the sand. Jack grinned, spotting the finish line just ahead. Only ten more yards to go and the battle would be won.

Then he was hit with a force that Jack couldn't believe, knocked to the sand with Eddie all over him. He'd gotten up in time to tackle Jack before he could cross the finish line. Eddie pushed Jack further into the sand, then tried to scramble off of him—but Jack grabbed onto his trunks and pulled him back.

It was a fight to the finish. Jack had to figure out a way to pull Eddie back and take the lead again, but he was as strong as a bull. Eddie lashed back with his fist, pounding on Jack's hands. He was screaming obscenities at him, trying to break Jack's grip.

But Jack wouldn't let go. With one hand latched onto his trunks, Jack reached out with the other and wrapped it around Eddie's legs, tripping him back down to the sand.

He climbed on top of Eddie, trying to get past him as the two intertwined, rolling in the sand. Their progress had stopped five yards short of the goal.

Which was all Hugh needed as he sprinted right by them, crossing the finish line with a shout. Maria passed beside them right after, coming in a close second.

Both Eddie and Jack stopped wrestling as they realized it was over. Jack rolled over on his back, sucking in the air, and staring at the sky.

He'd lost—but Eddie hadn't won.

Jack was thrilled.

And *The Ultimate Challenge* was finally over.

"You cheating..." Eddie swore, as he pounded the sand with his fist.

"Like pulling me off the wall wasn't?" Jack fired back.

"I should kill you, right here—right now, Forrest!" Eddie sat up, leaning over Jack as he blocked out the sun.

"Just like you did Stacy?" Jack challenged in between breaths.

"I had nothing to do with that!" Eddie screamed. "Just give it up, man. You just cost me ten million dollars—and you're gonna pay."

"Well, you can garnish my wages," Jack said with a laugh as he sat up, "but that might take awhile."

Eddie scowled at him, realizing the cameras were covering their every move. He left his threat hanging in the air and walked away, grumbling.

Jack glanced over at the finish line. Cameras surrounded Hugh as the staff around him cheered. Hugh received a congratulatory hug from Maria, but Jack could see by the look on her face that it was half-hearted. She was worried about what would happen next, and how Teresa and her mom would react to whatever secret she'd been keeping.

His thoughts drifted to his mom. How would she react when her past was broadcast to the world? Jack lowered his head, brushing his hand against the sand. He didn't know of any way to stop it—and his hatred of Zeke grew exponentially.

Then an arm was thrust in front of his face. Jack looked up to see Hugh offering him a hand up. Jack grasped it and held on as Hugh pulled him to his feet.

"You did it!" Jack smiled.

"Only because of you," Hugh answered. "If you hadn't stopped Eddie ..."

Maria came up and stood beside Jack, grasping his hand in hers. He knew she was seeking comfort, or maybe strength, for what was to come.

"You deserve the credit," Jack said to Hugh with a smile. "I might still be back there working on what Sam the monkey ate for lunch if not for you."

Jack pulled Maria close, then leaned down and whispered, "It'll be OK."

She looked at him as tears filled her eyes.

"It'll be OK," he repeated, trying to find comfort in the words as well.

"It seems your son has lost," Zeke proclaimed.

"So now he's *my* son?" Amanda pointed out. "Freudian slip? Or is there something you want to talk about."

"After all these years ..." Zeke seemed lost in a daze. "I watched him grow up, play football, graduate, coach. Someday I figured I'd see him get married—and he isn't even mine."

Zeke looked at her, the darkness in his eyes absolute. "You betrayed me."

"What did Travis show you?" Amanda asked softly. "The DNA results?"

Zeke nodded, his face struggling to hold in his emotions. "Yeah."

"I told you Jack wasn't your son, Zeke."

"But I thought you were talking figuratively." Zeke's voice rose bitterly. "You know, like Kevin was Jack's father because he loved him and raised him. I never thought in a million years you were cheating on me back then and carrying somebody else's baby. How could you?"

"Zeke," Amanda pleaded, "it's not what you think. I never cheated on you."

"Yeah." Zeke shook his head. "I've heard that one before."

Without another word, Zeke turned and started walking away.

"Wait!" Amanda yelled.

He turned back, looking at her in a way she hoped to never endure again.

"What did Travis say to you?" Amanda pleaded.

"Nothing more than the truth." Zeke spat the words out, then turned on his heels and headed back to the main building, leaving Amanda on the edge of the cliff alone.

• • •

The contestants were given an hour to freshen up before they were all to convene in the dining hall. Jack had gone directly to the pool and jumped into the deep end, allowing the cool water to soothe him. Maria and Hugh had joined him, and now all three were sitting on the steps of the shallow end enjoying the refreshing water. Even though the competition had ended, it didn't stop the camera crews from hanging around and capturing every sound and movement.

"So how were the maggots?" Hugh asked.

"Not something I'd make part of my regular diet," Jack said with a shiver. "Every time I close my eyes now, I have this nightmare that they're inside of me reproducing and someday I'm just going to explode."

"Yuck," Maria groaned. "Now I'm going to be worried about my worms."

"The octopus wasn't bad," Hugh said with a grin.

"So what are you going to do with all the money?" Maria asked him.

"I haven't really thought about it," Hugh chuckled. "It just seems so surreal."

"You could start your own law firm," Jack suggested.

"Maybe so. But for now, I think I'll just go on with my plans at the firm in San Francisco. Then I'll see what happens."

"I'm just glad you beat out Eddie," Jack said. "I couldn't bear to see him win this thing. I'm still thinking he was the one who pushed Stacy off the cliff and there's got to be some way to make him pay for it."

Amanda walked around the corner of the dining hall, and noticed Jack sitting in the shallow end of the pool.

"Mom, over here!"

She walked over and joined Jack, where he introduced her to Hugh and Maria. She marveled at Maria's beauty up close; she could see why Jack had been captivated with her.

"It's a pleasure meeting you both, and congratulations, Hugh."

"Thank you, Mrs. Forrest," Hugh acknowledged.

"It's nice to finally meet the mom behind this great guy," Maria smiled up at her.

Amanda smiled warmly back, noticing how Maria's eyes lit up as she glanced at Jack. She turned to Jack with an understanding nod. He grinned sheepishly, his face turning a soft crimson.

"Jack, I need to speak with you for a second, if it's OK."

"Sure." Jack rose from the pool.

"I need to go to my room and get ready anyway," Maria said, getting up as well. "We've got the big final meeting in a few minutes."

Hugh got out of the pool and joined Maria. Amanda watched the two of them walk off, wondering what would happen between Maria and Jack after this was all over.

"I'm sorry I lost, Mom," Jack stated. "I almost had it."

Amanda smiled. "Don't worry about it, Jack. It's OK. That's not why I wanted to speak with you."

"Really?" Jack said, rubbing a resort towel over his shoulders. "Then, what's up?"

"I thought we should talk before you see Zeke again," Amanda started.

"I'm not planning on seeing Zeke again," Jack said, then motioned his head toward the camera ten feet away. He leaned in and whispered, "Be careful what you say."

Amanda nodded. "He knows ..."

Jack nodded, understanding her unfinished sentence. "How?"

Amanda thought carefully. "The test results."

"Does he know the whole story?"

"No," Amanda shook her head. "I didn't tell him."

"I understand," Jack said. "Come on, why don't you wait in my bungalow while I get ready. The rest of this evening should prove rather interesting."

78

All of the people were assembled in the dining hall: the production assistants, all the camera crews, Vince and the head production team, and, of course, all of the remaining contestants. Set up at a special table, in front of where the large screen had been, sat the family members whom had been brought to the island the night before. Jack's mom sat beside Maria's mom and daughter. Teresa looked beautiful, the spitting image of her mother.

He glanced over at Maria, who still carried a grave look on her face. She was dreading what was to come, as was Jack. But his mother's attitude earlier by the pool gave him some hope that all might not unfold as he expected. He caught Maria's eyes and smiled, trying to reassure her a bit.

She didn't respond, just shrugged—the fear in her eyes never wavering.

Vince stepped up to his favorite position at the podium by the head table. "We have a winner!"

The room cheered, mostly by way of the production staff, but Jack and Maria added their applause enthusiastically. Eddie chose to stay quiet.

"But before we present the ten-million-dollar check," Vince continued over the applause, "We have some unfinished business to take care of."

The room quickly quieted down. Out of the corner of his eye, Jack could see Maria's shoulders slump down a bit.

Vince spent a few minutes debriefing the contestants, going over different parts of the final challenge to tape reactions for the television audience. For Jack, it was frustrating—the longer Vince kept going, the more Jack worried they were about to reveal his mom's history in front of the entire nation. Glancing over at Maria, he could see that it was agonizing for her as well.

"Jack." The mention of his name pulled his attention away from Maria and back to Vince at the podium. "You seemed to have created an alliance with Hugh fairly early in the game. Do you think that came back to haunt you in the end?"

Jack shook his head, irritated at having to answer and knowing Vince was just delaying the inevitable. "No, I don't. Without Hugh and Maria, I might still be back in the sand trying to figure out which monkey ate what and where."

The crew working around them laughed.

"I'm glad he won—and thrilled that Eddie didn't." He turned to Hugh with his hand outstretched as if he was giving a toast. "Congratulations. You deserve it."

Everyone but Eddie clapped once again for the winner.

Vince waited for the room to quiet down before continuing. "Nicely said, Jack. Now, we still have some important business to attend to before I can give Hugh that big check he's waiting for, so listen up. First, we have to deal with our three runners-up." Vince looked right at Jack, then moved to Maria, and finally to Eddie.

Jack tensed, sensing Vince was finally getting to the important stuff. His eyes shifted over to Maria, who grimaced and looked anxiously back at him.

"About your families being brought here for some untold secret ..." Vince paused, allowing the tension in the room to thicken, as the cameras captured every uncomfortable twitch, before he cracked a smile. "That was just our way of making sure you were all motivated. There will be no secrets unveiled today."

Maria gasped, bringing her hands up, palms together, in front of her mouth. She turned to Jack as tears of relief flooded her eyes. Jack smiled at her, pleased that whatever she'd been so worried about would stay hidden. But he wondered what was behind the decision. Did Zeke's knowledge of the DNA test alter this part of the game? Maybe his plan all along was to announce on national television that Jack was his son—and now that moment had been stolen from him just before the big finale.

Serves him right, Jack thought.

He glanced up at his mom, who was grinning back at him. She didn't look surprised—she already knew and hadn't told him.

Jack then looked at Eddie. He didn't seem to care one way or the other, which struck Jack as rather odd.

"The next announcement," Vince said, as his face took on a devilish grin. "Well, as the old saying goes, a picture is worth a thousand words ..."

He stepped back from the podium and opened a curtain behind him, revealing a thick cloud of smoke heavily backlit with a brilliant white light. A woman's silhouette stood against what looked like an intensely white cloud for a brief moment. Then, she stepped forward as a dramatic lighting cue brought the backlight down in pinpoint patterns through the smoke, and a front spotlight came up on her face.

Jack sucked in a quick breath before gaping. He couldn't believe his eyes.

It was Stacy.

And she was alive and well, smiling and posing as if she owned the world.

Jack was blinking in unbelief. He picked his jaw up off the floor and looked over to Maria, who was as shocked as he was. How could this be? He saw her with his own eyes—bloodied dress, broken neck, lying on the edge of the cliff.

But it had all been staged. He should have realized by the way the producers went on with the competition despite such a serious tragedy.

"Yes," Vince explained, "Stacy's death was nothing more than an elaborate makeup and special effects job. We told you she was an actress, but she's also a stuntwoman, and she really pulled a great one on you."

Jack shook his head—they'd completely fooled him. He was so sure she'd fallen off the cliff, and that Eddie had something to do with it.

Eddie stepped up in front of Jack, towering over him and scowling once again.

"You accused me of killing her, Forrest." Eddie got right into Jack's face. "I want an apology, now!" He held the menacing look for a second, then burst out in laughter.

For an instant, Jack couldn't figure out what was going on. Then Eddie pulled him to his feet, put his arm around him, and slapped him on the back. In a completely different voice from the dialect he'd been using all week, he said, "Actually my name is Eddie Thompson—I'm an actor from Thousand Oaks."

"Oh my." Jack felt his knees nearly buckle. A strong breeze could have knocked him over. He never would have guessed that Eddie was a plant.

But if Eddie was, then who else?

"I guess you've probably figured out by now," Vince said, "that a few of the people around you these past few days weren't real contestants. Stacy for one, and now, obviously, Eddie for another."

"Who else?" Jack grimaced.

"In all," Vince answered with a grin, "half of the contestants were real—the other half were actors."

"Oh, no." Jack shook his head, then immediately looked at Maria.

She was staring back at him, her eyes wide in shock and her head shaking back and forth. "Not me."

Vince chuckled. "No, Jack. She was as real as you. The other three plants were ..."

Vince paused as the curtain opened again and out stepped Whitney and Denny, smiling and waving at him.

Then, without warning, Hugh stepped up in front of Maria and Jack and humbly bowed his head. "And me."

"Hugh?!?" Jack exclaimed. "No way!"

Hugh grinned. "And I had a blast stringing you along, partner."

"I don't believe this," Maria exclaimed.

"My real name is Hugh Kokka. I'm also an actor and stunt man."

"You've got to be kidding me." Jack shook his head in disbelief. "What about the cliff? Here we're climbing up the rocks like Batman and Robin, and I'm stressed out about you. You're a stinkin' stuntman!"

Hugh laughed. "I couldn't believe you were doing it, man. If you ever need a job, come see me—we can use you in Hollywood."

"I don't think so," Jack assured him, then turned back to Vince. "So C. J., Spike, and Tara were all on the up-and-up?"

As if Jack had been the one to cue them out, the three of them stepped through the curtain.

"Pulled right out of their daily lives, just like you were," Vince answered.

"So what happens to the ten million dollars?" Maria asked.

"Ah, Maria," Vince said with a chuckle. "Always getting right to the point."

"You betcha," Maria shot back.

"There never was a ten million dollar prize, I'm sorry to say. You would've had to really study the small print on your contracts to see it, though. It was all part of our special version of *The Ultimate Challenge.* We did promise an incentive to our actors that if they made it all the way through and won—even as we were changing the game on them—they would get a one hundred thousand dollar bonus."

Hugh shrugged with a grin toward Jack and Maria. "Hey, it's not quite ten million, but I think I can live with that."

Eddie leaned in to Jack, towering over him once again and slipping into this South Central dialect. "You cost me a hundred G's, Forrest. I can't believe you tripped me right at the finish line. You're going to pay."

"Yeah, but you pulled me off the wall," Jack shot back.

"True," Eddie said, then laughed.

"What about the flare gun in the boat?" Jack turned back to Vince. "Stacy almost drowned—heck, any of us could have been hurt!"

"Not really," Vince said. "There was a team of scuba divers right below you, ready to lend a hand the second somebody got in trouble. We set Stacy up for her life jacket to get caught, but if Hugh hadn't been able to free her, the divers would've been right there to assist."

"And the fire?" Jack angled his head.

"No danger there either."

"Oh, come on—I nearly died," Maria argued.

"Not quite as close as you think." Vince grinned. "You had been drugged, Maria, to make it look like you were not breathing. Actually, there were two people in the room with you with fire-retardant suits and breathing gear. They kept you on oxygen right up until Jack crashed through the glass doors. They were also there to pull you out if Jack hadn't responded how we knew he would."

Jack glanced at Maria, who turned to him in shock. He hadn't saved her life after all, but was just a bit player in this theater called *The Ultimate Challenge.* "But the resort lost four bungalows ..."

"Yeah, but they're doing a whole remodel once we're done with the show and get off their island," Vince explained. "It was all just part of the plan."

"You guys seem to have thought of everything." Maria stood, amazed.

"And there's one more thing, Jack and Maria," Vince continued. "Even though you ultimately lost, for making it this far, and being such great sports, we're going to award you five hundred thousand dollars each."

Maria screamed right in Jack's ear. She jumped into his arms and hugged him for dear life. Jack laughed and twirled her around. That could hold him for quite a while until he found his next job—even if it was Zeke's money.

"We're also giving C. J., Spike, and Tara a hundred thousand dollars each for interrupting their lives the way we did," Vince added.

The three that had been knocked out earlier in the week jumped for joy, hugging each other and slapping high-fives.

"There is one catch, though."

Jack and Maria stopped hugging, wondering what it could be. "Yes?" they asked in unison.

"We need to recreate a bit of your hostage rescue from last night. Some of your heroics, planning, and, especially, the stuff in the control room, didn't get on tape. We need to re-shoot it all tonight; then we'll get you home first thing tomorrow."

Jack laughed, thinking how unreal reality television really is. "Whatever you say."

As the excitement was winding down, Jack made his way over to Vince and pulled him aside.

"I need to see Zeke before this is all over."

"I'm not sure that's possible, Jack. I'll have to check."

"Make it possible, please." Jack pressed.

"I'll try, but I'm not sure how much longer he's planning to stay on the island."

"Please," Jack repeated. "It's important."

Vince nodded, then stepped back behind the curtain. Jack wasn't sure what he was going to say when he saw Zeke, but he knew there needed to be some closure between them.

"What was that all about?" Amanda slid up next to her son.

"Nothing much." He tried to dodge the question. "So, how much did you know about all this?"

Amanda grinned. "Not as much as you might think. As far as I knew, everything in the game was real. Zeke just promised me there would be no secrets revealed tonight."

"He did, huh?"

"Yeah, he came to see me this morning."

"You couldn't have found a way to let me know?"

"I was locked in my room, remember—up until Zeke walked me out to the cliff," Amanda answered.

Vince stepped up beside Jack, "Excuse me for interrupting, but could I have a word with you, Jack?"

"Mom, if you'll excuse us."

"Of course." Amanda stepped away politely. "Meet me in my room when you're done."

Vince waited for her to be farther away, then turned to Jack. "Come with me."

Vince led Jack up the stairs and into the control room, which was now empty, except for Zeke sitting on the couch. Vince didn't stay, just turned around and walked out, closing the door without a word.

"Please." Zeke motioned beside him. "Have a seat."

Jack sat in the large chair opposite the couch, so it would be easy to speak eye-to-eye.

"What can I do for you?" Zeke asked.

Jack paused, suddenly not having a clue as to what he was going to say. He'd started praying the second Vince led him out of the dining hall. Now he hoped God would answer.

"Are there any cameras in here?" Jack asked.

"No," Zeke answered. "We're alone."

"So, thinking that I was your son, you brought me here under false pretenses."

"Right to the point. I would have expected nothing different."

"Are you disappointed?"

"That you're not my son?" Zeke asked.

Jack nodded.

"Actually, yes. I am."

"I'm not," Jack stated coldly.

"Why do you say that?" Zeke's brow creased.

"I can't imagine having you as a father after the way you've acted this week."

Zeke shook his head. "You're taking this way too seriously, Jack. Stacy's alive, nobody was hurt, and you're walking away with a half a million of my dollars."

Jack shrugged. "Your money means nothing to me."

"I've come to that same conclusion."

"Even with it all being an illusion—some demented way in your mind to rekindle a love lost with my mother, take hold of the long lost son you thought you had," Jack spat the words out. "I still can't get over how demeaning it was for you to offer Maria to me as if she was nothing more than a piece of scrap meat for the dogs at the dinner table. That was unforgivable."

"It was a test," Zeke explained. "Nothing more."

"What do you mean a 'test'?"

"It wasn't meant to degrade Maria, believe me," Zeke sighed. "*The Ultimate Challenge* was designed to get to the heart of your character."

Jack stared blankly at Zeke, trying to understand, but feeling totally lost.

"Look, I made a mess of my life," Zeke said, as he looked down. "Three failed marriages, kids that would just as soon see me die to get to my money. I wanted to see if your mother's life, and the values she had instilled in you, would really make a difference and actually work, even when under fire."

Jack was speechless.

"And they did." Zeke glanced up. His eyes had softened. "The carrot I dangled in front of you that morning was just to see how you'd react."

Jack grunted. "And I passed?"

"Unbelievably well. Any man I know, especially my sons, would've jumped at the chance, with or without the personal challenge. When you were willing to walk away from something that I know you desired, even if it cost you a hundred thousand dollars—that says a lot about you."

"I think it says more about Maria," Jack said. "You have a lot to learn about women."

"On that one, I actually agree with you."

"And that includes my mother," Jack added.

"What do you mean?" Jack had Zeke's full attention, but he didn't know how far he should go. If his mom had wanted Zeke to know the full truth, she would have told him.

"All I'll say ..." Jack struggled with the words. "Don't judge my mom. You don't know the full story."

"I know all I need to know," Zeke stated flatly.

"I don't think you do."

"Then please, enlighten me."

"That's between the two of you," Jack answered. "I'm sorry this whole thing didn't turn out the way you expected. Maybe, instead of it being a test for me, I wonder if it wasn't really a test for you."

Zeke scowled but chose not to respond.

"You've fallen under the spell of your own game," Jack continued. " 'No rules'—isn't that the motto? Sounds more like how you've lived your life, no one to answer to but yourself. Maybe it's time you realize there is someone greater than you—someone who's worth answering to."

"You sound just like your mother," Zeke said, cracking a smile.

"Maybe she's right."

Zeke shrugged.

"You should talk with her before she goes," Jack said.

"I have talked with her. If there's still something I don't know, then she obviously doesn't want to confide in me."

"You expect her to confide in the same man who gave her the ultimatum to get an abortion or he'd walk away from her?" Jack asked calmly.

Zeke looked at Jack in sorrow. "I see your point."

"Don't tell me—tell her." Jack got up and started to walk out of the door.

"Jack?" Zeke called after him.

Jack stopped by the doorway.

Zeke paused, tears welling up in his eyes. "I would've been proud to call you my son."

Zeke stayed alone in the control room, mulling over Jack's words. What could Amanda be holding back from him? He was the one who was betrayed.

He got up from the couch, struggling with whether he should go find her or not. He wasn't sure how he would handle himself. His eyes scanned over the huge bank of monitors in front of him. There was still a crowd in the dining hall, though a few people had gone back to their rooms.

Zeke's eyes caught movement in Amanda's room. She was on the screen, packing up her travel bag. He walked up to the switcher and punched the camera onto the colored plasma. He sighed as he took in her beauty and, for the first time, felt guilty for spying on her.

She closed her overnight bag and headed for the front room. Zeke looked at the other monitors that covered her bungalow, punching up the camera that showed the front door. Amanda came into view a second later.

When she opened the door, Zeke's heart seemed to stop.

Travis was standing there. Zeke reached for the volume, desperate to hear what was about to be said.

"Travis?" Amanda gasped. "What are you doing here?"

"We should talk," Travis said, stepping inside the room uninvited.

Amanda moved away from the door and into the kitchen area. She wanted to get the dinette table between them—anything to feel safer.

"I don't want to talk with you," Amanda stated in fear. "Please leave."

Travis wouldn't be deterred. "I know about the DNA test. Zeke isn't Jack's father."

"So?"

"So that means, you need to get packed and get off this island as soon as possible, and stay away from Zeke."

"What do you think I'm doing?" Amanda's anger flared instantly. After all these years, the only thing he can think about is getting her off the island and away from Zeke?

"I'm not going to let you ruin his life again," he said, moving closer to her.

"Stay away!"

"Don't be silly," Travis sneered. "I just want you to get your bag. I've got one of the choppers waiting."

"I'm not leaving without Jack."

"Yes, you are." Travis' voice rose. "I'm taking you right now. Jack has to stay to re-tape the rescue scene. He'll be home tomorrow."

"Wait," Amanda snapped. "You have no say over me."

"The hell I don't." Travis stepped closer, grabbing her arm and pushing her to the bedroom. "Now move it!"

His shove reminded her too much of the fateful night they'd shared many years before. She spun on her heels, faced him, and screamed at the top of her lungs, "Do not touch me!"

Travis jumped, shocked at her response.

"You keep your hands off of me," Amanda continued, bolstered by the sounds of her own voice. "I shouldn't have put up with it twenty-eight years ago, and I'm certainly not going to tonight!"

"You little ..." Travis swore, staring at her, as his eyes grew black as coal.

"Stay away!" Amanda interrupted his tirade, moving slowly toward the door. She backed away, as if escaping an enraged animal, trying to keep the panic from overtaking her.

"Yeah," Travis sneered. "You better be afraid."

Amanda continued to back up. "Afraid? How about disgusted. How many other women have you raped since me? Huh? Does Zeke know about you? Are you trying to protect him from me—or are you trying to protect yourself from him?"

"Shut up!" Travis shouted. "You wanted it, don't you try and deny it. You were a slut back then, and that's certainly what you are now!"

"I would never have wanted you!" Amanda screamed. "Admit it, you raped me."

Travis lashed out, whipping an open hand across Amanda's face. The force snapped her head to the side.

"Fine." Travis opened his arms to his sides. "I admit it! Somebody had to show Zeke what a tramp you were. You were probably sleeping around with everybody on campus. Zeke was just one in a thousand."

"No," Amanda stated firmly. "Zeke was the only one."

"But he's not the father!" Travis screamed.

Amanda bit at her upper lip, her eyes flashing with anger. "Do I have to spell it out for you, Travis?"

Travis stopped cold, his eyes shifting around the room. "What? You're saying I'm the father?"

Amanda nodded, ashamed to admit it.

"You liar," Travis snapped. "You're just here to ruin Zeke—and me in the process." He stepped toward her. Amanda tried to keep her distance, backing to the door. "You're not going to get away with it this time!" he yelled.

He reached out and grabbed her blouse with his left hand, pulling back with his right hand clenched. The door flew open, slamming against the entrance wall.

"You touch her, you're dead!" Jack shouted, pushing into the room and grabbing Travis's left hand. He pulled it off of his mom and stepped between them.

Travis kept his right hand cocked, seemingly trying to decide if he was going to throw a punch at Jack or not. Then his face turned ashen as he looked at Jack.

Standing face-to-face with him, Travis could see the resemblance he had refused to see all week. There was no way he could deny it any longer: *Jack was his son.*

Jack looked over at his mom, a painful expression etched on his face. "Is this him?"

Amanda nodded.

Jack pushed Travis away, which caused him to take a step back to keep his balance.

"I don't care if you are my biological father." Jack forced the words out through clenched teeth. "I'll flatten you right where you stand. I want you out of here, now!"

"Wait." Travis held his hands palms up in front of him. "It's not what you think."

"I think you were about to throw a punch at my mom," Jack said coldly. "How is it *not what I was thinking*?"

"No." Travis shook his head. "I'm sorry, I would never hurt your mother. I just lost my head."

Zeke suddenly burst through the door, stopping beside Jack, then looking back and forth from Travis to Amanda.

"Are you all right?" he asked Amanda first.

She nodded quickly.

Zeke turned back to Travis, his eyes blazing with anger.

Travis began babbling. "We've been through too much together, Zeke. I knew she was bad for you back then. You gotta believe me, whatever she says is a lie."

Zeke stepped within inches of Travis's face, his voice turning violently cold. "I heard it all—every word of it. You've been lying to me for thirty years."

"No," Travis whined. "It's not me, she's lying. She slept with everybody in the student body."

"I've got it all on tape," Zeke shouted, shutting Travis up. "I don't know if there's a statute of limitations on rape in Connecticut, but I'm going to find out. It finally makes perfect sense why you've been pushing me away from her. You were just covering your own sorry butt."

"It's not like that," Travis tried to explain. "You were destined for great things, you couldn't stop for a family …"

"Shut up!" Zeke shouted. "Get out of my face." Zeke stepped aside, opening the way to the door. "You're fired! I never want to see you again. Take that chopper and get off this island now!"

"You can't do this to me," Travis shouted back, swearing before he continued. "I made you. Without me you'd be nothing …"

"There's a reason why I never made you a partner, Travis!" Amanda could see the veins popping out on Zeke's forehead as he screamed. "That's so, right now, I could fire your butt—and there's nothing you can do about it. Now get out, before I let Jack here pummel you to the floor."

"You'll hear from my lawyers," Travis stated defiantly, finally leaving.

"Bring it on," Zeke growled as Travis walked by. The minute he was through the door, Zeke slammed it behind him.

"Thank God you came," Zeke said to Jack. "I took off the second he admitted raping …" Zeke couldn't finish the sentence. "I was afraid I wouldn't get here in time."

Zeke turned gently toward Amanda. "You're sure you're OK?"

She reached up and rubbed her left cheek, which she was sure was beet red by now. "Yeah, I'm fine. I'm so glad you both showed up, though."

"What was going on in here?" Jack asked.

Zeke turned to answer. "Travis was trying to get Amanda off the island before we had a chance to talk."

"How did you know?" Amanda asked.

"Jack and I had a talk in the control room," Zeke explained. "After he left, I saw Travis come into your room on one of the monitors. I listened in and heard everything."

"Everything?"

"Yeah," Zeke said. "I'm so sorry, Amanda. I had no idea."

"I think I'll leave you two alone," Jack slid over toward the door. "I'll be by the pool."

He left quietly as Zeke went to the kitchen and placed several ice cubes into a washcloth, then brought it back to Amanda and held it against her cheek. She placed her hand on his, before he gently released the washcloth to her.

"Thanks."

"You're welcome," Zeke answered. "Why didn't you tell me?"

"Then, or now?"

"Then."

Amanda shook her head, looking to the floor. "At first, I was too ashamed."

Zeke gently reached out and brought her chin up, meeting her directly eye-to-eye. "It wasn't your fault."

"It sure felt like it." Amanda fought back the tears building up. "You don't know what it's like. You get a bit flirtatious, just having a fun time. Then suddenly, it's not fun anymore, and you've got a guy who you can't control. You say 'no,' over and over again, but he's too strong."

The memories came flooding back, haunting her again as if it had happened the week before. She started sobbing. "And then it happens so quick, and he's gone and you're all alone—feeling so dirty, like it was something I did. Like I caused it."

Zeke pulled her close to him, enveloping her in his arms. "No, Amanda. No."

"I couldn't tell you. I didn't know how."

Zeke held her close as she shivered in his arms.

"You were already set on me ending the pregnancy. And then Travis threatened me," Amanda struggled to say through her tears. "If I didn't have the abortion, he would do something to harm me—and the baby. That's when I just left school. And you never called after that."

"If I ever see him again …" Zeke couldn't finish his thought. "So you suffered through it all, alone?"

"For a while," Amanda sniffed. "Then God brought Kevin into my life, and what started as something that could've destroyed me turned into something that really might have saved me."

Zeke pulled back to get a look at her face. "Jack *is* wonderful. I'd give anything to start over from the day you told me you were pregnant, to have another chance."

"It wasn't our time," Amanda whispered, placing her hand against his cheek. "I wasn't the person then that I am now. And neither are you."

"No," Zeke said. "I'm too much like the man I was then—and, at some point in my life, I need to grow up. Look at what I did this afternoon up on that cliff. The minute I got proof that Jack wasn't my son, I believed the worst about you."

"You had help."

Zeke paused, studying her carefully. "What do you mean?"

"Think about it, I saw the body language when you and Travis were talking. What did he lead you to believe?"

Zeke didn't have to think hard to recall. "That you had betrayed me."

"And isn't that the advice you got from him twenty-eight years ago?"

"Oh, my …" Zeke closed his eyes. "Of course. He led me right where he wanted to, didn't he? Back then, and on the cliff today. I'm so sorry, Amanda," he said with tears welling in his eyes. "I am so sorry."

Amanda moved closer, placing her head on his chest. "I should have told you, Zeke. But I couldn't. I just couldn't."

The two held each other for several minutes, both dealing with the ghosts from the past. Amanda prayed she'd never see Travis again. She hoped Jack wouldn't want to as well, even with what he'd found out today.

Zeke hurt beyond words. Whom he thought was his best friend for three decades had been the one to push him away from the only woman he'd ever loved. What could life have been like if they'd worked through it and stayed together? He would never know. For now, he felt lost, as if something had been ripped from him.

"I just wish we could turn back the clock," he finally whispered. "I should've been there for you. It's horrendous what he did to you, and then what I did to you on top of it. Can you ever forgive me?"

"Yes, I can," Amanda said quietly. "Listen … I've made so many mistakes in my life, Zeke. If God can forgive me, I can certainly forgive you."

Maria found Jack sitting by the pool. She sat down and joined him. "What happened to your mom?"

"She's having a long overdue conversation with an old friend," Jack answered.

"Really?"

"Yeah. Maybe I'll tell you about it someday."

"I like the sound of that," Maria said with a smile.

"Telling you about my mom's personal life?"

"No." Maria nudged him on the arm. "Talking about us as in … someday."

Jack grinned. "An interesting thought."

"Remember what you said a few days ago?"

"I said a lot of things."

"When you mentioned that we were just a product of the game, that our relationship was forced, not real."

Jack nodded. "Yeah, I remember."

"Do you still feel that way?"

He waited, thinking carefully about what to say next. He had a lot to sort out after this week: Zeke, a biological father who repulsed him, his lost job, and, most of all, his mixed-up feelings for both Maria and Kathryn.

Jack cleared his throat, trying to choose his words carefully. "What's amazing, Maria, even after all we've been through this week, is that other than Teresa, I don't have the slightest clue what's important in your life. Normally, that would be the first thing I'd talk about with somebody I'm interested in seeing. With you—it's been overshadowed by this unbelievable whirlwind romance."

"Jack," Maria sighed. "You can't stop your heart."

"No," Jack agreed. "But you can guard it, and I haven't. I should've found out what we both believe about the important things in life—about God—*before* I fell for you."

"You fell for me, huh?" Maria grinned.

Jack wished he could pull the words back out of thin air—he couldn't believe he'd slipped up. He waited anxiously, not sure what to say next.

Maria broke the silence this time. "Would it help if I told you I do believe in God?"

"Yeah," Jack smiled. "That's a start. But there's more to it than that."

"Is that what makes you so different?" Maria grinned. "You know, it's sad this week hasn't given us any time to talk like this. I'd really like to find out what makes you tick."

"You might be shocked," Jack said with a chuckle, then grew serious again. "If our relationship has any chance of being real, it would have to start on a whole different foundation—somewhere down the road."

"I'd like that." Maria looked over at him and smiled warmly. Her eyes seemed to glisten with the moonlight.

Jack leaned closer to her, pausing just before their lips met until she moved toward him. The kiss was the most innocent, and yet, the sweetest one they'd shared all week. It was also the shortest, as Teresa came running up behind Maria and jumped up on her back.

"Mommy," Teresa laughed.

Jack watched the two of them as a broad smile came to his lips. They were certainly beautiful together.

"So, what's next for you?" Jack asked.

"Well, we go home tomorrow. And I march right into the Luxor Hotel and quit."

"Really?" Jack smiled.

"With the prize money, I've got all I need to complete school and start a new life with my mother and little Teresa here. Right, kiddo?"

Teresa giggled.

"The second thing I'm planning, is to get serious about my relationship with God again, and I'm not saying that just for your benefit, Jack Forrest." Maria laughed.

Jack was taken aback. "Really?"

"Yeah, it's time—for me and for Teresa. We need to get our lives in order. Now, what about you?"

Jack shook his head. "I'm not sure. I'm hoping I can get my job back. I'll have to play that out when I get home."

"Well, the money should help, if not."

"Yeah, it doesn't hurt," Jack said with a grin. "Part of me feels like it's tainted money coming from Zeke—but maybe he's not that bad after all. Maybe I could use it to fly out for a little vacation to Las Vegas sometime."

Maria stared at him, her eyes filled with hope. "I'd love that."

"We'll just have to see what God has planned." Jack grinned as his stomach fluttered.

Later that night, Amanda sat by the pool, waiting for Jack to finish up the evening taping of the hostage rescue. The staff had brought out all kinds of snacks and drinks in celebration for the end of the show, but she hadn't been that hungry. She just wanted to go off to collect her thoughts. Maybe she'd go back to her room and Jack could find her later.

"How about a walk?" Zeke's voice nearly scared her, as he snuck up from behind.

"Uh, hi, Zeke." Amanda didn't know how to respond. "Are they done taping?"

"They are with me. Would you mind taking a walk with me?"

He led her around the main building, onto the grass, walking toward the edge of the cliff just as the moon began to rise on the horizon.

"I wanted to see the view one last time, with you."

Amanda smiled nervously, looking over the dark expanse of the ocean contrasted with the huge bright circle of a moon hanging just above the water line. "It certainly is beautiful."

"Jack's got his job back," Zeke mentioned casually.

"What?" Amanda turned to him. "How?"

"Let's just say that the Swanson family has had a change of heart. They won't be pursuing a lawsuit against Jack, or the school, any more."

Amanda cocked her head, as her eyes grew suspicious. "And how did you manage to work that out?"

Zeke grinned. "There are some benefits that come with money. Let's just say that along with some advice he had from a certain attorney you sent his way, Mr. Swanson seemed to be willing to let a few zeros convince him that his lawsuit suddenly wasn't in his best interest."

"Jack will be thrilled."

"I hope so. He's really quite a young man."

"Yeah." Amanda smiled. "He turned out pretty good."

Zeke leaned in to kiss her lightly on the forehead, then stood back and smiled warmly. "So did you."

They stood looking at each other for a moment, before Zeke spoke again.

"Can I ask you one last question, Amanda?"

Amanda nodded, trying to prepare herself for the unexpected. "Sure, go ahead."

"After all we've been through, and all you've told me about how you've changed … did you ever really love me?"

Amanda felt her eyes moisten, her heart snapping back to 1977 and the intense passion she had for Zeke. She reached up, gently touching the side of his cheek.

"Yes, Zeke." Amanda smiled warmly. "I loved you."

Zeke sighed, closing his eyes for a moment. When he opened them, Amanda noticed there were tears building. He reached his hand up and gently placed it on top of hers.

Amanda heard someone clear his throat behind her. "What's going on here?"

"Jack." Amanda turned to see her son walking up behind her.

"What are you doing out here?" she asked, pulling her hand away quickly, as if she'd been caught with her hand in the cookie jar.

"They gave us a break from the taping. What are you two doing out here is more the question?"

Amanda was sure her face was beet red; she hoped the darkness of the night covered it. "Zeke was just telling me that you've got your job back."

"I what?" Jack exclaimed, turning excitedly to Zeke.

Zeke nodded. "I was able to have a little chat with Mr. Swanson a moment ago—everything's been resolved."

"I don't know what to say," Jack stammered. "Thank you."

"You're very welcome," Zeke said, smiling. "It was the least I could do. And Jack, if I could offer one word of advice …"

Jack looked at his mom, then back to Zeke. "I guess so, sure."

Amanda watched Zeke intently, wondering what he was going to say.

"About Maria …"

"Yes?"

"What you two have is incredibly special. It was never part of the game." Amanda noticed Zeke's eyes were passionate, his voice nearly breaking. "A love like that may only come along once in your life. I suggest you don't let her go."

Jack sat beside his mom on the plush couch aboard the flying penthouse suite of Zeke Roberts Productions. They'd flown off the island the next morning by helicopter, directly to the waiting corporate jet, and were now on their way back to Chicago.

Jack had dutifully recreated most of the exciting moments of the heroic rescue of Maria from the hands of the rebels. Tara had still been there to play her role, as were Eddie and Hugh. It was even good to see Palau one last time. Jack had asked him to get the hatchling back to his cousin's family, and even told him what boat he'd taken the chair and net from. Palau promised he'd return the items.

Jack thought it hilarious for the director to try and get him to act out the lines he'd said originally. A lot of it had been taped from the cameras in his vest, but that only gave the production crew Jack's point of view. They needed his close-up from everything that had happened after he pulled his helmet camera off. Jack knew there was definitely not a career in acting in his future—it was a good thing he still had his coaching job.

"I had a long talk with Zeke this morning before we left," Amanda said out of the blue.

"And you're just now telling me this?"

"You seemed deep in thought after leaving Maria."

"Yeah, that was kind of hard."

"Do you think you'll see her again?"

"I don't know—we talked about it somewhat. I might have mentioned a possible trip to Las Vegas in the not-too-distant future."

"Jack." Amanda's voice sounded like it did when he'd been ten years old and misbehaved.

"What?" Jack asked innocently. "She's had a troubled life, but it sounds like she wants to make God a bigger part of it. Maybe I can help."

Amanda looked at her son and smiled.

"I know." Jack shrugged. "That's not my job."

"You're walking on dangerous ground. She's got to come to God on her own terms, not through you."

Jack looked at her with one eyebrow raised. "What if someone had given Dad that advice about you?"

Amanda froze, her eyes widening. "Ouch."

Jack grinned. "See, life isn't so black and white now, is it?"

"No, I guess not. I just know how much Kathryn went to bat for you, and how she feels about you. I'd hate to see her get hurt through all this."

Jack took in a deep breath. "Yeah, I know—I've thought the same thing. But I've just never had the strong, passionate feelings for Kathryn like I was hit with on the island for Maria."

"Maybe you just haven't let yourself go with Kathryn."

"What do you mean?"

"Well, you've always been so guarded back home," Amanda explained. "She's your boss, there's that working relationship that gets in the way, and she's kind of reserved. Before you make any decisions, you need to just let all that go and look at Kathryn for who she is—see what sparks are really there before you count her out."

"Oh, I haven't counted her out," Jack assured her. "And you have a great point."

"Of course I do," Amanda said with a smile. "A mother's always right."

The two sat quietly, as the hum of the engines filled the cabin.

"So, about Zeke." Jack broke the silence. "I had a thought last night."

"Really? And what would that be?"

Jack looked seriously at his mom. "Well, it was so great of him to talk to the Swansons and bribe them, or whatever he did to get them to drop their lawsuit…"

"Yeah?" Amanda listened intently.

Jack held his stern look. "How do we know he wasn't behind the lawsuit in the first place?"

"Oh, Jack." Amanda shook her head. "You're terrible."

"Wait, I'm serious," he said grinning. "With everything else that's happened, who's to say he didn't plan that part of it so I would be desperate to win?"

Jack could see in her expression that she was seriously thinking it over.

"I'm kidding, Mom," Jack laughed.

But the two didn't speak for a moment, as each mulled over the possibilities.

"Are you going to see him again?"

"Probably," Amanda said. "But whether it develops romantically or not depends on him more than me."

"What do you mean?"

Amanda sighed. "If he's really serious about changing his life and turning it over to God, then maybe there's a chance to rekindle something. But he's got a long road ahead of him, and I'm in no hurry to rush into anything. It's something to pray about."

"I'm sure it is. As well as what the heck I am going to say to Kathryn when I get home?"

Amanda laughed, "You better be fasting and praying on that one, son."

Jack laughed along with her, knowing she was dead-on. "I know one thing: if we're still dating when *The Ultimate Challenge* hits the air, I've got to find some way to keep her from watching it, or I'll be dead meat."

"Hurry up, it's about to start!" The woman's voice carried from the living room into the kitchen.

Jack pulled the popcorn bag out of the microwave, quickly tossing it into the sink before it burned his hands. He pulled open the top of the package, then poured the fresh popcorn into a large bowl. The aroma filled the kitchen, melting Jack's taste buds.

It had been four months since he'd returned from the island. He came home to find his job was indeed intact. Whatever Zeke had offered, combined with the work of the ACLJ attorney, had worked. The Swanson family had rescinded their demands and the threatened lawsuit.

Now with the end of summer, Jack was busy working out his new football squad and looking forward to a great season.

"Do you want anything else?" Jack called out.

"No, just get in here—it's starting and I miss you."

He wrapped his arm around the bowl of popcorn, using his hands to carry his Pepsi and her Diet Coke.

It was time. The first episode of *The Ultimate Challenge 3* was about to air.

The summer had been the most wonderful experience Jack could remember. He knew he'd finally found his soul mate—the one woman who shared his passions, dreams, goals, and hopes for the future. Jack turned the corner and walked into the room. He smiled, the vision of her sitting at the edge of the couch was stirring the passions within him. She'd come so far over the summer, breaking through on a level with God that he found astounding in her short walk. There was no need to guard his heart any longer; now the attention seemed to be needed to guard their purity.

She patted the seat next to her and looked up with a smile. "Come on, honey. I can't wait. This is going to be great!"

"I just hope the way they edited this thing doesn't make me look worse than I actually behaved."

Jack set the drinks and popcorn on the coffee table and snuggled in next to her. It would be interesting to relive that life-changing week that now seemed so long ago. Jack leaned back, put his arms around her and sighed, knowing that the true ultimate challenge really lay just ahead—building their new life together.

He looked at her, his heart racing. "Just remember as you watch this—I love you."